BIRDBRAINED

I cleared my throat and presented my idea. "Doves are white and pretty and pure. Doves are beautiful."

Diana looked up. "Yes, how right you are. Silly I didn't think of this days ago. After all, the product is called Bird Bath."

Suddenly, with Diana's sanctioned enthusiasm, everyone else became alert and hyperinterested. A marketing woman piped in. "What if we send a dove in flight to each magazine editor?"

Another marketing person continued the thought. "And we attach a packet of Bird Bath wipes to a chain around its neck."

"I got it! A Tiffany necklace that the editors can keep," said Winsome.

"I'll do you one better," Connie said. "With the press release miniaturized and tucked inside the locket."

"This is it," Diana said. "A dove will land on the windowsill of every New York beauty editor, and they will be so enthralled by its white avian splendor, they will throw open the window, take the Bird Bath wipes—and the Tiffany necklace, of course—and send the dove back to its roost." She trained her eyes on me. "Very cutting edge. Oh, and Marnie, since this was your smashing idea, you will be overseeing it."

The Immaculate Complexion

Edie Bloom

LEISURE BOOKS NEW YORK CITY

In loving memory of Estelle Leah Meyers
who knew the true meaning of the word
immaculate.

A LEISURE BOOK®

May 2007

Dorchester Publishing Co., Inc.
200 Madison Avenue
New York, NY 10016

ISBN-10: 0-8439-5856-1
ISBN-13: 978-0-8439-5856-0

The name "Leisure Books" and the stylized "L" with design are trademarks of Dorchester Publishing Co., Inc.

Printed in the United States of America.

Visit us on the web at www.dorchesterpub.com.

ACKNOWLEDGEMENTS

Many thanks to our peerless editor, Leah Hultenschmidt, and to our agents, Caroline Greeven and Marc Gerald. Also thanks to our publicist, Brianna Yamashita.

Special thanks to Pam Goeller, Lori Sterling, Sheri Weinstein and Marlene Adelstein for their invaluable editorial input.

This book would not be possible without the immeasurable help of Freyda Tavin, Christina Byers, Stacie & Seth Ernsdorf, Beverly Lorenc, Maryalena Salman, Émei Sheppard, Gail Wallach, Patricia Santillan, Glenn Chase, Susan Gabbay, Nicole Ellison and Terry Wolverton.

Immense gratitude to our families for their love and support: Gerald & Deborah Strober, Leah & Melvyn Wolff, Jonathan Strober, Bryan, Marley and Kai Sterling, Jeremy, Ran and Eyal Benjamin and Gabi Nocham.

Gene & Jan Meyers, Steven Meyers, Bruce Meyers, Cheryl & Marty Kahn, Norman Meyers, Liz Grebler, Harriet Kusnitz, Anita Lazan, Marsha Lewis, Nadine Simpson and in memory of Abe Kahn.

The Immaculate Complexion

FACE TIME

I had finally arrived. As I rocketed up to the LeVigne Cosmetics corporate headquarters in a high-speed elevator, it was impossible not to eavesdrop on the two fresh-faced, sylphlike women in front of me. They were so slim that, standing shoulder to shoulder, they barely made one person. The only oversized thing about them were their chunky golden highlights.

"Did you know having an orgasm burns twenty-seven calories?" posited the brittle blonde.

"You burn a hundred sixty when you fake it," retorted the Q-tip-thin brunette.

"Shut up!" said the blonde in disbelief.

I covered my mouth to suppress an incredulous laugh.

The brunette held out her hands and admired her glossy blunt nails. "Still on Sugar Busters?"

"Yeah, but somehow I keep gaining," sighed the blonde.

"You've got to try the Dolly Parton diet. It's mad awesome. Fist-sized portions of what you normally eat."

"Fistfuls of nothing work best for me. I'll eat when I'm dead."

The door slid open onto a blindingly white reception area. I exited and followed these power dieters as they approached the reception desk.

"Welcome back, Kyra. Cute Band-Aid," said the brunette to the stunning receptionist, admiring the Burberry-plaid adhesive strip affixed to Kyra's chin.

"Your jawline is definitely more defined," said the blonde. "Kudos to you."

"No, sillies. I was out having a butt lift. They blew it up like a little balloon. The bandage is hiding a zit," Kyra said, but the two stick figures had already walked down the hall.

I approached the desk. It was early October, and perched on a ledge behind Kyra was a foot-tall motorized witch wearing a black cape and a pointy black hat. She had a miniature broom wedged between her legs, and her pelvis gyrated in a choppy circular motion. The witch's nose was severely hooked, and at the tip of it was a rather large wart. She also had smaller warts and bumps on her face and neck. Next to her was a steaming black cauldron with little cosmetic pots spilling out of it.

"Hi. I'm Marnie Mann," I said to Kyra. "From Cross Temps. I'm supposed to ask for Tinsley Coughy."

"I'll let her know you're here," purred Kyra, her almond-shaped eyes resting coolly on the rhinestone poodle pinned to my vintage cashmere cardigan. "Interesting brooch. Very edgy."

"Thanks," I said proudly. "Scored it at the Hell's Kitchen flea market. Fifteen bucks."

Kyra wrinkled her nose. "We don't shop outdoors," she sniped as she punched a button on her phone console.

Ouch. Evidently these were not DIY girls.

"Your temp's here," Kyra whispered into the phone. She hung up and turned her attention back to me. "You've got some chocolate-chippy things on your forehead."

I clutched my head with alarm. "What do you mean?"

"They're age spots," Kyra said, holding up a hand mirror for me to see.

"No, they're freckles," I retorted, intently looking at the brown marks.

"Trust me, they're liver spots," Kyra replied emphatically. "They come with age. At least that's what I hear." She reached into the smoking witch's cauldron and pulled out a shiny black pot. "You'll be happy to know that Siesta, our brand for the more mature woman, has just come out with Sizzle. It's a cream to dissolve those pesky blemishes, warts, and skin tags so many women are plagued with. The active ingredient is arsenic. In minute quantities, of course. Here, take it," she said, coaxing it into my hand. "We don't test on animals— we test on you!"

Kyra's flawless visage was a whiter shade of pale. She grabbed her Dior handbag and opened a series of increasingly smaller logo purses nestled within one another like Russian matryoshka dolls until she found what she was looking for—a tiny tube of Paparazzi Sno-White Skin Brightener, which she slathered liberally on her face, neck, and arms.

I sat down on a white leather sofa in the reception area to wait for Tinsley Coughy. Safely shielded behind a tall vase of ivory calla lilies, I watched as the elevator spat out a dizzying procession of coltish, scrupulously groomed women. They were all wearing short fur chubbies; knee-grazing skirts in varying shades of buttery brown leather; tall, round-toed boots; and enormous purses the size of body bags; they all sported large mirrored sunglasses that obscured their chiseled faces and made them look like giant horseflies. Each one had long, lustrous hair and smooth, unlined skin. These were women who most definitely slept mummy-like on their backs. I, however, slept on my stomach, face squished into a drool-stained pillow, only to awaken resembling a wrinkly-faced Shar-Pei.

I glanced down at my work outfit, the one that had seemed quite chic (in a downtown sort of a way) when I locked my apartment door behind me. It was a 1950s sexy/serious librarian look—black cat's-eye glasses, wavy dark hair tied back in a loose bun, Donegal wool pencil skirt, vintage brogues, and the aforementioned sweater and brooch, which now seemed wan and inappropriate.

No one had come to fetch me yet, so I got up and walked over to the windows. The well-appointed LeVigne offices were high above Rockefeller Center. Down below, clusters of people skated on the ice rink's milky surface. Chubby families in bulky sweaters were carving out stiff figure eights, making mincemeat out of the Zambonied ice. It occurred to me that I had never skated on this rink or any other since moving from Los Angeles to New York almost fifteen years before. There was an outdoor rink in Prospect Park, near my apartment in Brooklyn, and it always seemed like something fun and romantic to do with a guy, but my ex-boyfriend, Nick, thought ice belonged in a tumbler.

Suddenly, a Junior Leaguer with a patrician snub nose and pin-straight blond hair galloped straight for me. She wore a white silk French-cuffed blouse, tan jodhpurs, and very expensive riding boots. She had psychotically good posture.

"I'm Tinsley Coughy, LeVigne's public relations office manager, and you must be . . ." she said with a tight smile, typing something into her CrackBerry, barely making eye contact with me as I smoothed out my molting skirt and offered up a hand.

". . . Marnie Mann," I replied with all the first-impression cheerfulness I could muster.

"Very glad to make your acquaintance, Marnie Mann," she said, her Locust Valley lockjaw elocution making her strangle every word. She thrust out a large-boned hand and vigorously shook mine. "You people have such interesting names."

I wasn't sure who "you people" were. Was she referring to my Jewish/Italian roots, or to the far-flung community of temps?

I followed Tinsley down a sparklingly bright hallway. As we walked, she cocked her head at a ninety-degree angle toward the wall. At first I thought she was admiring the impressive collection of framed photographs that lined the hall (Diane Arbus, Helmut Newton, Henri Cartier-Bresson), but then I realized that she was checking out her reflection in the frames' glass. As we continued along, I noticed several familiar LeVigne magazine ads hanging on the walls. They were from a famous Systems skincare campaign. In one, a woman's face was swathed in brightly colored paper streamers. The headline copy read, WITH CREPEY SKIN LIKE THIS, SHE'S NO LONGER THE LIFE OF THE PARTY.

Crepey skin. What a perfect description of how your neck and hands look when the ravages of age take hold. Another ad showed a beautiful woman's face

covered in tiny gray cobblestones. The copy read,
THERE WILL BE NO HORSE AND CARRIAGE FOR COBBLY SKIN LIKE
THIS. Yikes. They sure were playing the fear card. At
thirty-two, I had a face that was still quite status quo,
but I didn't take that for granted. I was straddling two
worlds, on the cusp of young and not-so-young. To my
great dismay, I was no longer getting carded. The pre-
vious week, on a phone call to my mother, she had reminded me to enjoy this time of life, that in your early
thirties you still have the same internal image of your
face and body that you developed in your teens. You
don't yet critically assess yourself in the mirror the way
you begin to do in your late thirties and early forties. I
touched my forehead. Did Kyra's suggestion that I use
Siesta imply that I looked like a "mature" woman?

As Tinsley and I continued down the hall, we passed
many identical cubes and offices that bled together
like a rear-projection driving scene in an old black-
and-white movie. Formidable-looking women in stark
offices talked on hands-free headsets, while their attractive young assistants sat in stark, unadorned cubes,
officiously pecking out missives on their ergonomic
keyboards. Even though it was quite chilly in the office, they were all wearing sleeveless muscle tees,
showing off biceps toned to perfection.

Tinsley stopped abruptly at a barren cube the size of
a rabbit warren. "Here's your little chubby, I mean
cubby," she said, assessing my size-10 body with a withering nose-to-toes once-over that ended with a deep
sigh at my scarlet brogues, which were, admittedly,
more nunnish than naughty.

"So, here's the thing," Tinsley continued. "You'll be a
floater, pitching in to help each brand when they need
assistance."

I liked that she was calling me a floater and not a temp. I envisioned myself floating on a fleecy cloud of delicately scented talc. Achoo!

"Have you worked in PR before?" Tinsley asked with a gimlet eye.

"No, but I vacationed there once," I replied with a nervous giggle.

She ignored my lame joke and continued. "To fill you in—this department is called Global Media Relations, GMR for short. We oversee all the LeVigne brands' public relations teams. Additionally, we keep the media at bay, putting out any fires regarding the safety and efficacy of our products or bad press that gets started by our nasty competitors. All the publicists sit on this floor. The other floors are comprised of product development, packaging, store design, education, marketing, and sales."

"There are five brands, right?" I said.

"No, four at present, but we always have our feelers out for profitable start-ups. Gobble, gobble!"

I couldn't believe how shamelessly she was talking about corporate buyouts.

Tinsley continued. "The easiest way to remember the four brands is by thinking of LeVigne Cosmetics as pricey New York real estate. Systems speaks to the suburban New Jersey housewife. Deeva is all-natural, earth-conscious Park Slope. Siesta screams ladies-who-lunch Park Avenue, and Paparazzi is all about the irrepressible celebrity of Tribeca."

Two lean, permabronzed women marched by in Louis Vuitton lockstep. One scribbled notes on a lilac steno pad while the other spoke. "Fall 2009. A fabulously candied color story. Working title: 'Tantalizing Tahitian Fantasy.' No. How about 'Tan-Tasy'? Yes. Corals, purples, ivory. A sarong for the lips. A lei for the eyes," she said, as they both stopped and stared toward Bora-Bora, sipping from tiny cans of diet cranberry juice through hot pink flexi-straws. "And don't forget to memo Research and Development. It's imperative that R and D be informed tiny heads are back."

Were they joking?

Tinsley stared intently at her own rather large head in the clear glass of a boxed fire extinguisher clamped to the wall. Were they creating a salve to make one's head smaller?

"My temp counselor told me you have a yogurt machine here," I said, trying to make conversation.

"Yes, and it's absolutely brilliant. Let me escort you to the pantry," Tinsley said as she led me into a state-of-the art kitchen and swiped her hand over the gleaming self-serve dispenser like a QVC hostess. "It's an Only 2 jobby," Tinsley continued, adjusting her pigskin head-band. "Only two calories per four-ounce serving, that is. Before we got it, many of our LeVignettes spent their lunch hours going out in search of Only 2, but now there's really no reason ever to leave the office, unless you have a dermaplaning appointment."

"I'm lactose intolerant," I said.

"There's actually no milk in it. It's all air and chemicals," she boasted, reaching out toward me. "There's something terribly unsightly on your forehead."

I covered the chocolate-chip spots with my hand, thinking how unabashedly rude she was, but I kept those thoughts to myself and said, "Yes, I know. Kyra gave me some Sizzle for it."

"Good, then. Please apply liberally," answered Tinsley.

The rickety brunette and her ditzy blond sidekick from the elevator came into the pantry. They were both

so perfectly groomed and accessorized that I felt out-
dated and obsolete, like last year's beat-up floor model.

"Juniper, should I slaughter you now or later?"
snapped Tinsley to the blonde, who was cupping a
beautiful Swarovski-encrusted compact in her hands.
"Is that not the limited-edition Paparazzi Oh! de Toi-
lette perfume solid? I thought I was first on the wait
list."

The slight blonde blinked back tears and meekly re-
linquished it to her.

"*Merci*," Tinsley continued, slipping the compact
into the side pocket of her riding pants. "Juniper and
Murfy, I'd like you to meet Marnie Mann. She'll be your
new Little Zero. Marnie, I have to make a phone call.
I'll meet you back at your desk in ten minutes sharp."

And with that, Tinsley turned abruptly on her riding
boots and left the kitchen.

Murfy made sure that Tinsley was out of earshot before she ripped into her. "If her jodhpurs were any
shorter, she'd be wearing culottes," she sniffed.

"It's a look," Juniper said sarcastically as she
tapped a packet of Crystal Light powder into a glass
of water. "And you could land a helicopter on that
forehead."

"I love your style," I said to them, hoping a compli-
ment might distract them from eviscerating me next.

Murfy immediately gave me the once-over and said,
"Juniper and I describe our style as dog-whistle fashion. Clothes with a pitch so high and astounding that
only the thinnest, most sophisticated women can hear
its call."

I glanced down at my sensible shoes and mentally
curled up into a little ball. With this kind of edict, how
would I survive the day, let alone my tenure here? "So,

what does Little Zero mean?" I asked warily, wondering how anyone here would consider me, at five-seven and 140 pounds, little.

Murfy explained. "Little Zero is what we called Mallis, the floater you're replacing, because she had no discernible body fat. She claims she contracted some mysterious illness and suddenly had to quit."

Juniper took a seaweed capsule from a baroque locket around her neck and swallowed it. "She told us it was mold spores in her bathroom, but I think it was a leaky boob. I told her not to get implants."

Before Juniper could further expand on the evils of implants, a sullen young woman in a white zip-front shift and foamy white shoes came into the pantry and started tidying up the counters. She had startling blue eyes and a beautiful square-jawed Eastern European face. She was so striking, she could have been a runway model.

"Saskia, take a bite out of that dark one and tell me what's inside," Juniper commanded, pointing to a pink box of candy from Fauchon sitting on the counter.

Saskia dutifully bit into it. "Mar-zi-pan," she said in a sexy Garbo accent, sharply spitting out each sweet syllable.

"Thanks, dude. You just saved me three hundred calories," Juniper said as Saskia hungrily popped the other half into her mouth, grabbed a bag of garbage, and left the pantry.

"She's very pretty," I said.

"The cleaning woman?" asked a mystified Murfy. "I never really noticed."

I looked at my watch. "I better get back to my desk to meet Tinsley," I said.

"Not so fast," said Juniper, grabbing my arm and

yanking me back. "Take off those kooky glasses so I can get a good look at you."

Afraid to disobey her, I slid my glasses into my skirt pocket.

Juniper gave me a long, hard stare. "If you don't mind my saying so, you strike me as a time bandit or possibly a nomad. Someone who hurries with her makeup and shifts from brand to brand. I'm a color junkie, and Murfy is a trendsetter."

Murfy got right up in my face. "You have beautiful blue eyes, Marnie. A little close-set, but really nice," she added. "The proper eye makeup makes all the difference in bringing your face into balance. You should think about doing a shimmer on the ocular ridge and maybe try applying liner with an outward swoop to widen them because, after all, don't you want your eyes to pop?"

"Actually, I prefer to leave them quietly in their sockets," I said.

"And one more thing," said Juniper, not getting my humor, her eyes darting around my face. "Shiny's out. You would benefit greatly from a manual exfoliator to dislodge oil and bring fresh cells to the surface."

Murfy handed me a Systems blotting paper to wipe the sheen off my nose. She turned to Juniper. "Definitely not an almond, categorically a cashew," she said as they giggled and strolled out of the kitchen.

I wanted to run after them to say that shiny was not a look I was working, that I had an ongoing battle with oily skin. As I walked back to my desk, I thought about how our faces define us. No matter who we are inside, the outside representation, at least initially, tells the beholder the story of who we are. I read somewhere that the mathematical difference between a pleasing and a not-so-pleasing face is something like one twenty-fifth of an inch. That's a one-millimeter deal-breaker, yet every face is made up of the same utilitarian, worka-day features—two eyes, a nose, and a mouth. Natural beauty is all about proportion, symmetry, and the sheer luck of superior genetics. So, with the help of Dr. Sapphire, I fudged the numbers. When I was eighteen, I had my nose fixed.

I had inherited Grandma Pearl's potato nose. It looked like a piece of molding clay that had landed *splat!* on my face. In high school, I remember being fascinated by the parade of older girls who would re-turn from winter break "ethnically cleansed." One night, my dad caught me lying on my bed, "retrain-ing" my nose. I had pugged it up with a lash of Scotch tape like Hailey Mills in *The Parent Trap*. Sometimes I missed my old nose. It was a lost piece of Jewish her-itage. As Dorothy Parker once said about the actress Fanny Brice: "She cut off her nose to spite her race."

When I got back to my desk, Tinsley was standing in my cube, tapping her foot impatiently. "For the time be-ing, you'll be answering phones until I talk to the brands and rustle up some real work for you to do. In the mean-time, here's some things you need to know. Connie Boyd is the new head of Global Media Relations. Murfy and Juniper work for her, and when they're away from their desks, you will pick up their lines. Do whatever they request of you. The password to your computer should be on a sticky in one of the drawers."

I nodded vigorously in obeisance.

Tinsley continued. "And this is the most important piece of information. If anyone calls regarding the whereabouts of Hattie LeVigne, the company's found-er, it's imperative that you send those calls immediately to me. Do not take it upon yourself to answer questions on her behalf. Can I trust that you will follow these instructions by the book and to the absolute T?"

"Is Hattie here?" I asked eagerly, excited to catch a glimpse of their infamous, venerable leader. Apparently Hattie had disappeared from the workplace many years prior, and recently there were rumors swirling in the press about whether the nonagenarian was even still alive. I knew quite a bit about the tough, tenacious Hattie LeVigne because September was Ballbuster Month on A&E, and they were airing her hagiography on heavy rotation.

Tinsley was taken off guard by my question. "Hattie's . . . she's around," she said cagily.

"Because I heard a rumor that—" I said.

Tinsley quickly regained her composure and cut me off. "Whatever you heard is a canard, and please do not ask me about Hattie ever again. *Comprenez-vous?*"

I nodded in the affirmative as I watched Tinsley trot away; then I rooted around the desk until I found the computer password—*bloat*. Once I started up Outlook, it never stopped dinging with annoying intranet bulletins that sped across the bottom of my screen like the CNN news crawl.

```
** This just in from WWD! Big
   heads, so passé. Small, pol-
   ished heads are here to stay.
** Harper's Bazaar declares: Carry
   a well-coiffed infant as an
   amusing costume adjunct.
** Cosmo trumpets: Hot new silhou-
   ette for spring: pale and con-
   fused with a hint of shimmer.
```

I looked around at my busy-bee coworkers. It was quite apparent that these high-maintenance women did not spend their lunch hours skulking around Hallmark stores and plastering their work areas with sappy personal ephemera. There were no clock radios playing Power 106 or Disney cruise photos tacked to their cube walls, just sleek flat-screen computers and silent bonsai trees.

At the end of the day, a gorgeous Latin guy pushing a mail cart stopped in front of my desk. He was wearing so much cologne, my nose began to twitch. " 'Sup, mami?" he asked with a sly wink. He had cocoa skin and a smokin' bod. I was so stunned by his hotness, I went mute. All I could do was smile at him and let out a loud and snotty sneeze.

It was eight P.M. when I finally got home from work. The train from Manhattan to Brooklyn had taken forever. I felt a little sad and PMS-y when I walked through my apartment door. There was no boyfriend or pet to greet me, just my oil-painting friends that hung on the walls. I collected vintage portraits (I had over twenty), and though I had no idea who these people were, they somehow comforted me. "Hi, Ricardo. Hi, Nan," I said pensively as I walked by them on the way to my bedroom. I had created little stories about each of them. Ricardo was a 1940s-era mommy's boy with pursed lips and a stand-up collar. Nan was a haughty, chain-smoking West Palm Beach divorcée in a Lilly Pulitzer caftan. We had a stormy past, Nan and I. She fell off the wall once and broke my pinkie toe.

I collapsed onto my bed, still in my rumpled work clothes. I was starving, but I was too weak even to pop my Amy's frozen enchilada into the microwave, so I turned on the Food Network for sustenance. Rachael Ray was making me really mad. On *Forty Dollars a Day*, she had just finished dinner in Pittsburgh and left another really bad tip. I switched channels and made a deal with myself: I would laze in bed for twenty minutes, and then I would get up and eat.

Suddenly there was a knock at my front door. "Marnie, you there?" cried a muffled voice.

"Open up, dude," shouted another.

Great. What were they doing here so late? It was my good friend and neighbor, Holly, with her husband, Dwayne, in tow. I opened the many latches, and Holly came shivering in with Dwayne two paces behind. Dwayne went directly to the radiator, warming his hands palms out like it was a roaring fire. Dwayne was a vegan, Holly a vegetarian, and neither of them wore any animal products or by-products. It was hemp, organic cotton, and Polarfleece. Consequently, in winter, they were almost always cold.

Holly stopped dead in her tracks and glared at my work outfit.

"Nice threads," said Dwayne, firing up a joint.

"No, they're not. You went to that job, didn't you?" Holly exclaimed.

I looked down at the ground, trying my best to feign shame and contrition, but inside I was beaming. I mean, I was working at the world's largest and most glamorous cosmetics company.

Holly got right in my face, the tiny bells in her blond dreads jingling wildly. "You know LeVigne does animal testing, in addition to clogging up the landfills with their nonbiodegradable packaging."

"But they're paying me twenty dollars an hour," I pleaded as I walked into the kitchen and pulled the enchilada out of the freezer.

Holly followed me. "I don't understand. You were making so much more as a camera assistant. I know you dropped that lens, but you worked on films for so many years. Won't they give you another chance?"

"No one will call me back. In this business, a mistake like that is unforgivable. I'm history."

"So cosmetics is your career change? What happened with that great temp job at the Ford Foundation?"

"I quit," I said, not telling her that Ford was a cheerless, paradoxical nonprofit where the toilet paper was the virtuous brown recycled kind, yet the coffee cups were curiously Styrofoam. After my demanding, peripatetic film life, I was ready for something totally glossy and indoors.

"We are not going to let you work for the man," Holly shouted, giving me the evil eye, sans mascara, of course. She yanked Dwayne over to the microwave and they stretched out their arms in front of it, forming a human chain as if they were at the entrance to the UN, protesting some injustice.

"Come on. I'm starving," I said, pushing them away.

Holly opened her Guatemalan purse, pulled out a small jar, and put it on the kitchen table. "Maybe this will stabilize your moods so you can think straight," she said. "Let's boogie, Dwayne."

Dwayne shot me a weak smile, and they were out the door.

"Don't be mad, Holl," I shouted down the hallway. "I'll put it on tonight. Promise." I closed the door and picked up the jar. It was a homemade yam cream that she claimed did wonders for PMS. Holly made perfumes and potions, often from a Wiccan book called *Kitchen Witchery*.

While Holly was an amazingly generous person, she could also be very dogmatic. It was easy for her to get all uppity on me. She had been able to "follow her bliss" by working as a masseuse at a holistic spa and volunteering at an animal shelter because Dwayne's mother had died and left them her huge co-op apartment.

After dinner, I put on a Queen Helene mint julep mask and slathered the yam cream on my stomach, praying that Holly wasn't casting some diabolical anti-corporate spell on me, like making me lose the ability to alphabetize or to wriggle into a pair of pantyhose. As I waited for the mask to dry, I reflected on what Holly had said about LeVigne's anti-eco business practices. I decided that while some of it might be true, I couldn't let things like mercury in makeup stand in the way of paying rent. And truth be told, I didn't want to intellectualize my lip gloss too much.

COSMETIC PUFFERY

Working at LeVigne was proving to be the guiltiest of pleasures because when my coworkers spoke passionately about exfoliation, they were not commiserating over the destruction of the rain forest, but rather plotting the global eradication of rough and cobbly skin. I was quickly learning that to get a face scrub to market, it took years of R and D, product testing, marketing, and publicity.

It was a thrilling world filled with tons of perks. There was lots of free food, because the meetings were catered and no one ate; I had access to every fashion magazine on the planet; and best of all, I had recently discovered the bountiful PR beauty closets where makeup and skin care products flowed like the chocolate river in *Charlie and the Chocolate Factory.* I summarily swiped fistfuls of lipstick, face creams, and moisturizers for me, and some to send to my mother. I felt like I had won the golden ticket.

I was learning all sorts of things about the company. I knew that LeVigne perfumes (or "juice," as they called it) were kept in a hermetically sealed cabinet, and it was best to hold your nose when it was opened. Most of the LeVigne scents were so heinous that I imagined a spike in homicides after they were launched. As if creating customized versions of the Twinkie Defense, people could claim that "Vienna [Hattie's original, cloying fragrance] made me do it." I also learned some interesting fragrance lingo. Phrases like *la persistence* and *sillage. La persistence* is the amount of time a fragrance lasts on the skin. *Sillage* means the trail of perfume the wearer leaves behind.

As I walked into the conference room for my first big staff meeting, pouty women with sunken cheeks and vacant expressions struck poses around a table laden with skinny food. I watched as they surreptitiously checked one another out, their well-trained eyes quickly scanning over someone's body in a visual T— toes to nose, clavicle to clavicle—cataloging the look as something they must, or in my case must not, copy. Very few of them were dressed in anything other than a minimalist designer uniform. I had been working here for about three weeks now, and I still hadn't gotten used to the brutally exacting way they dressed and carried themselves.

Connie Boyd, the new head of Global Media Relations, held court at the buffet table, gobbling down a cherry cheese Danish while the LeVignettes pecked at (depending on which diet they adhered to) mini–breakfast burgers (sans bun) or fruit salad. It was obvious that the LeVignettes were trying hard not to stare at Connie, this boyishly attractive woman in a conservative pants suit and chunky black loafers. I was sure they were hoping that her frosted hair and lack of lipstick did not imply that LeVigne-sanctioned salons and makeup applications were alien to her. With her ruddy complexion and crystal blue eyes, Connie was a cross between financial wizard Suze Orman and a professional golfer. I watched with fascination as she masterfully worked the room, vigorously shaking a series of bony hands.

This was Connie's first official GMR meeting since she'd come on board. Even though I was answering her phones, no one had bothered to formally introduce us. Nor had I officially met any of the publicists who were taking their seats and cracking open icy cans of Diet Coke.

The sun shone blindingly through the large windows, but instead of pulling down the shades, everyone except for Connie and me put on large, expensive-looking sunglasses. It was amazing how trendy people, no matter how silly they looked, always made the untrendy feel even sillier.

I was taking minutes at the meeting, and I nervously held my steno pad and pen at the ready. Normally Murfy acted as recording secretary, but she was out sick with a cold. Earlier, Tinsley had asked me if I knew Pitman. She made me so nervous that I nodded, even though I could barely take fast notes. The little secret was, not only did I not know steno, but my secretarial skills were less than average and I felt quite lucky to have snagged this job.

"Welcome to our first meeting together, folks," said Connie, squinting hard from the sun, using her hand like a tennis visor, trying futilely to make eye contact in a sea of polarized Gucci lenses. "As some of you already know, my background is in sports PR. I have an MBA from Wharton, and I worked at ESPN for ten years honing my corp-comm skill set. I'll be working hard to pump up the company's product placement positioning by getting our brands into movies, on TV, and on the skin of celebs. What else can I tell you? Kris and I have been together for ten fantabulous years, and we have two beautiful Chinese daughters whom we adopted in Shanghai."

"Did your husband go to China with you to pick them out?" Juniper asked.

"Yes, *she* did."

"She, Chris?" questioned Tinsley.

"Yes, she, Kris," Connie said proudly.

She Tarzan, she Jane, I thought.

The room broke out into nervous titters, and suddenly everyone became ravenously hungry, nibbling furiously on their heretofore untouched food.

"And now back to business," Connie continued. "I'd like it if each director could give us a heads-up on what's happening in her respective brand. But first, Tinsley, who is going to be my new point person, my go-to gal, will give us an update on some media kerfuffles that we all need to be aware of."

I noticed that Tinsley had winced when Connie

called her a "go-to gal." I'm sure she considered that beneath her.

Tinsley cleared her throat. "Kerfuffle number one: Siesta is facing more problems with *Primetime*. Remember the reporter who wrote that heinous exposé 'It All Comes Out of the Same Vat'? Well, we've been tipped off that *Primetime* is sending her out again to the department stores to try and show that Siesta's products are cosmetic puffery and that the counterpeople are doing hard-core link-selling."

I was ferociously scribbling. *Heinous, counterpeople, hard-core.* Unfortunately I was getting only every tenth word.

Connie rapped her large knuckles on the desk. "Now listen up, folks. If *Primetime*'s going to be there, we'd better make sure the counters are spotless, the beauty advisors are racially mixed, and there is absolutely no gum-chewing," she said. "We don't want the feces hitting the fan on this one."

Racially, chewing, feces, I scrawled. I suppressed a giggle and looked up from my notes while everyone else did their best to feign complicit agreement with Connie's locker-room metaphor.

A visibly rattled Tinsley spoke. "The next issue, as some of you already know, is that the Deeva PR director just resigned. I have a flotilla of interviews set up, and I will be working tirelessly to find a replacement, but until then Jacquie Wires will be doing double duty as PR director for both Deeva and Paparazzi."

Jacquie, who was clad in a beautiful man-tailored pin-striped suit, waved and nodded her head imperially. She sported Daniel Libeskind architect glasses, and her jet-black hair was cut in a severe Louise Brooks bob.

Tinsley continued. "And last but not least, kerfuffle number three: Systems is facing yet another class-action lawsuit. It seems that a group of women are claiming that Ass-stringent, the cellulitic butt tightener, is making them infertile."

Ass, butt, infertile, I quickly jotted.

"Sounds like a ticking time bomb," Connie said to Tinsley. "Let's talk later."

My writing hand went into a cramp, and when I dropped the pen to massage it, Tinsley shot me a look. I picked the Bic back up and angled the steno pad in such a way that she couldn't see what I was (or wasn't) writing.

Just then, a plasticky pregnant woman of indeterminate age stood up. She was the raven-haired Diana Duvall, the Systems PR director. She had probably been beautiful once, but all the face work made her look hyperfeminine, almost transgendered.

"Could someone please tell me which way is north?" she asked as she pulled out a powder compact from an embroidered antique satchel. "Because, as Hattie LeVigne says, northern light is the only light in which to apply one's makeup." Diana turned toward the window and powdered her nose with such flourish that a cloud of white talc enveloped her.

"Excuse me, Diana, I need to close the blinds," said Tinsley as she got up to lower them. "Leaks have been reported. We think Ronson's renting that office," she said, pointing to some darkened windows in the building across the street.

Schotzie Ronson was LeVigne's foremost cosmetics competitor, and I imagined slimy operatives in tatty trenchcoats reading our gloss-stained lips through high-powered binoculars. Ronson was always in the gossip rags. There had just been a juicy feature about him in *Vanity Fair*. He was a former celebrity makeup artist who dressed like a hip mortician in a sharkskin Beatles suit and seemed to intuitively understand the youth market.

Ronson relentlessly nipped at LeVigne's stilettoed heels. He would wait for a LeVigne product to launch, study their mistakes, and then bring out something virtually identical but with all the kinks worked out. It was even rumored that he planted spies at LeVigne so he could bring his version to market first and at lower price points. In the *Vanity Fair* article, it was implied that Hattie's disappearance was directly related to Schotzie's rise to powder-puff power. But where had she gone?

Diana Duvall grabbed a laser pointer and began a PowerPoint presentation. It was a good thing most everyone was still wearing sunglasses because she pointed the red dot with such reckless abandon that she surely could have burned out someone's retina. "We've all heard of separation anxiety, right?" she asked rhetorically as she clicked on a photo of Mount Saint Helens erupting with gooey lava. "Well, guess what teenagers have? It's what the dermatological community calls 'suppuration anxiety.'" She clicked to the next slide, which had a dictionary definition: SUPPURATE—TO FORM OR DISCHARGE PUS.

I scribbled to keep up, but she was talking too fast. *Anxiety, teenage, discharge.*

"Connie, let me give it to you straight," continued Diana. "We're rolling out an exciting new line of teen pimple products called AKNY. It's pronounced 'acne.' One day while I was having an oxygenating lymphatic-drainage fruit peel facial at the Systems spa, something dawned on me. I thought, why don't we take this pores-and-pimples show on the road? So we are conducting a major talent search to find America's hottest teens. The kids will live on tour buses and hand out AKNY samples at malls and high schools across America. We're calling it the Blemish Brigade."

Winsome, Diana's no-nonsense assistant, spoke. "You can't believe the breakouts AKNY's able to combat. Sebaceous cysts. Facial pustules. Whiteheads on top of blackheads."

Pimples, the great equalizer. I sighed to myself. Brad Pitt had bad acne scars, and this somehow made him more human.

Diana continued her spiel. "Our goal is to eradicate zits from the faces of America's adolescents. Marketing has projected that by the end of next fiscal year, we will have decimated thirty million pimples nationwide! And then we go global. Here's a little secret. Several days before the buses arrive, under the guise of a Christian outreach group, we'll be hosting teen pizza and pop parties. The grease-infused pepperoni has been specially formulated by our chemists, and they've determined exactly how many days it will take for the zits to reach full maximum yuck potential. Then we jump right in, handing out the solution."

"Sounds like your sales will explode," Connie chortled.

Beautiful skin took my breath away. With my large pores and sebaceous oil that starts reslicking the minute I dry my freshly washed face, I'm a sucker for velvety, peaches-and-cream derma. After years of my mother screaming at me for eating French fries and candy, I finally realized that it isn't the food we eat; it's the genetic cards we're dealt. Either you have good skin genes or you don't. Them's the breakouts.

After a few more equally ridiculous presentations, the Diet Cokes began to wear off and the women's eyes glazed over like the gloss on their perpetually parted lips. Connie raked her fingers through her closely shingled hair. "Excellent work, folks. Let's go hawk some makeup!"

As the meeting was breaking up, Tinsley whinnied over to me, "It would be terribly helpful, Marnie Mann, if you could type up those notes and have them back to me by the end of the business day," she intoned, trotting away before I could answer.

Connie sauntered over to me. "Hey, you. Didn't get your name," she said, ripping a bite out of a bagel.

"Marnie Mann," I replied, reaching out to shake her hand. "Nice to formally meet you, Connie."

I noticed that Connie had an eczema patch on her wrist. She noticed mine, and we both gave each other a knowing nod. "Keep up the good work, kid," Connie mumbled with a full mouth, walking back to her office. I didn't know exactly what "good work" I was doing, but it was nice to hear some positive feedback.

In the hall I bumped into Jarret, the PR art director, and he asked me to lunch. He seemed to be the only person who ate off-premises and certainly the only person interested in dining with me. Wearing the coveted Hermès leather wraparound watch and a black cashmere wifebeater, he was very cute, but no straight guy would have such immaculately groomed eyebrows or, for that matter, be wearing eye makeup.

Jarret was carrying a headshot of a LeVigne executive, which was marked up with grease pencil to suggest a major facial reconstruction.. "As Hattie LeVigne always says, there are no ugly executives, just unretouched ones," he exclaimed.

"Hattie? Is she around?" I asked excitedly as Jarret's cell phone rang and he took the call.

I went back to my desk to get my purse. While I waited for Jarret to pick me up, I flipped through the steno pages. Shit. My handwriting was practically illegible. I needed to sit down right then and transcribe the meeting from memory before I forgot everything.

"Let's go, ho," said Jarret, suddenly appearing at my desk.

"I don't think I can leave. I've got to do something for Tinsley."

He grabbed my arm and yanked me out of my seat. "Chillax. Do it when you get back. I mean, babygirl, you're only a temp."

We went to a Korean deli down the block. As I hungrily ate a greasy focaccia sandwich, Jarret tucked into a grilled chicken breast that lay atop a bed of steamed spinach. "Bread doesn't give you brain fog?" he asked, watching me stuff my face.

"I like bread," I said defensively.

"Your lunch would give me instant carb face," he chided sanctimoniously.

Suddenly my sandwich seemed a lot less appetizing.

"So spill it. How was the meeting? Any rad products coming down the pike?" he continued, staring at me with a paralyzing eye-lock.

For some reason Jarret seemed most interested in the AKNY Blemish Brigade campaign. I couldn't figure out why since his skin was clear and poreless. By way of explanation, he confessed that he suffered from back acne. I promised to show him photos of the cutest AKNY bus tour finalists that Diana had passed out at the meeting. It was good that we were talking about the meeting because it made me recall some of the details I had to type up later.

Jarret, who had seemed relatively normal in the office, launched into a series of fantastical stories about his personal life. He told me he grew up in Burbank, and his father worked the bubble machine on the *Lawrence Welk Show*; that in high school he was Peter Pan at Disneyland and got stuck in midair for ten hours on a broken wire; and that he was once part of the Witness Protection Program. When I asked why, he quickly changed the subject. He also told me he worked weekends as a motivational dancer at bar mitzvahs. That I could believe.

With his pumped-up chest, skinny waist, and protruding bubble butt, he reminded me of a satyr. He bragged that he was on anabolic steroids, and he lived for crystal meth. "It's called Tina. I'm on it right now," he said, bringing his face close to mine. He did seem rather amped, but then so did everyone at LeVigne.

"I've got to get back," I said. We both quickly retouched our makeup and got up to leave.

Outside, Jarret pointed to Giuseppe's Shoe Repair, a popular shoemaker where the LeVignettes and Condé Nasties had their Choos and Manolos resoled. "These puppies, my friend, are a result of sitting on the right lap at the right time. I'm going over to get them shined," he said, kicking up his very expensive J.M. Weston–shod foot. As he left, he imparted some more pearls of wisdom. "Marnie, did you know that Hattie LeVigne had the bottoms of her shoes cleaned and polished every time she wore them?"

"Why?" I asked incredulously.

"You can't make deals with dirty heels," he said, exasperated, as if this basic bit of information should have been hardwired into my brain.

When I finally got back to my desk, I started typing up the meeting notes, using the scribbles in my steno pad as a guide. After I dropped off the document in Tinsley's office (luckily she wasn't there), I took a different way around back to my desk. At the far end of a hallway was a true-to-size replica of a department store makeup counter, where Gentry Jones, the resident makeup artist (and as far as I could tell, the only African-American LeVigne employee) did touch-ups, demonstrated the latest products, and gave beauty advice. The makeup counter was shaped in a large square, and each of the four brands laid claim to one side of it. I stopped for a moment and looked at all the vibrant candy colors. The creams, the potions, the soft black brushes. It was like a cosmetics buffet. I wanted to dip my fingers into all the pots and palettes and play dress-up, but I was told that Gentry lorded over the counters with an iron fist and to stay away unless he invited you over.

As I headed back to my desk, the door to a conference room was opened a crack. Classical music floated out into the hallway. I tiptoed over and peered in. The room was dark, with the exception of several candles flickering on a credenza. When my eyes adjusted to the light, I had to cover my mouth so as not to gasp audibly. A group of women were sitting around a table, and a doctor in a crisp white lab coat was moving around the room with a syringe, deftly injecting their lips, cheeks, and brows.

I couldn't believe my eyes. They were getting their faces fluffed up, and at work, no less! Why visit your doctor when your doctor could visit you? It was instant gratification to the max. Holly, who had calmed down a little about my new job, was coming over for dinner that night. I couldn't wait to tell her about what I had just witnessed.

Eye Told You So

On the subway ride home, I scrutinized the faces of my fellow commuters. How many folks on this Brooklyn-bound train had had Botox injections? And how many were faithful users of LeVigne's antiaging products? I couldn't stop thinking about what I had seen in the conference room. It confused me. If LeVigne employees were getting shot up with Botox, what did that say about the efficacy of their age-defying unguents? Were they hawking products that they knew didn't work? The company made tanning lotions, yet all the PR girls went to tanning salons. They made exfoliating scrubs, but they all went to the doctor for dermabrasions. Despite the multitude of wrinkle creams, they were erasing their lines with the prick of a needle. No wonder they were all so attractive and perfect looking.

Shortly after I got home and changed into sweats, Holly arrived and we began to prepare dinner. I wanted to tell her straight off about the weird injection party I had witnessed, but I knew better than to plunge right into it when her blood sugar was low.

Holly put some jasmine rice in the rice cooker, and I heated up two Worthington tempeh Stakelets. I poured us some organic shiraz. "It's wine o'clock," I said as we clinked glasses.

"Good times," said Holly, her eyes crinkling up into a warm smile.

She could be such an enveloping earth mama, and I needed that right now. "I like that lip gloss you're wearing," I said. "Did you buy it at the food co-op?"

"I made it myself. I mashed up some organic raspberries, picked out the seeds, and mixed in some shea butter. Good color, right?"

I threw some onions in a hot pan and doused them with olive oil. "Really good."

"I know it's a little early to ask, but are you going to be making scents and stuff for Christmas gifts like you did last year? They were really great," Holly said.

"I think so, if I have enough spare time with this job and all."

We both loved to make handcrafted things. It was a direct response to our consumerist, throwaway culture. I also liked it because my family was so far away and it gave me a homey feeling. Holly had even been a contestant on the Style Network's *Craft Corner Death Match*, where she had to make a wedding cake out of Twinkies. As she'd slathered whipped-cream mortar between spongy yellow bricks, Holly looked at the camera and made an impassioned speech about junk food and fat camp for kids, which of course was edited out of the program.

Holly handed me a colander to strain the kale. "Do you want to come to a demonstration with me and Dwayne on Saturday? We're protesting Animal Planet," said Holly. "They have this reality show about bees, and it's from the bees' prospective. They're fitted with tiny little cameras. It's a disgrace!"

"Uh, maybe," I said, guiltily thinking about the clothes-shopping spree I had planned. Holly was so much more noble than I. She lived green and sub-scribed to a lifestyle philosophy she called "One Small Thing." The idea was that if everyone did just one envi-ronmentally conscious thing every day, the little incre-mental gestures added up and made a huge difference.

It was getting hot in the kitchen, so I pinned back my hair and rolled up my sleeves.

"What's that on your arms?" Holly asked, pointing to a scaly red rash that enveloped my elbows.

"Oh, nothing," I replied. "Just my eczema flaring up again."

"You know that's totally stress related."

"I'm not stressed."

"Yes, you are."

"Okay, maybe a little." I didn't tell her that part of the stress was from thinking about an upcoming date with someone I had met online. I had been on three dates this month, and they had all gone rather badly. This new guy was a doctor named Evan Milstein. Holly wouldn't want to hear about it because he practiced Western medicine.

In the past several months, Holly and Dwayne had set me up with a few of their guy friends, but they were all too crunchy and they all wore man-dals. An occasional pot smoker was fine, but most of them were burners in locked-in states whose idea of a pinup girl was Julia But-terfly Hill, the environmentalist who lived for 738 days in a redwood tree.

"Here, this is for you," Holly said as she handed me a glass vial filled with an amber liquid.

"What's that?" I asked nervously. In the four years I'd known her, I'd discovered that sometimes Holly's po-tions were sublime, sometimes as explosive as a mush-room cloud.

"It's a tincture from *Kitchen Witchery*, to help you

meet a man. Marnie, there's a guy out there, and if he can't find you, we're going to find him. You need to erase the bad energy from the past and start fresh," she said.

I rolled the cylindrical tube across the table to Holly. "I don't know about this. I'm not a desperado, at least not yet, and furthermore, *Kitchen Witchery* is not the way I want to meet a guy," I said.

"Trust me, *Kitchen Witchery* blows away all those girly-girl self-help books you like to read. I did a ritual purification bath right before I met Dwayne at Burning Man. And look at us."

"I'm sure the Ecstasy and naked dancing didn't hurt."

"I can tell by your negativity that you are not using my yam cream."

"I'm not being negative," I said. "I'm just being realistic."

"Chill," Holly said. "My potion will cleanse your chakras and bestow you with deity and power. It's made with organic essential oils like lavender, rosemary, and patchouli."

She had lost me at *chakra*. The food was ready, and we dug in.

"Tell me what's going on over at the evil empire," said Holly. As much as she didn't approve of my working there, she was certainly interested in hearing about it. It was like an antipornography activist who knew the intimate details of every raunchy film.

"Please don't say 'I told you so,' but working at LeVigne is turning out to be a bit peculiar," I said, cutting into my rubbery tempeh Stakelet, pretending it was a buttery filet mignon.

"Just a bit?" asked Holly.

"Well, maybe more than a bit. A few days ago, I was at my desk reapplying some lipstick I swiped from my mom when I was home this summer. Estée Lauder brand, you know, in that ugly gold ribbed tube? Murfy, one of my coworkers, came right up to me and asked where the mah-jongg tournament was, and then she snatched it out of my hand and threw it in the trash."

"That's so rude," said Holly, topping off our wine-glasses.

"I know, right? She told me never to bring the competitor on premises again. And all day long there's this steady stream of women—I call them silhouette junkies because they parade by my desk, preening and checking themselves out in every reflective surface. And as you can probably imagine, I'm the fattest one there."

"Survival of the thinnest," said Holly as she sucked in her cheeks like Kate Moss. "Years ago, when I back-packed through Europe, I met this guy in Sardinia. He taught me this phrase: *bella figura*. It means that you are willing to go to any length for beauty and perfection. It sounds to me like you're at *bella figura* ground friggin' zero."

"But what's wrong with looking good?"

"Nothing. It just takes the spontaneity out of life. If you're too busy searching for the perfect shoes, how can you see the beauty all around you?"

"But I love shoes." Holly shot me a look. "I mean, I just feel so dowdy there."

"What are you talking about? You always look cute."

"Thanks. Do you want to date me?" I joked.

"You'd have to become a veggie first," she retorted. We both laughed.

"Get this," I said, shaking some sesame seeds onto my kale. "A woman at work left early the other day to get her fat cells harvested. She's freezing them so that when her skin starts losing elasticity, she'll have them injected back into her face."

Holly shook her head in disgust. "We live in the weirdest times. Please don't go back there tomorrow," she implored. "Tell them you've come down with a gnarly flesh-eating virus."

"Are you kidding? They'd definitely want to catch that," I said. "This afternoon I saw a bunch of them, some younger than us, get shot up with Botox!"

Holly rolled her eyes at this news. "The receptionist at the spa just gave her notice. Come work with me. It'll be fun. They want me to make some all-natural products for the boutique they're opening in the spring. We can do it together."

The thing I couldn't tell her was that I was becoming addicted to working at LeVigne. I was using a Systems eye cream for puffiness and a Deeva hydrator that worked on the top layer of the skin to reduce the appearance of fine lines. They seemed to be making a difference.

After Holly went home, I did the dishes and drew a hot bath. *What the hell,* I thought as I lowered myself into the steaming water, trying to let the stress of the day dissipate, while I visualized my goals. The water felt good, but I couldn't relax.

My stress level heightened, and my mind went to its usual desperate and familiar outposts. I was past the big three-oh! What was I doing with my life? Wasn't I supposed to be zeroing in on a life partner? Why couldn't I get along better with my father? I hadn't told him I was temping, because that would have been way beneath a trial attorney's daughter's station. But in one of life's perverse little ironies, I had learned some secretarial skills during high school summers at his law firm. Of course, that was when the world was pre-Internet and post-Post-its.

The bleak, gray autumn days only magnified what was wrong with my life, and my fear was that when the days grew longer and warmer, and the tulips on Park Avenue pushed up, the sun would melt the ice floe that I was encased in and I would be left treading in its murky wake. Like Madonna, I needed to go on a Reinvention Tour and find something I loved to do.

I filled the tub with more hot water and tried to talk myself down from this chaotic mental ledge. I slowly let my stress dissipate while visualizing one of my elusive goals—the type of man I wanted to meet. Handsome, with a high FICO score. No. Good credit probably meant he was boring and had no life. Okay. Start again. Cute and artsy rambling man. But would he still be crashing on sofas into middle age? Was I even ready to meet the man of my dreams? Or did I just want to get my freak on for a while?

Enough of the histrionics. I closed my eyes and let Holly's chakra-speak fill my head. "Don't hold yourself back, Marnie. You have the power to change your life."

I steeped for a while longer, and when I lifted myself out of the tub, I felt more alive and conscious. I even saved a spider that was crawling on the sink. I coaxed it onto a tissue and let it out on the windowsill. That was a start. Now it was time to anoint myself. I inhaled Holly's fragrant love potion and stood sky-clad (Holly's word for naked) facing a northerly direction. I dabbed oil on the soles of my feet, on the base of my spine, and over my heart—as Madonna would say—for inspiration.

Dr. No

I was meeting Evan the Doctor at a pub in the Carroll Gardens neighborhood of Brooklyn. When I walked through the door, a man of Evan's description was sitting on a bar stool, nursing a drink. I quickly glanced at his shoes. Excellent. Brown suede Cole Haan lace-ups. Safe to proceed.

"Evan?" I asked excitedly, but I knew it was him—for once, a guy who looked like his online photo.

"Hey there," he said, getting up and giving me a kiss on the cheek. Wow, he was taller than advertised. I loved tall guys. Was it some hardwired, primal thing about feeling protected? Evan pulled out a stool for me and we both sat down.

"What would you like to drink?" Evan asked.

"I'd love a sidecar with a sugar rim."

"That's old-fashioned."

"I'm an old-fashioned kinda gal."

Before I had even settled in, Evan let out a big, languorous yawn and then quickly clamped his hand over his mouth. Was I boring him already?

"Oh, God. I'm really sorry. It's not you. I'm on this crazy schedule. I'm a resident in obstetrics. Sleep is this elusive, ephemeral thing. It's like the girl who got away."

"The nap that got away. You can sleep when you retire."

"But then there's golf," he said, stifling another yawn.

"Want to play a game?" I asked, taking a sip of my yummy drink.

"As long as I can do it from a sitting position."

"No problem. Who do people say you look like?"

He blinked a couple of times. "Uh, my uncle Irwin?"

If Uncle Irwin was as handsome as George Clooney. With his prematurely graying Caesar haircut and thick dark brows, Evan resembled the cutie-pie movie star. "I mean a celebrity."

He looked stumped. "I don't know. No one's ever really said."

"C'mon. Don't be so modest. You look just like George Clooney."

The bar door creaked open, and I turned to see who had come in. When I turned back around, Evan's eyes were shut and his head was lolling. I'd had a lot of things go wrong on dates, but no one had ever fallen asleep on me. At least not outside of the bedroom. I decided to let it slide. After all, he was a friggin' doctor. "Maybe we should do this another night," I said as I lightly touched his shoulder.

He blinked himself awake. "I'm sorry, Marnie. Okay, where were we? The game, right?" He rubbed his eyes and assessed my face, making all kinds of calculations, personal and societal, those private judgments and biases I would never know. "Has anyone ever said you look like That Girl?"

"Which girl?" I replied, looking around the room. It was just too easy to mess with a sleep-deprived person.

"You know. That Girl," he said.

"Oh, Marlo Thomas. No. I usually get Maggie Gyllenhaal."

The mention of pretty actresses seemed to perk him up. "You work for LeVigne, right?" he asked.

"Yeah." He got points for remembering our introductory phone conversation. Evan ordered us two more cocktails. "How was your day today?" I asked.

"Very long. I spent the morning inside Noelle."

Check, please! If I left now, I could make it home in time for *Law & Order SVU*, where I could get my molestation with commercial breaks.

He must have seen me eyeing the door. "No. No," he laughed. "It's not what you think. Noelle's the birthing simulator we use at school to practice deliveries."

"Sure she's not a blow-up doll?"

"Far from it. They made her realistic, yet not distracting. She looks like Ellen DeGeneres, actually," he said.

I nodded, and Evan bought us another round as I heard about head descent, cervical dilation, and the ins and outs of the all-too-pesky umbilical cord. "All I can say is, don't wait until you're forty to have children. It's complication city," he said with world-weary authority.

Wow. Evan was the first guy ever to broach the subject of kids on the first date. I smiled at him, and he gazed at me. Were we making a love connection? He was cute, and he seemed to have a heart. I felt really comfortable around him. I wondered what he'd be like after a solid night's slumber. He leaned over and gently touched my forehead. How sweet, I thought as we stared into each other's eyes.

"Forceps," he exclaimed.

"What?" I responded, wrenching myself back.

"I can see a small dent above the procerus muscle. The obstetrician who delivered you used forceps."

"I have a dent in my forehead?" I said, touching the spot. Just great. First the chocolate-chip spots, and now this.

"Don't worry. It's barely noticeable."

"Forceps? That's so nineteenth-century. My mother wouldn't have let her doctor use them."

"You'd be surprised to know that they were only taken out of general use in the late '70s."

Amazingly, all this clinical medical chat made me really randy, and before I knew it, we were kissing drunkenly on the street and then we walked around the corner to Evan's place. We made out on his couch for a while, and then he unbuttoned my shirt, feeling my breasts. If I hadn't been so tipsy, I probably would have enjoyed it more.

"Very good. No lumps," he whispered. "Although you're a little cystic. Might want to cut back on the coffee."

This was not my idea of "playing doctor," but two could play at this game. I groped at his crotch. "I feel two large bumps between your, uh, you know," I said shyly. "The prognosis is not good."

"Let's see what we have here," he said, spreading my legs apart. I was very wet.

I closed my eyes and imagined that I was at a tony Park Avenue medical practice. I was quickly led into an examination room with good lighting, and before I knew it, there was a knock at the door. The handsome Dr. Evan Milstein, in his starched white coat and good leather shoes, poked his head in and told me how happy he was to see me. As we chatted about my tipped uterus, it was like the world had melted away. There was only me.

Suddenly my eyes popped open. The real Evan, the bloodshot-eyed med student Evan with the attention span of a gnat, was haphazardly rooting around in my vagina like he was looking for loose change. "This one lady was as wide as the Lincoln Tunnel. I mean, the baby fell right out," he said, unzipping his pants. I could see his erect penis looming above me.

"Uh, I don't know about that," I said, pushing him away.

"What if I put it in an inch?"

"If I give an inch, you'll take a mile." This was all so wrong. While I appreciated the gratis gyno exam, I should have gone home, but the spins had taken hold and the train between his house and mine at this late hour was not running on a normal schedule. "Do you mind if I stay here and we just go to sleep?"

"That's music to my ears," he said as he unceremoniously passed out on top of me. His snoring was immediate and prodigious. I had to wriggle myself out from under him and put a pillow over my ears.

In the morning, the buzz of Evan's electric shaver woke me up. My head was pounding from a horrendous hangover. I looked at his alarm clock. Shit. It was almost seven-thirty, and we had the second half of the GMR product meeting this morning. When I heard him leave the bathroom, I ran in, threw on my wrinkled clothes, splashed some water on my face, and brushed my teeth with my finger. Then I went into the kitchen, where Evan was making coffee.

"I was kinda soused last night. What exactly happened?" he asked sheepishly, handing me a glass of extra-pulpy, calcium-enriched Tropicana.

"For starters, you didn't use a condom, and I'm not on the pill."

"What?" he yelped, the story of our illegitimate baby and his fall from grace written all over his terrified face.

"Just kidding. You passed out and nearly suffocated me. But that's okay. I lived."

Evan grabbed my hands and inspected my inflamed skin. "You've got a nice case of eczema there."

"I thought you'd never notice."

"What are you putting on that?"

"The dregs of a tube of Elidel. I'm kinda between in-surance plans right now."

"I'll call you in another scrip," he said. "Just let me know which pharmacy."

As I was leaving, Evan kissed me lightly on the mouth. "I like you, Marnie. I have crazy mad hours, with school and all, but I'd love to hook up once in a while," he said shyly. "Don't take this the wrong way, but it's got to be *really* casual."

By the time I left Evan's place, it was eight-thirty A.M. There was no time to go home and change, so I went directly to work. My disappointment at Evan's "casual" comment didn't hit me until I was halfway to Midtown. I thought I had healed from the breakup with Nick—it had been almost a year—but I was getting that hollow feeling inside again. When I got off the train at Rocke-feller Center, I walked by H&M. They were already open for business. I stopped and looked at my wretched reflection in the plate-glass window. I didn't want to wear the same clothes to work again, so I went in to buy a new outfit. God knows, shopping had such an insidious way of filling up that sad, empty hole.

As I waited in line for a dressing room (there was a line at this hour!), I spotted several other half-asleep, hungover women. We gave each other the nod of shame. I paid for my new clothes and raced over to Sephora to have my makeup done. Drats! They didn't open until ten. When I got to work, I rushed into the PR bathroom to change and gussy myself up. My hair was greasy and flyaway, and I reeked of last night's booze. I was exhausted and it showed.

I went into the pantry for a cup of coffee. Saskia was

wiping down the yogurt machine, which was dripping with vanilla and strawberry stalactites, Murfy was scraping out the innards of a bagel with a tiny pink shovel, and Juniper was in deep thought. "If I could just take Viggo's chin, Colin's manhood, Orlando's eyelashes . . ."

"And the Donald's wallet," I said, "you'd have the perfect man."

"How'd you know that?" asked Juniper, impressed by my grasp of the obvious.

"Because you're suffering from a bad case of Frankenstein Syndrome. Someday in the future, we'll be able to cobble together the perfect boyfriend. And won't that be nice."

I headed into the conference room to join the same group as last time for the second half of the GMR brand meeting. I was surprised that I had been asked back by Tinsley. Somehow, I had pulled off the first batch of minutes without blowing it. I sat down and nervously opened my steno pad. The only thing that was keeping me awake was my pounding headache. I took a deep, calming breath, hoping I could pull off this charade a second time.

Connie welcomed everyone back. "FiFi, we've all been waiting to hear about what's happening with Siesta," she said as we took our seats.

FiFi Langford, an Australian woman with a raspy Marianne Faithfull voice, long fringy bangs, and an oddly sun-worn face, got up to speak. With her smoldering kohl eye makeup and a white leather coatdress, she looked like the world's trendiest, unhealthiest dental hygienist. FiFi slowly circled the long table three times before she spoke in a croaky, spooky voice. "We are set to launch a revolutionary new firming night cream called Parachute, and mark my words, it will change the course of dermal history."

How did night cream know it was dark outside? I wondered.

FiFi continued. "Parachute was created by a brilliant Icelandic oceanographer named Olaf Olafson. His key ingredient is newborn sea anemones. The anemones are harvested according to a lunar calendar from the Greenland Sea, and then flown by private jet to our laboratory in Piscataway. Olaf Olafson is so concerned with quality that the harvesters must be nonsmokers and cannot wear nail polish or perfume, not even ours. The tincture is mixed with Greenlandian glacial water and then stewed for five months at very high temperatures in old wooden vats. To activate the distilling process, a surging Philip Glass score is continuously played until the miraculous juices are whipped at high speed into a luxuriously viscous poultice. It's going to be the most expensive product LeVigne sells."

Newborn, stewed, poultice, I quickly scrawled. They talked so damn fast and I was fighting so hard to stay awake.

"*How* expensive?" queried Connie. I got the feeling she wore drugstore brands just like I did.

"Price points are not an issue. This is a luxury demographic," scoffed FiFi with a dismissive wave of her hand.

"How much?" demanded Connie.

"It will retail at six hundred dollars a jar," said FiFi.

Connie and I gasped.

And with that, FiFi grabbed a jar of Parachute off the table and, with a sharp jerk of her thumb, pushed my chin back and fluttered some cream all over my face.

"Apply it with an upward stroke. Never down, because that will loosen the muscles and make the skin sag."

I tried to squirm away, but FiFi kept at it. Was this some sick sorority hazing?

"Do not rub or pat the unguent," FiFi continued. "You must apply it with fluttery dabs."

Everyone repeated her words like a magical mantra. "Fluttery dabs. Fluttery dabs."

Looking at her wizened skin, I was surprised that FiFi hadn't gone under the knife or the needle to erase her own facial road map. Maybe she was the ultimate LeVigne devotee, fervently believing that the products, given enough time and attention, would do their job.

"It's age-defying," Murfy exclaimed. Everyone oohed and aahed.

"Marnie, can you feel how nourishing it is? Doesn't your skin feel supple?" Juniper squealed.

"Stop. Please!" I pleaded. "I have really oily skin. This stuff will give me instant whiteheads."

The room went silent. "You mean to say you don't moisturize?" FiFi asked with abject horror, as if I confessed to doing my own mani-pedis. Which I did sometimes.

Juniper took a spoon and dipped it into the cream. "Parachute is good for the insides too. So pure, you can eat it right out of the jar," she exclaimed. "Olaf Olafson is known to put a dollop on his dessert." Juniper passed it around, and everyone took a taste.

"What's the trans-fat content?" asked Diana as she inspected the label.

The cream tasted horrible, but, trying to be a team player, I choked it down.

He's Catnip to the Ladies

It was finally Friday and, other than having scaly eczema arms, I felt great and was ready to start the weekend. After work, I went to the Duane Reade by my office to pick up the eczema cream that Evan had called in. That was really sweet of him. He shouldn't have. No, he should have. I waited a half hour in line only to find out that it wasn't there. I had the pharmacist check three times. My skin was on fire. Damn it. He must have forgotten. Just as well. Maybe I wasn't meant to use some toxic steroidal cream that might give me cancer.

It was a temperate mid-November night, and I didn't feel like going home yet, so I took the train to SoHo and walked around. I thought about how cute Evan was, but, sadly, how extremely unavailable. I didn't want to fall into that trap of pursuing someone who wasn't going to be there. And what kind of guy went into gynecology, anyway? With all the vaginas he saw, how would mine ever be special?

When I stopped in front of Dean & DeLuca to wait for the light to change on Broadway, I suddenly realized it was my turn to buy snacks for The Hookers, my craft circle, which was meeting on Sunday. I had no business being all bling, but instead of thriftily purchasing the provisions at my local Key Food, I ducked into the pricey gourmet market.

Pushing around a doll-sized shopping cart, I casually strolled up and down the savory aisles, pretending to be a wealthy New Yorker, when in fact, I was, for the first time ever, behind on my credit cards. I put crackers, olives, veggie pâté, grapes, and bread in my cart. The Hookers loved cheese, but I saved that purchase for last because: a) these days you needed to show up at a cheese counter clutching that hefty French food dictionary, *Larousse Gastronomique*, and b) in recent years, along with my myriad skin conditions and allergies, I had become severely lactose intolerant. Lactaid didn't work very well and it sometimes gave me gas, so subsequently I had to let go of my love of dairy, and in a sort of childish retribution, I grew to disdain it. Cheese had become my epicurean enemy.

I reluctantly wheeled my cart over and surveyed the vast selection. I blinked a couple of times, not having the faintest idea of what to buy. When I looked up at the elevated dairy counter, a tall Eurasian guy in a starched white apron was looking down at me and, surprisingly, he seemed ready, willing, and able to assist me. Usually, in places like this, the staff was soporifically blasé. He, on the other hand, was smiling and bright-eyed, behind square black Elvis Costello specs.

As I was about to speak—to explain to this stranger that, sadly, I could no longer eat cheese and I needed some remedial help with the huge assortment that lay before me—an older woman in a long mink coat hip-checked me and deftly swept front and center. She asked the cheese guy for a taste of something, which he obligingly cut from a large white wheel.

"Absolutely delicious, Paulie," she said rapturously as she popped the tiny wedge into her pursed mouth. "Mossy. Tastes just like a walk in the forest. Now give me something a little more raw and alive. Paulie, you taught me that the best cheeses are made from unpasteurized milk."

"Louis Pasteur is the devil," they chimed in gleeful unison.

As he obliged her, I stepped back to get a better look. Because of his nerdy glasses, I wouldn't have immediately noticed him, but upon closer inspection, he was strikingly handsome with a nice square jaw, thick spiky hair, and a well-groomed goatee.

Another well-heeled dowager sidled up next to the first. "I love how you cut the cheese, Paul," she said, apparently unaware of her sophomoric figure of speech.

He and I looked at each other, suppressing giggles. Apparently this guy had his share of groupies. When the women finally left empty-handed, he shot me a look that wasn't the usual "may I help you?" retail kind of look. I turned around to make sure there wasn't a supermodel towering behind me. And amazingly there wasn't. He looked at me. I looked at him. He smiled. I smiled. I yanked the sleeves of my coat down so that he couldn't see the eczema blooming on my wrists.

"After all that, they didn't buy anything?" I asked.

"They come in all the time. Never get a thing. Just lonely samplers, I guess." He was being modest. I had witnessed some full-throttle adoration. They didn't want cheese; they wanted a handsome gigolo.

"Would you like a taste of something?" he asked. But before I could say no, he handed me a thin curl he peeled from a huge orb the size of a Firestone tire. "Try this Reggiano," he said.

I waved it away, but he wouldn't take no for an answer. "How much for the wheel?" I joked, trying to deflect the fact that I was pretending to nibble it.

He looked at me dumbfoundedly. "You want to buy the whole wheel?"

"We Hookers like to eat."

He looked at me funny.

"Uh, I'm sorry. I mean my craft circle."

"Even so, that's eighty pounds of cheese," he said, looking at it uncertainly through his nerdy-cool glasses.

We stared at each other for a few beats longer than the normal customer/sales-associate allotment.

"What's the number?" he asked, positioning the knife over the cheese wheel.

"Uh," I said, hesitating, wondering why a guy this utterly model-cute would want my phone number. "Let me write it down."

"No, you can just tell me," he said.

"You must have a really good memory. I can't remember my own number sometimes."

Paul blushed. "Uh, I meant the number of people in your party."

"Oh. Six," I said, embarrassed and disappointed.

He suggested Bonne Bouche, a silky, pungent goat cheese, and a semihard cow's milk cheese called Tomme. "And this one has a mild, nutty flavor," he said, cupping something greenish-brown in his hands.

The cheese was beautifully wrapped in brandy-soaked chestnut leaves. How could I refuse something this exquisite? I bought everything Paul suggested, praying my Visa would go through.

"What's your name?" he asked.

"Marnie. And I guess you're Paulie?"

He blushed. "Paul, actually. Pleasure to meet you. I like your gap," he said, staring at my imperfect teeth.

"Oh, no, they're Levis," I bantered, feeling like we were "meeting cute" in a 1940s screwball comedy.

"I meant your great smile."

His handsomeness kind of frightened me. He must have gotten tons of attention from the ladies. "Uh, thanks," I said, blushing, not knowing what else to say.

As I was leaving, he pushed a pad and pen across the counter. "By the way, could I get your number? Phone number, that is."

My hand was shaking as I wrote it down. He was the cutest hottie that had ever come on to me. Was Holly's guy potion actually working?

I was bone tired when I got home, so I sank into the couch and turned on the TV. Ugh. If I had to be subjected to one more makeover show, I was going to slit my wrists. I didn't want to watch another sorry little stucco house get revamped. I didn't want to witness the transformation of yet another sloppy straight guy into a tidy metrosexual, and I especially did not want to watch another face get redone.

The phone rang. I looked at the caller ID. It was my father.

"Hi, Dad," I said. I could hear my stepmother's shrill, chirpy voice in the background. My father was married to Trudy "Everything I Touch Turns to Sold" Woolery, standard-issue wife No. 2 and a real estate broker, originally from Connecticut, who now hawked jerry-rigged condos in LA. Her cutesy suburban face was plastered on bus stop benches all over the So Cal beach communities. In the past couple of years, with all the competition between brokers for the ever-dwindling property inventory, she threatened to stand on the corner in satin hot pants in an attempt to hook for listings.

Trudy was petite, frosted, and wore sequined blousons. Her tops were bedazzled to such excess, it looked like the designer had taken a hit off a crack pipe before creating his "Fernando Originals." Her colorful clothing had always entertained me, but now, after being held captive in LeVigne's Hermès halfway house, I winced just thinking about her getups.

I still had a vivid memory of the day my mother had thrown a pickle tray at my dad and splattered Trudy's crisp white suit with Gulden's mustard when she discovered their deli tryst. During my parents' acrimonious divorce proceedings, I slipped out of LA basically unnoticed and went to study at NYU.

"How's the job hunt going?" asked my dad in his raspy ex-smoker's voice.

"I've been temping," I confessed.

"You're what? After all the money I spent on film school? And you were working with Ridley Scott."

He didn't have to rub it in. "I know, Dad. I think I just needed a major change. I got a job at LeVigne Cosmetics."

His tone suddenly changed. "LeVigne? Really? We did legal work for them some years back. Extremely profitable operation. Sounds like a good thing. So you're working there full-time, I take it?"

"For right now, I'll be moving around from brand to brand."

"Stop dabbling! You've got to pick something and stick with it," my dad lectured.

"You don't want to be a serf your whole life," inserted a female voice from thin air.

I gasped. It was Trudy. She must have been listening on the other extension. "Marnie, my psychic sees big changes for you in the upcoming year. She thinks you're going to get involved with a man whose first name begins with an O."

"How utterly specific," I said.

"Marnie, there's no need for sarcasm," snapped my father. "You know that Trudy and I only want the best for you."

"I don't know if your father told you, Marn, but I just found out I was a robber baron in one of my many illustrious past lives. Isn't that neat?"

"Watching any golf, Dad?" I asked, trying to change the subject.

"Hell with the Tiger," said Trudy. "Give someone else a chance."

My father was semiretired and, as he uncharacteristically put it, looked forward to some "La-Z-Boy living." But since when did he watch such pedestrian shows as *Judge Judy* and *Desperate Housewives*? He used to be such a news junkie. I always assumed that in retirement he'd be married to the golf course, but since Trudy didn't want him to be married to anyone but her, she dreamed them up an "act." My dad played the piano, and Trudy had a pretty good voice, so she created "Paunch and Trudy." It was a burlesque-y vaudeville show that traveled from one geriatric restaurant to another. It had all started when Dad and Trudy's condo was robbed. They were featured on *Cops* and considered that their official Hollywood debut. This gave them the showbiz bug, and they were hooked.

"Why don't you try and make it out for Thanksgiving? Your brother is having it at his house," said my dad. "I'll get you a last minute JetBlue ticket."

"Since I'm trying not to *dabble*, I need to stay here and work," I said pointedly, although it was a generous offer and I would have loved to spend some time back in LA. If I stayed in New York for turkey day, I'd surely be eating tasteless Tofurkey and kumquat quinoa stuffing at Holly's.

"Larry! *Jeopardy!'s* coming on," Trudy shouted.

"Love you, Marn. Gotta go," said my dad.

Hanging up the phone, I thought about this new touchy-feely man. What had happened to the short-tempered, buttoned-down guy I remembered from my youth? I knew how much this Paunch and Trudy togeth-erness irked my mother. She said it was always the sec-ond wives who got the mellow, more forgiving versions, while the first wives got the control freaks. I guess the same was true for the children. It kind of tore me up in-side how tough he was on me, yet how accepting he was of Trudy and all her crazy schemes and vanity projects.

Later, as I checked my emails, I looked down at my splotchy eczema hands. This was the last thing I needed to be sporting at work. That afternoon, a huge bottle of industrial-strength antibacterial liquid soap had appeared in the bathroom, and Saskia had been instructed to swab down communal surfaces with Clorox wipes. They were acting like I had Ebola.

The tube of Elidel was running out, and it wasn't even working. I needed to take a different route, so I searched Google for some all-natural skin remedies.

FELT SEW GOOD

It was a chilly Sunday afternoon in the East Village. I ar-rived at Petra's fifth-floor walk-up as the Hookers were gathering around her teak boomerang coffee table and excitedly pulling out their crafting projects.

Petra was knitting cute little mohair iPod cozies. Tanya was making a disco ball out of smashed up AOL disks. Jana was creating charms for necklaces made out of fake fingernails that had little sunsets and *Playboy* bunnies airbrushed on them. Carina, a dedicated "felter," was making a matching felt beret and poncho set for her dachshund. Holly, who recycled virtually everything, was making a Buddhist altar out of Red Bull cans and old Altoids tins.

Playing in the background was the documentary *The Gleaners & I*. It was about these off-the-grid French citizens who lived off the land by eating what others threw away.

"Dwayne wants us to become freegans," Holly coolly announced. "There's so much people toss out. Why pay for stuff?"

"Gross," replied Carina. "Why would you want to pick things out of garbage cans?"

"Restaurants throw out perfectly good food. Think of all the money we'd save," Holly said, unfazed by our disapproving faces.

With some upper-crust awkwardness, I timidly pulled out the bountiful assortment of Dean & DeLuca delicacies and arranged them on a platter.

"Who's been screwing the cheese guy?" Petra asked as she spread some goat cheese on a cracker.

I blushed and didn't say anything.

"Did you finish that sweater, Marnie? I really loved that fair-trade yarn you were using," Jana said, referring to a cardigan I was making for my mother.

"I'm almost done. I've been knitting on the train."

I pulled some products out of a shopping bag. Extra-virgin olive oil, beeswax, cocoa butter, and a packet of dried bright orange calendula flowers.

Jana watched me assemble the ingredients on the counter. "Ooh. Are you making gifts for Christmas? Hint, hint," she asked.

"Not tonight. My eczema's flaring and I'm going to make a salve with this stuff. Marigolds are known to have excellent healing powers because of their anti-bacterial properties."

"Do you need help?" asked Holly. "If you want, I can check in *Kitchen Witchery* for a recipe."

"Thanks, but I've got it under control," I said, my arms itching like crazy.

"Whatever," Holly tartly replied, pulling her glue gun out of its warmer and wantonly wagging it in my direction.

This was turning into Kitchen Bitchery, but I needed to take matters into my own hands.

"Any issues we want to share?" asked Petra, our gracious hostess, as she poured each of us a healthy goblet of wine. She had a small, open kitchen, so while I stood over the stove, melting my mixture, I could participate in the discussion.

Carina raised a metallic pink knitting needle like a long E.T. finger. "Does anyone know a good doctor? I fell down the subway steps yesterday and really messed up my coccyx bone."

"I know a great osteopath," said Holly. "He does really rad work, although he's a little intrusive."

"Intrusive how?" I asked.

"He puts a finger up your butt during the adjustment."

"I don't even let my boyfriend do that," Carina said as she went back to assembling her felt outfit.

"I know a doctor. But he's in obstetrics. I had a date with him," I said wistfully.

Holly looked at me funny. Shit. I had outed myself about Evan.

"How'd it go?" Tanya asked

"We fooled around, but it's not meant to be. I met this new guy. He's really fine. He looks a little like Keanu Reeves. I hope he calls."

Petra took that as her cue to tell us about a hot affair she had on a silent knitting retreat in Vermont. She monkishly knitted by day, and at night had wild, unsilent sex with the hunky groundskeeper.

Later in the evening, when we were all bitching about our jobs, I told them about the striving LeVigne women who obsessed about antioxidant shields and neutralizing free radicals. This seemed to perk them up again. "Freeing radicals?" Tanya excitedly asked. She was an ACLU lawyer.

"Keep your mittens on. She's not talking about Squeaky Fromme," said Holly.

I really wet their whistles when I told them about the huge closets filled with a bottomless supply of makeup and skin care potions. "I can get you full-size, not samples," I bragged.

"I wash my face with yogurt, tone it with apple cider vinegar, and moisturize with olive oil. Don't you guys want to try my regime?" Holly pleaded.

"No, not really," Petra said, hungrily licking her chops. "Hook us up, Marn."

Holly shot me an angry look. "Marnie, it's like you live for that place. You've got a bad case of Stockholm syndrome."

"Love your compacts," I said, smiling at her, trying to lighten Holly up.

When I got home, I slathered my still-warm homemade eczema balm on the affected areas and went to sleep. In the morning, I turned on my bedside lamp and lifted my hands to my face. The rash was still there, but it looked a tiny bit better and it wasn't itching nearly as much. I got up and inspected my legs and arms. I didn't want to get excited, but the redness seemed to have faded slightly.

THE COMPANY YOU KEEP

Before I had a chance to put my things down the next morning, my desk phone rang. Tinsley's name lit up on the caller ID. My hand visibly shook when I lifted the receiver. "Hello?" I said in a pathetically weak voice.

"I finally got around to reviewing your minutes from the second GMR meeting, and they are an utter disgrace. Get in here now, Marnie Mann!" she shouted through the phone.

I knew this was coming. When I had finished typing the transcript, there was so little text, they could have called it "seconds," not "minutes." I didn't know why I had bothered handing it in. I skulked into Tinsley's office, pale as the palest LeVigne talc. I hovered anxiously in the doorway. One foot in. One foot out.

"I'm not feeling very confident about the way things are going. I think we should . . ." But before she could finish her sentence, Tinsley's eyes moved to the homemade patchwork handbag slung across my chest. "What on God's green earth is that atrocity?" she bellowed, pointing at it like it was a giant scuttering water bug.

"My purse?" I responded uncertainly.

"It's a parody of a purse," she shouted, her perfect Waspy head floating before me like a Macy's parade balloon. "By working here, no matter how fleetingly, you are a representative of fashion and beauty. You need to adhere to Hattie LeVigne's 'Five-Foot Test,' wherein you stand five feet away from a full-length mirror and walk slowly toward it. As you approach it, please ask yourself the following questions: Is one thing preceding my entrance? Are my lips, eyes, cheeks, clothes, hair jumping out at me? If you answer yes to any of these queries, you are not finished and should not leave the house! Tell me something, Marnie Mann. What would Hattie think of that ghoulish purse?"

"Hattie probably wouldn't like it," I whispered defeatedly.

I couldn't believe her audacity. And what did her Jesus-like Hattie reference mean, anyway? Was Hattie still around, pulling the corporate strings from some secret hideaway? Sometimes I imagined she had gone the way of Walt Disney, frozen in a lipstick-shaped cryonic chamber with instructions to be thawed out only when someone invented an antiaging serum that really worked. "Freeze! Wait! Reanimate!" That was the Life Extension Society's slogan. Or would the company have Hattie live on in product perpetuity, encapsulated in a little oval portrait like Aunt Jemima or Betty Crocker?

Tinsley's phone rang and she took the call, motioning for me to sit down. I slid into an uncomfortable Philippe Starck Plexiglas chair and surveyed her office. After she hung up, her eyes focused on me. "You skated by the first time, Miss Mann," she said, waving the minutes in the air, "but this is an utter mockery. How can I trust you to do the most basic of chores?"

I sat there, speechless, my eyes rapidly blinking, my face turning bright red. *Fire me already,* I thought. *Just do it. On second thought, please don't fire me. My rent is due.*

"Hell's bells. Gone mute?" she said, putting on her fur-lined Burberry trenchcoat and grabbing a giant pink snakeskin carryall, which apparently was not a parody of a purse. "It has come to my attention that Connie Boyd has a flotilla of work for you to do, and she will surely put you through your paces. I want you to pack up your desk and get over there now. And please don't forget, pretty lips and fingertips!" she said imperiously and left the room.

I was surprised she would send me to Connie, considering my less-than-stellar skill set. Maybe she just wanted to torture me for a while longer before she kicked me to the curb. If I were to quit now, Sheila Buckle, my counselor from Cross Temps, would surely never send me out again. The thought of going to another agency and retaking all those maddening tests seemed like a miserable idea. Maybe working for Connie would turn out to be all right.

When I approached Connie's office, she was standing, legs apart, straddled between Juniper's and Murfy's desks. She was making a valiant but futile attempt to teach them how to work up a financial spreadsheet, searching for the appropriate words in their vapid language. She talked to them very slowly, as if they were nonnative speakers.

"Why don't you think of the budget as calories, and you can only eat a certain number until July or you'll blow your diet," Connie said, shaking her head in frustration. Connie looked up and saw me. "Ah, here's

Marnie. Maybe she can show you." And with that, Connie hightailed it back into her office.

I quickly discovered that Murfy's and Juniper's secretarial skills were far worse than mine. Therefore, I got to do the real work, while Murfy and Juniper were essentially put on ice, stuck doing grunt work like pumping the pedal on the creaky signature machine that spat out stockholder letters from the ephemeral Hattie. Apparently the last straw had been when Connie caught Juniper in the copy center, hovered over the Xerox machine. "I pray this works," Juniper said, tears streaming down her face as she desperately fiddled with the reduce/enlarge buttons.

While Juniper and Murfy could beautifully calligraphize place cards and masterfully arrange complicated seating charts for press functions and dinners, they were virtually incapable of doing even the most mundane office chores. LeVigne, where beauty and fashion were the orgasmic focus of many of its employees' lives, was more like a finishing school than a twenty-first-century workplace. I was promptly told where to order the individual splits of champagne (they called it "champ") and fat-free, "color-appropriate" cupcakes for the endless round of LeVigne "life events"—birthdays, weddings, baby showers, reaching one's goal weight.

Murfy told me that when she was a teen, she and her mother went on a busman's holiday to Europe, retracing Hattie's original steps through the Parisian department store makeup counters. Juniper confided that since junior high school she had been on a lifelong quest for the perfect red lipstick (this was prominently noted under "hobbies" on her resume) and she had worked at LeVigne's cosmetics counters during col-

lege summers. And apparently Tinsley never threw a
dinner party without color-coordinating her nails and
lip color to match the border on her china, because
she wanted to "belong to the table."

There was a word in Japanese, *enryo*. It meant "total
devotion to the group." That was them; they were
cultishly devoted to their jobs.

I too was fascinated by Hattie's story. The bio I had
seen on A&E presented her as the quintessential
American rags-to-riches tale. As a young child, Hattie
LeVigne, nee Koenig, emigrated with her family from
Kiev to Brooklyn. She married her childhood sweetheart, Harold Levine, and together, their kitchen stove
bubbling over with pots of creams, they sold makeup
and beauty potions at Catskills hotels, beach clubs,
and Hadassah luncheons. When sales were sluggish,
Hattie added more products to the line and, always
careful to keep the Brooklyn from showing, changed
the Semitic "Levine" to the French-sounding "LeVigne."

Harold died in the late 1970s, and by that time their
only child, Sidney, had already joined the company,
working his way up the ranks to his present position as
president and CEO. Hattie, the tiny spitfire, the super-
persuader, was known for her hard-sell tactics. In the
show, they had flickering newsreel footage of her at department store counters, cupping products like rare
jewels, applying them carefully to a woman's eager
face. With a hand mirror perched at a high angle to
eliminate a double chin, Hattie would show the shop-
per the "miraculous" results and then grasp the
woman's hand and not let go until she bought at least
one product. When Hattie went to Harrods in London
to hawk her wares and was snootily ignored, she had a
fit and spilled a bottle of her signature fragrance, Vi-

enna, on the selling floor. Impressed by her doggedness, the management agreed to carry her line.

In old publicity photos, she was a jarring blend of Queen Elizabeth and Gloria Swanson, resplendent in her regal veiled hats and dramatically arched eyebrows, throwing lavish dinner parties for the rich and jetty. She said she always dreamed of being an actress, but would settle for her name lit up on compacts and atomizers.

One retired marketing director, his back to the camera and voice altered for anonymity, spoke about Hattie's favorite method of terminating employees. She would send the hapless worker a terse telegram at home, instructing them not to come back. A former LeVigne publicist, who sat disguised in a wig and dark shadows, talked about the day she worked a press launch and her water broke. She was soaked and contracting, yet Hattie demanded that the publicist stay until the event was over.

While Hattie was mysteriously missing, her family carried on. Her son, Sidney, was at the helm with his wife, Marion, who was known as "the nose" for her perfume-sniffing abilities. Hattie's fraternal twin granddaughters, Summer and Rebecca LeVigne, had offices here as well, and once or twice I'd caught a glimpse of them prancing about.

I must confess that I, like lots of other American girls, grew up revering Summer and Rebecca. I remember how Hattie used to drag them out like show ponies on the talk show circuit. Hattie would play the accordion, and the girls would be used as face models so Hattie could show us philistine viewers the proper way to apply blusher and eye shadow. I remember blowing my allowance on stacks of *Sassy*s and *Seventeen*s just so I

could look at them. *Click!* Young Summer and Rebecca
in Palm Springs, sitting by a piano-shaped pool, drinking Shirley Temples. (Were they visiting Hattie's pal, Uncle Liberace?) *Click!* Rebecca and Summer in matching
sailor suits, clamming on Nantucket. *Click!* The twins at
their thirteenth birthday party, a big black mammy holding an enormous cake in the background. As a thirteen-
year-old, I could relate to them both. I could aspire to be
the beautiful Summer and commiserate with the plebeian Rebecca.

These days, though, not only did they not resemble
the fresh-faced girls I remembered from my youth, but
they had become charter members of the *titerati*, with
their unnaturally large bimboobs and possibly in-
flated butts. Jarret had told me how Summer (the
older twin by three minutes—isn't it sad how I could
recall that?) was constantly bragging about her outrageous sexcapades.

I was happy to see that Rebecca had kept her original, rather prodigious schnoz, but for someone so obscenely wealthy, she seemed inexplicably wan and
forlorn. What could she possibly be so glum about?
Geez, wasn't she in line to inherit her family's out-
landish fortune?

I shuddered to think what Rebecca's and Summer's
lives would have been like had their grandmother not
been a self-made, enormously driven businesswoman.
Would they be chunky baby machines, living on
Staten Island with cop husbands, loading up their
shopping carts at Costco? If I had Summer and Rebecca's money and privilege, I sure as hell wouldn't
want to punch a time clock.

I'm Fondue of You

"Marnie, why are you so smiley today?" Murfy asked. "Did you fast on Thanksgiving like I did and lose five pounds?"

"No. I had a meat-free, wheat-free dinner with friends," I sighed, wishing I had flown home and had my mother's scrumptious turkey supper. I told Murfy and Juniper I was smiling because tonight was my first date with Paul. I also told them that he was a cheese buyer at Dean & DeLuca.

While most everyone had the day after Thanksgiving off, we had to work on Friday. Sometimes this place felt like a high-end sweatshop. Holly reminded me that the day after Thanksgiving was "Buy Nothing Day," a protest against consumerism. But it was also "Black Friday," and when I went to lunch, it took all my willpower not to run into Saks and cruise the sales racks.

All afternoon, I kept imagining Paul, wondering what his body would be like. He looked lean and athletic, but I had only seen him from the waist up and he was wearing a long apron at the time. What if he was nice, but didn't make me laugh? What if he was a great kisser, but he didn't like my collection of sex toys? What if he had tiny feet and licked his fingers when he ate?

Toward the end of the day, Murfy and Juniper came by my desk. "So where's this cheesehead taking you?" teased Murfy.

"To Melt. Ever hear of it?" I asked.

"Sure," Juniper replied. "It's a fondue restaurant in Brooklyn. Near the Manhattan Bridge."

Good to know. Now I'd have to run to Duane Reade,

buy a bottle of Lactaid pills, and pray I didn't fart my way through dinner.

"Sounds like the guy lives and breathes cheese," said Murfy. "I was on Atkins, and I seem to recall that the diet was quite lenient about eating dairy. I gained instead of lost, so I would say cancel."

Leave it to Juniper to find a way to connect cheese and fashion. "Did you know that the original owners of Coach handbags sold their company to start a cheese making business upstate called Coach Farm?" she said.

"Really?" I replied, thinking I could steal that tidbit of information if I ran out of things to say to Paul.

"Marnie, be forewarned. Cheese can give a girl gnarly cellulite," cautioned Murfy.

"That's okay, I don't do dairy either."

"Thank God," Juniper said.

It was almost time to leave for my date, so I ducked into the bathroom to get ready. I washed my face and put on a brand-new Systems lipstick. There was something so thrilling about trying on a new color. Would this be the perfect shade that would transform my face and make me irresistibly kissable? It occurred to me that the act of making up was such an ancient ritual, like Holly's witch-crafted potions. You painted your face to cast a spell.

When I got off the train, I wrapped my scarf tightly around my neck. It was cold outside, and the news had predicted a snowstorm. As I walked to Melt, I popped some Lactaid pills and queasily recalled the colorized recipe photos in the Betty Crocker hostess cookbooks featuring avocado green fondue pots and viscous cheese melted by the blue light of Sterno cans. I could have kicked myself. Why hadn't I told Paul on the phone about my lactose problem? Why did I feel the need to be such a people pleaser? I was sure he would have understood. Now, on top of being nervous about the date, I also had to be nervous about the dreaded cheese and the concomitant flatulence.

Melt was in a low, warehouse-style brick building that was practically underneath the Manhattan Bridge. Paul was bundled up, waiting for me by the door. He put his hand lightly on my back and ushered me inside. The joint was jumpin'. A tall model-waitress handed us menus and took our drink orders. I was stunned when I took a look at the food options. I assumed that there would be something like a veggie plate or grilled salmon for us dairy duds, but no such luck. It was cheese, cheese, and more cheese. The sharp molten smells wafting from the neighboring table made me green.

"Are you okay?" Paul asked.

"Fine," I answered.

A jazz trio played Thelonious Monk near the crowded bar. Paul intently studied the menu. "I definitely think we should get the smoked Gouda. The Grana Padano and Gruyère sound excellent too. And what about the Brie and basil?"

"You're the expert. Whatever you think is good," I said quietly, slugging down a big gulp of my cabernet.

"It's all good. They order their cheese from me," Paul said, as he took a swig of his wine. "This may sound kind of weird to you, but my father hates cheese," he revealed in a deadly serious tone.

"Really? Why?" I asked. Considering my own dilemma, that didn't sound weird at all.

"He never acquired a taste for it. It's not part of the traditional Chinese diet," Paul said, leaning in conspiratorially. "But how could he hate something so amazing?"

I let out a nervous chuckle. "Kind of ironic, considering what you do for a living." I should have fessed up right then and there, but our model-waitress arrived with the fondue bowls and I lost the moment. I was such a wimp.

As Paul speared a cube of sourdough bread with a long, slender prong, I checked him out. He was wearing his black Clark Kent glasses, a striped vintage ski sweater, a corduroy blazer with suede elbow patches, and groovy tan chukka boots. I liked his casual, understated style.

"Aren't you taking any?" he asked.

"You go first," I said, stalling.

"Ladies first."

"No, really. You go," I repeated. He probably thought I was like so many girls in New York, on some sort of starvation diet, but deprivation chic was definitely not my bag.

As Paul happily dunked the bread into the fondue, I noticed his strong, well-manicured hands. Guys' paws were such a turn-on. He must have been a little nervous too, because during the meal he absentmindedly scratched the label off the wine bottle.

"How did you get involved with cheese?" I asked.

"After college, I bummed around Europe for a while, trying to figure out what I wanted to do with my life. When I got back home, I worked on a farm near Madison that made French-style chèvre. One day, Steve Jenkins, the guy who started the cheese department at Dean & DeLuca, showed up on a buying trip. We got to talking and he offered me a job in New York," Paul said, dipping a cube of bread into the cheese and handing it to me.

"Thanks," I said, holding it in the air, imagining that it was a creamy lollipop.

"My dad still can't believe that I've devoted my life to dairy," said Paul. "I think he's still waiting for me to go to grad school or something. But I'm twenty-eight now, and I want to get my career off the ground and become a consultant. I would advise restaurants on what kinds of cheese to buy. Cheese isn't just a food anymore. It's a lifestyle. What about you, Marnie? Have you met your parents' expectations?"

I coughed nervously, and my right eye began to twitch. "Hardly. It's mostly my dad who's on my case. After my parents divorced, he wasn't around a lot, and now, all these years later, he's suddenly decided to jump in and play Daddy. I'm his little pet project now."

"It sounds like Jewish fathers and Chinese fathers have a lot more in common than one might think."

"You know, you're right," I said, thinking how intuitive and sweet Paul was.

I wasn't sure whether it was accidental or intentional, but I kept losing pieces of bread in the gelatinous sinkholes. The waitress must have caught this because she smiled at me and said, "The rule here is, if you lose a hunk of bread in the fondue pot, the guy sitting closest to you has to kiss you."

Paul blushed, leaned over the table, and gave me a tender buss on the cheek. Now I knew why they called this place Melt. I was liquid. His sweetness trumped his cuteness, and it made me more relaxed.

When we could focus on talking again, Paul asked me why I left the West Coast.

"I always dreamed of living in New York. My mother grew up in Queens. She'd tell us stories. And when we'd come back with her to visit, I kind of knew I'd end up here someday."

"Do you miss LA?"

"Not really. The pace is too slow and the sunshine can be relentless," I said. "There's no weather there. Although I shouldn't be saying that. You probably had too much weather in Wisconsin."

"New York's not much better in that department," Paul said, looking out the window at the falling snow.

I raised my glass in a toast. "Here's to us masochists."

"Cheers," he said, clinking his glass with mine. "I was in LA once. Everything out there reminded me of a movie set. Like the buildings were facades with nothing behind them."

"Are you sure you're not talking about the Universal Studios tour?" I joked. "No, I know what you mean. I think that's what happens when you go to a place you've never been before. Your references often come from the movies, so when you actually visit the place in person, you think you're in a film."

"Life imitating art imitating life," Paul said.

"Imitation of imitation of life," I retorted.

"You're really funny," said Paul.

I smiled and blushed. I loved a guy that got my sense of humor. "But seriously, LA makes me feel kind of agoraphobic and exposed," I said. "All that flat space. What I love about New York City is the verticality. Some people feel alienated and closed in by it, but it makes me feel snug and secure."

"Like those huggy machines for autistic kids?"

I smiled and discreetly spat some milky matter into my napkin.

"I'm glad you're here. In this restaurant. In New York,"

Paul said, giving me a big warm grin. Suddenly there was an awkward silence, as if he had said too much.

"Do you have any hobbies?" I asked, trying to fill the void, my tone sounding a bit officious, like I was interviewing him for a job.

"I'm really into cycling. I just did a five-borough ride, and I'm shopping for a lightweight speed-racing bike to ride in Central Park. What about you?" he asked.

"I'm bad about exercising," I said, nibbling on a piece of bread that had the faintest coating of cheese.

"No, I mean interests in general. You mentioned you were a hooker," he said with a Cheshire grin.

Wow, he remembered. "By way of explanation, the name got started because at first we all did knitting, but now we're a full-service crafts group. I've always been good at doing things with my hands," I said, suddenly blushing, realizing how X-rated that sounded. "I mean, you know, like for holiday gifts. This year I'm whipping up some homemade fragrances and bath products for my friends."

"That's cool."

"Right? It's nice to get something handcrafted, that no one else has. Everything's so mass-produced these days."

"It's the same with cheese. There's the bland, over-processed Kraft stuff that's been boiled into submission. I mean, doesn't it disturb you that their Parmesan doesn't melt, it browns?"

"Never really thought about it," I said as I anxiously nibbled some bread.

"Sorry to go off like that. So you were saying . . ."

"I also love the movies," I continued. If I couldn't tell him about my lactose problem, at least I could come clean about my checkered job history. Amazingly, when I told Paul why I was temping and how I had gone from a something to a nothing, he didn't bat an eye. Paul seemed refreshingly nonjudgmental and supportive.

By the time we left the restaurant, the streets were blanketed in white fluffy stuff. "Let's walk over the Brooklyn Bridge. It's only a couple of blocks," Paul said as we wrapped ourselves in face-obscuring hats and scarves. My apartment was in the opposite direction, but how could I say no? I was really grooving on him, and I didn't want this night to end.

In all the years I lived in New York, I had never walked over the dazzling Brooklyn Bridge at night. I had crossed it a few times on summer days, but it was much better after dark. Puffy storm clouds pushed back the velvet blue sky, tugboats with strings of white lights moved up and down the river, and the glittering skyline grew increasingly twinklier as a carbon monoxide high kicked in from the roaring traffic below.

New York was still incredibly awe-inspiring to me. Holly, who had been born and raised here, said she was jealous of the way I could still get slack-jawed and glassy-eyed when I walked around the city. I guess residing as an adult in the same place where you grew up could never give you those magical feelings. Not fully. You know every nook and cranny, and you get jaded. When I first moved here, I had wanted to swallow the city whole. No place could be more different from LA, and that was exactly what I wanted. If California was a Kodachrome picture in a slide carousel, then New York was a torn and precious sepia photograph.

Paul and I walked close, almost touching. It was freezing out, but I could feel heat radiating between us. I was smiling behind the blowhole that was all that was left of my swaddled face. It was such a beautiful night. The streets were deserted, and we just kept strolling.

"This is my hood," Paul said as we reached the corner of Mulberry and Spring, the intersection where SoHo and Little Italy collide. To me, Nolita was one of the coolest neighborhoods in the city. It had a European feel to it. Cozy bistros, great boutiques, little old Italian ladies kibitzing on the stoops.

As lacy snowflakes floated down and landed on my face, I leaned against a streetlight and took it all in. "What I wouldn't give for a rent-controlled apartment in the city," I sighed.

Paul shifted from one foot to the other. "Want to come up?" he blurted out. I didn't know it, but we were standing in front of his redbrick walk-up.

I was out of breath when we reached his fifth-floor apartment. It seemed that everyone I knew in the city lived on the highest floor in buildings without elevators. After we wended around and around and around, it felt really good to finally sit down on Paul's couch. He put on a Zero 7 CD and sat down next to me. Suddenly, after the flowing, animated dinner conversation, we were at a serious loss for words. Sitting nervously side by side, we said nothing. Every sound in his apartment was amplified. My stomach growled angrily from lack of food. The clock ticked louder than Big Ben. The radiator clanked out a cacophonous tune. Why was this part always so unnerving?

During this awkward silence, I studied Paul's living room. My eyes were drawn to a dusty collection of Stonehenge-assembled candles that loomed on the coffee table and a vast assortment of angels and plump little cherubs that were spread out all over the windowsills and bookshelves. But instead of judging

Paul on this unflattering clutter, I dismissed it. After all, he was a straight guy, and I remembered something a friend of my mother's once said when I mentioned that her husband was a spiffy dresser. She thanked me and recited a line I would often recall when feeling queasy about a paramour's clothing taste or design sense. "You realize Harry didn't come this way."

"Would you like something to drink?" Paul finally asked, jumping up to break the silence.

"Sure. That would be great."

While he was clanking around in the kitchen, I further eyeballed his place. Across the living room was an aquarium. In it, I could see a turtle happily basking on a rock while a gurgling treasure chest pumped out oxygen bubbles in the water. The radiator banged some more, drowning out the CD. Then the phone rang, and the machine picked up. "Hi, Paulie. Are you there?" said a sexy, accented female voice. "Haven't heard from you in a while. Wondering what's going on in the Big Apple." Of course he had a fan club. "Call me. Can't wait to see you. Love and kisses."

Paul came back with two icy-cold beers and handed one to me.

"I think someone just left you a message. I didn't mean to listen. But the volume was up."

"Who was it?"

"A woman with an accent. German, maybe?"

"Dutch."

Great. I imagined a tall, blond Valkyrie in wooden clogs.

Paul smiled. "No worries. That would be my mother."

Relieved, I took a refreshing sip of beer. "She sounds so young. I take it you're half Chinese, then."

"I like to call it 'honkinese,'" Paul joked. "I'm a half-breed. My parents met when my dad was doing graduate work in Chicago. She was an exchange student who stayed on in the States. My dad's a retired physics professor. He taught for years at the University of Wisconsin. They still live there, in the house where I grew up."

"Wow. Still married. That's amazing," I said.

"Yeah. My mom and I are really close, and so am I with my dad, minus our career-choice differences."

"That's great you're all so tight. I wish I had a better bond with my dad."

"Yeah. Parents. It can be hard," said Paul. "But you should try to patch things up. They won't be around forever."

After we had drained our bottles, Paul leaned over, cocked his head to the side, and kissed me. It was a kiss so deep and soulful, I felt weak and buzzingly alive at the same time. His lips felt cool and sweet from the beer. *Wow*, I thought. It felt so good to carnally communicate with someone who was so on my wavelength. Paul took off his glasses, and that was when I saw his pure, unadulterated beauty. He was a Chinese matinee idol with gorgeous high cheekbones and a long straight nose. I reached under his shirt. He had the tight, hard body of a kung fu fighter.

As we made out, my hand accidentally brushed Paul's crotch. His pants were propped up like a Boy Scout tent.

A fat black cat jumped between us. "Down, Jeffrey," Paul whispered as he shooed the cat away. Paul reached under my skirt and placed the palm of his hand over my tights and on top of my pelvic bone. "Mar-nie. Marn-ie." He sounded out my name slowly and carefully. "Marnie. I like that. It's different."

"Thanks," I said breathlessly as we kissed some more.

"How did you get your name?" he asked as he gently, teasingly caressed me through my clothes. He was evidently the kind of guy who liked to talk during nookie. I tried to answer him, but with all the tonsil hockey, I was tongue-tied. Finally, after a long kiss, I answered him. Jeffrey stared jealously from a chair.

"My name? Uh. Hitchcock. The movie. My parents' first date," I whispered.

His next question was more in line with what was happening between us. He put on a fake English accent and cleared his throat. "Shall we shag?"

I laughed at his bad Austin Powers impersonation. "Not gonna happen," I said, which was exactly the opposite of what I wanted to happen, but after my disappointment with Evan, I had let my chastity pelt grow back in to prevent myself from doing something untoward.

"Sorry," he said, pulling back.

I didn't want Paul to think I was rebuffing him completely, so I pulled him close and gave him some tender Eskimo kisses. After a few rapid lashes with my lashes, he pulled back again, but this time his face hovered in front of mine. He looked at me so intensely that I had to shut my eyes. An hour and a thousand delicious smooches later, I was glistening with a pheromony sweat. I sat up to catch my breath, and my eyes fell on the clay tchotchke cherubs.

"Wow, you have a lot of stuff," I remarked.

Paul put his glasses back on. "Yeah, I guess I do," he said, intently studying the room as if for the very first time. "I'm so used to it all, I barely even notice."

"You must really like angels," I said. I had counted twelve.

"No, no, I don't. I mean, yeah, angels are nice, but most of the stuff's my ex—" He cut himself off.

"Did she live here?" I asked casually, wanting to sound curious but not intrusive.

"No, but we went out for about two years. You know how it is. Things accumulate. She gave me a lot of gifts and things."

"What does she do for a living?"

"Kendra's in the acting program at the New School, and she works at Dean & DeLuca."

"You two work together?"

"Well, not exactly. She's in *poisson*."

I laughed. "You mean the fish department?"

Paul rolled his eyes in solidarity. "The store's a little pretentious that way." Jeffrey the cat jumped into Paul's lap, and Paul rubbed his cheeks. "We got Jeffrey there. Kendra found him in the alley eating out of a Dumpster. Poor guy."

"I take it you got him in the divorce settlement?"

"Something like that."

We started up another round of deep kisses. It was nearly impossible to pull myself away, but I had to go. Paul threw on his coat, walked me downstairs, and put me in a cab. It had been a wonderful night, and I wanted to savor it. I leaned back against the seat, and with plaintive Indian music blasting from the tinny speakers, I replayed the whole evening in my head.

A BIRD IN HAND

"So? How'd it go with the curd nerd?" Juniper asked on Monday morning as we rode up together in the elevator. "Was it a complete waste of mascara?"

"Definitely not," I said.

Juniper looked disappointed, her schadenfreude shining through. "Don't forget, you have to go to Diana's product meeting this morning," she said.

Systems was launching a new skin care product called Bird Bath. It was a multipurpose "three-in-one rejuvenator," which in layman's terms meant a whitening, antiaging, and cleansing wipe all in one. Bird Bath was positioned for the fluttery, fast-paced girl-bird who desired that all her skin care needs be managed by one easy pad. The wipes fit into a small compact that fit neatly into a purse, pocket, or diaper bag.

Diana Duvall, the Systems PR director, was in charge of the launch, and she was holding a groupthink to try and brainstorm a compelling "theme and delivery system" for the Bird Bath press kit, i.e., how it would be uniquely presented to beauty editors. She wanted the theme and delivery system to be one—form and function seamlessly merged.

Press kits were a sore spot with magazine beauty editors. The original point of the kits was for editors to receive information about a product, sample it, and then write a story or blurb about it in their magazine. There were countless beauty products on the market, and with new ones coming out practically every day, the wooing was ongoing and never-ending. The editors received armloads of press kits from every imaginable makeup, skin care, and perfume company. It had gotten back to LeVigne PR that the spoiled editrixes didn't want sample-size products and boring press releases. Their idea of a rousing press kit was a high-end designer handbag stuffed with full-sized Chanel product, or, if you were the low-rent Revlon, then a high-end designer handbag stuffed with fancy sunglasses, jewelry, or a gift certificate to a fancy spa. Anything less fabulous was tossed in the trash or passed around the office and viciously gossiped about.

Diana had asked that Connie sit in on the Bird Bath groupthink, and in turn Connie had me and several marketing people sit in on it too. Diana's assistant, Winsome, came in carrying a tray of Diet Cokes, and everyone but me grabbed one and cracked it open. Diana shoved a straw into her soda can and took a long, ravenous sip. She looked down at her baby bump, and her frozen Botoxed mouth struggled to form a tiny frown. "Do I look fat?" she pouted, cupping her hands on her little bowling ball of a stomach that couldn't have housed more than a couple of embryonic kittens. "I've worked all my life to be thin, and look what's happened. Why couldn't I have been born a seahorse, where the males carry the babies?"

I wondered what a steady stream of Diet Coke and Botox was doing to her developing fetus.

"Don't say that, Diana. You look gorgeous! Simply luminous! Skinnier than Mary-Kate!" were the comments that the group dutifully uttered.

These comments seemed to soothe Diana's outsized ego, and she was ready to get down to business. "I am vividly seeing white for this launch, so I'd like to pose the following question," she said, holding up a box of Bird Bath wipes. "What, to you, is white?"

There was a flurry of answers from the marketing team. "Noguchi lamps, nonfat yogurt, the new Balenciaga coat, Carr's Table Water Crackers, my bichon frise."

Diane spoke again. "And what is beauty to all of you?"

No one spoke. To them, that was way too obvious a question.

I thought about the Bird Bath product. I thought about what was truly beautiful, and suddenly a magnificent image of a soaring white dove popped into my head. *Say something, Marnie.* No one else was speaking. *Just say something. Anything.*

"Doves have a special kind of beauty," I said sheepishly.

"Doves," repeated Diana robotically, not really paying attention to me, focusing more on draining her second can of Diet Coke.

I looked at Connie. She nodded in the affirmative, as if to say, "Go on." I cleared my throat and continued. "Doves are white and pretty and pure. Doves are beautiful," I said.

Diana looked up. The second caffeine boost must have centered her. "Yes, how right you are. Doves are pretty and white and pure. They're aspirational, really. Yes. This product story is about doves!"

I rolled my eyes at Diana's daftness.

"Attagirl, Marnie," said Connie, slapping me on the back, right on a tender eczema patch.

"How silly that I didn't think of this days ago," Diana cooed. "After all, the product is called Bird Bath."

I smiled, pleased that I was able to impress the seemingly impenetrable Diana.

Suddenly, with Diana's sanctioned enthusiasm, everyone else became alert and hyperinterested. A marketing woman piped in. "I have an idea for the launch. What if we send a dove in flight to each editor?"

Another marketing person continued the thought. "And we attach a packet of Bird Bath wipes to a chain around its neck."

"I got it! A Tiffany necklace that the editors can keep," said Winsome. "Monogrammed, of course."

"I'll do you one better," said Connie. "With the press release miniaturized and tucked inside the locket."

Diana closed her eyes in thought, then popped them open and spoke. "This is it. A dove will land on the windowsill of every New York beauty editor, and they will be so enthralled by its white avian splendor, they will throw open the window, take the Bird Bath wipes—and the Tiffany necklace, of course—and send the dove back to its roost." Diana trained her eyes on me. "Very cutting-edge, Marnie. It will be the talk of the town," she said. "I want you to check our press launch database to make sure this concept has never been actualized by us or a competitor. Oh, and Marnie, since this was your smashing idea, you will be overseeing it."

She couldn't possibly be serious, I thought. Winsome gave me a death glare, probably upset that Diana was singling me out rather than asking her for assistance.

Diana continued. "Oh, and Marnie, would you be so kind as to do some research in an effort to find out where we might locate the highest-quality, most angelic doves to deliver Bird Bath to the editors."

"Excuse me for saying so, Diana," Connie said, "but while I do think it's a great idea, I don't think doves are capable of performing such a complex task."

"Excuse *me* for saying so, Connie, but this is LeVigne, and we are known as a company that raises the bar. If we don't aspire, astound, and astonish, then we are not worth our bath salts, now, are we? I am requesting that Marnie access these doves and find a way for them to appear on the editors' windowsills, even if she has to crawl out on the ledges and put them there herself."

Winsome smiled broadly when she realized it was better me than her.

With the task at hand, I trudged back to my desk and made a couple of reluctant calls to pet shops. "Got doves?" I asked, explaining my situation. I was laughed off the phone. Connie must have smelled my abject panic because she beckoned me into her office.

"Diana must be joking," Connie said, absentmindedly throwing a series of Nerf balls into a hoop that hung over her plasma TV. With the blinds drawn and a game blasting, her office had the dusky feel of a sports bar. "Everyone knows doves can't fly distances, and they have no homing abilities. And even if you were somehow able to crawl out and place them on the window ledges, that would be extremely dangerous. What if you fell off? Do you have any idea what kind of lawsuit we'd have on our hands?"

Thanks, I thought. I wasn't a viable person whose life mattered. Just a nameless, disposable temp whose dead body splayed out in front of the Condé Nast building would create bad press and a wrongful death suit initiated by my family.

"Diana's pretty adamant about this. What should I do?" I asked.

"For the life of me, I can't figure out those PR heads. One of the reasons Sidney hired me was to rein in the escalating budgets. Get them to cut back on their launch expenses, but they won't budge." She sunk a Nerf ball into the hoop. "By God, I think I've got it," she continued. "What about pigeons?"

I almost choked on my Chiclet. "Dirty, filthy pigeons?"

"Yes. Pigeons."

"Diana will freak."

"Aren't pigeons really gray doves anyway?" she said with a devilish grin.

I smiled in complicity. "Or are doves really white pigeons?"

"I like the way you think," she said. Connie got up from

her desk and paced the room. "You could use carrier pigeons to fly to your editors' locations. Kris and I once went white-water rafting, and they used pigeons to ferry down film that a photographer had taken of the group. When the trip was over, the pictures were already printed and waiting for us to purchase."

"But what about the gray factor?" I asked.

"Gray is the new black is the new pink is the new white is the new gray."

She kind of lost me there. "But, Connie, you heard Diana. She wants white doves and only doves."

"Let me think. Just let me think," Connie said, squeezing the life out of a Nerf ball.

"Maybe we can dress them in little white outfits," I said jokingly.

Connie had a sinister gleam in her eye. "That's it, my friend. Bingo! We'll bleach them. We can smear the pigeons with Paparazzi Sno-White whitening cream. We'll do it on the q.t. Diana won't find out. The editors won't know. It will be our little secret. Pinky swear," she said, hooking her ringed pinky finger around mine and yanking it like a wishbone.

"Okay," I said meekly, not knowing what I was getting myself into.

THE CAT CAME BACK

It had been almost a week since my first date with Paul. We had had a couple of really fun, teasing, getting-to-know-you phone conversations, and now we were meeting for dinner in Nolita, at Café Habana on Prince Street. As I approached the restaurant, I could see him in the distance, waiting outside. He looked so cute, slouched against the wall with his hands in his pockets. Several attractive women checked him out, and I was relieved to see that he didn't do that cruise-the-girls head swivel most guys did when they thought you weren't looking. I walked up behind him and tugged on his long striped scarf.

"Hey, cutie," he said, turning around and grinning a big grin.

"Hey back," I said. We stared at each other for a long, hard beat. He kissed me lightly on the lips, and we went inside.

Paul studied the menu. "I've had the Mexican-style grilled corn here. It's really good. They coat it with *queso blanco* cheese, chili powder, lime, and paprika," Paul said as we drank mojitos and played footsie under the table. I loved that Paul was a foodie, except for the cheese thing. His culinary knowledge was sexy, and I was looking forward to a long, languorous meal. Eating was such a sensuous way to escape reality. Lots of sniffing and tasting. Gustatory bliss.

"How was work today?" I asked after he ordered empanadas, *masistas de puerco* (pork marinated in a garlic and citrus sauce), *ropa vieja* (a classic Cuban steak dish), and sweet plantains.

"I smelled something really funky this morning at work," he said. "It's a cheese called Desoto, made in Louisiana, from cow's milk. It looks like provolone, but it gets very, very strong when it ages. It smells like . . . ass."

"Yuck," I replied. This wasn't where I thought the conversation would be going, but I was glad not to be thinking about doves. "I've got one even grosser," I said, taking a sip of my minty cocktail.

"Bring it on," he said with piqued interest, folding his arms across his chest.

"Today I was reading some files at work, and apparently some of the LeVigne perfumes are made with this stuff called ambergris. They use infinitesimal amounts of it, and what it is, is . . ." I said, looking around to make sure none of the other diners were paying attention to our gross-out conversation. "It's—well, there's really no delicate way to put it."

"Just tell me!" said Paul.

"Ambergris is. . . . whale vomit."

"Oh my God is that revolting," he said in mock disgust.

I brought my voice down to a whisper. "The whales puke it up, and the oily black stuff ferments on the surface of the ocean for, like, ten years. When it gets really good and rancid, hunters come along in their boats and skim it off the water and sell slabs of it at very high prices to perfume companies."

"I wonder what it smells like," he said.

"It's supposed to be an aphrodisiac, with a musky marine odor, and when the chemists mix it with other, more pleasant scent molecules, it becomes very sensual, very animalistic."

"Okay, you win. Ambergris is definitely grosser than Desoto cheese," Paul said as we clinked glasses and changed the conversation to more palatable topics. "People often complain about the high price of certain cheeses," he continued. "When I have a customer who's turned off by the cost, I try to convey the enormity of the journey. That this lady cheese maker who lives in a remote village in the Spanish Pyrenees has to get her product down the mountain, on a train and then a plane, through customs, and into our store. It's really a small miracle."

I told Paul about *sillage* and he told me about *affinage*, which is what they called the aging of cheese. I smiled to myself, thinking about how the process of aging was so dramatically different in our two industries. In his world, aging was good; in mine, aging was something vexing to be creamed and injected away.

"Do you like the Wong Kar-wai film *In the Mood for Love*?" I asked, images of vintage, after-hours Hong Kong and Maggie Cheung's tight floral cheongsam flickering in my head.

"Love it," he said. "We should watch it together sometime."

I was swooning. Paul had just passed a major hurdle. It was terribly judgmental of me, but that movie was a litmus test. If a guy didn't know about it, that was bad. If he had seen it and didn't like it, that was unpardonable.

The food arrived. As a ruse to not have to eat the cheese coating on the corn, I told Paul it was too buttery, and I wiped a lot of it off with my napkin. He looked on in horror as I denuded the cob. Eating it was still a mistake, because it smeared my lipstick and we both had kernels embedded in our teeth. I went into the tiny bathroom to try to repair the mess. When I came out, there was a dish of pumpkin flan waiting to be shared, but I slugged down a tequila shot instead.

Paul's apartment was only a block away from the restaurant, but it took us a heavenly half hour to get there. We pawed, we necked, we groped, we fondled in every darkened doorway we could squeeze ourselves into. I was in that all-embracing tequila haze where everything around me was a blur and I didn't care who saw what because I couldn't see them and who the hell cared anyway. We ducked into a deserted alley. Paul swept back my hair and caressed my neck with his lips. "You smell fantastic, like pears mixed with musk and honey," he said. "I could lick it right off you."

Please do, I thought. Fragrance could be liquid emotion, and my gastronome was describing exactly the essential oils I had mixed together to make a new homemade holiday scent. We had a long, messy kiss. "Women supposedly have a better sense of smell than men," I remarked, coming up for air. "But yours is exceptionally good." We stumbled into a doorway and kissed some more. "Did you know that you lose your sense of smell when you get older?" I whispered, inhaling him, sniffing a minty shampoo and a mild aftershave I could not identify.

"You smell so good, I could eat you up," said Paul.

Hearing this made me weak in the knees. When we finally got up to Paul's place, we fell on the couch. "Now, where were we?" he asked as we resumed kissing. Although loitering in the street was certainly less comfortable, it proved better for my head, because when I lay supine, the drunken spins took hold. Jeffrey the cat pounced on my tender boobs, and I bolted upright with a painful jolt.

"Oh, good, Jeffrey's back," Paul announced as he shooed the cat off the couch and sent him darting under a chair.

"He's back? Where did he go?" I asked, wondering whether Jeffrey had his own key and let himself in and out of the apartment.

"Kendra, my ex, had him for a few days. She must have dropped him off while we were out."

Hmmm. I thought I had caught a whiff of Calyx perfume upon entering Paul's apartment.

"Let's go into the bedroom," Paul said, fondling my bottom.

"Uh. I like it out here," I replied, not ready to venture into sex quite yet. Plus my chastity pelt and dove-induced stress eczema, which was spreading by the minute, would surely scare him away.

Paul palmed my 36Bs, lightly squeezing them. "Mmmm," he said dreamily. "They have the spring and consistency of two fresh mozzarella balls." The guy certainly had an interesting take on foreplay.

I straddled him, sitting down on his lap, pushing his hand up toward my eager nipples. After he tenderly stroked my breasts, we exchanged some deep soul kisses and then he slowly slid down the length of my body, hit the floor, and began teasingly dry-licking my crotch right through the resin-coated jeans. Ohmygod-didthatfeelgood. But the tag said DRY CLEAN ONLY. Was his wet tongue going to ruin the glossy finish? What was I, nuts? *Enjoy the moment.* And so I did.

After an hour of some serious seminude groping, Paul got up to use the bathroom. The lights were on, and the trusty, dusty cherubs were staring down at me from on high, judging my body against this mysterious Kendra's, who apparently let herself in and out of Paul's apartment. I wondered what she looked like, how her mozzarella balls stacked up against mine. I supposed only the cherubs knew for sure. Paul came back in.

"I really better go," I said reluctantly. "It's getting late, and I've already got a hangover."

"No. Stay," said a groggy Paul, reaching out for me.

"I shouldn't. I can't," I said, stroking his hair. "You know, in some species, after mating, the female kills the male and eats him, so you better be careful."

"Then we'll just hold hands all night," said Paul.

"I've heard that before," I said, lightly kissing his cheek. Paul reluctantly walked me downstairs and hailed me a cab. He stuffed some money in my hand, and when I tried to give it back, he insisted that I take it. I was nauseated and I needed some fresh air, so I cracked the window open as the taxi sailed across the Brooklyn Bridge. Why hadn't I stayed? I had unquestioningly, unself-consciously slept over at Evan's, yet I wouldn't stay at Paul's. I wasn't trying to play head games with him. As much as I wanted to get my ya-yas off, I didn't want to screw things up, and I certainly didn't want him hearing me puke in his bathroom.

WINGING IT

There were only four short days to find the "doves" and make the Bird Bath launch happen. I was thrilled that Diana was entrusting me to oversee such an important event, but it was scary and nerve-wracking.

Of course this was the week that Connie was on a major warpath. She stomped around the office, proverbial balls out, screaming irritating acronyms like "MLMO" (I'm in major-league meeting overload) or "RUTUS!" (Round up the usual suspects, i.e., get her all the daily newspapers plus *Barron's* and *Baseball Weekly*). I was discovering that Connie was just as bad as a male boss. In some ways she *was* a male boss, masquerading in a skirt and hose.

"Juniper, you move like a snail! Have you had your thyroid tested?" Connie would yell over the din of the rabidly cheering fans from some sporting event that blared on her flat-screen TV. The next day she'd come in and offhandedly apologize. "Sorry I was such a whore, ladies. Sometimes I get stressed and skip the civilities."

So much for Sisterhood Is Powerful.

I tuned Connie out and focused on finding the doves. Finally, on AnimalPlanet.com, I found out about a guy, Salvatore Ruggerio, who trained carrier pigeons on his Coney Island rooftop. Pigeon enthusiasts were a dying breed, and with his phlegmy, hacking cough, it sounded like Sal was about to kick the bucket himself. I asked him about the doves. He had only one, and he used it for weddings. "It flies up in da air and comes right back down. That's all it'll do. You want doves? Call David Copperfield," he said.

I agreed to use his pigeons (he didn't know about the whitening cream yet), and I called him at least four times a day with frantic questions. What time will the birds leave? How will they know where to go? When will they get there? Will they wait on the ledge until someone comes to open the window? In the meantime I went to Tiffany, express-ordered the monogrammed locket necklaces, and got the product samples ready.

To take my mind off work stress, I made a batch of men's cologne, which I put in a tightly stoppered glass bottle. It was made from lavender, rosemary, musk, and bergamot. The base ingredient was vodka. Who knew vodka could be so versatile? Kind of like the chickpea. I figured that if Paul and I were still dating by Christmas, I would give it to him—but the recipe said to store it in a dark place for three months to a year, so it might have to wait.

The cologne I chose to make was called Courage, an apt name for two reasons. First, it had taken courage to sit tight and wait for the right guy to come along, and second, now that I found a guy I really liked, it was going to take courage to be patient and see where this romantic journey might take me.

* * *

The day before the birds were to fly, I called Sal to finalize the plans and to get directions to his place. When he answered the phone, I could hear the soothing coo of birds in the background, and then I heard him screaming at someone.

"Butchie, the broad from LaFine is on the line. Get me dat contract, would youse?"

"Fug you, Dad."

"I sez ders a lady on the phone, you ingrate," Sal yelled back. I could hear the sound of a file cabinet creaking open and papers shuffling. After about a minute, Sal got back on the line.

"Okay, I sees we got five boids goin' to Candy Nasty, five goin' to Hatchet Philip, and three goin' to the Times Weiner building."

"That's correct," I said. "Are you sure they'll know exactly what floor and windowsill to land on?"

"We've gone dru dis a thousand times. These boids got iron deposits in their brains that work like a compass."

"How long will it take them to get to the offices?" I asked.

"Yo Butchie, any storms forecasted for tomorra?" he yelled. I heard a muffled, "Naw." "Good," continued Sal. "So if the boids leave at eleven A.M. and they fly at an average speed, give or take, of fifty-five miles per hour, with easterly tailwinds, they'll arrive by noon."

"Sal, listen. Noon's too early. I need the birds to arrive at two P.M. That way the editors will be back from lunch and sitting at their desks when the birds land. They're going to some very important people. Like Anna Wintour at *Vogue* and Glenda Bailey at *Harper's Bazaar*."

"Aye, aye, el capitan."

"And another thing my boss wanted to know. The birds won't be—how can I say this?—dropping excrement on the windowsills? Because that would be a major problem."

"Zowie, lady. Dees ain't no street rats. Youse is getting the Cadillac of boids. Thoroughbreds of the sky, is what I call dem."

"There's just one more thing," I said hesitantly. I told him about the whitening cream and was thankful when he didn't seem fazed. He seemed more interested in the money.

"Don't furget the check tomorra."

On Friday, my clock radio went off at 6 A.M. "Is your face resembling the palm of your hand?" blared the DJ in her husky New York accent. "Are you saggin', baggin', craggin', and draggin'? Is your skin feeling crinkled and cluttered? Then try Chamonix. It will take years off by propping up and smoothing out your saggy, wrinkled mug."

I looked in the mirror at my tired, cluttered face. I felt like this job was taking years off my life. I showered, got dressed, and nervously got on the Q train with my shopping bag filled with the whitening cream, Tiffany necklaces, miniaturized press releases, and the packets of Bird Bath samples. I was traveling out to the last stop on the line, Coney Island. Sal lived on the top floor of a five-story walkup, and he greeted me at the door in a dirty wifebeater, stained sweatpants, and Adidas knockoff shower sandals. His apartment was done up in high mafioso splendor. The living room was wallpapered in black-and-white raised flocking. Above the red velvet sofa was a black velvet Don Quixote paint-by-number, and from the ceiling hung a gold-leafed cherub that dripped mineral oil from the filigree walls of its metallic cage. Paint-by-number pigeon art lined the walls.

"Dat's a painting of Monty. A true champ, may he rest in peace," Sal said, pointing to a rather handsome-looking bird.

In the distance, I could see a heavyset greasy-haired guy hunched over the kitchen sink. He was eating cereal out of a huge mixing bowl with a wooden spoon. He didn't bother to turn around and acknowledge my presence.

"Ever since Butchie's mother died," Sal said loudly enough for Butchie to hear, "he ain't never been the same. Don't leave the house much."

"When did Mrs. Ruggerio pass away?" I whispered.

"In 1988."

"Oh," I responded. It was *On the Waterfront* meets *Grey Gardens*. Even though they lived on the top floor, Butchie was what I called a basement boy: a grown man who still lived with his parents. I followed Sal up to the roof, where the bird coops were kept. It was windy and freezing, so I zipped up my coat and pulled my hat down over my ears. There were dozens of pigeons nestled up together, cooing in a soothing cacophonous rhythm as Sal threw bird feed through the chicken wire. "Ever taste pigeon?" he asked, lighting up the first of a series of Pall Malls.

"No, can't say that I have."

"Very tender. Kinda like squab, but more like squirrel," he said, leading me into a glassed-in observation deck that was set high above the coops. It was about the size of a subway token booth and reminded me of a widow's walk. It was outfitted with two metal folding chairs, a space heater, a desk, a clock, and an old rotary phone. I looked out at the sky.

"Weather's nice and clear," I said.

"Yeah. Dis is where I watch them fly back in," Sal said.

Sal had a beautiful view of the stark winter ocean. From his roof, you could also see the Cyclone roller-coaster and the old parachute jump. I stared out at the crashing waves, longing for a hot summer day.

"Nice beachfront property, huh? You won't be getting a view like this in Mah'ha'un," bragged Sal.

"You're right about that," I said, looking nervously at my watch.

"My boids is my life. If I wasn't flying dem, I think I'd be dead," he said, pensively gazing out like a sea wife on the lookout for a long-lost sailor husband.

We finally left the observation deck and he led me back to the coops. Sal took a jeweler's loupe out of his pocket and grabbed a bird. "This one's a winner. You can see it in his eyes."

"Yes, yes," I impatiently agreed, glancing at my watch again. "We better get to work."

"Ready to fly to Midtown, boys? On your way back, will youse pick me up a coupla dogs at Gray's Papaya, mustard, extra onions?" he said to them.

I reached into the shopping bag and pulled out a Tiffany chain.

"Tiffany. Nice," said Sal. "That's my niece's name."

I donned rubber gloves and opened a jar of whitener. "Can you hold a bird while I slather this on?" I said, bracing myself, not wanting to touch the pigeon.

"Whoa, whoa, whoa, lady!" Sal said, looking at the cream. "What is this?"

"I told you on the phone that we needed doves, so instead I'm going to whiten the pigeons."

Sal stuck his hand in the jar and rubbed the viscous whitener between his fingers. "You can't use this stuff on feathers. It's too thick. Between the cream and that heavy chain, it'll weigh dem down. They'll never get there."

"What are we going to do?" I said in a panic.

"Wait here," said Sal as he retreated into his apartment. I stood there shivering, staring at the poor helpless birds. What had I gotten myself into? Suddenly, big greasy Butchie appeared in the doorway.

"Hi," he grunted shyly, casting his feral eyes to the ground.

"Hi," I said back, looking away, afraid to make eye contact with him.

He sidled up next to me and stood really close, his breathing strained and heavy. He pulled an asthma inhaler from his pocket and took a hit off it. Like a bull ready to charge, he scraped his foot against the rough tar floor. My heart was racing. I wanted to run, but I was frozen in place. Was this some sort of setup? Were they going to hack me up and feed me to the pigeons? We stood there for what seemed like forever until finally Sal reappeared with a big bottle of Gold Bond talcum powder. I never thought I'd be so happy to see him.

"You want 'em white, I'll make 'em white," Sal said, sticking his head into the coop and liberally sprinkling the birds with powder. "Nice and white for your fancy VIPs." Sal grabbed a pigeon and presented it to me. "Look at your pwetty wittle dovey now."

It did look like a dove, which made me happy, but I was desperately trying to convince myself that we weren't really hurting the birds. Sal held out the pigeon, and I carefully placed a chain around its neck.

"Da chain's heavier than I thought," said Sal, fingering the thick, highly polished necklace. "I don't think the boid can fly wid dat weight around its neck. Listen, just leave it all wid me. I'll try to rig something up around the ankle."

I gave him a worried look. "You're going to attach the Bird Bath wipes, right?" I asked. "It's crucial that they get attached."

"No sweat. We'll take it from here," Sal said.

"Are you sure?" I asked.

"We got it covered," answered Sal.

"Okay," I said reluctantly. As much as I wanted to supervise, the vibe on this roof was deadly, so I started toward the staircase.

"Go on," Sal said, shooing me away. "But can youse take Butchie wiccha? He hasn't been out in a while."

My eyes widened. Butchie smiled at me with crooked yellow teeth and licked his chapped lips. In my head, I could hear the eerie backwater strains of the *Deliverance* "Dueling Banjos" song. I ran down the stairs, reluctantly leaving behind the thirteen blue Tiffany boxes and the product samples. My stomach was in knots. On the way to the subway, I stopped in a bodega to get some Mylanta. If this was what every product launch was like, I wasn't sure I could hack it. As I waited for the train on the elevated track, I saw a flock of white birds soar across the sky. I closed my eyes and sent positive affirmations to them, believing that they would do their job. If this went off without a hitch, maybe I could get promoted out of the land of low-paid lipstick lackeys and into a permanent, stable position.

The train ride back to the city was excruciatingly slow. It was after two P.M. when I finally arrived at Rockefeller Center. If everything had gone as planned, the birds would have already landed and done their thing. When I got out of the station, I checked my cell.

Good. No messages. I rewarded myself with a Frappuccino for a job well-done.

Murfy and Juniper met me in the hallway. "Hey, guys," I said to them, taking a sip of my drink.

They crossed their arms in unison and glared at me. "We hope you have your last will and testament in order because Diana's about to off you."

My stomach dropped. "What happened?" I cried. "Is it the doves?"

"Doves? Ha!" said Murfy. "They were gray pigeons, and they crashed through Anna's window. All thirteen of them! They got stuck in her bob and tore most of her hair out. She was medevaced to Brad Johns for an emergency hairendectomy. Can you even imagine?"

Juniper piped in. "She has cuts and stitches all over her body, and she had to have a rabies shot."

"*Vogue*'s going to pull our advertising accounts. I just know it. We're in some deep, deep guano," said Murfy.

"Connie's crazy mad. You betrayed her. She thought you were getting doves," said Juniper.

I couldn't believe it. The pigeons were Connie's idea! That two-faced witch was letting me take the fall. I sat slumped at my desk in a cold sweat. When I saw Diana marching down the hall, I got up and hid in the bathroom. When I came back out, Connie's door was shut. I manically checked all the Internet news sites. The story was already on Gawker and Defamer. Sure enough, Anna had been airlifted off the top of the Condé Nast building. And, always thinking on her feet, she immediately called Cher's wig maker and ordered three identical bobbed lace-front wigs that she could wear while her ravaged hair grew back. Suddenly, Connie's door flew open, and she, Tinsley, and Diana marched into the hallway. I grabbed my purse and was about to make a run for it.

"Stop right there, Marnie Mann," barked Tinsley.

I put my hands up like a two-bit fugitive.

"Put your arms down, Marnie. I've got some good news to report," Connie said.

"Anna's recovered and back at work?" asked Juniper.

"Even better. I pinned the whole blasted thing on PETA. I anonymously leaked it to the *Post*. For some reason, the products were not attached to the birds, so they can't trace it back to us. Anna thinks PETA was trying to take her out with a bunch of rabid pigeons. Mum's the word, folks."

"You're like Teflon, Connie. Nothing sticks to you," said Juniper.

"You're the master of spin," added Murfy.

Diana trained her hollow anime eyes on me. "You've got some explaining to do, young Mann."

"Tout de suite," added Tinsley, tapping her foot.

I felt like I was being lowered into a shark cage. Connie came over to my desk and protectively put her arm around my shoulder. "Look, Diana, the doves would never have worked anyway. Marnie tried something that in my opinion was rather ingenious, but unfortunately it didn't work. Leave the poor girl alone."

"Fine," Diana said, staring at me, "but with your inferior work ethic and unattractively hearty appetite, you'll never do a launch in this town again." She stormed away with Tinsley in tow.

That was low. I had worked so hard on the launch. What had happened with the doves wasn't my fault. I couldn't believe how cruel they were being. I had to get out of this place.

"Marnie, I have one question," Connie said once Diana and Tinsley were gone. "What do you think happened to the Tiffany necklaces?"

"I bet the assistants swiped them when they pulled the birds off of Anna," said Juniper.

"Yeah, you're probably right," I said, knowing full well that Sal and Butchie had kept them. I grabbed my purse and ran back into the bathroom. I sat in a stall and began to sob. This was all too much. Connie's blaming the dove disaster on PETA was pure evil, and I was being demonized. When the tears finally subsided, I wiped my eyes and dialed a number on my cell phone. "Sheila Buckle, please," I demanded. I was swiftly put on hold.

A prerecorded announcement in plummy Britspeak harrumphed in my ear. "At Cross Temps, the more you know, the more we pay."

"Sheila Buckle here," she finally announced.

I could hear a swipe, a wipe, and a flush in the next stall. "Sheila, it's Marnie Mann," I whispered.

"Is there not a better place to work than LeVigne Cosmetics?" she said, not altogether convincingly.

"To be honest, I don't think things are working out." There was a gag, a heave, and a flush in another stall.

"Doll, you made a commitment to Cross," Sheila said sternly, as though I was a wayward nun who had broken her pledge to Christ.

"What if I'm not happy here?" I implored.

Sheila let out a cruel cackle. "I never promised you happy."

"I'm being abused and the bathroom smells like vomit," I shouted.

"Occupational hazard, sweetie. I need you there."

"Sheila, I don't think I'm cut out for this. My eczema's flaring. I have to leave."

"I've got no one to replace you, doll, and further-more, where do you think you can go with those terri-ble test scores and your lack of office experience? I wouldn't even waste the time going to another agency. You're looking, at best, at a ten-dollar-an-hour filing job."

This revelation was shocking. I knew I hadn't done great on my tests, but she hadn't told me how bad my results actually were. It was obviously a fluke that I had gotten this job. What was I going to do? My rent was due and so were a pile of mounting bills. I felt power-less and desperate.

"So what's it gonna be, kid? I'll try to find you a re-placement, but I can't make any promises."

I was stuck between a rock and a hard place. I knew she was lying about finding a new temp. It was obvious that they couldn't keep anyone in this spot, and that was why Sheila had ignored my test scores and hired me. She was probably right. If I went to another employ-ment agency, who knew where they would send me.

On the upside, there *were* parts of my job that I actu-ally liked. The perks were great, the offices were beau-tiful, and I was learning some interesting things. Since I was a fungible, invisible temp, my coworkers would often talk shop in front of me, as if I weren't there, so I was learning a lot about the company, about how this monolithic business was run. That was the part I found fascinating.

"I guess I'll stay, then," I said through gritted teeth. "But not forever."

"I knew you'd see the light," said Sheila. "LeVigne is one of our best clients, and we need our temps to shine."

I wanted to tell her that I did shine, but mostly from my nose.

* * *

The next morning I picked up the *Post* on the way to the subway. Red Is the New Gray, screamed the headline, with a picture of a bloody, scratched-up Anna being carted off on a stretcher. The head of PETA had taken Connie's bait. As with the dead raccoon they had thrown on Anna's Four Seasons lunch plate and the tofu pie that they smashed in her face, PETA had punked Anna again, but this time they didn't have to put out a penny. I guess it was all good.

Apparently, unflappable Anna, bald patches, stitches, and all, was back at her desk the next morning. Connie sent her a big bouquet of white parrot tulips and a basket of Bird Bath wipes, since bathing was not yet an option.

SPACED OUT

After taking the fall for the Bird Bath debacle, I was summarily demoted and forced to stuff press kits and tend to the press clip books. I was feeling sorry for myself, but I couldn't complain to Holly, because I didn't want her to know about the birds, and I didn't feel comfortable enough to lean emotionally on Paul. We were still newly dating, and I wanted to be on my best behavior.

Murfy asked me to stuff press kits for Siesta. They were introducing a new face serum called Launch Pad that was said to have—surprise!—age-defying properties. Astronauts had performed senescence studies in outer space, and the LeVigne chemists had translated this invaluable research and put it into their wrinkle products. Included in the press kit mailer were a fancy four-color informational booklet, a sample of the product, and two packages of freeze-dried NASA-endorsed astronaut food (an ice cream sandwich and a bag of strawberries) that were to be put in a specially designed box made of heavy cardboard stock with a beautifully crafted snug-fitting lid. The booklet stated oxymoronically, "Launch Pad works instantly and over time."

"Stuff and seal," screamed Tinsley as she galloped by my desk. "Stuff and seal."

When I was done assembling the kits, I stuck some extra samples of the freeze-dried ice cream sand-wiches into my purse, and with the rest of the leftovers, like a good NASA scientist, I decided to perform an ex-periment. I put the packets on the counter in the pantry and stood around to see what would happen. Sure enough, a cluster of LeVignettes crowded around them to inspect the nutritional chart. When it was de-termined that one small bite equaled only five calo-ries, a melee ensued, and they gobbled up the pieces.

Later on, Murfy accosted me in the hallway and led me to several large cardboard boxes that were now at the foot of my desk. "The Systems gals are really tied up right now and they need your help with another press kit mailing. They're marketing a new under-eye con-cealer called Pow! The beauty editors will be getting kits that include a sample of the product, a pair of sil-ver boxing gloves, and a press release. These items are to be put into those purple knapsacks and FedExed out ASAP," she said.

When the kits were done, I went to lunch. My cell phone rang and I excitedly answered it, thinking it was Paul. He was on an unexpected cheese buying trip to Northern California because his boss had gone to a cheese rolling competition and was injured by a giant cheddar wheel. Paul called it "the running of the bulls for cheese."

But, alas, it was my dad. With him, there were no customary pleasantries like "Hi, how are you?" He just launched into his spiel. "Do you know how to use the eBay, kiddo? Trudy wants to bid on a spiffy pair of shoes for my costume."

"What costume?" I asked the king of non sequiturs.

"Larry, can you let me explain this to Marnie," said Trudy on the other extension. "We're doing Dickens in the Square again at the Cerritos strip mall. You know, where they recreate an old English village in the parking lot by Payless and Pep Boys? Your father is going as Scrooge, and I found him the most perfect pair of pilgrim shoes on eBay, but it's Greek to me."

"Marn, you're never going to guess what Trudy's going as," my dad said.

Trudy piped in. "A chimney sweep with my face all sooty."

"Doesn't that sound cute?" added Dad.

I pictured them dressed as ragamuffins, belting out Christmas carols in eighty-five-degree weather against a backdrop of fake falling snow.

"I hear you have a new Oriental beau," Trudy pried, always hungry for any stray tidbits about my life.

"He's Asian," I corrected. Why was it that people of their generation often used "Oriental"? It was cringeworthy. Why had I told my dad about Paul?

"That's wonderful, darling," gushed Trudy. "I hear Asian men are very gifted down there."

I nearly choked.

"You two talking about the Oriental fella?" my dad added, tuning back in to the conversation.

They were beyond hopeless, but I needed to accept

the fact that Dad and Trudy were never going to change, and as hard as it was, I had to come to terms with this. "How's your day been going, you two?" I asked with forced cheer. Anger into love, I repeated to myself. As difficult as it was, I forced myself to be positive, and surprisingly I felt better when I got off the phone with them. Plus, Murfy had told me that when you get angry, your body releases cortisol, a hormone that accelerates the aging process, and we didn't want that!

At the end of the day, Murfy and Juniper broke out the champagne. "I have an imperfection," whined Murfy.

"No, you don't," I said as I looked her up and down. The girl was absolutely perfect, if you didn't count her sallow skin and red-rimmed sloe eyes, which were probably due to a recent trip to the vomitorium.

It was then that I realized they were CAPs— Cosmetic American Princesses—with their capped teeth and capped faces.

"Don't you see it?" Murfy demanded, shoving her enviably poreless skin in my face. "I have phantom acne. My dermapharmacologist says it's because my face isn't centered."

"You've got the most symmetrical features I've ever seen," I said.

She stomped her feet. "Of course my features are centered. I was blessed with a very good head. That's not what I mean. I mean, my mind isn't centered, so my skin's off balance."

Maybe because of all the toxic injectables coursing through her size-zero body.

"Murfy, if I told you once, I told you a thousand times: you should really try Deeva's Witch Doctor facial revitalizer," said Juniper. "It imparts clarity, depth, and dimension."

Murfy took a sip of her champ and stared intently at my face. "Yikes, Marnie. You're starting to look like an old Dannon yogurt woman. Since you've been working here, I've noticed that your nasolabial folds have gotten way deeper," she said.

"My labial wuh?" I replied, blushing.

"Your smile lines, silly. It's from years of repeated facial movements. You have fifty-five muscles in your face, and I implore you to stop using them."

"Okay, then. No eating, smiling, laughing, or frowning," I said.

Juniper clapped her hands together. "Exactly," she exclaimed with a vacant expression. "But in the meantime, to correct the damage that's already been done, you can either use a dermal filler like Restylane or you can do a fat transfer from your tummy and inject it into your face folds. It would significantly decrease the step-off between cheek and lip to plump up your marionette lines. They give you a sad look," she said, cocking her head like a limp sock puppet.

"From here on I'm going to throw my voice. I will never move my mouth again," I mumbled stiffly, like a ventriloquist.

Juniper started to laugh and then stopped herself, making sure to relax her face into a crease-free zone. "Marnie, you really should pay a visit to Dr. Lurvey. He's the Svengali of skin. Wrinkle maintenance is a staple, like coloring your hair. It's something you do on a regular basis. You should also ask him to touch up your frown creases and worry lines," she said, pointing to the furrow between my brows and the horizontal lines spanning across my forehead like a set of Levolor blinds.

Murfy chimed in. "There's this botulinum toxin called Placiderm. It's like Botox, but with a slightly higher protein load, which makes it last a few months longer. What do you think?"

"Bella figura," I sighed.

"What's that?" asked Juniper.

"Oh, nothing," I said. I was desperate to move away from the subject of their faces.

It was almost seven P.M. "Look at the time, you guys. Why are we all still here? Even Connie's gone. I mean, it's only lipstick," I said blithely.

"Only lipstick?" Murfy spat out indignantly.

Their cube rage became tube rage.

"You're not being a team player, Marnie," said Juniper. "Maybe you should find another job. Like at a nonprofit."

If they only knew.

"Or go across the street and work for Schotzie Ronson," Juniper continued. "Murfy can tell you all about that hellhole."

"Please don't make me tell her," Murfy whimpered, cowering at her desk.

I was jonesing for some gossip about Ronson's company. "I didn't know you worked there," I said. "C'mon. You've got to tell me. I've heard he has magnifying mirrors attached to the back of the toilet seats in the executive men's room and that he tests his makeup by wearing it to bed."

After tense negotiations where I promised to stay and finish an organizational chart they couldn't quite figure out, Murfy finally fessed up. "What you just said is true. He also saves his blackheads in a jar and he breaks wind in meetings. A woman in packaging once remarked that one of his creams looked like mucus, and he had her tires slashed. He works you to death, and I'm not joking. The week I quit, the girl next to me dropped dead at her desk. She had blood gushing out of her ears."

"Oh my God," I said incredulously. "Tell me more!"

"I think I've said enough," cried Murfy, running off to the bathroom.

"Now look what you've done," Juniper said, running after Murfy. She turned around and shouted, "See you at Diana's baby shower tomorrow night, Marnie."

When I got home, I ran to the mirror because the mirror doesn't lie. I did have a furrow. It was big and deep and ugly. It made me look haggard and confused. Was it this job or the natural aging process?

The phone rang. It was Paul. He was back from his trip! I hopped into bed and got under the covers.

"Marnie, I had such a great time in Napa. The second the plane hit the tarmac, I was off and running to the cheese farms. I went to a couple of vineyards. It's very *Sideways* out there. All these looky-loo tourists who kept repeating that annoying merlot line. But that said, the wine was outrageous."

"I've never been. I'd love to take a trip there one day," I said.

"The coolest part was, I met Francis Ford Coppola at his vineyard. Sofia was there too. That girl really knows her cheese. She's spent time in the Loire valley, where a lot of the raw-milk chèvres come from. We talked for hours and hours."

I was a little taken aback. He and Sofia Coppola had talked for hours and hours? In interviews, she always seemed so reserved, almost mute. I always thought of her as the beautiful mute girl. Sofia was the chick I loved to hate. She had everything. An Academy Award, wealth, talent, the honor of being Marc Jacobs's muse, and, ugh, now cheese connoisseurship. While Paul was sipping California chards and hobnobbing with Hollywood royalty, I was home nursing a Bartles & Jaymes wine cooler that I found at the back of my fridge, and self-medicating my eczema rash. But I silently forgave him because he was so sweet and adorable.

"I really missed you," Paul said. "And I can't wait to get my hands on you."

Hearing this made me horny, and I reached into my goody drawer for my trusty vibrator. I revved up the quiet metallic bullet as I told him about my week at work. We were still in that wide-eyed exploratory stage where you could gab on the phone for hours. The conversation was going great until Paul very matter-of-factly mentioned that he had to go to Vermont for a couple of days to visit a cheese farm and that his ex, Kendra, would be coming over to feed Jeffrey. Whoa. Major buzz kill. Literally. I snapped the vibrator off and threw it to the side of the bed. But what was wrong with me? I had no reason to be proprietary so early on. I mean, we hadn't even had sex yet, but he could have asked *me* to feed Jeffrey. Why did it bother me so much that his ex was coming over to take care of the cat? Okay, *their* cat. But still. I realized exes had all sorts of custody arrangements with children, so why not pets? It just seemed a little strange, was all. I was getting the subtlest vibe that he wasn't totally over her.

"What are you doing tomorrow night?" Paul asked.

"I was going to ask you the same thing," I said. "I

have to go to this baby shower for work. Would you like to come?

"To a baby shower? Isn't that an all-girls thing?"

"Oh, didn't you hear? *Vogue* declared that all-girl showers aren't cool anymore, so it's a coed affair."

"Sure. I'll go," Paul said, and with that he proceeded to indulge me with stories about farmstead cheese-making. "I learned this great French phrase from Sofia. *'Regardez ce quart de Brie,'* which loosely translates to 'look at the quarterwheel of brie.' It's used when describing someone with a large nose. Isn't that great?"

"Leave it to the French," I said. And Sofia, with her own sizable nose.

"What are you wearing?" Paul asked seductively.

"Not much," I purred.

"Sounds sexy."

And with that, I quietly turned the vibrator back on.

"I wish you'd been there with me to try the most incredible Brie. The supple rind broke at the slightest touch. . . ."

"Ooooh, really," I panted.

"It was liquid heaven."

". . . Oh my God," I cried as I stealthily had the most jammin' orgasm.

"Wow," said Paul. "You sound really into it. I'm definitely going to bring over some Fromage de Meaux, then."

After we hung up, I lay there in a half-dreamy state. Then I jumped out of bed and opened the closet to check on my Courage cologne. I did what the recipe said and gave the marinating bottle a brisk little shake.

DESIGN FOR LIVING

Tonight was Diana Duvall's surprise baby shower, so I went shopping for a new frock. At H&M, I was mowed down by a bunch of screaming prep-school girls, so I hightailed it over to Banana and Bloomies.

Diana lived near Paul, so I swung by to pick him up. I was rocking a really cute look that involved sexy black tango shoes and a glittery red beret.

We had an impromptu make-out session where he threw me on top of his combo washer/dryer. We turned it on for the extra vibrational action. If it hadn't been for the party, I think we would have consummated our relationship right there on the Maytag, but, alas, I had made a commitment to go to the party. As we walked to Tribeca, I got excited just thinking about how we would resume things later.

As we approached Diana's building, Murfy and Juniper were already there, ringing the buzzer. We all rode up together in the elevator. Thank God Tinsley had gone away for the weekend, so I wouldn't have to see her nasty face.

Juniper looked me up and down. "Marnie, do you have really big feet, or are those just incredibly long shoes?"

Paul shot Juniper a look like she was crazy. Good! I liked a man who would come to my defense.

"Thank God I'm a sample-size seven," she continued. "I don't know what I would do if I had your boats."

Paul and I traded glances.

"You must be Paul," said Murfy, ogling him. "We've heard all about you."

I shot her a look. When we reached the top floor of Diana's building, the door slid open into an enormous minimalist loft. I looked around. It seemed that we were the first guests to arrive. My eyes were drawn to the center of the room, where an outsized Silver Cross Balmoral pram sat. It was black, with big whitewashed wheels and a giant pink satin bow wrapped around it. It was old-fashioned, but in a creepy way. It looked like something straight out of *Rosemary's Baby*. All it needed was an upside-down cross dangling from it.

A tall, perfectly groomed man in horn-rimmed glasses came rushing over to us. He was Hickory Jones, famous British portrait painter and husband to Diana Duvall. He hugged Murfy and Juniper. "The last time I saw you two daffodils was two years ago at the Christmas party," he said. "Remember all the absinthe we drank?"

Murfy and Juniper giggled. "That night was mad awesome. I think I lost five pounds from all the barfing afterward," Juniper said.

"Your place looks amazing," cooed Murfy over the jazzy strains of Herb Alpert and the Tijuana Brass.

"We just had it redone. Isn't it divine?" he lisped.

Hickory looked at me quizzically and at Paul lasciviously.

"Oh, Hick, I'm sorry. How rude," said Murfy. "This is Marnie Mann, our PR floater."

"Nice to meet you," I said. "I love your work. I'm an avid portrait collector myself."

"But do you have one of mine?" pried Hickory presumptuously.

"Doubtful, on her salary," said Murfy, cutting me off.

"Listen, Hick. If you need Marnie to do anything, she's yours for the asking."

I wondered if I was going to be sold off at a slave auction.

"I didn't think I was on the clock tonight," I muttered to Murfy with a tight smile, eying two topless, chiseled catering waiters wearing nothing but bow ties and out-sized cloth diapers held together with huge metal pins. One guy was setting up the bar while the other pulled some yummy-smelling appetizers from the oven.

"And who might this be?" Hickory asked, offering up a limp wrist to Paul.

"This is my date, Paul," I said.

"Charmed, I'm sure," Hickory said, shaking the tips of Paul's fingers. Was this guy really Diana Duvall's husband? He seemed sooooo beyond gay. Maybe he was just another SoHo puss, "puss" being the endearing term for a certain kind of finicky straight guy who ironed knife pleats into his jeans, never missed a tele-vised ice dancing competition, and knew all the lyrics to the *Pippin* songbook.

I grabbed Paul's hand. "Let's find a place to stash our coats," I said as my eyes took in the cavernous loft. Nothing was more satisfying yet ultimately dishearten-ing than examining how the other half lived. This ex-quisitely photogenic apartment was certainly ready for its close-up.

"Boy, they sure have a lot of books," Paul said as we scanned the spines on the floor-to-ceiling, wall-to-wall bookcase.

"But they're all picture books," I whispered. Lots of design tomes, photography journals, and a million coffee-table books. The only thing text-driven was Hat-tie LeVigne's authorized biography.

"Weird that they don't read," whispered Paul.

"No one reads at work either," I explained to him. "They all get subscriptions to the *Times* and the *Journal*, which they promptly lift up with an aloe tissue and throw into the trash. The *Post* is only good for Page Six."

We continued our tour. We were like two people strolling through a museum: Paul had his arms folded behind his back, and I stopped every few feet to look at some objets d'art with my head cocked and my hand curled pensively under my chin.

"Would you like to live in a place like this?" I asked.

"Naw," he said in a low voice. "I prefer rooms. Plus, I would love a basement for my cheese cave."

"Are cheese caves the new panic rooms?" I joked.

"What about you?" Paul laughed, grabbing my hand as we strolled on through the massive space.

"I like proper rooms too," I said, giving his hand a tight squeeze. "If I could live anywhere, it would be in a stately Village brownstone. Clean, spare rooms. White walls. An eclectic mix of modern and antique. A fireplace in the bedroom. A small backyard. A flower garden. A stackable washer and dryer." And with that, we both giggled, thinking back on our earlier tryst.

Wow. I had verbalized what I wanted. It seemed like such an impossible dream—to be a homeowner in this town—that it hurt even to think about it. At the moment, all I could hope for were some Isaac Mizrahi sheets from Target and a new set of dishes.

We walked over to a table that had appetizers artfully arranged on it. Paul picked up two hunks of crumbly cheese. He put one in his mouth.

"Gran Canaria from La Valle, Wisconsin. Deliciously pungent. Hickory sure knows his cheese."

I opened my mouth to say something, and Paul

popped the other piece in mine. I felt a little violated. I wouldn't just shove a piece of gefilte fish into his mouth. I was just about to out myself about my dairy problem when Murfy and Juniper motioned to us from the open high-tech kitchen.

"Yo, Marnie, we've got nipples to cut," Murfy yelled. "I need you and Paul over here pronto."

I gave Paul a searching look and grabbed a napkin to surreptitiously spit out the cheese that was wedged in the corner of my mouth. We walked over, and Juniper handed both of us a pair of scissors and a box of plastic baby bottles.

"Snip the tips. We're putting booze in them," Juniper said in a completely blasé way.

I shot Paul a look.

"Hey, it's cool," he said, trying to mollify me. "I mean, who doesn't like playing with nipples?"

A cater waiter approached Murfy and Juniper and whispered something to them. Murfy whispered something back, and the three of them laid eyes on me. He handed Juniper a tote bag and went back to readying the hors d'oeuvres.

Juniper placed her hand lightly on Paul's arm. "Paul, do you know what happens when a madam's best call girl is out with a yeast infection?" she asked.

"You get another call girl?" he said.

"Bingo!" Murfy retorted, grabbing the tote bag from Juniper and handing it to me. "Marnie, we have a really big favor to ask. The cater waitress called in sick, and we need you to pitch in and take her place. There's a uniform in the bag. You can change in the bathroom."

I gave her an evil death glare.

Juniper came over and put her arm around my

waist. "Could you, please? Pretty please? Play bartender tonight?" she asked.

They were so great at playing good cop bad cop.

Guests wandered in and drifted over to the coveted Balmoral carriage, placing their baby gifts inside it. I didn't want to make a scene in front of Paul, but I didn't want to leave him alone in this room of Botoxed barracudas.

He must have read my mind. "Marnie, it's okay. Do it for a while," coaxed Paul, "and then I'll take your place. It'll be fun."

I smiled at him. He was such a good sport. Jarret had arrived, and I waved to him as I reluctantly went into the bathroom.

There was a knock at the door. No one said anything, but I knew it was Murfy, so I didn't respond. I unzipped the tote bag and pulled out the contents. If this wasn't a sexual harassment suit in the making, I didn't know what was. This was no prim maid's uniform. This was far worse. It was a gag outfit cobbled together from the Pink Pussycat and A Pea in the Pod: a foam breastplate with huge porno boobs (one was pierced) and a white cotton nursing bra (size 42DD). I sat down on the tile floor. I was going to puke. They must have been getting me back for the Bird Bath fiasco. I looked up to see if there was a window that I could escape from. No such luck. There was a knock at the door again.

"Listen, Marnie. I'll make it up to you. Really, I will," said Murfy as she jiggled the handle.

"Go away," I replied tearfully.

"You can add these hours to your time sheet," she said.

"I quit."

"How does time and a half sound?"

"I'm so out of here."

"Double time?"

"Triple time," I said. "I bought a new outfit for tonight. I thought I was an invited guest. My date's out there and I'm starving."

"Okay, fine, then. Triple time. Now let me in."

I got up and reluctantly unlocked the door. Murfy came in and with great relish helped me with the breastplate and nursing bra. "Aren't they great? They're Dolly boobs," she said, squeezing one like she was shopping for melons.

I wrenched away from her and started out of the bathroom. At least the huge bra covered up the grotesque foamy mammaries.

"Hold up, missy," Murfy said, yanking me back. "We're not done yet. For triple time, you're gonna have to show them off." She unlatched the nursing cups from the top so they dropped down, exposing both obscenely large breasts for the world to see.

I skulked out into the vast living room with the tote bag blocking my "naked" chest. This felt incredibly surreal, like an anxiety dream where you went to school without your clothes on. As I walked to the kitchen, I could see Paul and Jarret yucking it up, standing at the bar, making milk-based cocktails. Juniper yanked the tote bag away from my chest and let out a yelp. Paul stifled a laugh. "Sweet," he said, flicking off the blender and lasciviously gazing at my bawdy bundles.

"The wet nurse is here. We're off duty, Paul," Jarret said, grabbing two chocolate-milk martinis and leading Paul out into the buoyant crowd.

Paul looked over his shoulder. "Sorry. I'll be right back," he mouthed to me.

Jacquie Wires, the PR director of Paparazzi and

Deeva, bellied up to the bar. "White Russian. Skim. And step on it. Where's Connie?" she asked, not the least bit fazed by my outsized breasts.

"They found a gun in her daughter's lunchbox," I said as I made her a drink.

"Damn breeders," she replied, taking a sip and walking away.

Hickory dimmed the lights and shushed everyone. He had been alerted that Diana was on her way up. There were lots of giggles and whispers in the dark. Finally Diana burst through the door. "Surprise!" everyone shouted. Diana mustered up as much shock as her paralyzed facial muscles would allow. I don't think she had expected to find porno-me, diapered waiters, and her coworkers getting sloppy drunk in her pristine apartment. I noticed that Paul, Murfy, and Juniper were off in a corner, whispering in a tight little huddle. *Whatever,* I thought.

Diana approached the bar. "Get me a glass of oblivion," she cried dramatically, stroking her pregnant belly. But I had been instructed not to let her drink. I made her a virgin chocolate-milk martini and put it in one of the baby bottles. Someone grabbed me from behind and squeezed my rent-a-boobs.

"Shake your moneymakers, girlfriend," Jarret purred, spinning me around.

Paul came over and put his arm around my waist. "You're turning me on with those hooters."

I knew he was trying to make me feel better about my outfit and about my having to work, but it had the reverse effect, making me feel worse.

Juniper sauntered over. "Paul, you seem so bored," she said, dragging him away again and back into the crowd.

As I wearily whirred the blender, poured more drinks, and snipped more nipple tips, a young woman came up to the bar. She had a homeschooled complexion and the athletic ramrod posture of a drum majorette. She definitely looked intimidated by this extreme crowd.

"Hey there, I'm Tawny Brinkmore, FiFi's new assistant," she said with a sweet nasal twang.

"What can I do ya for?" I said, suddenly channeling my inner bartender.

"Milk, straight up. I've been here a week, and I think I have an ulcer."

"How old are you?" I asked the authentically youthful Tawny.

"Twenty-one. I graduated from Florida State last spring."

As I handed Tawny a martini glass filled with whole milk, I realized that if she started getting Botox now, she could truly be Forever 21.

The crowd gathered around Diana as she opened her shower presents. In addition to the Silver Cross carriage, which was a gift from Sidney and Marion Levigne, she received a Chanel diaper bag, a deluxe-edition Maclaren stroller, and a high-tech Braun electric breast pump with a crocodile-skin travel cooler and battery pack. It reminded me of the jet pack Woody Allen wore in *Sleeper*. I winced as I watched Diana unwrap my Old Navy onesie.

Patrick, Murfy's cute-brute hedge fund boyfriend, sidled up to the bar. He looked exactly like Robert Chambers. "None of this milk shit and no baby bottle. Grey Goose martini, straight up, olives. Nice headlights, by the way," he said, staring at my permanipples.

I filled a shaker with ice. "Thanks," I said, thrusting

them out, trying to make some sort of peace with my ta-tas.

I had to pee. I needed a break. I motioned for Paul, but he was too busy picking up wrapping paper off the floor and handing it to Tawny. Patrick rambled on about the bear market, his irritable bowel syndrome, and his waning interest in his girlfriend, who was heading straight for the bar. I was quickly learning that in any setting and in any outfit (or lack thereof), a barmaid was a confidante, a psychiatrist, a nonjudgmental ear.

Murfy wrapped her arms protectively around Patrick. "Don't get any ideas, Marnie," she said.

I guess it was okay for her and the other CAPs to flirt shamelessly with Paul, but even as a captive audience, I wasn't supposed to talk to her boyfriend. Suddenly a scream emanated from amidst the crowd. "Get that thing off of me, you animal!" Diana shouted.

I couldn't help cracking up. Tawny had thoughtfully made the traditional baby shower bonnet fashioned from a paper plate and shreds of wrapping paper and ribbons, and was tying it under Diana's chin.

Hickory came rushing over to Tawny. "No, no, no, my dear. This is Tribeca. Not Tallahassee. We don't do that sort of thing here," he said as he grabbed the flat hat and flung it, Frisbee-style, across the room, whereupon it clocked Jacquie Wires in the head.

Diana ran shrieking into bathroom, and everyone made a mad dash for more drinks. Someone grabbed my boob and then everyone rushed over to cop a feel.

"Will someone please touch mine?" said a drunk Juniper as she stuck her small cashmered chest out for anyone to feel. "They're real. I swear. And they haven't been groped in years." When no one took her up on the generous offer, Juniper grabbed Diana's breast pump from the pile of gifts. She sat down on the couch, whipped out a boob, and turned on the machine. It made an electric whirring noise that sounded just like sex moans. "I want a baby. I want a man to suck my titties," she slurred.

Hickory came rushing over. "Goodness gracious, Juni. This is not *National Geographic*. Cover yourself up," he said, shielding her chest with an oversized Taschen coffee-table book.

"Get outta my way, Dickory," Juniper garbled, pushing him aside. And then she fell off the couch and collapsed onto the floor.

Paul rushed over to help her up. With all eyes on Juniper, I snuck into the bathroom and put on my civvies. I tentatively gazed at myself in the mirror. I looked like shit. I threw the stupid costume in the trash can and did my best to restore what was left of my cute but now wrinkled outfit.

I found Paul and grabbed his hand. "Let's get out of here," I said.

As we sped away in a cab, he stroked my hair. "You looked really hot in that costume."

"You're crazy. I looked like Pam Anderson's ugly stepsister with those flotation devices."

"No, you didn't. I thought it was really funny and kinda sexy." He nuzzled into my neck and then pulled away.

"What's wrong?" I asked.

"You smell a little milky, is all," he said.

I smelled milky? Look who was calling the cheese white. He sometimes had a slightly sour, cheesy smell. Occupational hazard, I guess. But I kept my mouth shut.

"That was really fun," Paul continued. "Thanks for

inviting me. Your work friends seem nice. A little over-
the-top and kind of plastic, but nice."

"They're not my friends."

"Don't be so mean. I might have some new cus-
tomers. They said they want to come in and buy
cheese. I gave them my business card."

"Paul, please. Those girls don't eat cheese. Don't you
get it? They're coming in to see you."

"What are you talking about?"

"Hellooo? They were flirting with you, and you were
being so nice to them."

"What's wrong with being nice? I was just being me,"
Paul responded.

"Then don't be so charming. It's irritating, okay?" I
said, staring at his Lees.

"What are you looking at?"

"Your jeans are so dated. You need some new threads."

I caught myself sounding petty. What was wrong with
me? He *was* really charming, and that was one of things
I loved about him. He was from the Midwest, after all,
and who cared about his clothes? I was used to New
York and LA guys, who were never friendly just to be
friendly. Just the way the LeVignettes didn't eat cheese
just to *eat* cheese. He wasn't getting it, but I had to stop
myself from sinking into a really bad mood. Wearing
that stupid outfit when everyone else got to look great in
their party clothes made me feel insecure and bitchy.

When we got back to Paul's apartment, I collapsed
onto the sofa from sheer exhaustion. Paul sat next to
me, kissed me, and then slowly unbuttoned my shirt,
sliding his strong hand across my breast. I still felt
tense, and he could sense it. "Come on, snap out of it,"
Paul said. "I'm sorry you had such a bad time tonight.
We should have just stayed here."

"No, I'm glad we went. I wanted to show you off to my coworkers. You're way cuter than Patrick."

"Ya think?" Paul said, stroking my stomach and then the tender skin right below my belly button. I was starting to calm down.

"You feel so smooth. Like fine china," he said.

My nerve endings were dancing. I was jittery with anticipation, knowing this was going to be our first night. We had the most intense chemistry, he and I. The kind where time stops and everything in the periphery becomes hazy and wholly insignificant. "You feel velvety, like a bloomy-rind cheese," he said, easing his fingers into my slippery slope. I lay back and melted into a pool of clarified butter.

"Fine china. I like the way that sounds," I murmured, basking in a room that felt sauna-hot from the heat that was emanating from our bodies.

"You're really beautiful, Marnie."

Music to my ears. I reached for his crotch. I always loved the feeling of a guy's hard dick through his clothes. What you didn't see was sometimes the biggest turn-on, almost more erotic and exciting than touching the actual flesh. "Let's take a shower à deux," I said grabbing his hand and leading him into the bathroom.

I turned on the faucets and we slowly took off our clothes. I got into the shower first, and Paul followed. The hot water drenched us as we bubbled each other up. His warm hands on my wet, lathery breasts made me light-headed and tipsy.

As we continued to explore each other's bodies, Paul looked into my eyes. I looked intently back. I hoped this night would last forever. Having sex for the first time with someone new could be amazing. The intense connection. The exploration. Paul cradled my face in his hands.

His fingers traced the outline of my jaw, cheeks, lids. "Remember when I told you that the holes in Swiss cheese are called eyes? Well, when the cheese ripens, droplets of moisture flow out. They call it weeping and . . ."

I put a finger over his mouth to shush him. The only crying I wanted to do was from sheer ecstasy. "Sshhh," I said as I pulled him out of the shower and led him to the bed.

THE LOOK OF LOVE

As I walked to work the next morning, I found myself humming the disco anthem "You Make Me Feel (Mighty Real)" by Sylvester. Paul and I had consummated our relationship, and I felt absolutely ravishing, inside and out. It occurred to me right then that sex was nature's original beauty potion.

But my sexual reverie came to a crashing halt when I thought about the humdrum reality of birth control. Paul had used a condom, but if this was going to be an ongoing thing, I needed to get a prescription for the pill. However, without health coverage, I would have to make an out-of-pocket trip to the gynecologist. I was showing up every day at LeVigne, but I wasn't reaping the benefits of a full-time employee. Maybe I should inquire about a permanent job with a 401(k) and a pension plan.

As I made my way to my desk, a nattily dressed man suddenly grabbed my arm and yanked me into a conference room. "Ooh. Fresh meat," he said, backing me up against a credenza and dousing perfume on my pulse points.

"What the hell are you doing?" I yelled as he snogged the nape of my neck.

As I struggled to get free, a woman joined him and hungrily sniffed my inner wrists.

"Stop it," I demanded as I tried to kick her.

"I'm getting two profound chords here," the woman exclaimed. "Nice top note. I like the asymmetry. I'm smelling donut shop. Dog fur and plastic baby dolls. Not traditional at all, but with good depth."

After I accepted the fact that I was being used as their flesh-test dummy, I relaxed into the sniff.

The man pinched shut his nasal passages and took in several deep snorts. "Amazing whiffability. I smell candy corn, hashish, and expensive brown leather."

As quickly as they had assaulted me, they abruptly walked away, obliviously scribbling down notes.

Their fragrance mauling left me with a nasty headache, so I stumbled into the pantry for an aspirin and a glass of water.

"Marnie, you stink. Did they get you again?" Jarret asked. "I told you, don't hug the walls, and stay clear of doorways."

Jarret was busy hanging a homemade sign about the dangers of Aspartame over the boxes of pink, yellow, and blue artificial sweeteners.

Juniper came in, ignored the posted warning, and chugged down a Diet Coke.

"Hey, cowgirl, slow it down. You're pickling your body with that toxic stuff," Jarret said to her.

"This is nothing," Juniper said. "Jacquie Wires drinks like thirty cans a day."

"There's anecdotal evidence that diet soft drinks can cause brain tumors," I said.

"Die young and stay pretty . . . thin," Juniper replied

as she grabbed another one from the fridge and ran out.

After all the devil's dandruff Jarret had smoked, it seemed inconceivable that he was waging a war against Equal, but I guess everyone has his cross to bear. I reached over Jarret to grab a napkin and I caught a whiff of something out of place, yet very familiar.

"That's not Schotzie you're wearing?" I asked.

Jarret stepped back a few paces. "That would be scandal. I'm cloaked in Sidney," he purred.

But he did smell of Schotzie.

To compete with Ronson's bestselling fragrance, Schotzie, LeVigne was rolling out their own epony-mously named perfumes. The first to hit pulse points everywhere was a fragrance called Sidney. Sidney's tagline was "It's not all over you like a cheap suit." Last year, Marion had brought to market a sickly-sweet scent of her own, called Morning Dew. Jarret referred to it as Mourning Doo. To me, it was just another form of air pollution, which seemed to be favored by the *mature* woman who didn't want to be rendered invisible. She wanted her *sillage* to trail close behind her.

Later that day, I was in the women's room when I heard Murfy and Juniper come in. I could hear them talking by the powder-room mirror. I tucked my feet under me so they wouldn't know I was there.

"I desperately need some new shoes," whined Murfy. "I'm going downtown to Sigerson Morrison. Wanna come?"

"You're going to Siggy Mo in NoHo? So not fair. I've got a hair appointment with Sally Hershberger," lamented Juniper. "I'm getting my blondness refreshed."

"And I desperately need a trim. It's that half inch that makes all the difference, don't ya think?"

My bladder was about to burst. *Hurry up and get out,* I thought.

"How do you work it with Sally? Do you do a trade?" asked Murfy.

"Half in product, half in cash. Sally wants the new Siesta cream," replied Juniper.

I was so jealous that they could afford even half of Sally's outrageous fee (half being four hundred dollars) and that they could buy Sigerson Morrison shoes with such wanton abandon. I lusted after every single unaffordable pair.

"Do you think Jarret uses testosterone?" asked Murfy. "His forehead juts out like a Neanderthal man. It makes him cute by half."

Leave already, I screamed in my head.

"Right? And can you tell me why Juan brings that big stack of magazines into the men's room? Nothing kills a crush like a dump announcement," scoffed Juniper.

Juan was a fox with a smokin' bod, but I never thought that he would be one of Juniper's midnight players.

"And most importantly," Juniper continued, "can we even discuss the studliness of that guy Marnie brought to the shower?"

"He's a tasty snack. Like, what's the deal?" asked Murfy.

"Don't really know. Do you think she's got a trick vagina?" posited Juniper.

I shoved my fist in my mouth so as not to audibly gasp.

"I guess Hattie LeVigne was right when she said there can only be one peacock per relationship," said Murfy.

What evil little bitches! I was glad they thought Paul was cute, but what was I, chopped liver? Was I really a parakeet to his peacock?

"And furthermore," Juniper said as they were leaving, "she's got to do something about that knitted corrugator muscle. It's a fright. Didn't we tell her about Dr. Lurvey, like, at least ten times? He's such a great shooter."

When Murfy and Juniper were gone, I finally peed and ran to the mirror to assess my face. They were right. The tension that had been sexually released last night was back in full force. I had gone from haggard to ravishing and back to haggard again. That was it! I was going to buy a box of Frownies at Zitomer on Madison. Who needed expensive Botox when a low-tech piece of paper glued to your forehead overnight could do the trick? The only problem was, I couldn't use them on the nights I saw Paul. It was too soon in our relationship to be revealing a woman's beauty secrets.

On my way back to my desk, I passed Juan and his mail cart. Damn, he was cute.

"Hi, Marnie," he said with a wink.

"Hi back," I said with a shy smile.

"How's it going?" he asked. "They working you too hard? 'Cause you always have a freaked-out look on your face."

How could I explain that my "angry" appearance was due to my furrow?

I remembered the gossip Jarret has spilled one day at lunch, and wondered if Juan and Summer really had done the nasty in Hattie's office. I was dying to know what was going on between them. Summer didn't have a furrow.

"Summer's kind of pretty, isn't she?" I said, nonchalantly fishing for information.

"Kinda? She's way hot," he said defensively. "Big glossy lips. Decent rack. Could be bigger. But I hate her bony white ass," he said. "You got a boyfriend?"

"I'm dating someone," I said, blushing.

"Too bad," he replied. " 'Cause you don't look like the cheating kind."

I blushed even harder and had to run into the kitchen for a glass of ice water.

"Smile, girl! Things aren't so bad," said Jarret as he buzzed out of the pantry.

But I *was* smiling. It was my damn knitted corrugator muscle that made me look cross.

ALL BLOGGED DOWN

It was less than two weeks until Christmas, and when I heard the slightly warbled female computer voice reading my nearly negative bank balance over the phone, I almost fell off my chair.

Deirdre from Paparazzi chose that moment to seek me out. She had a blunt blond bob and wore a beat-up fur coat of about the same shade. I stared at her coat, wondering if she was ever pelted by the politically correct Deeva employees.

"I know what you're thinking. It's vintage, and it was already dead when I bought it. Are you busy this Saturday?" Deidre asked hurriedly, probably on her way outside to smoke.

"Just gonna lay low."

"Wanna work?"

"On the weekend? Are you joking?"

"Here's the thing. Paparazzi is hosting its annual Tranquility Spa for the Daytime TV Glammy Awards, and I'm a bridesmaid in my cousin's wedding in Westport. If I don't find someone to cover for me, Jacquie'll have my head."

"I wouldn't want to be on the wrong side of Jacquie

Wires either, but my weekend's my weekend. I really don't know what to tell you," I said, sympathetically shrugging my shoulders.

"We'll pay you time and a half," Deirdre said desperately. "Believe it or not, those soap opera guys are really sweet, and some of them are even straight. They've been RSVPing like crazy. It's your basic swagfest. Nothing really to it. Just smile and sign them in."

"What's swag?" I asked.

"Stands for 'Stuff We All Get.' It's the shit in the gift bags."

I thought about my bank balance. "I'll do it for double time," I shot back.

"Sold." We shook on it.

Deirdre looked at my forehead. "I see you're using Frownies."

"Yeah. I'm glad they're working."

"Well, your furrow is gone, but beam me up, Scotty. I can see the triangular mark that the paper strip left behind."

"That's just great," I said, touching the spot. At least Deirdre was forthright enough to tell me. Juniper and Murfy were probably snickering behind my back.

I accompanied Deirdre on her cigarette break, and as she blew smoke at the passing tourists, she told me a few things about the event. To win brownie points with Sidney, Jacquie Wires had come up with the idea that Summer and Rebecca would hang out at the spa to meet and greet the daytime-TV stars, and then Marion had upped the ante and decided that they would actually administer select spa treatments. Rebecca would play the part of the "hairdresser," and Summer would make a cameo appearance as the "aesthetician."

* * *

The night before the Tranquility Spa event, I slept over at Paul's place. We ordered Chinese. "Can you have them bring over a Diet Coke?" I shouted from the bathroom.

Paul placed the order and hung up. "Since when do you drink Diet Coke?" he asked.

"I don't know. I kind of started drinking it at work. That's all they have in the pantry."

"Whatever," Paul said coolly.

After we ate, Paul took a shower. While he was scrub-a-dubbing, I decided to send a quick e-mail to my mom, giving her a heads-up on a FedEx cosmetics package I was sending her. I touched the keyboard to wake it up out of sleep mode. There was something called Pandora's Box on the screen. It was a MySpace page. Oh my God. It was a blog by Kendra. As I quickly scanned it, a song began to play. It was an awful version of an already atrocious song—"Papa, Can You Hear Me?"—but it wasn't Barbra singing. Was it Kendra? I quickly muted the sound.

Pandora's Box. Open it and find out . . .

<u>*Today Pandora is:*</u> *Cold, Grouchy, Crampy, Horny*

<u>*Things Pandora loves in no particular order:*</u>
Bras with no underwire because since my
augmentation, I certainly don't need it!
My natural red hair and no, you can't make me prove it
Being sore from too much nookie!
Parking meters with time left on them

<u>*Things Pandora's addicted to:*</u>
Tickle deodorant and my sexy silk camis
Being thrown from the mechanical bull

Things Pandora wishes she had done:
Kept her old rock concert T-shirts
Paid more attention in Spanish class

Things Pandora wishes she would do more:
Smile at strangers (but only if they're cute because if
you're not cute and you hit on me, I will cut you!!)
Hang out more with my ex!!!
Do Kegel squeezes (my gyno says I have weak vaginal
muscles and could "leak" later in life)

Wish List:
Stripper pole
Getting a meaty acting role: I'll do crippled, I'll play
crazy crack whore, I'll even wear a crooked nose
Red Bull and vodka and a baby from Africa

Rant of the Day:
Roger Ebert called that little brat Dakota Fanning the
most talented woman in Hollywood! Can u believe? I'm
so sick of hearing that precocious 13-year-old twerp go
on about her craft, working with De Niro, and how Scors-
ese is such a genius. Dakota: I invite you to a duel. Let's
you and me read some Ibsen monologues and see who's
the better actress. Bring it on, beeatch. I will cut you!

I wanted to read more, but I heard the shower faucets
squeak off, so I hopped onto the couch and pretended
to read a book. I couldn't focus on the words because I
was reeling over Kendra's retarded blog. When Paul
opened the bathroom door, I grabbed him and led him
into the bedroom. He said he was tired, which was
good, because I had to keep him out of the living room
until his computer went back to sleep.

As soon as Paul started snoring, I snuck into the bathroom and did some face-firming gymnastics. I stood in front of the bathroom mirror, extended my neck like a swan, pushed my chin forward, and thrust out my lower lip. With my face in that position, I slowly turned my head to the left and then slowly to the right. I did this twelve times to strengthen my throat and less-than-piquant jawline.

When I got into bed, I spooned against Paul and thought about Kendra. I couldn't believe how tacky and self-absorbed she was, probably the type who wore a sequined butt advertisement on her sweatpants, like "Guess" or "Juicy." Whenever I saw the word "Juicy" printed on a girl's behind, it made me think of the word "sluicy," which made me think of diarrhea. One thing was for sure: Kendra had a bad case of blogorrhea. What did that mean when she blogged about spending more time with an ex? Was Paul that ex? She'd better stay away from my man. As I lay there stewing, I constricted my vaginal muscles. If Kendra was doing her Kegel squeezes, I guessed I'd better be doing mine.

I arrived at the W hotel Tranquility Spa suite the next morning at eight A.M., bleary-eyed and still somewhat bothered by Kendra's blog. I thought I was early, but it seemed that the whole gang was already there. Rebecca was teasing Sidney's puffy red and black hair, which looked like a fiery cotton-candy cloud. Summer was in a hushed huddle with Anya, a burly Romanian aesthetician in a white smock. Anya was instructing Summer in how to give simple facial massages and basic pore-tightening masks.

I sat down at the check-in desk. Behind me on a credenza were the gift bags. I peeked inside one. They were each loaded with an iPod Nano and lots of Paparazzi products. Deirdre had told me that we'd have a full house and to look out for soap-star biggies like Susan Lucci, John Aniston, and especially heartthrob Austin Peck, of *Days of Our Lives* fame. There were several well-dressed people sitting in the waiting area, but no one I recognized and certainly no hunks. Maybe they were still getting their beauty sleep. One well-dressed older woman got up and approached the desk.

"Hello," she said sunnily. "I'm Barbara Wagner. I'm here for my facial."

I opened the appointment book and looked for her name. "I see a Jack Wagner."

"That's my son," she said proudly. "He's on *The Bold and the Beautiful*."

"Is he with you?" I asked, eying the room.

"Oh, he couldn't make it, so he sent me along in his place."

I was a little confused, but I gave her a robe and led her into Summer's treatment room.

The phone rang. It was Mary-Kate and Ashley's personal assistant. They were up for an award for their daytime chat show. They had to cancel their beauty treatments because they were "dehydrated." Uh-huh. "But could you messenger over their gift bags?" asked the snotty assistant.

Then Minnie Driver's henchwoman called. In a plummy British accent, she inquired about the contents of the gift bag. "There's an iPod that's pretty cool," I said.

The woman laughed. "Minnie's got oodles of iPods." The assistant must have lost interest because suddenly all I could hear was a blaring dial tone.

I scanned the guest list. I didn't see Minnie's name on it, and for that matter, was she even on daytime television?

A husky man in a tracksuit approached the desk. "Good morning, my dear. I have a facial appointment scheduled for ten thirty. Name's Vieira," he said.

I looked at the book. "Meredith?"

"Very funny. Leonard. Meredith's my sister-in-law, and she's got another engagement, so she sent me."

"Okay," I said. I thought this was rather strange, but I led him into Anya's treatment room.

A few minutes later, Marion LeVigne rushed in, laden with shopping bags filled with Paparazzi products. "Hi, guys," she said to Sidney, Rebecca, and me. She looked around the room and gasped. "What happened here? Where is the color? I told Deirdre I wanted the room blanketed in hot pink gerbera daisies. I wanted a magnificent carpet of flowers."

I helped Marion unpack the bags as she continued talking. "Marnie, I thought we could make a little sales counter, and you could recommend some of these products as people leave." Suddenly Marion shielded her face with her hands. "Rebecca, watch it with that hair spray, will you?" Sidney smiled into the mirror, seemingly pleased with his lacquered column of hair.

"Mommy, come take a seat," Rebecca said to Marion.

"I think we might want to let our guests take their turns," Marion said, looking around the crowded waiting area. She turned to me and talked in a very low voice. "I don't watch much TV, but who are these people?" she asked.

"I was wondering the same thing. Susan Lucci had a ten fifteen, and it's now ten forty-five," I said to her. "Maybe she's running late."

The youngest "hunk" in the room was a Bob Barker look-alike. Or maybe that *was* Bob Barker. Then Barbara Wagner hobbled out of Summer's treatment room. Her head was cocked to one side, and she was wincing in pain.

"What's wrong?" I asked.

"You've got to tell that girl in there that she's too rough."

"*That girl in there* happens to be my daughter," Marion snapped.

Barbara Wagner looked over my shoulder. "Those aren't goody bags, are they?" she asked hungrily, suddenly cured of her injury.

Marion steered Barbara over to the Paparazzi counter. "Have you tried our bestselling Don't Blink! eye brightener? You won't believe the difference in just three days. Look at my peepers. It's scientifically proven!"

What a liar. Her peepers had been brightened by Botox.

Barbara went back to cradling her neck. "What I really need is a long hot shower and one of those goody bags."

Marion reluctantly handed her one and watched the woman walk out the door. "Greedy little things, those celebs," Marion whispered to me.

Sidney came over to my desk and surveyed the crowded room. "Now that's what I call a turnout," he said proudly.

I was about to tell them who Barbara Wagner really was and that Meredith Vieira's brother-in-law was in Anya's room, but before I could speak, Jacquie Wires stormed through the door. She was wearing a black wool pants suit and her signature Libeskind glasses, and she was carrying two life-sized photo cutouts of

Summer and Rebecca. According to Marion, every celebrity was going to get their Polaroid taken with the "cardboard" twins as part of their exit gift.

Jacquie propped the cutouts against the wall behind the desk and gave Marion an air kiss. "Susan Lucci. Facial. How'd it go?" Jacquie asked, speaking in sharp machine-gun bursts. "Can't wait to call it in to Page Six." It was then that Jacquie saw all the motley pedestrian faces. "What the hell is going on here? Is the W hotel sequestering jurors?" she continued. She came behind the desk and stood over me, frantically scouring the appointment book. Many of the names were scratched out because people had been calling and canceling in droves.

The phone rang. Jacquie snatched it out of my hand. "Paparazzi Tranquility Spa. May I help you?" she said in her fakest, sweetest voice. "Oh, really. Is that so?" When she hung up, her face was beet red. She turned to Sidney and Marion. "That was Connie. Apparently Schotzie Ronson's doing a Roman bath thing at the Mercer. He's giving them Prada wheelie suitcases as big as chariots, stuffed with thousands of dollars in swag."

When Jacquie discovered that everyone in the room was a "regifted" relative of a no-show invitee, she took the bull by the horns. "Okay, folks. Listen up. I've got to see some ID. If you don't have the same last name as the person who RSVP'd, I'm sorry, but you'll have to leave."

Grumbles rippled through the room. An old man stood up. "I'm Kelly Ripa's grandpa, but not on the Ripa side."

"It took me two hours to get here on the Peter Pan

bus," cried a teenage girl who claimed she was Judge Judy's niece.

"Everyone will get their turn," shouted Sidney as he escorted Grandpa Ripa into Rebecca's waiting chair.

After scrutinizing her British passport, Marion begrudgingly led a woman who claimed to be Finola Hughes's sister into Summer's treatment room.

Jacquie leaned toward me. "Quietly take the iPods out of the gift bags," she whispered.

Summer's Birkin bag was tucked under my desk. When her cell rang, she rushed out of the treatment room to take the call. "Cool. We'll be there by five. My driver's got the directions. Never been to Brooklyn before," she said as she clicked her phone shut.

"Where are you going?" Marion asked Summer.

"Didn't Becca tell you? We're going to the Coney Island aquarium before the awards show. We're swimming with dolphins. To decompress."

Suddenly a high-pitched shriek emanated from Summer's room. Anya ran in and came right back out. "Oh, dear Lord. You won't believe it," she cried.

"Holy shit," said Summer. "The peel. Did I leave it on too long?"

"What kind of peel did you leave on too long?" demanded Jacquie.

"Salicylic acid," Summer whimpered.

Marion ran into the room and back out again. "Why did you let Summer give a chemical peel? The woman's been excoriated," she said to Anya.

Anya shook her head frantically. "I tried to stop her. I told her to stick with masks and light massages. I was the one who was supposed to do peels," she said as she angrily went back to the room.

"Who's in Summer's room?" Jacquie asked me.

"Finola Hughes's sister. Finola's on *All My Children*," I said.

"But her sister isn't," scoffed Jacquie.

Sidney and Jacquie quietly peeked into the room. When they came back to my desk, they were ashen-faced.

"Marnie, quick. Call Dr. Lurvey," commanded Sidney. "Get him down here right away."

I called Dr. Lurvey's office and then went into the bathroom to pee. I snuck a peek at my face. The Frownie had worn off, and my angry furrow had risen up again like a throbbing earthworm. When I went back into the swag suite, Summer and Rebecca were in a huddle.

"Becca, let's bail," whispered Summer, grabbing her purse and tiptoeing toward the door.

Rebecca left Kelly Ripa's dozing grandfather in mid-comb-over as she and Summer scurried off to the outer boroughs. Jacquie stood between the cutouts of Rebecca and Summer and turned to the agitated crowd. "We have officially closed the spa. Please exit immediately."

"What about our gift bags?" someone shouted.

"There are no gift bags," Jacquie said emphatically.

There were angry murmurs reverberating throughout the room. "I see them!" someone yelled. "The bags are behind the desk."

I stared nervously at the crowd. They were hungry-eyed frothing zombies, and they were coming straight for us! Someone charged the desk, and they all followed. A melee ensued, and Jacquie rolled up her sleeves and engaged in hand-to-hand combat.

"Marnie, hold them back," shouted Marion as she cowered in a corner next to Sidney.

Jacquie had an old woman in a headlock. I sort of pretended to stop the zombies, but I didn't really care if they took the bags.

"Jacquie, Jacquie, please. It's not worth the lawsuit," Sidney said, pulling the old woman away but not bothering to see if she was okay.

In under ten minutes, the room had been ransacked. All the bags and relatives were gone.

"Marnie, go in there and see if Finola's sister needs anything," Marion said wearily.

I could hear Finola's sister's labored breathing as I slowly walked toward her. I kept my eyes half shut, afraid of what horrors I might find. I stood before her, clenching the table on which she lay, and slowly opened my lids. Her face was red but not nearly as burned as they'd made it out to be.

"Are you okay?" I asked, relieved. "Can I get you some water?"

"Just don't leave me until the doctor comes," she pleaded, grasping my hand.

"I won't. I promise," I said. I reached into my pocket and pulled out a pot of my new homemade eczema cream, which contained black currant oil (an omega-6 fatty acid known for healing) and chamomile (a natural anti-inflammatory agent). If it had cooled and soothed my itchy rash, maybe it would help this poor woman's face. I gently applied some.

"That feels good," she said.

"You'll be just fine," I assured her. And rich from the lawsuit, I thought. I held the poor woman's hand as we waited for Dr. Lurvey.

When Dr. Lurvey arrived in his white knee-length lab coat, he took one look at my furrowed brow and disdainfully shook his head. "Ach. Do I start with you or her?" he said to me in his thick Czechoslovakian accent.

Bottled Nature

Holly and I were putting the finishing touches on the holiday bath and beauty products we were making for the girls in The Hookers. We were using autumnal essences like cider, pomegranate, and maple.

It was times like these that I really enjoyed the creative process, the camaraderie with Holly, how well we worked together. The way the mixing and measuring got me in the zone. It was so satisfying to create something by hand, put it in a jar, and give it to someone to enjoy. It was kinda Zen.

As Holly blended a cranberry-pumpkin enzyme mask, I thought about the cosmetics industry. How ironic it was that most beauty products on the market today (and certainly most everything that LeVigne sold) were filled with chemicals, preservatives, and stabilizers; yet lately the trend was to include ingredients straight out of the forests and health food stores—pistachios, moss, kale, rose hips, alfalfa, green tea extracts. I guess they figured that if they threw in some healthy stuff, no one would notice the bad.

I marveled over how many products had food-based scents and tastes. Since so many women were on diets, and eating was such a twisted source of obsession and denial, the cosmetics companies came up with a clever conceit. They put "edible" ingredients in their formulations and used confectionary adjectives like "whipped," "creamy," "frothy," and "buttery" to describe them. They smelled and tasted so real, they could almost be a lunch alternative. But what a nasty tease because you couldn't actually eat the toxic stuff.

It was said that Hattie LeVigne's original creations contained real butter and raw eggs (an effective way to shore up a puckering décolletage, according to Hattie). Company folklore claimed that one winter when a group of workers were snowed in at the lab, they resorted to eating the eggs that had been slated for one of her lustrously rich creams.

"It's too bad LeVigne's products can't go back to the way they used to be," I said wistfully to Holly. "Without all the chemicals. Out of all their products, there's just this one cream that seems to work. I think it's Hattie's original creation."

"I'm sure there's all kinds of crap in it now. Now that Hattie's no longer around," said Holly.

"I know, right? I wish I knew the original recipe. Someone at work told me that Happy Rockefeller was a devotee of Hattie's early creams, and she kept them in the refrigerator because back in the day, the products didn't contain preservatives to keep them fresh at room temperature. The dampness from the fridge made the labels fall off, and once, when she had a dinner party, the cook inadvertently served the stuff on the guests' salads."

"It was probably delicious," Holly said. "You know that rose petal vinegar astringent I make? Sometimes I mix it with olive oil and use it as a salad dressing."

Hmm. I seemed to recall eating one of her salads that had tasted vaguely like facial toner.

"Christmas is next week. Do you want to invite Paul?" Holly continued.

I knew this invitation was coming. I wanted to have
the meal at my place, in a more controlled environ-
ment, but I knew Holly wanted to do it at her apartment. "That would be great," I said, not wanting to
upset the organic apple cart. "I can't wait for you and
Dwayne to finally meet him."

The next night, I broached the subject with Paul. "What
are you doing for Christmas?" I asked as we cuddled
on the couch.

"Spending it with you, I hope," he said.

"Oh, great," I said excitedly, giving him a hug. "Would
you mind terribly if we had Christmas dinner at Holly
and Dwayne's? I've really been wanting you to meet
them, and I know they want to meet you."

"That would be great," he said.

Trying to ease him into the prickliness of Holly and
Dwayne, I said, "If the food is really bad or if things get
weird, we can leave and eat at the diner around the
corner from my house. My treat."

"Marnie, don't be so negative," said Paul. "I'm sure
it'll be fine."

"You can just give me a signal. When you're ready to
go, blink your eyes really fast, and if I'm ready to go
first, I'll give you this little squeeze," I said, pinching his
love handles. I had been noticing with some amuse-
ment and alarm that he was developing a midsection
from all the cheese he was eating.

"Hey, stop it," said Paul as he wriggled away from me.

"Sorry. It's just that—"

He gave me a "don't even go there" look, crossed his
arms defensively, and began to sulk.

I went into the bedroom and turned on the TV. I
watched Suze Orman for a while. God, her teeth were

white. Maybe I should bleach my teeth. Suze was talking about home financing, making it sound so easy and attainable, while I could barely afford to be a renter. As Brooklyn's borough president so astutely said, "Blessed are those who bought early." It was all too depressing, so I snapped off Suze and went into the bathroom and dabbed some Vienna on my pulse points. It was kind of pungent, but Hattie swore that it saved many a relationship. I put on a pale yellow baby doll negligee and brought a kitchen chair into the living room. I straddled the chair and threw my head back in a *Flashdance* sort of move. My erotic dance number seemed to get Paul's attention.

"That's good, Marn. I like that. You put so much energy into it," he said.

"It's because I just had a colonic. At the Deeva spa. I get forty percent off. I feel light in my loafers," I said as I Jazzercised around the room.

He reached out for me, but I was playing hard to get. I lasciviously licked my lips and slowly took off the negligee. "I was thinking about installing a stripper's pole right there," I said, pointing to a spot in the corner. Since Kendra talked about it in her blog, I thought it might be my ace in the hole, so to speak.

"You don't need to install a pole, Marn. This little performance is working just fine."

"I read in the *Wall Street Journal* that a high-end stripper can pull in three hundred K a year," I said as I shimmied down the wall to the floor with my knees spread wide, and then slowly worked my way back up again, knowing full well that I'd be really sore tomorrow. "Oh, I forgot to mention, the woman who gave me the colonic told me that cheese is a real clogger," I said as I bent over and lifted my butt in the air, giving it a coy little slap.

Paul sat up straight, slightly annoyed. "I eat cheese every day and I feel just fine, thank you very much."

What was wrong with me? Sometimes I opened my big trap and really stupid things flew out. I sauntered over to him and dragged my Vienna-scented wrist under Paul's nose. He took one whiff and turned away in disgust.

"You stink," he said.

"What do you mean?"

"That perfume. It's rancid."

I realized with regret that this was our first official fight. But then I dove right in.

"And sometimes you smell like your cheese," I exclaimed.

"And you always look angry when I see you after work," Paul said, pointing to my corrugated forehead.

How dare he! "I'm not angry. It's my furrow. It's hereditary. I get it from my dad." Now I was really mad. Paul had started this fight, and I was going to finish it. "Well, for your information, you twitch your leg like a teenage boy, and your toenails are as sharp as the devil's claws. They scratch me in the night. And let's not forget this," I said, grabbing at his doughy midsection.

Paul went silent. It looked like he was regrouping. "Your forehead is spotted like a cheetah, and your boobs sag," he revealed.

I felt sick. "My boobs are not saggy," I retorted, covering them with my hands. "And even if they were, so what? That's what happens in the real world where women don't use their student loans to get boob jobs."

"Are you talking about Kendra? How did you know that?"

"Because you told me once. Pillow talk. You said everybody's doing it with their Sallie Maes."

Paul went into the bedroom and slammed the door. I ran into the bathroom and slammed the door. I lowered the toilet lid and sat down to think. Had Paul been mentally comparing me all this time to Kendra and my attractive, put-together coworkers? Is that how he wanted me to look? Paul had sure seemed fond of the attention they gave him at the baby shower. And from what I could tell, Kendra was certainly more like them than I was. Desperate to scrub off the Vienna, I turned the faucet and shoved my wrists under the hot water, but it just lingered, giving me a nasty headache.

I gazed at myself in the mirror. My eyes went directly to my throat. It didn't look as taut as I had remembered. Was I seeing the beginnings of crepey skin? How many more years would it be before I was styling my hair into "neck and cheek bangs" like Goldie Hawn and Candice Bergen? The cruel turtleneck years would be here before I knew it.

Was the bloom already fading off the rose? Was Paul going to find someone prettier, perter, and facially smoother? Maybe I should have pointed out all my flaws in the beginning of our relationship, carefully going over each anomaly with a penlight so he couldn't take credit for "discovering" them and then get some perverse satisfaction when he used them against me.

Maybe it was in everyone's best interest if I switched it up a little, but how could I ever compete with the CAPs without spending a boatload on beauty treatments and expensive clothes? Did Paul want me natu-

ral or not? I was dying to ask him, but I was afraid of
what the answer might be.

When I realized that Paul was not going to break
down the door and scoop me up in his arms, I left the
bathroom and got into bed. Paul scooched over to
spoon me, and I grabbed a mini Dictaphone recorder
and spoke into it. "Call Jane about product comps. In-
teroffice Connie's expense report to Accounting."

Paul ignored that I was working, and grabbed my
breast.

"Not too saggy for you?" I asked pointedly, putting
down the recorder.

"Come on. Stop it," Paul responded, trying to get
frisky.

"Do you think we can fast-track this?" I asked. "I
mean, if we're going to screw around, we need to
power through it and close the deal."

"Corpospeak really turns me on," he said, pulling
away.

"Listen, I'm exhausted and I have to get up early."

We rolled to opposite sides of the bed and fell
asleep in steely silence.

When I got to work the next morning, there was a message from Paul apologizing for his cranky behavior. All
was forgiven. I had been irritable too. I cared so much
about him, and all I needed was to know that he
cared back.

Later in the day, I called my dad. I had made a promise to myself to try to get closer to him, and I needed to
be better with the follow-through.

"Yello," said Trudy, intercepting the call on the first
ring.

"Hi. It's Marnie," I said, closing my eyes, trying my

hardest to be nice. Why did she always have to answer the phone?

"Guess what? I was seduced by an octopus today," she bragged.

"Really? How wonderful," I said with forced enthusiasm.

"Your father and I had a really intense session with our life coach, and afterward we treated ourselves to lunch at the Fish Grill on Beverly. You know, where they have that aquarium? Well, out of nowhere, this octopus swims right up to the glass and locks eyes with me. He did the most wonderfully erotic dance."

"That's great," I said, wondering if it was anything like the dance I did for Paul.

"I hope this happens to you one day," she added.

"Me too," I said through clenched teeth. Anger into love.

"Larry, Marnie's on line two," she screamed. " 'Bye, Marnie."

My dad picked up. "Hi there, kiddo. Trudy tell you about the octopus? Well, your handsome father got some attention too. When I was walking to my car yesterday, guess who was cruising me in an old Jag."

"Who, Dad?"

"None other than Charo, and I'm not kidding you— her head was practically hanging out the window."

"Maybe she wanted your parking spot," I said right as Murfy and Juniper marched by my desk, carrying two large white shopping bags stuffed with food. "Gotta go, Dad. Love you. Talk to you later."

"Lunch is here," barked Murfy. I ran into the kitchen and was jabbed in the ribs by a cluster of women who circled the food like a pack of salivating wildebeests. When I saw what they were pulling out of the bags, I decided that it was a complete abuse of the word "lunch."

"Who has the side of kale and vegetable moo shu, steamed not fried, no rice, no pancakes, no hoisin sauce?" yelled Murfy.

"Ooh, the chuckwagon's here," said a Skeletor who grabbed her spartan lunch and threw some cash on the counter.

More like the upchuck wagon, I thought.

"Who's got the half an avocado?" asked Juniper. Winsome grabbed it.

Then Murfy pulled something heavy from the bottom of the bag. "Fried chicken?" she said in a deeply troubled voice.

I snatched it from her and started to make a run for it.

Juniper grabbed me. "Fried? Isn't that rather low-income, Marnie? I mean, don't you want to fit into all the cutest clothes?"

"It's not fried, it's broasted," I said defensively.

"You're killing yourself, Marnie," yelled Murfy as I ran down the hall. "It's a slow, horrible death."

Juniper ran after me. "Did you know that every calorie you eat takes a second off your life?" she intoned. "There's a monkey on a calorie-restricted diet and he's, like, a hundred fourteen years old."

"Leave me alone," I said emphatically as I ran outside and ate my lunch on a bench in Central Park. My broasted chicken certainly tasted less yummy after that verbal beating. I could never tell whether they were trying to help me or just ridicule me. I ate half of it and threw out the rest, looking around for a healthy-food cart. I loosened the notch on my belt. I had been gaining weight, and the eczema was flaring up again. I needed to start taking better care of myself, but I was not about to become a member of the flush-'n'-brush crowd. The LeVignettes could run on fumes, but I couldn't function like that.

As I turned my head skyward to bask in the weak December sunlight, I thought about LeVigne's well-trafficked internal staircase, which spanned their five floors. It was lined with fabulous photographs and gorgeous paintings from their corporate art collection. Every day as I trucked down the stairwell on errands, I would see the Fendi foot soldiers who bounded energetically up the steps as though they were pumping a carpeted StairMaster. When they passed me, their tight butts seemed to mock me, and they would let out a derisive sniff and avert their gazes when they saw what I was wearing.

Even though I couldn't relate to most of my high-maintenance fembot coworkers, to my horror I found myself desiring to look like them, to exude a certain je ne sais quoi like them. It was as if their constant harping had begun to have an effect on me.

When I got back to my desk, I found an e-mail message from Dr. Lurvey's office in my inbox. Because I was working at LeVigne, I was eligible for a "onetime only" Botox injection for the very low price of fifty dollars. Yowza! That was insanely cheap—the shots normally cost four hundred dollars.

What the hell. You only lived once. I called Dr. Lurvey's office and made an appointment for the following week. The price could not be beat, and I wanted to look great for New Year's Eve. But was Botox the gateway drug to full-on plastic surgery? I pushed that thought out of my mind, because I needed to focus on getting Paul safely through Holly's Christmas dinner. Which reminded me. I needed to ask Paul to bring some goodies from Dean & DeLuca. They might be the only edibles there.

<u>CHILLY SCENES OF WINTER</u>

It was Christmas day, and it had snowed all morning. The city was a winter wonderland, and Brooklyn had never looked more pristine.

At six P.M., Paul and I walked over to Holly's place and buzzed. And buzzed and buzzed. In an attempt to get their attention, we made snowballs and pelted them up at the windows.

"Dwayne! Holly! Let us in," I screamed. Finally the buzzer sounded and we walked up the four flights of stairs. Dwayne's voice traveled toward us down the hallway. "Die, loser, die," he yelled.

"Are you sure you want to go in there?" asked Paul, stopping dead in his tracks.

"I warned you," I whispered pointedly.

Holly came to the door to greet us. "Sorry, I didn't hear you. Dwayne's playing video games and I was whirring the blender," she said as she ushered us in. Their dogs leapt up and kissed our faces before Holly even could. She was wearing a 1950s vintage apron and checkered oven mitts. "Excellent to finally meet you, Paul," she said, shaking his hand with the mitts still on and then giving him a big Holly bear hug. She pushed a humping dog off Paul. "Don't mind the kids—they can get a bit rambunctious. Let's go into the kitchen."

We followed her down a long hallway, passing room

after messy room until we got to the chaotic kitchen. The sink was filled with dishes. Every cabinet door was flung open. There were splatter marks on the walls, and it looked as if she had been cooking for days. I suspiciously eyed the room, wondering if they had Dumpster-dived for any of the food.

Paul handed Holly two big white Dean & DeLuca shopping bags. As we unpacked the food, Paul carefully pulled out two baseball-sized white globes. "I picked these up at JFK this morning. The fashion designer Valentino specially ordered this mozzarella for his Christmas dinner in New York. It comes from Naples. I ordered two for us."

"You're being so delicate with them. It's like you're handling nitroglycerin," I teased.

"They're really fragile, and you're not going to believe how delicious."

"What can I do to help?" I asked Holly.

"I'm preheating the stove for the Tofurky. You can get it out of the freezer."

"How long have you been a vegetarian, Holly?" asked Paul.

"Since I was nine, when I cradled the Thanksgiving turkey and wouldn't let my grandma cook it. I'll be right back. Gotta take a cheese whiz," Holly said, winking at Paul as she left the room.

"That's a good one," said Paul, smiling. "Gotta remember that."

Dwayne suddenly appeared in the doorway, suspiciously eyeing the goodies that we brought.

"Oh, hi Dwayne. I'd like you to meet Paul," I said.

Dwayne wouldn't budge from his spot, so Paul chivalrously walked over and shook Dwayne's hand. Dwayne was wearing a T-shirt with a picture of Sasquatch on it.

"What's the latest on Bigfoot?" asked Paul, trying to make friendly small talk, but Dwayne didn't respond.

"Is that cheese I see?" inquired Dwayne.

"Yeah, but I brought some vegan stuff too," Paul said. "Do you like tempeh?"

"But of course. It's a staple," he replied coolly. "Since I don't eat anything with a face or a father."

Thanks, Dwayne, I thought. That image would surely haunt me through dinner. When I was finished putting tomato slices and basil around the mozzarella, Dwayne took it from me. "I'll put it in the living room, Marnie."

"Thanks, Dwayne," I said, surprised by his helpfulness. I took a deep breath and put the Tofurky into a roasting pan. We'd had one at Thanksgiving, and that was already one too many. Paul pitched in and made the salad dressing.

Suddenly there was a commotion coming from the living room. The dogs were growling and Holly was screaming. "Dwayne, what the hell is wrong with you?" she yelled.

Paul and I ran in as Holly was pulling a hunk of white cheese out of a growling dog's mouth. The platter had been eviscerated, and Paul looked like he was going to cry.

"I'm really sorry about that," Holly said to us, shooting Dwayne a nasty look and heading back into the kitchen.

As was my fear, things were getting off to a bad start. Dwayne flopped down on the sofa, lifted up a tall glass bong, and took a long, gurgly hit. Paul sat down next to him.

"Dude, you need to relax. This is some choice foliage. You in?" Dwayne asked Paul, his face enveloped in a cloud of smoke.

"I'm cool for now. Got any napkins?" Paul asked,

bending down in an attempt to clean up the food dregs that were all over the floor.

"We try not to use paper products in this house," said Dwayne. "It's cloth towels all the way, buddy."

"They do, however, use toilet paper," I said to Paul, giggling nervously. "See that bookshelf over there? Dwayne's a carpenter. He made it himself. From reclaimed wood that he found at salvage yards."

"Sweet," said Paul.

The bookshelf was hypothetically very nice, but it was only half built, covered in an inch of dust, and listing sideways like the tower of Pisa.

"It's a work in progress," bragged Dwayne.

Holly came back in with a bottle of wine. "Maybe if he cut back on the peace pipe, his carpentry business might flourish."

Dwayne ignored Holly, took another toke, and got up. "Wanna take a tour of the pad, dude?" Dwayne asked Paul. The THC must have kicked in because Dwayne was finally warming up.

I shot Paul a pleading look. Dwayne was probably going to show Paul the dreaded cat room—an extra bedroom with litter boxes strewn around like Monopoly property. It stunk to high heaven, and I was convinced that some of the cats were feral, because once, when I'd house-sat, one of them attacked me and scratched up my face.

"Sure, I'll take a tour," Paul said, getting up and following Dwayne down the hall. "I bet you've got a low-flow toilet."

While they were gone, Holly showed me the hemp teddy Dwayne had given her for Christmas.

"Ooh. I love the pink pleather trim. Very sexy," I said as I helped Holly set the dinner table.

"Remind me to give you some great chem-free water-based lube I've been working on," Holly whispered. "Sometimes I feel like I'm saving the planet . . ."

"One orgasm at a time," I finished. We high-fived each other.

In keeping with an old English tradition, there were colorful paper favors at each place setting. At dinner, we pulled the little strings on them and they turned into delicate tissue-thin hats. We wore them while we ate, resembling a band of medieval knaves and damsels.

"Listen, dude. Question for you," said Dwayne to Paul as he tucked into the ersatz turkey. "If you were on a dark country road and there was an animal and a person crossing, and you only had a split second to swerve out of the way, would you save the person or the animal?"

"Well, I'd like to think I would try to save both."

"Not me, dude. I'd only save the animal," said Dwayne. "In my experience, people generally suck."

"That's cool," Paul said with his characteristic diplomacy.

After dinner, we retired to the living room. Dwayne put on a Neil Young album (this was a vinyl-only household) and we all sat on the battered L-shaped sectional. Paul and I lounged on the short part, Holly and Dwayne on the long. When Dwayne lit up the bong again, to my surprise Paul reached over and took a hit. We all did, actually.

The pot loosened Paul up and made him very lovey-dovey. Paul and I made out, and so did Holly and Dwayne. It reminded me of high school. Heavy petting in flagrante, privacy not yet a cherished requirement. Paul and I came up for air and did another bong hit.

"Hey, did you ever think about how racehorses don't

need to eat animal protein? They get their speed from hay and carrots," Dwayne remarked.

"Wow. That's pretty trippy," I said, leaning my head on Paul's shoulder and seeing two miniature sumo wrestlers dancing on his face. Great. I was hallucinating.

Holly turned on the Travel Channel and we watched a show about haunted houses.

"Sometimes I think my mom haunts this apartment," said Dwayne.

"If she did, you'd be cleaning more," retorted Holly. "Have you guys ever seen a ghost?"

"Sometimes I think I see my brother, Calvin. Definitely in dreams, but sometimes I really feel his presence around me," Paul said.

Was Paul tripping too? "What? Who's Calvin?" I asked.

"I'm sorry, Marn. I never told you," Paul said.

"Told me what?"

"I had an older brother."

Holly quickly turned the channel to the yule log station.

I had goose bumps. I moved closer to Paul. "Really? What happened to him?"

Paul's eyes watered. "He died when I was twelve."

"You don't have to talk about it if you don't want to," said Holly.

"No, it's okay. It makes me feel better when I do."

I stroked Paul's hand, and he continued.

"Calvin was two years older than me. It was a really snowy day in Madison, and we went down to the lake to play ice hockey. It was freezing cold but the sun came out, and I remember how it warmed my face. We met up with some kids from the neighborhood and knocked around some pucks. The sun was going down and we were getting ready to leave when suddenly I heard a scream. I turned around. I could see Calvin way out in the distance. He was down in a hole in the ice, his arms flailing wildly in the air. As we all skated toward him, he kept going under and coming back up again."

"Oh, my God," I said, putting my arms around Paul.

Paul closed his eyes for a minute and then continued. "He was a great swimmer, but the water was freezing and he panicked. We tried to save him, but by the time we reached him, he was gone." Paul turned away. Tears streamed down his checks. "Drowned at age fourteen."

"Paul, I'm so sorry," said Holly.

"Me too, man," said Dwayne. "What a bummer."

"I didn't get to him fast enough. I could have saved him."

"There was nothing you could have done," I pleaded.

"It's weird. Sudden death is something you never fully get over," Paul said.

"Whoa," said Dwayne. "That's heavy."

I started to cry. So did Holly and Dwayne. Dwayne lit a sage stick to cleanse the weighty vibe, and Holly led us in a Buddhist chant for the dead. Then Paul and I broke off into a long, emotional hug. I could feel the most intense energy flow between us.

"Okay, everybody," said Dwayne, sitting down at his Korg keyboard.

"No Jerry Garcia, please," said Holly pointedly.

Dwayne played the theme song to *Shaft* and sang along in a surprisingly deep voice. Paul and I nodded our heads to the rhythm.

Holly put her hands over her ears. "Enough. Your voice sucks."

Dwayne gave Holly a dirty look and awkwardly transitioned into an instrumental TV Land lineup of all the shows he was missing tonight. After a while, we were all back to kibitzing, and then the four of us dozed off on the sofa. At some point, I gently woke Paul up.

"Ready to go?" I whispered.

"If you are."

On our way out, I left gifts for Holly and Dwayne and wrote "Merry Xmas" on the dusty credenza.

When we got back to my place, I made us some hot tea. The radio softly played an old Sinatra Christmas song. Paul came up behind me and nuzzled his face into the back of my neck. I felt so close to him. I reached under the coffee table and pulled out a wrapped box.

"This is for you," I said.

"Thanks," Paul answered excitedly as he unwrapped the package. It was a gel seat that I had purchased for his new speed bike. He stood up, leaned over imaginary handles, and stuck the seat under his butt. "You must have read my mind. I was just about to buy one."

Paul went over to his knapsack and fished something out. Its flat, square shape betrayed the secret of what lay beneath the cute reindeer wrapping. But it wasn't just a store bought CD: he had made me a mix.

"I hope you like it," he said, blushing.

"Thanks so much," I said, giving him a hug. "Merry Christmas."

I got up and opened my desk drawer. "I hope this isn't overkill, but I have something else for you," I said, handing him a Yao Ming bobble-head doll.

"How did you know he's my favorite player?" asked Paul, examining the card.

"You mentioned it at dinner one night."

"This is so awesome. I wonder what kind of cheese Yao Ming likes."

Paul put me on his knee and bounced me up and down like a randy ol' Saint Nick. "Should I put on the CD?" I asked, opening the jewel case.

"Uh. Maybe you should listen to it another time." He seemed embarrassed, so I sat down next to him, pulled off his socks, and massaged his feet. I was so eager to hear what songs he had chosen for me, but I understood how he was feeling. Making a mix for someone you really cared about could be incredibly personal and soul-baring. It was usually best that the recipient listened to it alone the first time.

"How often do you go back to see your family?" Paul asked.

"For years I couldn't go back a lot because I was always working on a movie set, and now with this temp job, if I don't work, I don't get paid, and I really need the cash. But I've been working on my relationship with my dad, and you can't just do it over the phone."

"You should go visit him. And your mom."

"I know. I will soon."

Paul was sensitive and caring. I realized now how much I wanted to build a life with a stable, kind man. I wanted to dig in deep and put down roots.

<u>Spinning Summer</u>

Though the workweek between Christmas and New Year's was historically quiet, the LeVigne family had chosen to stay in town and drive everyone berserk. Bright and early Monday morning, Sidney and Marion called a meeting with an image consulting firm. Connie asked me to sit in and take minutes because Juniper and Murfy had laser resurfacing appointments with Dr. Lurvey, then a lunch-hour French lesson in the conference room with Monsieur Pierre. Surprisingly, Tinsley hadn't clued Connie in on my steno skills.

In the new year, Sidney wanted Summer and Rebecca to have more than a titular role in the company, because at present, they would torpidly sit in their offices for an hour or so and then go out shopping for the rest of the day.

After a recent sex scandal that played all over the tabloids, the family had sent Summer away on a cool-hunting expedition, a trend-trekking trip where she was instructed to follow in her grandmother's footsteps and forage for groovy objects that could be translated into color statements and packaging designs.

LeVigne was always looking for new angles to make the products fresh and innovative. Years ago, Hattie's collection of Fabergé eggs had been used to create a container for the solid-fragrance version of Vienna, and the opulent whorled patterns on an old tortoise-shell hairbrush were copied for Siesta's packaging.

While we waited for Summer and Rebecca to arrive, Marion got up and smelled the air. "What's that delicious scent?" she asked. She marched around bulldog-like, sniffing everyone in the room. I was about to make a run for it. I was not in the mood to get snoggled again.

"It's you, Marnie, isn't it?" she said in a tone that was at once praising and accusatory. "What are you wearing? It's unfamiliar to me." She came over and smelled the crook of my arm.

Wow. I couldn't believe it. The "nose" was complimenting my homegrown fragrance made from nutmeg, cinnamon, and figs. I couldn't wait to tell Holly.

Before I could answer, Rebecca minced in and stole my thunder. But that was okay because what would I have told Marion anyway? That I whipped something up from some stuff I grabbed out of my kitchen cabinet?

I smiled at Rebecca, and she weakly smiled back. Her ironed-out hair was teased up into a big, bubbly sixties hostess helmet, and she wore a sedate, genteel outfit—black silk blouse, tight taupe boot-cut slacks, and a million golden bangles. She sat down and stared dead-eyed and unsmiling at her well-shod feet, probably contemplating a chauffeured trip around the corner to buy more Choos.

Summer barreled in fifteen minutes later with her teacup Chihuahua, Gringo. Today she was looking very "street," with ghetto-fabulous blond cornrows, chunky gold chains, a sparkly bra top, and acid-washed hip-huggers so low, you could see the wormy veins crisscrossing her rock-hard belly like a freeway interchange. I was transfixed by her creamy white skin.

It must have taken a lot of work for Summer to evolve into this pseudo-unconventional manqué. The attention to detail was impeccable, from the airbrushed nail bunnies to the gold tooth on her bicuspid, far enough away from the front teeth not to be gauche, but visible enough to know it was there.

"My God, Summer," said Sidney. "How you stomp around in those clodhoppers. Footsteps like that are fine for soldiers, but ladies should walk softly. If your grandmother saw you, she'd fire you on the spot."

"Then put me out of my misery," shouted Summer.

Marion got up and waltzed across the room. Her

spindly legs resembled two atrophied Tofu Pups. "Watch closely, ladies. Pull up your instep. Tense the leg. Heel to toe. Heel to toe," she said, wrinkling her nose at Summer's six-inch dominatrix pumps. Then Marion shot a look at my shoes du jour, a pair of emerald green Charleston pumps that Jane Fonda might have worn in *They Shoot Horses, Don't They?* I quickly shoved my feet under the table. What could I ever wear that would please them?

To drown out Marion's lesson in ladyhood, Summer turned up the volume on her iPod and break-danced to a raunchy 50 Cent song. "Do you mind?" she said to me, gesturing to my water glass. Before I could answer, Gringo the dog was on the table, thirstily lapping out of it.

"Don't worry. G's got clean germs." And to prove it, she and Gringo tongue-kissed.

"Enough of the shenanigans," snapped Sidney. "Let's see what you gathered on your transcontinental trip, Summer."

The image consultants, Gainsley and Khaki, laid out a bunch of mass market items on the conference table. A Care Bear cell phone cover from Sweden. Acrylic glitter leg warmers from Rio. A box of "Nippless" brand nipple shields from Tokyo. A plastic laundry bag from the Hotel Costes in Paris and a carton of Gauloises.

"Is this all?" asked an exasperated Marion.

Sidney fingered the nipple covers. "You could have taken a forty-dollar round-trip cab ride to the Village to find this junk," he said.

"Dude, that Gauloises blue is totally awesome for an eye shadow color! And the script on that laundry bag is a must-do packaging font."

In the 1970s, Gerald Ford had offered Hattie the ambassadorship to Monaco. She turned it down to focus on her company's growth. While Summer was globetrotting around the world, she acted as the ambassador to lipstick, handing out over one thousand tubes of gloss. Lipstick was the universal denominator, breaking all language and cultural barriers. Cheer up, Youzhi Xian of Hunan province. You may work in the fields and not have enough to eat, but your lips sure look luscious.

The image gurus gave Sidney and Marion some mumbo jumbo about how prescient Summer was, but it was obvious that, left to her own devices, she couldn't coax cool out of a cucumber.

Marion spoke. "Maybe Summer could be a style correspondent for E! A name behind the brand. A face behind the products."

"With the look Summer's working, I can probably get her on the WB," Gainsley said wanly.

"You guys are so uncool. I want my own reality show, or I'm going across the street to work with Schotzie," she whined. "I'm really just a Schotzie girl at heart."

"Don't even joke about a thing like that," hissed Sidney.

Exasperated, Marion excused herself and left for the ladies' room.

Gainsley closed his eyes in deep thought and then popped them open. "Okay, I'm seeing it now. Summer reporting from the front row at the Paris collections. Summer as Karl Lagerfeld's most inspiring muse. Summer launching her very own signature fragrance."

They could call her perfume "Ennui"—for the girl who has absolutely nothing to do, I thought.

"Are you through yet?" asked Summer. " 'Cuz I've got

to go down to Dr. Lurvey and have a tattoo lasered off my ass."

"One more thing before you go," Gainsley said to her. "We need to give you a disease."

Marion had just come back from the bathroom.

"I already have chlamydia," Summer said, scratching her crotch. "Isn't that enough?"

Marion threw up her hands. "No. He means something for charity. Like MS or ALS or ADHD."

Which she obviously had. "Maybe she should go with cancer," I said facetiously.

"Yes. That's fantastic, Marnie," said Sidney. "Something totally incurable. This way she doesn't ever have to switch out causes."

"Great idea," Connie muttered. *This is all so twisted,* I thought.

When Summer left for her appointment, the group started in on poor Rebecca. As they fired off questions, she bit her nails and twirled a brittle tendril of fried hair around her finger. They asked what she wanted to do with her life. "Nothing," she sighed. They asked her about her passions. She said there was only one. "Balenciaga." Then, after a long silence, Rebecca continued. "I want to work with Grandma."

Everyone gasped. "You know Gammy's infirm, Rebecca," said Marion.

My ears perked up. So Hattie was alive.

"Didn't Dr. Lurvey say there's a new drug for her that's about to be approved by the FDA?" asked Rebecca.

"This is not *Cocoon,* young lady," Sidney snapped.

What did this all mean? I was dying to get the 411 on Hattie.

As more ridiculous ideas were bandied about, Rebecca spoke again. "Is it curling?" she asked as she touched her ever-expanding hair. It had been raining all day, and her hair was bushing out like Weird Al Yankovic's.

Marion reluctantly nodded her head in the affirmative.

Rebecca stood up and pointed at me. "That is what I want," she cried, hungrily reaching out toward me.

All eyes went in my direction. I sank low in my seat. Should I be flattered that she had a crush on me?

"You want her?" asked a horrified Marion.

"No! Her hair," answered Rebecca.

Oh, well. She wasn't my type anyway.

"I've battled the frizzies my whole life, Mommy," continued Rebecca. "If I could do just one thing, it would be to start a hair care line, create some products that really work."

Little did she know, I had flat-ironed my hair that morning.

Connie was jazzed. "A hair care line. That's a fantastic idea, Rebecca. It would really open our product base to brand segmentation."

Rebecca was the luckiest little girl in the world. Because of her birthright, she had the infrastructure to start her own product line by just uttering the desire.

Gainsley and Khaki were off to the side in a heated huddle. Finally Khaki spoke. "To create the proper buzz, we could generate some great behind-the-scenes stories. For example, we could do a reality show where Rebecca goes to beauty school at Vidal Sassoon, or she could apprentice with a celebrity hairstylist like Sally Hershberger."

"I don't want to work with that skanky-ass Skeletor. Even I'm not dumb enough to pay eight hundred dollars for a haircut," bristled Rebecca.

"Okay. No problem," Connie said, feigning patience. "If you could pick anything in the world, what would you like to do?"

"I told you already, bitch. Listen when I speak," said Rebecca, showing a new and cheeky side to her personality.

"Darling, language," said Marion.

"I just want to create some decent products to prevent the frizzies," Rebecca whined.

"I'm seeing it now," Gainsley effervesced. "We could do a photo shoot at the Bronx Zoo with Rebecca and a bunch of alpha monkeys. It seems they get better hair care than the lazier monkeys because they get their minions to groom them, like, ten times a day."

Gainsley must have pulled this one out of his ass, I thought.

Marion was livid. "An heiress to a billion-dollar company has no place in a gorilla cage," she said to him sternly. Marion touched her helmet hair. "Personally, I'd love to see some antiaging hair care products. A shampoo and conditioner with built-in collagen and a rejuvenating antioxidant shield."

With budding confidence, Rebecca looked at me again, critically. "Now that I really look at you, I see your hair is limp. You'd look a lot better with wild, unscripted beach hair. A piece-y, wrecked kind of look that could be achieved with a spray of kelp extracts and salt water."

"Kind of like a wave crashed over me?" I said.

Rebecca clapped her hands together. "Exactly!"

Why had I spent even a moment feeling sorry for her?

"And you two," Rebecca sighed, staring at Marion and Sidney. "Where do I begin?"

PONCE DE LEVIGNE AND
THE FOUNTAIN OF YOUTH

Paul's eclectic mix CD was playing softly on my computer at work. He had recorded some Barry White and Roxy Music, ending with Donna Summer's very subtle—not!—eight-minute orgasm song "Love to Love You Baby."

It was hard to get anything done because I was thinking about him so much. I was starting to fall in love with him, and I hoped that his musical choices were an indication of how he felt about me. On Tuesday, Paul called to firm up our Friday New Year's Eve plans. The sound of his deep voice heated up my crotch faster than a Hot Pocket in a microwave. We were going to celebrate at the Cowgirl Hall of Fame in the West Village. His friend Darcy, a Patsy Cline impersonator, was performing with her band. Darcy worked in pastries (oh, excuse me, I mean *patisserie*) at Dean & DeLuca.

And this little cherry tart had to pretty herself up. This afternoon was my Botox appointment! It didn't hurt. Just a little prick. I was told most emphatically by Dr. Lurvey not to bend over for at least four hours, or I might develop a horrendous Cyclops bump at the site of injection. "Ach, perfection!" he exclaimed. "Your skin speaks to me in Czechoslovakian!"

I kept sneaking peeks at myself in the mirror. I was on a major high mentally and physically. I looked totally refreshed, as if I had just come out of a cave after a long winter's hibernation. After work, I went to Victoria's Secret in an effort to downsize my vast collection of Hanes Her Way granny panties. With my chin lifted high as a reminder not to bend my head, it was hard to find things in my purse, but I confided in the salesgirl and she gladly helped me extract my Visa from my wallet.

At work the next day, I wore one of my new thongs under a pair of slacks that had always given me terrible panty line. For the first few hours, I felt fantastic and confident. In my bronze Capezio shoes that tango dancers wear, I stood taller and shook my booty to and fro. Later, though, as the thong gravitated closer and closer to the center of the earth, my mood shifted. I became anxious and irritable. I felt like I was being cut in half by one of those mandolin cheese wires I'd seen at Paul's place. No wonder everyone at LeVigne was so bitchy!

Juniper stopped at my desk and stared at my face. "You look fantastic!" she said.

I was absolutely stunned to hear her praise. The CAPs were so weird about compliments. Seldom were they administered, even to each other. What was so wrong with telling someone they looked good?

"Could you be a love and go to the cashier on the thirty-first floor and get me some petty cash?" Juniper asked sweetly, handing me a reimbursement form.

"Sure," I said.

"And, Marnie, maybe after New Year's, we all could go out for cocktails," she said.

"That would be great," I said excitedly. I had finally cracked the code. It was just that simple. A little fifty-dollar shot of botulinum toxin allowed me into their exclusive club.

But before I went to the cashier, there was something I urgently needed to do. I grabbed a pair of scissors and slid them into my pants pocket. In the stairwell, under the watchful eye of a creepy Matthew Barney photograph, I dug the thong out of my crack, snipped it in half, and yanked it out of my pants. I stood there for a moment, holding the mangled panties in my hand. An icy chill ran down my spine. What was I doing? Transforming myself into a card-carrying CAP wasn't as easy as I thought. Last night I'd noticed that my toe skin was bagging.

On the subway ride home that night, I looked around at the weary faces of my fellow passengers. The man across the aisle had dry and flaky skin. The woman next to him had ruddy rosacea patches on her cheeks and dark circles under her eyes. It occurred to me that I could really do wonders for their troubled skin. A lightbulb went off. If Hattie LeVigne could start her own company from spit and vinegar, why couldn't Holly and I create a line of skin care products? We had both been making our own beauty concoctions, and I had been absorbing relevant information at LeVigne like a sea sponge.

I thought back on some of the twentieth-century cosmetic giants, like Elizabeth Arden, Charles Revson of Revlon fame, Estée Lauder, Max Factor, and Helena Rubinstein—how they had gotten their starts. They were all first-generation entrepreneurs who began with a drive and passion that took them to heights they never dreamed possible. There had always been tremendous competition in the beauty industry. In the old days, if you weren't a bona fide European countess, a Transylvanian ladies' man, or a Waspy horse trainer, then you changed your name and pretended you were by creating an elaborate story about your bloodline and lineage. Glamorous living and lavish spending surely helped. A brash ruthlessness and some peculiar peccadilloes were also encouraged.

Today it seemed the opposite was true. At least on the surface. Contemporary cosmetics moguls seemed to downplay their roots. The British fragrance guru Jo Malone boasted that her childhood was downright Dickensian, and Roxanne Quimby, the founder of Burt's Bees, weaved a chilly tale of New England frugality. Even Schotzie Ronson claimed that he'd spent his formative years at the Omaha Home for Boys.

One way or another, you needed a personal narrative to connect to your customer. If Holly and I were going to do this right, we needed a schtick, some kind of angle to differentiate ourselves. What would our narrative be? Holly was certainly more colorful than I, and she'd had a dramatic childhood. She was raised by a peripatetic alcoholic mother, and, when Holly was thirteen, she disappeared and lived for a month under a freeway with a bunch of runaways. At age thirteen, I was playing softball and singing in the chorus.

What could I bring to the down-and-out table? Well, as a kid, I had chronic ear infections; my creepy high school math tutor ate my dog's Liv-A-Littles and forced me to eat them too; and my schnoz was certainly Dickensian before it was remanufactured. More recently, my cable was disconnected, and lately I was surviving on protein bars and the leftover freeze-dried ice cream sandwiches from the NASA launch. This didn't seem dramatic enough, but I guess it would have to do.

Could a beauty business be a way out of my adult-onset destitution? A golden ticket for my never having to temp again and Holly's not getting carpal tunnel from all the massages she'd have to give in her lifetime? But where were we going to get the start-up money? Did I know any venture capitalists? No. Wealthy relatives? No. Sugar daddies? Most definitely not. My own daddy? Doubtful. Bank loans? Hell no. My credit was on the fritz. But I wasn't going to lose sleep over this.

I'd have to run this exciting business idea by Holly.

Holly had finally gotten rid of her smelly, furry L-shaped sectional sofa, and invited me over to see the new one.

"Let's show Marnie the new couch, shall we, Dwayne?" Holly said pointedly as she ushered me through the door.

I couldn't believe it. The "Woody Harrelson Collection" hemp sofa that Holly and Dwayne had scrimped and saved for was completely in shreds. There were tear marks all over it, and Dwayne was trying to push the stuffing back into the armrests. "Don't worry. We can sew it back together," he said optimistically.

"I never wanted cats," Holly cried, collapsing in a heap.

I was stunned by her antifeline admission. "You didn't just say that, Miss I-love-all-creatures-great-and-small?" I said.

"I confess. I'm a dog person at heart."

"Cats will be cats," said Dwayne, protectively scooping up a rotund orange tabby in his arms. "They are living, breathing organisms."

"With very sharp claws," sighed Holly.

"They're predators," said Dwayne. "You can't take away their natural-born right to scratch, especially when we keep them captive in our totally oppressive human domains." Dwayne pointed at the shredded couch. "It's nature. Don't you see? It's the animal kingdom playing itself out right here in our living room."

"Go tell it to Animal Planet," Holly said defeatedly.

"Don't step on my buzz, Holly," he said, suddenly mesmerized by my face.

Shit. Dwayne's eyes were trained on my Botoxed forehead, and he wouldn't look away. I got up and walked over to the window, staring out into the blackness so he couldn't see my face.

Dwayne walked right over and stared at me. "Am I tripping, or is your forehead, like, totally frozen?" he asked.

I pulled my plaid tam down tightly over my head. I was going to kill him. Holly slowly came at me like a zombie from *Night of the Living Dead*. She yanked the hat off and poked at my forehead.

"Oh my goddess. You got Botoxed! LeVigne has put a spell on you!" she screamed.

I stood there paralyzed. "It's not what you think."

Holly continued to drag me over the coals. "What's next? A face-lift? Why don't you just embalm your whole body while you're at it," she said angrily.

"You need to lighten up," I yelled. "I was feeling really ugly."

"Don't you think I'd like to take a shortcut to looking younger and prettier? Don't you think I'd like to stop using menstrual sponges and be able to buy all those cute sweatshopped clothes at the mall? Well, I can't. I know too much."

"But it's hard not to be seduced," I said. "I admit it. I'm weaker than you."

"I'm outtie," said Dwayne, looking around uneasily. "Gonna get another grow light and some wood at Home Depot. See ya, Marnie." And with that, he left.

I had to do something to deflect Holly's anger. And it had to be good. I knew it was a low blow, but I had no choice. "I know something about Dwayne that you might be very interested in," I teased.

"What?" Holly demanded. "And don't tell me he's

screwing someone because I won't believe you. He can barely drag his stoner ass away from the tube."

I laughed. "No, it's not that. Although it's something you might find even more disturbing."

"Tell me," cried Holly. "What is it?"

"Apparently he told Paul on Christmas that once when he was out, he ate a hot dog. And I don't mean a tofu pup."

"You must be joking," Holly said with a laugh.

"You're not mad?" I asked.

"Well, don't tell anyone, but the other day I relapsed too. I ate a few marshmallows. Those tiny ones in the Swiss Miss packet. They're made from gelatin, which is made from horse hooves, but, boy, did they taste good."

So Holly wasn't so perfect after all. "Everybody slips," I said. "You can't beat yourself up."

"I shouldn't be telling you this, because I'm so annoyed with you, but Dwayne told me that on Christmas Paul told him how much he likes you," Holly confided.

"Really? That makes me so happy," I said excitedly. A flattering remark like that could fuel me for weeks. Now I felt really bad about ratting on Dwayne. "Hey, I almost forgot to tell you. Marion LeVigne complimented me on that nutmeg-fig fragrance I made."

"I know I should be glad for you, but praise coming from her? That sounds a bit suspect."

"Oh, lighten up. She's got the best nose in the business."

"The nose knows," Holly said in a haughty voice. "Hey, if you can't beat 'em, join 'em. Maybe you should sell LeVigne your secret recipe and make a ton of money."

"Maybe we should start a business and make our own goddamn money."

"Ya think?" said Holly.

"Yes, I think. I mean we don't have any formal bath-and-beauty experience, but we've been doing this for a while now and our stuff is really good."

"What should we call ourselves?"

"So you're into it?" I asked.

"Totally."

"The name. Hmm. Let's see. We're doing fresh, all-natural products that are earth-conscious and environmentally friendly," I said.

"How about Beautyfarm?"

"I like the sound of that."

"I think we're on to something," she said.

"We can be the new movers and shakers of the organic beauty world," I said.

"Movers? I think not," said Holly, touching my smoothed-out forehead. We hugged each other and made some hot chocolate with the tiny contraband marshmallows.

Later I called my dad to tell him about our Beauty-farm business idea. I wanted to include him in this somehow—to show him that I could turn my life around and maybe to get some entrepreneurial advice from him. When I told him, he wasn't nearly as negative as I thought he would be, but in his inimitable heavy-handed fashion, he was unintentionally setting me up for disaster. He was already talking about sales figures and department store counter space.

"Dad. Stop! We haven't even perfected our first product yet."

"It's never too early to celebrate, kiddo," he said.

"Dad, let's not break open the Moët until we make our first sale, okay?"

"It'll have to be wine because the bubbles upset Trudy's stomach."

ST. PAULIE GIRL

By the time Paul and I got to the Cowgirl Hall of Fame on New Year's, it was nearly midnight. We were so busy canoodling at his apartment, we almost didn't make it out of the house.

"I need a drink pronto. What would you like?" Paul asked as we stumbled into the restaurant.

"Frozen margarita, por favor," I shouted cheerfully over the din. "And can you get us some chips? The salsa's really good here."

"Coming right up, señorita," he shouted. "And by the way," he said before he squeezed toward the crowded bar, "you look really beautiful tonight."

I smiled a big smile, confident that Paul hadn't clued in to my immobilized brow. I nabbed a table and looked around at the raucous New Year's revelers, some single, some coupled off. I was very lucky to have met Paul. He was so fine. All the men in the room paled in comparison. Paul came back with the drinks and chips. As I took my first salty sip, the room began to disappear. We were mooning over each other as the noisy revelers receded into the background and became near-invisible.

I was about to tell Paul about Beautyfarm when a buxom redhead appeared at our table. I was at eye level with her pierced navel.

"Hey ya, Paulie. How the hell aaaaare you?"

"Oh, hi Kendra," said Paul a little too brightly.

So this was the infamous Kendra. She and I could not have been dressed more differently. I was decked out in a demure bottle-green velvet skirt and a butter-

cup yellow cashmere beaded sweater. It might have
been all of seven degrees outside, yet that hadn't
stopped Kendra from wearing a short leather skirt,
black fishnets, and a cropped sleeveless turtleneck
that showed off her large breasts and scrawny body. I
referred to this reedy type as "tits on a stick." She
looked like a Tenth Avenue hooker.

Flirty Kendra put her hand on Paul's shoulder.
"Aren't you just so excited to see Darcy perform?
Funny, until yesterday, I thought she only decorated
cakes," she said pityingly.

And you only gutted fish, I thought. Paul tried to introduce us, but Kendra kept on talking.

"Guess who I saw yesterday. Remember Snaggle-
tooth? She's finally engaged to Dumbo. And Cruella De
Vil, that chick who was dating Kombat Kenny? She
landed a part in *Les Mis*. I'm so insanely jealous."

"But I thought you told me that Granny Clampett got
it," he said with more concern than seemed warranted.

Paul and Kendra were talking and talking as if I
weren't there, batting around silly nicknames like long-
term couples do. Barf. Paul had never mentioned any
of these people to me.

"Here I am just yammering away," Kendra said, finally laying her hazel dagger eyes on me. "Paul, who's
this? Please introduce."

"I'm sorry. Kendra, this is Marnie," Paul said. "Marnie,
Kendra. Do you want to sit down?" he said to her.

No way. He did not just invite her to join us.

Before she could answer, someone caught Kendra's
eye. "Tiffy's here," she said as a statuesque blonde sauntered toward us. Kendra intently studied my face. "Nice
to meet you, Marsha," she said as she grabbed Tiffy's
hand and they disappeared into the crowd.

I couldn't believe she was calling me the wrong name. What a bitch.

"That was really weird," I said to Paul as Darcy started up a rousing rendition of "Crazy."

"Kendra's an actress. She can get a little dramatic," yelled Paul over the music.

"I thought you said she was in acting school," I yelled back.

"She's been in a couple of things."

Like dinner theater in Stamford, I thought. Paul's back was to them, but I could see Kendra and Tiffy whispering about us. Why was there always a jealous ex lurking in the wings, ready for an encore performance? But why should I care? I was here with Paul. She wasn't. The countdown had begun. Ten! Nine! Eight! This incredibly trying year was going to be over in exactly six seconds. The new year would prove to be fantastic, with all kinds of exciting possibilities. I pushed the chip basket away from me. No more hydrogenated oil after the clock struck twelve.

Happy New Year! Paul leaned across the table for a long, sensual kiss, when suddenly something moist hit my nose. I thought it was Paul's tongue, but then it landed in my lap. I looked down. It was a large martini olive with a red pimento sticking out of it like a pert little nipple. I looked up. Kendra was standing over me, with Tiffy as her backup.

"I'm so sorry. Did that hit you?" Kendra said.

Tiffy was very drunk and clutched on to whatever she could of Kendra's skimpy sweater.

I was incensed. I looked at Paul for help. He looked at me searchingly. He was acting really weird. Why wasn't he backing me up? I couldn't take this sitting down. So I stood up. As tall as I was, Kendra was even taller.

"I don't appreciate having things thrown in my face," I said, puffing out my chest.

"It was an accident," said Kendra.

"Really?" I chortled.

"She said it was an accident," retorted Tiffy.

"I wasn't talking to you," I said, wagging my finger in her face like a hoochie mama.

Paul finally stood up. "Hey, now! There's no reason to fight. It's New Year's. Everybody get happy," he said, waving his finger in the air like a 1940s band leader.

"Let's hit the road, Kendra," slurred Tiffy.

"Good luck, Marsha. Hope you like cheese," Kendra taunted as they both wobbled to the door.

Once they were gone, Paul and I sat back down. The silence between us was killer. Luckily the band started up again and we pretended that nothing had happened. When the band took a break, Paul pulled his chair around to my side of the table and tried to make nice, but I pulled away. "There's like a thousand bars downtown. Why did she pick this one?" I asked.

"I guess she wanted to see Darcy."

"More like she wanted to see you."

"Or maybe you," Paul confessed. "I told her about you."

"I wish you hadn't. She was so rude to me. Calling me the wrong name and acting out like that. It's so immature."

As we walked back to Paul's apartment, I had a sick feeling in my stomach. I was glad that he had told her about us, but he wasn't very apologetic about her atrocious behavior. Should I be worried that he had gone out with such a psycho?

Paul grabbed my hand. He stopped and turned to me. "I . . . uh . . . I . . ." he sputtered. "I wanted to tell you . . ."

Say it, you fool. Say that you love me.

"I . . . uh . . . really love . . . your eyes. You look beautiful in the moonlight."

"Thanks," I said, trying to keep the agony of defeat under wraps. While I was happy that he found my peepers attractive and hadn't pinned my restful, beatific glow on the Botox, I didn't want to have a State of the Union address about the state of our union. It was painfully clear that we were in the throes of an I Love You showdown. Was he hesitating because he wasn't over Kendra? *Please, Paul. Don't make me say it first.*

YOU'RE KIDDING ME?

We were a week into the new year, and Connie was furiously multitasking. She stood behind my chair, and as I typed, she composed apology letters to angry consumers while she simultaneously clipped her fingernails. The sharp little boomerangs shot every which way as Connie's hot breath hit the back of my neck.

"Dear Ms. Montgomery," Connie bellowed, clearing her throat. "Let me begin by saying how sorry we are about your dreadful accident. Never before has a bottle of our nail polish exploded. We will pay all damages, and hope that your extensive facial scars heal with Godspeed. . . ." And then we were on to the next perfunctory letter. "Dear Mrs. Dunne: Sorry the salt scrub lacerated your feet and ruined your Christmas. . . ."

Suddenly the hallway filled up with wild little girls, all wearing minikin Juicy Couture velour jogging suits. It was LeVigne's First annual "Bring Your Daughters to Work" day.

Kris (on crutches) hobbled over and pushed their daughters, Brita and Seiko, toward Connie. "Good luck, Con. They're all yours," she said with sadistic relish.

Kris Gotbaum, Connie's hummingbird of a partner, often stopped by the office. Just last week, she'd dropped off a tux that Connie needed for a gala. I often chatted with her on the phone when she called Connie to complain about the kids. From what Murfy told me, Kris had given up a career as a nurse and a heterosexual to become Connie's life partner.

"I'm through for the day," Kris continued. Apparently, Brita and Seiko (all of eight years old) had tried to take Connie's Jaguar station wagon out for a joyride, but an eagle-eyed parking attendant stopped them in the nick of time.

"Kris, what happened to your leg?" I asked.

"I messed up my knee doing the nut allergy triathlon. Marnie, I don't remember getting your pledge money for the fibromyalgia walkathon."

"Uh, I'll write you out a check now." Damn her. Why was she shaking down a destitute secretary?

The minute Kris left, Brita and Seiko somersaulted down the long hallway. There were events scheduled every ten minutes. There was an art class where the girls used crayons to color in the faces of the three Paparazzi ad campaign models for Idée Fixe, their long-lasting lipstick.

Then I was asked to give each girl a skin analysis and a goody bag filled with products culled from the four LeVigne brands. Upon opening her gift bag, one tiny tot wailed, "This is the gift-with-purchase junk my mommy gets at Bendel. I want eight-ounce jars or larger."

By three P.M., the girls were totally out of control. Some of them were getting high from huffing Liquid

Paper, while others were using tubes of lipstick to graffiti the walls.

A jar of Deeva camphor hand unguent was turned into finger paint; the girls' tracksuits covered in minty green handprints. Red string bracelets that they received in Kabbalah class had been gnawed off their wrists, and littered the floor. Then the Oops! Patrol, two men outfitted in crisp white jumpsuits, arrived. They got down on all fours to clean up little puddles of kiddie vomit that was the upshot of the spicy Indian buffet catered by Dawat restaurant.

Tinsley had been sequestered in her office all day. It was obvious that she wanted nothing to do with this miniature mayhem. Brita brazenly opened Tinsley's door and walked right in. I knew I should have stopped her, but I didn't; instead I watched from the hallway.

"Hey, let me see your bling," Brita squeaked as she grabbed Tinsley's watch. "Yo! That Roley ain't real."

I couldn't believe that little Brita was astute enough to spot a Canal Street counterfeit and, more unbelievably, that Tinsley was actually wearing one!

The two of them were making me sick, so I walked into the pantry when suddenly bloodcurdling screams emanated from Tinsley's office. When I got back there, Tinsley was crying in a corner. I had never seen her so weak. Brita was obliviously wrestling with another girl in the hallway.

"Brita bit Tinsley," whispered Juniper, her eyes lighting up like a Christmas tree.

"And it looks like Tinsley bit Brita," I said, pointing to Brita's reddened arm.

"Yowza," replied Juniper.

"I have to make a poopie, Jupi," whined Brita. "Someone take me. My arm hurts."

Juniper looked at me. "You take her and put some Neosporin on it. I'll watch the other kids."

I gave Juniper a withering glare and took Brita into the bathroom.

SPIDERMAN

It was the middle of January, and I was in the midst of a call with a producer from HGTV (or, as Jarret called it, Horrible Gay TV) about a segment featuring Summer and Rebecca's side-by-side Park Avenue panic rooms, when Tinsley came marching over to my desk.

"There's a Tootie on hold for you," Tinsley said brusquely. "She's called three times. I don't know how in the world she got my extension."

I picked up the line with the blinking red light. "Hello?"

"Marnie, it's Trudy. Boy, are you hard to reach."

Strange. Though she was in the habit of intercepting calls, she was not in the habit of calling me directly. "Is everything okay?" I asked.

"It's your father. He's very ill. He's in the hospital with an infection."

"Oh my God. What kind of infection?"

"He begged me not to tell you, but I just had to. I'm so upset," she said, sobbing. "He's got a one hundred and one-degree fever. They think it's a staph infection in his leg. The doctor said something about amputation."

"What?" I yelped. "He's so healthy. How could this be?"

"A few weeks ago, he was cleaning out the storage unit and he got bitten by a brown recluse spider."

"Why do they call it a recluse spider if it comes out to bite people?"

"Now is not the time to figure that out, Marnie. All I know is, it started with an angry-looking ring on his leg, like a bull's-eye. He said it didn't hurt. Then it blistered and scabbed over. Then white sores began to spread down his thigh. Your dad thought it would just go away. But it didn't. On Saturday night, we did a twelve-hour tangothon for rheumatoid arthritis. I thought it would be too taxing for him, all that dancing, but you know your father. He's the Energizer bunny. And then yesterday we rode our tandem bike on a four-hour jaunt to Malibu. When we got home last night, he had a fever and was extremely weak," she explained.

"This is so horrible. I'm in total shock," I said.

"He's on a boatload of antibiotics. The kind they give leprosy patients. They don't want the infection spreading to his heart. I love your dad so much. I haven't left his side since it happened. I just spoke with my assistant at Century 21. The brokers are holding a prayer vigil, and I've been praying to Jesus nonstop."

"Jesus? I thought you were Jewish," I said.

"Never mind about that."

"Can I talk to my dad?"

"He's sleeping. Everything was going so well. We wanted to plan a trip to Hawaii with you kids."

Why was she talking in the past tense?

"Life is short, Marnie," Trudy continued. "Your father told me about your business idea. Get going with that. Your dad and I are really proud of you. I'll keep you posted." And then she hung up.

I started to cry. I knew Tinsley was staring at me, but I didn't care. What if my dad's immune system couldn't fight the infection? What if it spread to his heart? I had always thought that Trudy was out for her own self-interest, but she seemed genuinely upset about my dad's illness. I had grossly underestimated her love for my father. My negative attitude had never let me see that they were soul mates and life partners, and as annoying as she was, she loved him.

The thought of losing him terrified me. He and I were getting closer. I couldn't imagine my life without him. He might never walk me down the aisle. He might never meet his future grandchildren. The new year was getting off to a terrible start, and the rest of the day only got worse.

Tinsley ushered me into her office and sat me down in the guest chair. "The foreign beauty editors are arriving next week for the Parachute launch, and FiFi in Siesta is in dire need of help."

"But I'm working for Connie."

"You're working for whomever I say you're working for. *Comprenez-vous?*" Tinsley said.

My eyes welled up with tears. "I just got a call from my stepmother. My dad's really . . ."

Tinsley raised her hand. "Stop. Please do not bring your sordid personal problems to this job. Gather your things and go to FiFi's office immediately. But before you go . . ." Tinsley got up from her chair, pulled a huge doorstop of a book from the shelf behind her desk, and dumped it in my lap. "Take this with you."

It was a copy of *The Secret Language of Birthdays*, a tome that gives in-depth two-page horoscopes for each day of the year. Holly owned a well-worn copy, and whenever a new person came into her life, she pored over it, analyzing the natal day to determine whether she could be friends with a person born on, say, August twentieth. Why the hell was Tinsley giving me this book?

When I arrived in FiFi's office, she was on the phone. She had a floor-to-ceiling window with a jaw-dropping view facing north. Her Aeron chair was positioned directly in line with the uptown traffic, so it looked like the cars and cabs were zooming between her Blahnik-clad feet. I stood in the doorway while she spoke in her warm Aussie accent.

"Hello, my dahling Chantal," FiFi said into the receiver as she complicitly rolled her eyes at me. "Can't wait to see you in America next week. I'm so very glad you like the hotel we've chosen. It's very hip-hip, very intimate-intimate. It's where all the action is. Yes, I know you expected a big suite, but this hotel is what we call twee hip. Yes, and the little miracle jars are already waiting nestled in the gift bags. Yes, yes. We're delighted to fuel your addiction. Stay beautiful, dahling. Be beautiful. Ta," she said in her singsong accent as she put the phone back in its cradle. She looked me squarely in the eye. "I can't stand that French cow. My God, how those editors complain about the accommodations. It's as if there's AstroTurf around the pool and twenty-nine-cent shower curtains."

A young woman clutching a pad and pen sidled up next to me. She seemed slightly out of her league in a too-short mini and too-high heels. She turned and gave me a big tooth-whitened grin. "Hey, Marn. Wus up, girl? It's great that you're working for us."

Was I supposed to know her?

"Marnie, I hope you had a restful holiday because we've got gobs and gobs of work for you to do. Do you two birds know each other? Marnie, this is my assistant, Tawny Brinkmore."

"Feef, chill it on the intros. Marn and I met at Diana's baby shower."

I gasped. I hadn't even recognized her. Evidently, over the ensuing months, this seemingly guileless baton-twirling coed had transformed herself into a card-carrying mini-CAP. As they say in the beauty world, "Polish or Perish." I noticed that her formerly normal lips resembled two overinflated inner tubes.

FiFi got up and put on a pair of white bamboo sunglasses. "Well, then, Tawny-Tawn, while I'm out, why don't you explain to Mamacita Marnita exactly what to do."

FiFi was unveiling Parachute to the foreign markets and was flying in twenty top international magazine beauty editors. They would be wined and dined (but since none of them really ate, they would mostly be wined). Lavish gifts would be showered upon them, including complimentary jumbo-sized pots of the very expensive Parachute, and when they jetted back with their bags of swag, they were expected to write glowing articles about how the products worked like manna from heaven, instantly making them twenty years younger.

"Oh, I see you have the book," said Tawny. I was cradling the heavy *The Secret Language of Birthdays* in my aching arms. "Why don't you get comfortable? You'll be inputting that into the computer," she said sadistically.

"What? You can't possibly mean the whole book," I asked incredulously.

"The whole book. Is there a problem?" she asked as her stilettos crunched over an anthill of paper clips that she dropped and neglected to pick up.

I quickly did some mental arithmetic. 366 birthdays multiplied by two pages per horoscope was 732 pages. To type. "Not a problem," I said angrily, heaving the book onto my new desk.

The idea for this project was that each foreign editor would receive a personalized horoscope reading for their natal day. But it wasn't enough to just photocopy the pages. FiFi wanted the oversized book to be typed into the computer, and then the horoscopes would be printed out on expensive paper and presented in some sort of gifty way.

All day long I typed pages from this evil, misguided tome until my gnarled fingers experienced early rigor mortis. By four, I had only gotten through the first eight days in January. I calculated that, at the rate I was going, it would take me over three months to complete the project.

When I get home, I called my dad. He sounded weak and groggy, but a little better. I told him how much I loved him. Then I called Holly, and we talked about Kendra. "I just don't get it," I said. "Kendra's so tacky and obnoxious. What did Paul possibly see in her?"

"I hate to break it to you, Marn, but he might just be into big fake boobies."

"Then what's he doing with me?"

"He's with you because you're amazing," Holly said. "But it's always like that. The former girlfriend is nothing like you. She's usually some kind of flashy fuck puppet, and if you draw a line from her to you, you wonder what the connection point is."

"I get a really weird feeling about her."

"You should. From what you've been saying, she sounds really shady."

"She's like a hacking cough that won't go away."

The next morning, sad and bleary-eyed from worrying about my dad and obsessing about Kendra, I began typing in my own "secret language of birthdays," a language of petulant missives that would surely send the French beauty editors into tailspins. Someone born on April twenty-eighth got the reworked sentence: *You will always be fat, even though you smoke three packs of Gauloises a day.* July twenty-fifth got: *Your bland leek soup is killing you. To fill up, try McDonald's pommes frites instead.* And October fourteenth received: *You are skinny, boring, and will probably never marry.*

Tawny kept coming by to tell me that I wasn't working fast enough. *Merde, merde, merde,* I typed over and over again like Jack Nicholson in *The Shining.* Tawny was such a bossy-boots, acting like she owned the joint. I was at my breaking point with my dad's illness, Kendra's antics, and this crap at work. I got up and stormed into the bathroom to call Cross Temps. I asked Sheila whether she had found me a replacement and still the answer was—surprise—no. We had a blowout fight, where I threatened to walk. What did I have to lose? My skills were a lot better now, and if I wanted, I could probably find another job that was less oppressive than this one. Sheila surprisingly offered to increase my salary to an enticing $24.75 per hour. Much better! I accepted her raise with the hope that at some point I would abandon office work entirely to launch Beautyfarm with Holly. Right now, though, I would begrudgingly collect the coins I was offered.

When I returned to my desk, Tawny was at hers, beginning the meticulous process of reapplying her makeup. "I used to be a temp once," she said condescendingly. "During college. Can you believe it? Me? A temp? I have a lunch appointment. I'll be back in an hour." Yank, yank on the ass-riding mini. Sniff, sniff of the nose. She was probably meeting her dealer. Maybe

her nose would crack off from all the coke she was
snorting.

After she left, FiFi came out of her office and spoke
to me. "Oh, Tawny-Tawn. Ain't she a peach? You can
take the girl out of Florida, but . . . that one doesn't stop
moving, does she? What the hell is she on, anyway?"

I shrugged. I didn't give a rat's ass if she was speed-
balling in the bathroom. What I really cared about was
that my father got better.

Ex Marks The Spot

A few weeks later, my dad was on the road to a full recovery, and I could finally start to relax. It turned out
that it was a regular brown spider and not a recluse. After what he had been through, he was a little disappointed that it wasn't a little more venomous—it was
as if he wanted to be a CDC statistic.

Paul and I were just coming back to his place after a
wonderful dinner. I had told him about Beautyfarm,
and he loved the idea. Paul opened the door, letting
me in ahead of him. I flipped on the living room light.
I screamed. Kendra screamed. She dropped the cat
carrier and I dropped my leftovers.

"What are you doing here?" Paul yelled.

"No reason to raise your voice, sweetie," said
Kendra, suddenly composed. "It's my weekend to take
Jeffrey, remember?" She kneeled down, opened the
cage door, and dramatically stroked the mewing cat.

"Oh, hello, Marsha," Kendra said to me.

"That's not my name!" I shouted as I stormed past

them to seek refuge in the bathroom. I had a splitting headache, and opened the medicine chest. There was a homeopathic tincture called Emotional Relief. Interesting. And a bottle of Natural Break-Up Spray with Ester-C. Very interesting. Were these Paul's break-free-of-Kendra elixirs, which weren't exactly working? When I came back out, Kendra and Jeffrey were gone.

Paul followed me into the bedroom. "I'm really sorry," he said. "I forgot she was coming by."

"How wonderful. The four of us are a happy little family now," I said bitingly.

"You're overreacting."

"Well, it's a little disconcerting, finding her here like that. She scared the shit out of me." I walked over to the bed. "I don't believe this," I yelped.

"What's the matter?"

"Kendra was lying on your bed!"

"Get out," he said, rushing over in disbelief.

"Look," I said, pointing to the shape of a human form. "There's a deep indentation in the down comforter."

"Jeffrey must have been sleeping there," Paul offered.

"If Jeffrey were five foot ten." I leaned in closer and saw a long red hair on one of the pillows, looped over like an AIDS ribbon. "What's this, then?" I asked, picking it up and waving it in front of him.

"I have no idea," Paul said, backing away.

"Unless an Irish setter was here, it's Kendra's. You still have a thing for each other, don't you?"

"That's ridiculous."

"You don't think it's weird and inappropriate that she lets herself in, especially now that I'm over here all the time? It's disrespectful. Maybe you should arrange a mutually agreed-upon time for her to pick up Jeffrey."

"I tried."

"And?"

"She shows up whenever she wants."

"That is so not cool. Don't you have any say regarding what goes on in your own home? She must still have feelings for you, and she uses Jeffrey as a way to hold on," I said.

"I can't control how she feels."

"No, but you can control other things. For starters, you can get her key back. She almost gave me a heart attack. You've got to tell her that all pickups and drop-offs must be done on the street," I instructed.

"You're being harsh," Paul said, grabbing me from behind.

"Why are you defending her? I don't think I'm being harsh. I think I'm being fair."

I fell on the bed and pushed my face into the pillow, the one without the hair on it, to hide the fact that I was crying. This was bringing up all kinds of emotional issues. I wanted to believe him about Kendra, but my track record with noncommittal guys made me wonder if I could ever have a mature adult relationship with an honest, up-front man.

Paul turned me over to kiss me, but then he stopped. He stared at me. "There's something different. About your face."

I turned away. "No, there isn't."

He ran his finger over my forehead. "What did you do to yourself?"

My face turned bright red. "I had a little procedure. Nothing big. Botox. It was done by a doctor at work."

"Marnie, you're insane."

"But I look better, don't I? You even said so."

"Botox? At your age? Marnie, what's up with that?

You've been living on astronaut food and Diet Coke. All you want to watch are stupid awards shows. It's like you're turning into a different girl."

"No, I'm not. I'm still the same old me," I said, desperately trying to rev up my dormant furrow.

"I don't know why you're doing this to yourself. You look like a painted lady with all that makeup you wear now. I like you natural."

"If I'm going to be running a business, I need to represent. And furthermore, you're the one who complained about my furrow, don't you remember?"

"We were in a fight. I didn't mean it."

"Yes, you did."

We got into bed, but I couldn't sleep. My mind was racing. First Kendra appeared unannounced in his apartment, and now Paul was mad at me for trying to look more attractive. He needed to get used to the new me. If his career was going places, so would mine.

In the morning, Paul seemed better but a little distant. I still felt weird about Kendra, but I wanted to move on from our fight. Paul had some work to do from home, so I left him there and planned to be gone all day, running errands and buying provisions to make a delicious dinner.

When I got back, Paul was out on the street, wearing a down coat and gardening gloves. It was late afternoon, and I was loaded down with shopping bags. He was holding a spade in one hand and a jar of some kind of oil in the other.

"What's up, Martha Stewart?" I said with a laugh, wondering what he could possibly be doing.

Paul pointed to a fenced-off patch of dirt in front of

his building. "I was slathering pumpkin-seed oil on my formaggio di fossa. I do it every few months."

I was dumbfounded. "There's cheese down there?" I asked, pointing to the freshly tilled soil.

"Yeah. It's buried. It's best to age it for a year. I've got about four more months to go."

"Wow," was the only thing I could say. As we walked upstairs to Paul's apartment, it struck me how similar we were in our passions. Against all odds, Paul was lovingly nursing a hunk of cheese in a dark urban space, while I was patiently nurturing my Courage cologne in a darkened closet.

When we got inside, I immediately noticed how tidy his apartment looked. He must have been working on it for hours. "Your place looks fantastic," I said.

"Thanks," said Paul as he led me into the bedroom. "I'm trying to get rid of some junk. One of my New Year's resolutions."

We tumbled onto the bed. "I'm impressed that you can keep your promises. I make them, and break them five seconds later," I said, kissing his neck, so happy that we had made up.

Paul unhooked my bra. "There's something in that Febreze that brings out the tiger in me."

"Ooh. I like the sound of that," I purred.

"Let me be your slave," he said, ready to ravish me in any and all ways of my choosing. I moved on top of Paul, letting my "trick vagina" work its magic. After several hours of acrobatic antics, I got up to use the bathroom. On the way back, I noticed a photo that was propped up on Paul's dresser. "What's this?" I asked, snapping on the bedside lamp to get a better look. It was a framed shot of Paul and Kendra with Jeffrey sandwiched in between.

"Oh, that?" Paul said nonchalantly, rubbing his eyes

and lifting himself up on one elbow. "It's Jeffrey. And me. And Kendra."

"I realize that, but what's Kendra doing on your bureau?"

"I don't know. I found it this afternoon. It was buried underneath a pile of stuff," he said cavalierly.

"You don't even have a clue, do you? Don't you think having a picture displayed like that is just going to encourage her?" I asked.

"What does that mean?" he said defensively. "You're acting like she's some sort of force that I can't control."

"Isn't she? I feel like there's unfinished business between you two."

"You're being ridiculous," he said.

His impassive attitude about Kendra fueled me, and all of my insecurities and frustrations resurfaced.

"I know about *your* past, but you never ask me about mine. Don't you want to know about any of my exes?" I asked indignantly.

"No," he said. "Why would I?"

Guys could be so infuriatingly black and white. "Well, at least I don't have pictures of them strewn all over my apartment," I said, my eyes welling up with tears.

"Marnie, you're exaggerating. It's one picture."

"It's more than that. First it's the olive, then she comes over here whenever she feels like it and naps on your bed, the bed where we just made love. She calls me the wrong name and you don't even correct her, and now the picture," I said. "I feel disrespected by both of you."

Paul went into the kitchen while I sat brooding on the edge of the bed. I didn't know how to explain to him how really vulnerable I was feeling. Something wasn't right. He didn't say he was getting rid of the picture and he didn't say anything about changing the cat arrangements and getting her key back. I was starting to wonder if our commitment level was matching up. We clicked in so many ways, but where were we going as a couple?

Suddenly this weekend felt like a movie running in reverse. The love stuff that had made my boy-cut panties deliciously wet was being sucked back up inside my body. I threw on my clothes, grabbed my overnight bag, and walked backwards to the door.

"Hey, where are you going?" Paul asked.

Maybe I had just imagined the I Love You showdown three weeks ago. Maybe that wasn't what he had been thinking and stuttering. One thing I knew was that I was petrified of getting hurt by him. He still had a connection to Kendra, and if he was in love with her, so be it, but I wasn't going to stick around to get my heart broken. There was nothing wrong with being friends with an ex, but only after the wounds had healed. It was obvious that there were still strings attached, and I didn't want to be a bystander as those strings were either snipped apart or stitched back together. I had to make a decision. I had to take care of myself.

I took a deep breath and plunged into the abyss. "When you take Kendra off your dresser, give me a call, okay?" I yelled as I bolted down the stairs.

Paul stood on the landing and shouted down at me. "Okay, fine, then . . ." he stammered. "Then you . . . can call me . . . when your forehead wakes up."

About-Face

I was so glad the weekend was over and I could go back to work. I had taken too many Ambiens and eaten too many Marie Callender's complete frozen dinners in front of the tube. Work was a distraction from my angst about Paul. How could Paul have treated me so callously and let me walk out the door? Had he really been that repulsed by my using Botox? And furthermore, what kind of weirdo keeps a wad of cheese buried in his yard? Not normal! I should have been working on some Beautyfarm formulations, but I was too depressed. I called Holly but she was chained to a fence in Vermont on some protest.

In the morning, Tawny was acting really strange. I thought maybe she had discovered my nasty additions to the birthday book. She was jumping from one task to another with no real attention span. After lunch, she told me that she had been rolling on X all weekend, and she was finally coming down.

"Marnie, I've had a life-altering vision. I'm editing down my entire wardrobe. Going forward, I'm only wearing clothes that are black, silver, and red," she said, grinding her teeth and nervously tapping her black, silver, and red strappy shoes on the carpet. Dressed in her new color scheme, she resembled a can of Diet Coke.

On Wednesday, the foreign beauty editors finally arrived, and FiFi and Tawny were out for the rest of the day, taking them on a tour of the plant so they could observe how Parachute was made. I kept checking my voice mail, hoping Paul would call and apologize. But nothing. I knew we'd had a bad fight, but I didn't think we had broken up. I realized the phone worked both ways, but his disappearing act reminded me so much of Nick's behavior that my reaction was to stick my head in the sand. Was Paul turning out to be like him— headstrong and detached?

Later in the day, when I got really bored, I read the paper insert in the Parachute box. "Using this product night and day for a lifetime can dramatically change your skin. And when used in combination with the supporting ancillary products, you won't believe the difference!"

I got out a calculator and did a mathematical computation. Let's say a woman started using Parachute at age forty when, in a panic, she began noticing fine lines around her eyes and the turkey-gobbler skin at her neck. A jar costs six hundred dollars and, as FiFi said, it would take three months of daily religious creaming to use it all up. If this woman kept at it, by the time she was eighty she would have spent, not including tax, just under $100,000. And that didn't include the strongly suggested ancillary products, which, if used as directed, would probably set you back another fifty grand. They wanted you to drop a hundred grand on this tenuous crap. And throngs of people used it! Maybe the secret was in the pricing. If it was promising a fantasy, then it needed to have an obscenely high price tag.

I was dying to know the Parachute formula. I had taken a jar home and was using it every night. It did seem to have some rejuvenating properties. My neck skin seemed firmer. If the active ingredient was natural, maybe Holly and I could modify the formula and use it in our own products.

My cell phone rang. It was Evan Milstein, the doctor. I had totally forgotten about him.

"Hey, sexy," he whispered. I could hear an ambulance blaring in the background. Was he calling from the ER? "You were so hot the night we met."

It was amazing how guys had a sixth sense for when a chastity belt had been unlocked.

"And how many months ago was that?" I asked. I guess he didn't get out much.

"Sorry. I've been crazy busy. Do you want to get together?" he whispered lasciviously.

"Where? Like in the hospital broom closet?" I whispered back.

"I'm going to be off for the next twelve hours. A little nookie might be good for your eczema," he said.

"I cleared that up myself, thank you. I'd be up for dinner, maybe, but that's about it."

There was silence on his end. "Uh, actually, I'm kind of stuffed. They gave us Carnegie Deli sandwiches for discharging patients early."

"That's a good incentive program."

"So? You wanna hook up?"

"Where's your bedside manner? I'm at work and I've got to go," I said, clicking him off. I was so depressed about Paul that sex, even hot-doctor sex, was the last thing on my mind.

Right then, FiFi and Tawny swept back in. "It was a raving, tearing success, Mamacita Marnita!" FiFi bellowed. "The tiny hotel rooms worked miracles. We held back on them, and the editors said it was the first time they felt that they weren't being bribed. And Tawny got to witness all kinds of things. Didn't you, my pet?"

"It was sort of like when I worked at Bennigan's and they sprayed grill marks on the burgers," Tawny said.

"Really?" I asked, wanting to know more.

"Enough," FiFi snapped, "because if you tell her, I'll have to drown you in a vat of Parachute. And one more thing, Mamacita Marnita . . ." she said with a raised eyebrow.

My heart dropped.

"Those birthday messages you typed."

"FiFi, I'm really sorry about that."

"There were a couple of French girls who were sent back early in tears."

"Oh no. They were crying?" I asked, feeling really bad.

"Oui," FiFi firmly replied.

My hands were visibly shaking.

"Marnita, get a hold of yourself."

"That was very wrong of me to do," I said.

"Yes, it was. But I loved it," FiFi exclaimed. "Those demanding frogs drove me batty. They deserved it."

After FiFi left for a meeting, I tried to coax the Parachute secret out of Tawny by promising to give her some Systems products I had stockpiled at home. But the little tramp upped the ante by insisting that I run to Scoop to pick up an outfit she had on hold. "But it's pouring," I said, looking out the window at the lashing rain. She wouldn't take no for an answer.

When I got back, I was utterly soaked. "Spill it, Tawny," I said as I handed her the plastic garment bag, which was a lot drier than I was.

"Sweetie, to be perfectly frank, I don't think I can."

I was shivering. My face pulsed with rage. She hadn't even acknowledged that I was standing in a pool of rainwater. "Sweetie, I think you can. I was up late watching TV. I mean, what would FiFi think if she saw your antics in that *Girls Gone Wild* video?" I asked, pantomiming a Shakira butt shake.

Tawny went white. "You saw that? Promise you won't tell her."

I crossed my arms over my clammy chest and waited. After a long staredown, Tawny led me into FiFi's office and closed the door. She told me that there was no such person as Olaf Olafson. He had been fabricated by a branding company. She said that the so-called Greenlandic sea anemones were actually hijiki seaweed you could buy at Whole Foods. She said that the cream was made in fast-track stainless-steel vats, not in the touted slow-fermenting wooden barrels, and without the aid of the tranquil Philip Glass score. (The lab workers preferred the thumping disco beat of Power 106.)

Tawny also told me that FiFi had sent her down to the East Village to wrangle up a bunch of Ukrainian waitresses. They outfitted them in white smocks and hairnets and had them sit at a worktable, hand-decanting jars of Parachute while the foreign editors watched. "Normally it's all packed by machines," whispered Tawny. "And System's Especially Affable Lotion for Terribly Cranky Skin is made from the same exact formulation as Parachute. They just dye one light blue and the other petal pink. The six-hundred-dollar jar is costing them less than a dollar to produce."

"No wonder everyone is getting injectables," I said.

I had been duped like the rest of Parachute's fervent fans, believing that the cream contained a magical ingredient that could rid me of my facial road map, the unfolding story of my bittersweet life.

SIGGY MO HO

It was ten days now, and I still hadn't heard from Paul. I removed his text messages from my phone, tossed his toothbrush in the trash, and threw out his moldy cheese from my fridge. I went on Kendra's blog and saw that she had written giddily about having spent time with one of her exes. I was convinced that Paul was seeing her again, and I needed to know whether this was true. In an effort to find out, I took my lead from the master infiltrator Schotzie Ronson, and cooked up a scheme to spy on Paul.

It was Saturday, and Holly and I were standing on the northwest corner of Broadway and Prince, catty-corner from Dean & DeLuca. We were both wearing dark sunglasses and baseball caps. Holly's said "Brooklyn," which I found irritatingly redundant, considering that she lived there. At 3:05, the action began. We watched Paul and Kendra exit the store in animated conversation.

"I knew it," I said angrily. "I just knew it!"

"That's your competition? That tits-on-a-stick?" Holly scoffed, loudly enough for passersby to try and get a glimpse of who might fit such a crude description.

"Can you believe it? That bastard got back together with her."

We watched as Paul and Kendra leisurely strolled south on Broadway. When they crossed over, we hopscotched to the other side and watched from a doorway as they stopped in front of the makeup emporium Sephora.

Kendra pointed inside and Paul nodded. She sniffed

the inside of her wrist and said something. They laughed, and she sauntered off down the street. Paul walked into Sephora.

"I guess she needs some more Calyx," I sniped. "Let's split up. I'll shadow Paul. You tail Kendra. Stay in touch on the cell. Go!" Holly bolted down the street, and I watched Paul through the window. He inspected a couple of bars of soap and some tubes of lotion. Then he quickly moved to another aisle. I raced over to another window to get a better look. He was sniffing bottles of perfume. A beautiful saleswoman approached him. She said something and he chuckled. *Ha, ha, ha,* I thought. She sprayed a scent on a tiny white strip and held it under his nose. He sneezed. She handed him a tissue. More laughs. She sprayed another and another. Finally he nodded enthusiastically and pulled out his wallet.

My cell phone rang. It was Holly. "I'm trailing Kendra. She's moving east on Prince, crossing Mulberry," she said. "She just pulled a *New York Post* out of the trash. Wow! A budding freegan."

Paul exited Sephora, and I jumped into a doorway. He passed me, whistling and swinging a little black-and-white-striped shopping bag.

"Are you still there?" asked Holly.

"Uh-huh," I said, following Paul south on Broadway. "What's Tits on a Stick doing?"

"Oh, you won't believe it. A woman walking in front of Kendra dropped her sunglasses and Kendra picked them up and put them in her pocket. Now she's going into a shoe store called Sigerson Morrison."

"Keep talking, Holl. What's she doing now?"

"Kendra's trying on a pair of brown pumps with ties that lace up the leg. Not too high but, I hate to admit it, extremely sexy. Where are you?" she asked.

"I'm still tailing Paul. He bought a bottle of perfume at Sephora and now he's in a bodega buying a lottery ticket. Stay where you are. I'm on my way over. But keep talking. What's going on now?"

"Kendra's prancing around the store," she said.

The fact that that tacky bitch was buying pumps at the divine temple of exquisitely gorgeous shoes was almost worse than her tramping around with Paul.

"She's coming out." I heard a clank and a bang. "Ow! Shit," screamed Holly. "I just tripped over a stupid Vespa parked by the door."

"Where's Kendra?" I yelled as I ran to Holly's corner.

"I lost her."

Panting, I gazed in the window of Siggy Mo and hungrily surveyed the untouchable tootsies from outside the glass fishbowl. The store was filled with tall scarecrow models carrying tiny doll purses.

On the subway ride home, Holly and I instant-replayed the afternoon over and over again.

"I know you're feeling down, but you've got to remember that Paul's not the only game in town," Holly said, motioning generously to the subway car full of men.

"You're right," I said, trying to sound upbeat, even though half of them looked like subterranean mole people. I found myself staring at their troubled, pock-marked skin, thinking how a salicylic chemical peel would really even them out. Everyone that crossed my path now received a mental makeover. "I thought Paul and I were going places," I said wistfully.

"Marnie, maybe you're putting too much pressure on him. He's not even thirty yet."

I guess the age thing could have had something to do with it, but the fact that he let me storm out of his apartment and didn't come running after me or call to apologize about Kendra's picture or ask me to explain my behavior made me realize he was either too imma- ture for me or a heartless cad.

"Marn, you've got a really faraway look in your eye. You're scaring me. We've got to start focusing on Beau- tyfarm," Holly said, pulling out a tweezer from her purse. Suddenly Holly pinched me with it.

"Cut it out. That hurts," I exclaimed, pulling away.

"Good. That's what you're going to do now every time you think about Paul," Holly responded. "It's be- havior modification."

"You're right, Holl. From here on, I'm gonna pull my- self up by my bra straps, put guys on the back burner, and focus my energies on Beautyfarm." Don't dream it; be it.

PLOT LINES

After the Siesta launch was over, I was sent back to work for Connie. While I was very relieved to get Tawny out of my craw, my deepening crow's-feet (aka perior- bital lines) were really digging in. Screw MIA Paul. I was going to get another injection. To be a businesswoman and compete in the cutthroat world of beauty, I had to look my best. Holly would just have to understand.

I e-mailed Dr. Lurvey's office, inquiring about an- other shot. The nurse emailed me back, saying it would cost $600 for Botox injections around my eyes. Yikes. I couldn't afford that. How did people finance this stuff when it was going to wear off in six months? Would it be rent or Botox? Botox or rent?

I told Jarret what the nurse had said. "Don't go to

Lurvey," Jarret said. "Gentry does the same thing for less than half the price, and he's a really good shooter."

I immediately called Gentry, LeVigne's resident makeup artist. "Girl needs some beauty support? If you keep it on the down-low," he whispered, "I can shoot you up for fifty bucks. Cash. You in?"

I felt like a depraved druggie, but fifty dollars did sound awfully reasonable, and I'd just gotten paid. I scheduled the appointment for 5:30 P.M. that evening at Gentry's makeup station.

That afternoon, Sidney was in Connie's office. The door was ajar, and I could hear him bellowing about LeVigne's' flagging antiaging cream sales. Were the creams becoming outmoded? Redundant? Obsolete? How should LeVigne position itself so people would find their products relevant and effective?

As far as I could tell, they were fighting a losing battle until they could figure out how to put dermal fillers directly into the cream. Even the shopping malls were getting a leg up on LeVigne. Medical spas, where shoppers could drop in for a quick Botox shot and laser hair removal before hitting the department store white sales, were opening up in malls across America.

When I got to Gentry's makeup counter, he minced toward me in pink wool elephant bells and a purple silk tunic. He had such an exaggerated swing to his walk (his arms and hips moved generously in unison) that he reminded me of an Olympic speed skater.

Gentry sat me down in a high director's chair and, as a ruse, he pretended to give me a makeover. I wished he hadn't been pretending, because he made everyone he touched look like a million bucks. But, alas, I was here to have my eye wrinkles uncrinkled. Gentry reached into a drawer, and I watched as he stealthily drew a vial of botulinum toxin into a syringe. I closed my eyes and mentally prepared for the sting.

"Gentry wields the needle like an artist's paintbrush," he said. "Duchess, this will fluff you up like a little down pillow."

"Oh, good, Gentry. You're still here," said a shrill, unfamiliar voice that emanated from somewhere behind me. "I've got the *Cosmetic News* awards tonight, and I need a shot of B and some Artecoll on the double."

I opened my eyes. Standing before me was a tiny uber-CAP swathed in head-to-toe Versace. She must have worked on another floor, because I didn't recognize her.

"Sorry, sister-girlfriend," Gentry said sotto voce. "Duchess here has got the last shot of B. The new shipment's coming in tomorrow. And you know I don't do that other stuff."

He raised the needle to shoot my furrow.

"Who's this?" asked the CAP, training her overdone eyes on me.

Before Gentry or I could answer, she assessed that I was a member of the peasant class and attempted to bodily remove me from the chair.

"What the hell?" I said, holding on to the armrests for dear life. "Who the heck are *you?*"

"I'm a woman who's about to look ten to fifteen years younger," she said, giving me a karate chop to the arm.

"Get off of me, you lunatic. I was here first," I said, raising my fists in a "bring it on" kind of way.

Gentry gave us some loud, fierce diva snaps. "Break it up, ladies, or Gentry won't be helping either of you hoochie-mamas."

The crazy Versace woman patently ignored him and,

with superhuman Pilates strength, she hoisted me out of the chair and threw me to the ground.

"I'm going to report you to Human Resources," I yelled, rubbing my sore butt.

The woman hopped into the chair. "I am Human Resources," she cackled sadistically as Gentry injected her in the forehead.

Classic, I thought as I stormed down the hall.

"Sorry, child. Come back in twenty minutes and I'll do your maquillage," Gentry shouted after me.

I ran outside and began to cry. I walked for a while, directionless and enraged. When I got to Forty-fourth and Madison, I stopped. Why was I going to let that prune-face get me down? If Gentry, one of the best makeup artists in the world, was offering to do my face, why was I not taking him up on it? I guessed I could wait one more day to have crease-free eyes.

When I got back to the makeup station at the assigned time, Gentry wasn't there. I sat in the chair and flipped through an Italian *Vogue.* I bet he was going to flake. After another ten minutes, Gentry skated in, holding a pale green boba tea. "Are those lines around your eyes, or were you just worried I wasn't going to show up? You needn't fret, child. Gentry is going to serve it like a legend. You will represent."

Gentry liked to work with his subject lying down, so he unfurled a yoga mat on the ground next to the cosmetics counter. He handed me a pillow and had me lie down on my back. "I don't know why that girl likes her Artecoll so much. That's some nasty-ass shit. They put tiny beads in the collagen, and when the body absorbs it, hard little bumps get left behind."

"Like in a Beanie Baby?"

"Exactly right, duchess." Holding a makeup brush between his teeth like a long-stemmed rose, and a palette of colors in his large, mittlike hand, Gentry went to work, kneeling over me and then standing to assess his work, kneeling and standing. It was his trademark. "Gentry's had 'em all down here on the floor. Liza has lain down for La Gentry. Miss Diana Ross has communed with the dust bunnies for Mlle. Gentry.

"Gentry does hair too. She can rat a wig like nobody's business," he continued as he put down the brush. "Gorgeena! Your man is going to eat you up."

"I don't really have a man."

"Then your bitch is going to eat you up."

"Nope. Don't have that either."

"Shame, shame, shame," sang Gentry as he hoisted me up and we stood in front of the mirror. The blood rushed to my head and there were silver spots in front of my eyes. "What do you think, girl? Gentry is the master, isn't she?"

I blinked a few times to focus, and then a sultry, glowing girl slowly appeared. Wow. I looked amazing, like a better, prettier me. This could be addictive. No wonder women had been beautifying themselves for thousands of years.

"Let me take a picture. It will last longer," he said, picking up a Polaroid camera. He took his finger and gently pushed my lips apart. "Always keep your mouth slightly open, enough to put a penny between. It'll make your lips look fuller."

He snapped a shot and handed it to me. "Marnie looks good," I said in third person, imitating Gentry.

"Hang on to this. Might be worth millions someday."

He pulled out a card from his drawer and punched two holes. "I'm giving you one in advance for tomorrow's B shot and one extra for that nasty throw-down earlier. Six punches, and the seventh injection is free."

I gave Gentry a hug. He was an absolute genius.

By the time I left the office, it was ten P.M. I wanted to go out somewhere with my pretty new face, but I didn't want to go alone and it was getting too late to call anyone. When I got off the train in Brooklyn, I thought about getting a quick drink at Rhythm & Booze, but when I looked in the window, it was practically deserted. "Here, kitty, kitty," I said, leaning down to pet the bar cat that was hanging out on the corner. "Look at me. Look at me," I said desperately, but the cat hissed and ran away.

My last hope was the corner bodega. At least I could flirt with the cute counter guy. Damn. It was his night off, so I bought a Captain Nemo carrot cake to console myself. I stared at the bearded fisherman on the label. So much for Gentry's "your man's gonna eat you up." More like I was gonna eat him up.

When I got home, I lingered in front of the mirror, reluctant to wash off Gentry's artistry. I opened my mouth seductively like Gentry said. Was the imaginary penny supposed to sit lengthwise or widthwise? I put the Polaroid on my nightstand, got undressed, brushed my teeth, and carefully laid my head down on the pillow. If I was careful and slept on my back, I hoped to get another day out of the makeover. I wished Paul could have seen me look this beautiful. Oh no. I grabbed my tweezer. If they could cure people of their fear of flying, and had camps to turn gay kids straight, maybe reprogramming could work for me. Pinch, pinch. Ouch, ouch.

Femme Fatality

I was so worried about mussing my face that I got a terrible night's sleep. My mascara was smeared and the eye makeup was now blending into the rouge, but I did my best to repair this melting facial spumoni.

When I got to my cube, Connie's door was shut, but I could hear a muffled speakerphone conversation. Juniper and Murfy were in a huddle, whispering near the pantry. I put my things down and started walking to the bathroom, but Murfy put out her hand to stop me.

"Did you hear what happened?" she asked.

"No."

"Charlotte Warlick is in intensive care at St. Vincent's," said Juniper.

"Who's Charlotte Warlick?" I asked.

"The head of Human Resources," added Murfy.

My pulse began to race. "Is she built like a spark plug with short curly hair?"

"Yeah," said Juniper. "She's paralyzed and in and out of consciousness."

"What happened?" I asked, thinking back on last night's drama.

"No one knows exactly. The doctors think it was a Botox injection. Her husband said she was planning on getting some age maintenance done, but he didn't know where or by whom," said Juniper.

"At first they thought it was Lurvey, but he swears he didn't do it," Murfy said.

"Apparently there's a B knockoff going around that's

ten times stronger than the real thing," exclaimed Juniper. "Poor Charlotte. You get what you pay for."

My heart was jumping out of my throat. Oh my God. Could it have been Gentry's shot? Chills ran down my spine. If Charlotte Warlick hadn't nearly broken my neck to get at the syringe, that would be me in ICU right now. My emotions were conflicted. I felt bad for her (even though she was a total psycho), but I was never so happy to be hip-checked in my entire life.

It was obvious that they hadn't guessed it was Gentry. Should I alert Connie before he wielded his poisonous needle again? But before I had the chance to tell anyone about Gentry, Charotte did. She mouthed his name right before she slipped into a coma.

Holly and I had made a pact that if either of us ever lapsed into a coma, the conscious would pluck the unconscious. We would become each other's chin-hair custodians. What happened to Charlotte had given this a whole new meaning.

Word quickly spread through the office. When the cops came to the office looking for Gentry, he ran down the hall and barricaded himself in the Xerox room two doors from my desk.

Gentry was not going down easy. There was a standoff where he shouted to the police through the door that he had a loaded gun, and he taunted them by saying he would shoot any officer that wasn't hot. Then he sang the entire *Liza with a "Z"* album a cappella.

Eventually they brought in a battering ram. They wanted the floor evacuated, but there was a big launch happening and no one would leave. I watched the whole thing from my desk as the cops bashed the door down and sprayed mace inside. Whoa. My eyes began to burn. I looked over at Juniper and Murfy, who were still pecking away at their keyboards, oblivious to the mini-Waco that was unfolding a few doors down.

The medics arrived and carried out an unconscious Gentry. He was wearing a shaggy, cropped black wig and had done up his face like Liza in *Cabaret*. His heavy eye makeup dripped down his face. He had a pink Saturday Night Special in one hand and a needle dangling out of his arm. Had he tried to OD on Botox? Poor Gentry. He was sunk. He could be looking at a long jail sentence for what he had mistakenly done to Charlotte. One thing was for sure: the convicts at Rikers would never look better.

I could hear Connie shrieking behind closed doors in her office. What was going on in there?

When Connie finally emerged, she was smiling broadly. "Time to celebrate," she said, opening a bottle of champagne.

"Is Charlotte better?" I asked, assuming that she had made some sort of speedy and miraculous recovery.

"God, no. She's on a feeding tube and completely out of commission, but we're not."

I looked at her, puzzled.

"Marnie, don't you get it? We're back in business," Connie said. "There are stories coming in from all over the country about people dropping like flies from bad Botox. Disfigurement. Immobility. Dare I say death?"

"What do you mean, we're back in business?" I asked, timidly touching my blessedly craggy crow's-feet.

"With all the bad press that's going to snowball, everyone will be so terrified of using injectables, they'll go back to good old-fashioned skin care products. Fortuitously Siesta's about to launch G-Force, a putty that pulls the skin back. It's a face-lift in a tube, and it is safe. Sales are going to skyrocket! We've got bragging rights now!"

"I get it. No shots. No surgeries. Just the power of cream. Exactly the way Hattie intended," I said.

By the time I got home, I had really worked myself up into a lather. I was extremely shaken up by the course of events. My makeover, like an eighteen-hour-bra, had finally given out, so I scrubbed the remnants off my face. I made a cup of tea and curled up on my couch, shivering under the afghan my grandmother made for me when I went off to college. I couldn't stop obsessing about how it was just a quirk of fate that I wasn't the one lying supine in a hospital bed, fighting for my life. And all in the name of beauty. Why was I conforming to some impossible standard of perfection? Attractiveness was overrated anyway. It was fleeting, and it came with its own distinct set of problems. I don't think it made even the prettiest people any happier. No wonder I had scared off Paul with my erratic, self-absorbed behavior.

I reached for the phone and dialed Paul's number. He picked up and, through a veil of snotty tears, I blurted out the whole horrible story of Charlotte and the Botox.

"I'm coming right over," he said.

An hour later, Paul was at my side. We hugged for the longest time and then we curled on the bed in complete silence, like two intertwined bonsai.

"Can I ask you something?" he said.

"Of course."

"Are you seeing someone else?"

"Someone *else*? I didn't know *we* were still seeing each other. I thought it was over."

"You ran out of my apartment without letting me explain," he retorted.

"What was there to explain? You had a picture of your ex-girlfriend in your bedroom."

"I know you don't believe me, but I didn't realize the picture was there until I found it under a pile of stuff. I care so much about you, Marnie," he said, trying to hug me.

"Then where were you?" I said, backing away.

"I needed to set things straight with Kendra, and I needed some time to think. You're not the only one who can be withdrawn and moody. I can get that way too."

"If you were so gloomy, then why didn't you call me? I would've cheered you up."

"I thought you hated me, the way you ran out that night. You have to believe me when I tell you that it's over with Kendra." I was dying to tell him that I had seen them together at Sephora. Paul took me in his arms. "I did a lot of thinking, and I told Kendra that we couldn't be friends, that it wasn't fair to you. I also realize now how weird the cat thing is. I was being oblivious and insensitive to your feelings. I had a talk with Kendra about keeping Jeffrey at her apartment, and she told me the most incredible thing. She got this gig overseas singing for the USO, and she's leaving the country for a year. Jeffrey's staying put, and she'll be gone."

"Really?" I said incredulously.

"Uh-huh." Paul nuzzled my neck. "Marnie, you mean the world to me. I've never met anyone like you. I just can't take these ups and downs. I want things to be good between us. This whole thing with Kendra has given me major stress."

I thought about how much I'd missed him.

"And there's something else I want to discuss. When you got that Botox shot, it really freaked me out. You've been tinkering around like a mad scientist."

"I just wanted to be a better me."

"You're perfect just the way you are," Paul said.

"I'll never do injectables again. I promise."

"Pray tell me, milady, that no one has stolen your heart," said Paul.

I stepped back to visually drink him in. "Someone has, actually. He's six-one, has dark spiky hair, and is really cheesy," I giggled.

"Valentine's Day is coming up. Are you free?" he asked.

The icicles began to melt. "Yes, I'm available for a playdate," I replied.

I excused myself and reached into the closet for the bottle of Courage. It wasn't yet at full optimum strength to decant, but I could wait no longer. I opened it and took a sniff. Just as I had hoped. It had intoxicating whiffability. Marion would have been delighted.

"I made this for you," I said, proudly handing it to him. "Think of it as an early V-Day present."

Paul opened the bottle and took a sniff. "Nice scent. I can see it at Bloomingdale's. A runaway success." He turned the bottle over and dabbed some liquid on his neck, chest, pits. "Do I smell irresistible?" he asked, his body close to mine.

"Truly, madly, deeply," I said, dreamily falling into his arms.

"I . . . I . . ." Paul said, slightly hesitating.

No time for beating around the bush. Say it, you fool. Say it.

"I love you."

I put my gun back in its holster. The I Love You showdown was finally over. I had won without firing the first shot.

"I love you too," I said, holding him as tight as I could without breaking him.

On Valentine's Day, Paul took me for a romantic dinner at Manchego in Brooklyn. At the table, he presented me with a black-and-white-striped Sephora shopping bag. Inside was a bottle of perfume. I looked at the label. It was a scent I was not familiar with called Eau de Stilton. Without really thinking, I spritzed a little on myself.

"No, don't," Paul exclaimed.

It was too late. I smelled like dirty socks.

"I wasn't really thinking you would wear it. It's a novelty item. I was thinking it was more for show and tell at work."

"Thanks. It's really unique," I said as I reached across to kiss him. Paul recoiled. When I was in the bathroom washing it off my neck, I realized that this must have been what he bought the day I went spying on him. My gift to Paul, well . . . he'd get that later.

"You look beautiful," Paul said dreamily as I sat back down. "And your furrow is back."

"I know. Isn't it great? Now I can frown again." I opened the menu. Ugh. It turned out manchego was a kind of Spanish cheese. The menu boasted 178 cheeses in its refrigerated vault. My stomach tightened. I quickly snuck out two Lactaid pills from my pocket and swallowed them with some wine.

"What's that?" Paul asked.

"Vitamins."

This cheese lie really needed to come to an end.

Paul pored over the list of offerings, studying it like the sports stats, then ordered. A little while later, a small bearded man (the maître fromager) wheeled up a glass box with a little latched door. It was sealed to prevent any malodorous whiffs that might offend less adventuresome diners. The maître fromager cut six chunks and put them on a long Lucite tray. In addition, he gave us a basket of raisin bread and little clear ramekins filled with olives, walnuts, and dried figs. I hungrily dove into the side dishes.

"You know, Kendra never really liked cheese," Paul said casually, taking a sip of wine. "It was sort of a problem."

The cheese lie could not come to an end. I took a gulp of wine to steady myself and surveyed the little uneven wedges that were propped up irregularly like Stonehenge. The wedge in the middle looked the least threatening, so I took the knife and sliced into it. Paul gently grabbed my hand.

"Actually, the cheese is arranged in the order it should be eaten, so your palate can adjust to the different tastes. It goes from mild and soft to hard and veiny."

Was he describing an erection? If I looked at the bright side, this cheese chat was really turning me on.

"Tonight we're sampling rustic farmhouse cheeses. Wabash Cannonball, Cheshire, Double Gloucester, Shopshire Blue." Paul cut a hunk and put it on a piece of bread. "Here, try this. It's soft."

"It looks really firm to me," I teased, playing footsie under the table.

"This is the kind of assortment I'll set up when I'm a cave master."

"Sounds kinky," I said, refilling our wineglasses. "What's the job description for a cave master?" I asked, imaging him as a Neanderthal in a fur pelt, dragging me by my ponytail into a craggy cave.

"It's a fancy way of saying cheese consultant."

When Paul talked about cheese, he was totally in his element. "You really found your calling."

"And so have you, with Beautyfarm," he said. "I'll be your test monkey if you need one."

"Whatever you do, don't say 'test monkey' in front of Holly."

It was now time for dessert and dessert wine. "Have you ever had Sauternes?" asked Paul as our waiter uncorked a bottle of wine and decanted it into Paul's glass.

"No," I said, a little embarrassed by my ignorance.

"It's a sweet French wine made from rotten grapes," he said, swirling the golden liquid around in his glass and taking a snorty sip.

He gave the waiter an approving nod, and the waiter poured us each a healthy goblet.

"Rotten grapes," I repeated, inching the glass toward my disapproving mouth.

"You have to realize that mold is good," Paul said, recognizing my apprehension. "That mold is our friend. In cheese. In wine."

"In my shower," I added. When I finally took a sip, it actually tasted delicious. The first taste reminded me of honeyed flowers, the second like woodsy bananas.

After dinner, we went back to my apartment. "There's something I want to give you," said Paul as we walked into the bedroom.

"Yeah?" I asked excitedly.

"Reach into my pocket."

"Ooh, baby," I said, slipping in my hand and going for his crotch.

"No. That's not what I meant," he laughed.

"Oh, sorry," I said, suddenly embarrassed by my forwardness.

He redirected my hand to the other pocket. There was a key inside. Kendra's key. I pulled it out, and he took my hand so we were both holding it.

"You've got to ease it in and give it a quick jiggle," he said, thrusting my hand back and forth.

"Just the way I like it," I said, kissing him.

I was still wearing my coat, and Paul pulled me closer, sticking his hands in my pockets.

"Ouch," he said, extracting the reprogramming tweezer that I had forgotten was there.

I quickly grabbed it away from him. "Remember how you said you admired the wispy hairs on the Fleur de Maquis cheese?" I said, stroking an ersatz beard on my chin. "Now that I'm going natural, I won't be needing a tweezer anymore."

"You don't have to go *that* natural," he said with a sweet laugh.

GENE, GENIE

Fifty-seven people nationwide were in Botox-related comas. Some were paralyzed, some on respirators fighting for their lives. There was a barista at my neighborhood coffee place who sometimes wore a t-shirt that read MAKEUP IS EVIL. After recent events, that seemed quite quaint. Injectables were the enemy.

In their inimitable sharklike fashion, the LeVigne family took this tragic incident and used it as an opportunity to make lemonade from lemons. As Connie predicted, the demand for injectables had dropped significantly, and LeVigne planned to fully exploit that fact. If Sidney was looking for a way to reinvigorate the skin cream market, now was his golden opportunity. They couldn't have orchestrated something better if they tried. There were rumors that Schotzie Ronson was the mastermind behind the bad Botox. That he had purchased the excessively strong solution, mixed it without fully diluting it, and sold it to cut-rate clinics that in turn advertised dermal filler blowouts, all in an effort to create bad press for injectables and a renewed interest in the cosmetics industry's flagging skin care market.

Sidney and Connie were in negotiations with Dr. Nicholas Von Heedle, a Swiss scientist from a company called Vector 21. He had created a custom face cream that was formulated from a person's DNA. Skin cells were swabbed from inside the cheek, and the genes were then sequenced in a centrifuge. Cells that were believed to increase the production of collagen were isolated and captured. Then they were mixed into a time-released creaming agent that penetrated the skin's surface and were absorbed into the layers below. According to the good doctor, the results were remarkable. It was like you were cloning yourself—your younger, more elastic self—by putting fresh, nubile cells back into your skin. Just like Murfy and Juniper had hoped, you could now actually be reborn.

Collecting and tailoring each customer's DNA would be extremely costly on a mass-market level, so LeVigne decided to streamline the application. Since Summer's new fragrance, Inertia, had been such a monstrous success, they decided that instead of individualizing the creams, they would use Summer's exceptional DNA for the product. They had even hired Frank Gehry to do the Bilbao-like architectural packaging.

One day I found myself in a meeting with the Le-

Vignes and Dr. Von Heedle. Dr. Von Heedle was stroking Summer's face. "You are a raging beauty," he said in his Swiss-German accent. "Everyone vants a piece of Summer, and now they can get it."

The doctor took a tiny ruler from his pocket, measured Summer's perfectly symmetrical face, and scribbled some notes on a pad. Then he took out a calculator, punched in some numbers, and exclaimed, "We are looking for stray microscopic enzymes that degrade the stratum corneum and attack the structural integrity of—"

Marion cut him off. "You're blinding us with science, Dr. Von Heedle," she said. "All we want to know is that it works."

"Let me get a sample to the lab. Open wide, Summer," he said, wielding a long-stemmed Q-tip.

Summer took a big wad of gum out of her mouth and handed it to Sidney. Getting close enough to French-kiss her, the good doctor swiped the inside of her mouth and daubed the Q-tip on a glass specimen slide.

"What about my DNA?" whined Rebecca. "Can't we market some of mine?"

Sidney put his arm around his less-than-gorgeous daughter. "Darling, I don't know how to put this, but Summer's DNA will drive traffic to counters. While your DNA is quite special, Summer's is a little more special."

Rebecca started to cry.

"Honey, we're running a business here," said Marion. "You have to look at the numbers, the bigger picture."

"Well, Mommy and Daddy, if your DNA wasn't so screwed up, I wouldn't have come out looking like this. Good thing you didn't have another child because you might have given birth to Quasimodo."

"I have an idea, Rebecca," said Dr. Von Heedle diplomatically. "As a gift to you, your very kind parents, and the company for taking me on, I will do a complimentary customized DNA cream for you and for everyone in this room. I'll leave behind some swab kits. Have someone collect the cells and messenger them over to the lab. Auf Wiedersehen," said Dr. Von Heedle as he donned his black felt fedora and swept out of the room.

Connie looked at me. "Get to work, Marnie," she said, pointing to the Q-tips and glass specimen slides.

Everyone eagerly lined up in a single file before me. They all seemed excited about this new, incredible-sounding product. Since injectables had (at least temporarily) gone out of vogue, they were all looking a little rough around the edges. A new mother's little helper was in short order.

I assigned each slide a number, and on a sheet of paper I wrote down the number and corresponding name. But what a disgusting job this was. When I was done with Marion, Sidney, Connie, and Jarret, Connie had me go out and swab Murfy, Juniper, and Tinsley. At first Tinsley didn't want me anywhere near her mouth, but when I explained what she would be receiving, she opened wide.

There was no mention of me either way, so I took the liberty of swabbing my own cheek. After this dastardly task, the least they could do was give me a customized DNA cream. I realized I had promised Paul that I had sworn off all artificial beauty enhancements, but this was my own DNA, so it didn't really count.

When I got back to my desk with all the slide specimens, there was a message from my dad. I rang him back, and of course Trudy intercepted the call.

"How's your business plan going, Marnie? My cousin Annette made a fortune in Avon. She sold makeup to the natives on the Solomon Islands. They still trade in beads."

"We're kinda working on a smaller scale, making our own products," I said. "Natural stuff."

"Let me give you Annette's number. She'll answer all your questions."

God, couldn't I do anything without her getting involved? *Okay, calm down. Think nice thoughts. Anger into love. Smiles all around.*

"Thanks," I said to Trudy. "I really appreciate your interest."

Trudy's shrill voice interrupted me. "Get outta the john, mister, and say hi to the next Mary Kay. 'Bye, Marnie," she said, clicking off.

Dad and I talked for a few minutes. When I reached to grab a pen, I knocked my grande latte over and it spilled on my desk. "Damn," I said. "That coffee cost me four bucks."

"Still drinking the hard stuff?"

"Dad, it's only coffee, not heroin. What's been going on out there?"

"I've been doing a little work for Trudy."

"Legal stuff?"

"No. She has me dress up in a foam costume. It's shaped like a key. I've been waving a sign in front of her new condos. It's working like dynamite. She's already sold four units."

It was amazing how Trudy had been able to transform my dad, the pit bull attorney, into a docile puppy dog. My dad must have read my mind. "Don't get mad, Marnie. It's kinda fun. Sorta like performance art. I'll tell you one thing. If she sells two more units, we can go on that safari she keeps nagging me about."

"*Access Hollywood* is on," screamed Trudy.

"Gotta go, Marnie. Everything's fine. I feel great," said my dad. And with that he hung up. He was warmer and fuzzier than I'd ever heard him. I was starting to like this new, improved guy.

As part of my research for Beautyfarm, I was hunched over the Xerox machine, surreptitiously copying some natural skin care formulations I found in a beauty trade magazine, when suddenly I smelled smoke. All morning long, the sounds of jackhammering had been reverberating from the floor below. I figured the smoke was coming from the construction crew hotwiring something downstairs. About a minute later, Murfy came tearing down the hall. "Aren't you from LA, Marnie?"

"Yeah, why?"

"There was just an earthquake out there," she said. This sudden, scary news made me forget about the acrid smell that lingered in the air.

As I ran back to my desk, I bumped into Juniper. "Well, that's just swell, isn't it? The media coverage is going to screw up my whole night's TV lineup," she said, stomping her feet.

I clicked on Yahoo! news. The epicenter was in West Hollywood. It was a magnitude 5.0. I didn't know anyone in WeHo, but I was going to call my family just to check in. I wanted to tell Paul, but I remembered that he was in the subterranean refrigeration rooms at the Artisanal Premium Cheese Center, and cell phones didn't work down there.

As I was about to dial my mother, our fire alarms went off. Thick smoke came pouring down the hallway, and Tinsley shouted into a mini megaphone, "There appears to be a fire emanating from the accounting department. Everyone please use the stair-wells and evacuate the building immediately."

Suddenly the lights went out. There was some day-light coming in through the windows, but the smoke kept getting thicker and it was hard to see. I found a flashlight in my desk and quickly grabbed my knap-sack and cell phone. I put on my sneakers and threw my work shoes into the growing pile that was heaped under my desk. As I hustled down the hall, the CAPs were in a bizarre state of panic and preening—touching up their makeup, tying back their hair into sensible ponytails, and grabbing bottled water and en-ergy bars for the forty-three flights down.

I turned on my flashlight and led a small group of women down the hallway. Apparently they didn't know where the stairwell was: the day of the fire drill, they were all out at a Stella McCartney sample sale. Saskia and I had politely listened to the fire marshal's spiel and by default we were anointed as official floor monitors and given little orange vests and first-aid kits.

The dark stairwell became very crowded as new people joined us from the floors below. As we walked, I tried LA on my cell, but the circuits were busy.

The women walked very slowly, struggling in their towering-inferno heels. Why in God's name were they wearing those ridiculous shoes? Then I realized none of them had a stockpile of sneakers under their desks. These women arrived at work every day wearing the same shoes they went home in. It was only female pharmaceutical executives and secretaries like myself who "saved" their good shoes for the office and wore their comfies to-and-fro.

I tried to push past them, and just as I was about to break free, someone pulled on my knapsack and yanked me back. I turned around and beamed my flashlight in the face of this rude offender. It was Summer. With Rebecca in tow. Rebecca must have been having her hair and makeup done when the electricity went out, because only half her face was painted and only one side of her head was smooth and kink-free.

Wobbling in her tower-of-power pumps, Summer grabbed my arm. "Hey, listen, I'll give you a hundred bucks for those. . . . those things on your feet," she whined as she pointed to my beat-up Jack Purcell tennies.

I thought back to how rude they had been and how they basically ignored me at all the meetings. "They're not for sale," I said emphatically.

Not used to being said no to, Summer harrumphed and blinked her false eyelashes in utter disbelief. "Since you seem so attached to them, are they at least for rent?" Summer asked, coming to a dead stop, simply not caring that she was preventing a throng of coughing, terrified women from seeing daylight. But, alas, no one would dare speak up to a LeVigne.

"Well, are they?" she asked again, thrusting her ample cleavage in my face.

If she was trying to fake-flirt with me, it wasn't working. "No, they are not," I said, crossing my arms across my comparatively scanty chest.

Throats were politely cleared while a standoff ensued.

"I'll give you two hundred dollars for them."

"Not a chance," I said.

"What size are they?"

"Nines."

"Well, I'm a ten, but now that I've had my toes shortened, they should fit," Summer said.

"I'm not selling them."

"Three hundred."

"No," I barked. Wait! Was I crazy? I could use the money for Beautyfarm. "Five hundred dollars, and give me your Manolos," I extorted.

Summer gasped. I stood there, stock-still. Precious seconds ticked by. Begrudgingly, she handed over her gorgeous magenta suede pumps, opened her purse, withdrew the cash, and slammed it into my hand. I took off my sneakers and kicked them in her direction.

"Any more shoes in the backpack?" Rebecca inquired, painfully shifting from foot to foot. She was clutching three large bottles of Evian water.

"No."

"I could use that filthy rucksack to carry my water in," she said, grabbing at my pink JanSport.

"You can have my bag for seven hundred and fifty dollars. Firm," I said, coughing from the smoke.

"Now you're getting greedy. I'll give you four hundred dollars for it, but you carry the water," said Rebecca.

Fine. I'd be their sherpa for a grand total of $900. I stuck the Manolos in my coat pocket (I would certainly wear them, but not today) and trudged in stocking feet ahead of them, shining the light so they could see, continuing the slow traverse down. I tried LA on my cell again, but I couldn't get through to anyone. Where had my dad said he was working? It couldn't be West Hollywood. Trudy sold in the beach cities.

"Do you think we should have the driver take us to the Hamptons for the night? I need to breathe some clean air," Summer said as she coughed her way down another flight.

"Maybe we should just jet to Paris. To that oxygen bar that Donatella goes to in the Place des Vosges," said Rebecca.

"Ya think? Let's just go hang in my panic room. Mommy had the new generators put in, so the fridge will work, and we've got that new PlayStation."

"With all these calories we're burning, I think we should treat ourselves to my secret sugar stash," added Rebecca. "I bought some candy-by-the pound at Dylan's."

"Naughty," said Summer, as she stopped to tie my/her shoe. "How recherché. I haven't worn shoe strings since my freshman year at Spence," she continued, marveling at the white ribbons that the rest of us called laces.

"One thing's for sure, we've got to tell Daddy to screw the view. After this, we need office space on the ground floor," huffed Rebecca. Then she turned to me and jabbed at my knapsack. "You. Whoever you are. I'm parched. Water, please."

I was very preoccupied with the fact that I hadn't heard from anyone in my family, so I robotically opened my knapsack and handed Rebecca her Evian bottle.

"I'd offer you some, but I've got herpes," she said to me.

"So do I," chimed Summer.

Ick. Did they give it to each other? Did her dog, Gringo, have it too?

"Why the long face?" Rebecca asked me.

"Didn't you hear?" I snapped. "There was an earthquake in LA, and I can't reach my family out there."

Summer turned to Rebecca. "Too bad Mummy and Daddy weren't out on the Coast. We'd be billionairesses right now."

Rebecca let out a sinister chuckle.

"It's not funny!" I yelled. "People could be dead."

"I think that would be my sister's point," chided Rebecca.

Summer put her arm around me, and I tried to wriggle away. "It's not that bad, really. Imagine death like this," she said avuncularly, eager to impart her Mikimoto pearls of wisdom. "It's as if somebody went to Bergdorf's and never came back."

That was it. I'd had it. I dumped the knapsack at their feet and pushed my way down the stairs. As I slowly made it to daylight, I could hear grief-stricken cries in the stairwell. I assumed it was coworkers worried about loved ones who might have been caught in the LA temblor. It wasn't until later, when I saw the CAPs clopping down Fifth Avenue in their flattened-out, turned-up clown shoes, that I realized their anguished cries were from having to crack the heels off their Manolos and Choos so they could walk down the stairs with some modicum of speed and comfort.

When I bumped into Saskia ten blocks from the office, I realized I was barefoot. She reached into her tote bag and gave me an extra pair of her spongy white nurse's shoes. I hugged her, and we went our separate ways. When I got out of the station, my cell phone rang. It was my brother Mark.

"Marnie, I've got some bad news."

"Oh, no. What happened? Is it Dad?"

"It's Trudy. She's dead. Dad was helping her show a condo in West Hollywood, and the building collapsed. Flat like a pancake."

"Oh my God. I can't believe it! Is Dad okay?"

"He was wearing some crazy foam suit that saved him. Physically he's fine. Just a little beaten up. But mentally. Well. That's another story."

"Can I talk to him?"

"They gave him a really strong sedative. He's totally out of it."

"How's Mom? I've been trying to get through to you guys for hours. The lines were all jammed."

"Mom's fine, but we're all in a state of shock about Trudy."

When I got in the house, I called Paul. He rushed over as fast as he could, and when he got to my place, I fell sobbing into his arms. We held on to each other for a very long time, our faces wet with mingled tears.

"I'm so sorry about your stepmother," Paul said, unloading a Dean & DeLuca shopping bag filled with very expensive comfort food. Later, as we lay in bed, Paul massaged my feet and we talked about life and death, the fleetingness of things, and how life could change on a dime. We talked about Paul's brother Calvin.

"I think about him all the time," he said, putting his arms around me. "It's like part of you is stuck in that moment and you can't completely move forward. It's going to be hard for your dad. You've got to go out there and be with him."

"Do you want to come with me?" I asked.

"You need some quality time with him," he said, wiping away my tears. "He really needs you. Now more than ever." Paul scooped me up in his arms. "I'll be right here when you get back. I love you so much." Paul was the voice of reason. He was so logical about things.

DEATH VALLEY

Tinsley gave me a hard time about going to LA, but there was a death-in-the-family clause in my Cross Temps contract that gave me a leave of absence (unpaid, of course), and I was only going to be gone for a week. As it turned out, most of my coworkers were getting part of that week off anyway: during the fire, the sprinkler system had flooded the PR floor (including millions of dollars of artwork), and a crew was coming in to clean up the mess.

I called Holly from the airport to go over some Beautyfarm marketing ideas, and when I got on the plane, I opened a dog-eared copy of Suze Orman's *The Money Book for the Young, Fabulous & Broke*, which put me in a twilight sleep. A memory came to mind of the first time I met Trudy. I was seventeen. My Dad took Trudy, Mark, and me to the Old Spaghetti Factory in Hollywood (some sort of teen concession for our benefit). As we walked to the restaurant, my dad and Trudy strolled a few paces ahead, holding hands as we skulked behind. As we approached a XXX theater, they stopped to look up at the marquee. The film was called *Insatiable*. Trudy grabbed my dad's unruly back curls, which had grown longer than a lawyer's should ever be.

"Larry. You're insatiable," she whispered coyly.

My dad shushed her, knowing we were within earshot. Ugh. I was going to barf. Who was this two-bit floozy? At the table, Trudy clutched his thigh, a little too close to his crotch. To make matters worse (if they could get any worse), I found what looked to be a Q-tip in my spaghetti. The lovebirds never bothered to notice that I hadn't touched my food.

Suddenly something cold and metal hit my leg.

"Watch your feet. Cart coming through," said a frosted flight attendant, jostling me awake.

I closed my eyes again and thought back on the first time I'd seen my dad and Trudy ("Paunch and Trudy") perform at Kiki's Hideaway, a Polynesian restaurant in Hermosa Beach. It had taken ten minutes of drawn-out hellos and dramatic air kisses from the old coots in checkered sports coats and their markedly younger wives in slabby platforms and plunging necklines for them to get to the stage and for me to reach my reserved table.

The restaurant was filled with Dad and Trudy's doctors: the cardiologist, the ENT, their plastic surgeon, even my dad's metal detector beach buddies. With all these *alter kochers* cheering them on, Paunch and Trudy could never bomb. When they scatted a tripped-out psychedelic version of "Muskrat Love," with Trudy singing in screechy highs and guttural lows, half the room reached up to fiddle with their squawking hearing aids.

"There's so much love in this room," Trudy cooed into the mike. She was clearly in her element.

I realized that she had been good for my dad. I had spent so many years being exasperated by her that I didn't get to see the true person. Until it was too late. And now I felt horrible.

After we landed, I zipped through the accordion and entered the LAX terminal. My dad stood all alone by the baggage claim. His eyes were bloodshot. He looked older and drawn. I gave him a big warm hug.

When we got back to the condo, we sat in the den, just the two of us. The place was eerily quiet without Trudy's outsized personality filling up the rooms. We stared at each other. I couldn't remember the last time we were alone together. I couldn't take the silence.

"I'm going to take a shower before we meet Mark for dinner," I said, jumping up from the sofa.

"Before you go, I want to give you something from Trudy," he said, going to the credenza and pulling out three giant Ziploc bags filled with tiny bars of hotel soap. "Take these. She collected them. You'll never have to buy soap again."

"Thanks, Dad. I love you," I said, hugging him as he cried into my shoulder.

Later, the elevator journey down to the parking garage was heartbreaking. There was a framed poster of my dad and Trudy attached to the metal wall. JOIN US FOR THE COMIC STYLINGS OF PAUNCH AND TRUDY, it read, boasting a photo of them in matching his-and-hers flecked sweaters with whipstitched pleather patches.

I tried to open the little glass box, but it was locked. "Dad, we've got to get them to take this down," I said, standing in front of it to block the sad image.

"We looked pretty good back then," my father sniffed. He traced the outline of Trudy's face with his finger. "The poor girl had a voice that wouldn't quit."

As odd as it sounds, my mother held Trudy's memorial service at her house. My father's place was too small, and Mom loved to host an event, even if it was for her ex-husband's dead second wife—or maybe, secretly, because of it.

Mom lived in a gated/guarded Tarzana senior community called Valley Mews. The complex was built into the hills, so her condo had spectacular views. At night, the shoppers' triumvirate, Target, Home Depot, and Costco, formed a heavenly constellation.

"Marnie, which place is your mother's?" asked Dad as we drove through the gates.

"Keep driving straight. I'll let you know when we're there," I answered.

As we drove past house after house of identical two-story peach stucco structures, my dad spoke.

"I want to make a trip out to New York to see you

and to fulfill a wish of Trudy's. She wanted her ashes spread in Connecticut over the site of her first real estate transaction."

"That sounds great, Dad. Just let me know when. I'd love to come with you and help."

We pulled up into my mother's driveway and I quickly got out of the car. She and I hugged for a long time and then she pulled me back to drink me in.

"You look wonderful, Marnie."

"Thanks, Mom," I said, so happy to see her. "You look great too."

"Beverly, I want to thank you for having the service here," my dad said, coming up to us.

My mother gave him a hug. "Larry, I am so sorry about Trudy," she said. "It's just so tragic."

"I'm going to go in the house now," Dad said, trudging sadly up the driveway.

"He looks terrible," whispered my mom. "I have to tell you: there's not a lot of Trudy's family here. Mostly real estate friends. It's a sea of frosted hair."

My Uncle Vic, Aunt Sadie, and one of my mom's mall-walker friends, Midge, gathered around the dining room table, loading up their plates with chopped liver, lox, potato salad, and pastrami.

"What Hitler didn't finish, the delis surely will," muttered Uncle Vic.

"Now, tell us what you've learned at your makeup factory, Marnie. Do the products really work?" asked Midge.

"All I can tell you is, don't drink, smoke, or tan," I instructed. From the looks I was getting, I thought they might pelt me with bagels.

"It's a little too late for that," said Aunt Sadie, who had lived a full life and had a beautifully wrinkled mug to prove it.

"Marnie," my mom said, "I saw on Oprah they're using infant foreskin cells to fill in wrinkles."

Everyone gasped.

"That's true," I said, looking out into the living room, wondering which real estate broker might have a little boy's pecker plumping up her cheeks.

The service was starting, and we sat in the living room on rented folding chairs. As people gave their touching eulogies, there wasn't a dry eye in the house. When everyone was done reminiscing about Trudy's amazing sales records and how she expertly guided anxious homeowners through their buyers' remorse, my dad inched toward the piano and, before anyone could stop him, he performed a slow rendition of "Burning Down the House" by the Talking Heads.

My mother and I stood in the shadows and watched this rather entertaining train wreck.

"How did Trudy do it? I could never bring out that side in him," marveled my mom.

"What about his fashion sense?" I asked.

"From Brooks Brothers to this? I dressed him so well," my mom lamented as we quietly inventoried my father's thin gray ponytail, piling Sansabelt trousers and the tasseled Italian slip-ons that were so beat-up, the left shoe was missing its tassel.

In addition to her passion for real estate, Trudy's other obsession had been remodeling my father. Over time, my mom had forgiven Trudy for stealing Dad away, but not for what she had done to his appearance.

"I remember how Trudy used to keep the beat by yanking on his ponytail," I said sadly as I watched my dad tickle the ivories.

BUSINESS CASUAL

When I got back to New York, I dove energetically into my Beautyfarm work. It was mid-March, and I was searching for a manufacturer that made glass containers and recyclable paper cartons for our earth-conscious products. As I scrolled through a list on the Internet, Juan appeared at my desk with a big box. The personalized DNA creams had arrived from the lab. Murfy and Juniper swooped down like hungry vultures to get theirs. I shooed them away because the creams had to be accounted for first. Even though I had given the lab the list of names and the corresponding numbers, for some reason each jar had only a number on it. I suppose they were trying to preserve a sense of anonymity, but it was irritating because now I had to find the list (thank God I'd made a copy), match up the names with the numbers, and make identifying labels for each jar.

When I was done labeling them, I walked around to everyone's desk to distribute the jars and deliver this firm edict: "Dr. Von Heedle strongly recommends that the cream be applied twice a day and used for several months to reach full effect." Who knows if any of them were listening, since they were so busy grabbing the jars out of my hands.

All week long I diligently applied the cream twice daily and spent a lot of time in the bathroom mirror staring at myself, but to no avail. I didn't look like a younger, fresher me, just my same old tired self with a worsening furrow. (I was back to using low-tech Frownies.)

One afternoon, on my way to the pantry, I spotted Juan and Summer in a little passageway that led to the service elevator. Because LeVigne was about to launch Summer's DNA cream (which they had christened Gene Cream), Connie had instructed me to report any odd or inappropriate behavior exhibited by Summer. You couldn't open a magazine or turn on the tube without seeing a story about her latest sexcapades, and they didn't want any more bad press to mess up sales.

Juan had Summer pinned against the wall with his mail cart. I could see them, but they couldn't see me. I watched as Summer animatedly told him some idiotic story. He smiled and laughed, leaning over his cart to grab her breasts.

"Where you been, girl? I've seen your titty, but I haven't seen you."

He was referring to Summer's birthday party photo in the *Post,* where her boob had fallen out of her tube top and dipped right into the cake.

"My titty's right here," she said, guiding his hands over her firm body.

"I miss your Singapore grip, mami," he said, stroking her face.

"A little birdie told me your girlfriend doesn't wear makeup. Is she really that pretty?" Summer was wearing gobs of it.

"Not as bonita as you," Juan purred as he patted her high, tight butt.

I rolled my eyes and walked away from their cheesy *telenovela*, deciding not to sing like a canary and tell Connie what I had witnessed.

Holly had given her boss at the spa some samples of our Beautyfarm products, and she loved them. She wanted to carry them in their boutique, so I went over to Holly's bright and early on a Saturday morning to get ready for our first order. We were making a batch of lemon maple foot scrub called Sweet Feet and an age spot remover called Crop Circles made from Japanese seaweed, saffron oil, and yuzu extract. I was still trying to get rid of my forehead spots.

When I got there, Dwayne was on all fours, sifting through the shag rug. "Check this out," he said, pointing to a fishbowl filled with loose change. "I found all that in the carpet. It's like two hundred dollars."

"That's great. Where's Holly? In the lab?" I asked, pointing to the kitchen.

"Oh, shit, if you're making stuff, I'm outta here. I'm not letting Holly near me again," he said. "Not after this." Dwayne ripped the bandana off his head. Whoa! There was a crew cut where his long, luscious locks had been. He was still cute, but it was shocking to see him without the security blanket of his hair.

"What happened?" I asked.

Holly came out of the kitchen. "Remember that soap I was making? I put the lye in an old conditioner tub and Dwayne used it by mistake. It burned off all his hair. Accidents happen," she said with a chuckle.

"You're polluting my vibe, Holly. You better watch your back," said Dwayne as he marched out of the apartment and slammed the door.

"I bought him some high-potency vitamins. You know how guys' hair grows. It'll be back in two years, tops," she said, shrugging it off.

"Well, the place looks nice and bright," I commented, looking around at the shiny-clean living room.

"Thanks. Dwayne finally quit smoking weed. For the first few days, he was really moody, but now he can't sit still. He's been screwing in compact fluorescent bulbs and washing windows. It's great."

Holly and I sat down at the kitchen table and I pulled out some documents from my tote bag. "I downloaded a business contract for us to go over," I said, handing it to her to read. "The only thing we're missing is the start-up funding," I said.

"It'll come, Marnie. We're both saving money from our jobs, and my credit's good enough to get us a bank loan."

"You're right. I'm not going to worry. At least not yet. So, if we're going to start a successful business," I said, "we need to set up some ground rules. Number one: no outsourcing."

"You're preaching to the choir," said Holly. "Number two: no animal testing. Only cruelty-free products."

"But of course," I responded. "And no artificial anything. No methyls, ethyls, propyls, parabens, sodium laureth sulfates, or cocamide DEAs."

"If you can't pronounce 'em, we denounce 'em," said Holly. "Number three—or is it number four? Ten percent of our profits goes to North Shore Animal League. And another ten percent should be donated to the Dressed to Kill Foundation, educating women about the link between underwire bras and breast cancer. And our employees will work a thirty-five-hour week with all holidays off and paid maternity leave."

"That sounds great," I said.

"And numbers five, six, and seven. I want to be CEO and president, and you can be CFO."

"Have pod people invaded your body? For someone as proletarian as yourself, you're awfully concerned with titles," I joked.

"Marnie, that's how companies work. I've been reading *Forbes*," she said.

"Very impressive. I've been thinking. There's this big health-and-beauty expo at the Javits Center in September. We should get a booth there. Retail outlets, e-tailers, and mail-order catalogues all go. It's major exposure."

"Those booths are really expensive. Maybe we should start a little smaller with, say, the Renegade Craft Fair in Williamsburg," said Holly. "It's coming up in June."

"Yeah, I guess I'm getting ahead of myself. If you're ready to get to work, so am I," I said, rolling up my shirtsleeves, confident that the business side of things was starting to gel. I held up a small vile of cardamom extract. "To Beautyfarm: an apothecary of botanicals and essential oils."

Holly chimed in. "To Beautyfarm: where recipes are made to be broken."

"I don't know if that's the best message to get across," I said.

"Yeah, I guess you're right."

BRIDEZILLAS

A few weeks later, Connie bolted out of her office and stood at my desk. "I think congratulations are in order," she boasted as she flicked a business card onto my desk. It read NANCY RAMEKIN, WEDDING COORDINATOR, CHÂTEAU HOLLOW, MANHASSET, LONG ISLAND. "I've finally proposed to Kris, and she has very wisely accepted. Marnie, you will be closely involved in organizing this auspicious event."

"Congratulations," I said through clenched teeth, wondering how much work this would entail.

"Set up some face time with this wed-co woman,"

she shouted from her office. "Just make sure it's not on Kris's carpool day."

I grabbed a steno pad and went into Connie's office. "Château Hollow. I've heard of that place. Isn't that where Rosie and Kelli got married?"

"Rosie's the one who told us about it."

I guessed high-powered lesbians shared recipes like everyone else.

"And according to Rosie," Connie continued, "the place is very Kris. English manor house, roaring fireplaces, a jaunty equestrian theme, sorbet between courses. A real class act. Kris wants an *InStyle*-style wedding."

"Do you have a date set?"

"No, but we need to nail it down. Kris wants a biological baby, but she doesn't want a shotgun wedding, so we need to get married ASAP before we turkey-baste her."

Shotgun wedding? Jeez. Lesbians were becoming more old-fashioned than us straights.

When I got back to my desk after lunch, my message light was blinking. It was my dad again. He was calling me two to three times a day now. He was my new BFF, and since Trudy's death, I felt a strong desire to protect him. He was so fragile. Isn't that what happens in the bittersweet cycle of life? The child becomes the protector and parent.

"Your father's packed on a few pounds, so I've been using Trudy's TrimSpa. It's just loaded with hoodia," he said. "Which is evidently an appetite suppressant. I haven't been hungry in days."

"Is that stuff safe?" I asked.

"Sure it is, kiddo. Should I send you some? It's giving me lots of pizzazz."

"Thanks, Dad, no. What else is going on?" I asked.

"I've been out looking for another Trudy."

"You're ready to date so soon?"

"No, it's not like that. Kiki's Hideaway called. They want me to continue the act, so I'm auditioning singers."

"You've really got your work cut out for you. Trudy was one of a kind."

My dad began to cry. *Extract foot from mouth*. I quickly said good-bye as I saw Tinsley storming out of her office.

That week, when Billy the IT guy was fixing a problem with my Web browser, he accidentally gave me access to Connie's e-mail account. Now I no longer had to imagine her well-heeled domesticated life; I got to vicariously live it. It was like Billy had inadvertently given a ravenous voyeur a pair of night-vision goggles.

Right after they met with the wedding planner, frenetic emails began flying between Kris and Connie.

```
Conster:
Have Marnie "Starr Jones" around
for our wedding gift bags. Also, we
haven't really talked about The Di-
amond, but have Marnie make a prelim
call to Harry Winston's PR girl and
press them about some sort of makeup
trade for life.

In addition, do you still have an
in at Le Cirque? Sirio could do our
catering—I'm sure he's got a large
family in Italy that needs shampoo,
etc. It would also be nice to have
```

a really great singer at our wedding. Not some middle-aged guy from
Queens who teaches trig by day.

Connie responded with:

Dear Kris:
Get off my case about Marnie. She
has other work to do besides planning the Wedding of the Century.
The makeup trade doesn't seem to be
working. Pepperidge Farm will donate a giant fishbowl of cheddar
crackers for cocktail hour, and
that's it!

A few days later, I stayed late to work on Connie's
ever-growing wedding invite list. After she left for the
evening, I eagerly dipped into her e-mails. I was so
ready to punch Kris out.

Condiment:
Regarding your interest in inviting
Marnie—it all depends on my elderly
Aunt Pyper, who really counts for
two because we'll have to invite
her caregiver.☹ Does Marnie have a
special someone in her life? I hope
not, because you wouldn't believe
how expensive salmon is! I'm putting "wild" on the menu, but actually it's farm-raised. Mum's the
word, 'kay? Let's make sure you & I
order the chicken!

Brainstorm: If we invite Marnie
only to the ceremony, the money we
save on her meal can go toward a
vodka ice luge or the sign language
interpreter—your choice.

FYI—If you feel obligated to invite
certain coworkers, pls consult me
first. Anyone prone to table dancing
(we heard about Juniper & the
breast pump) may pose a threat to
the fragile wedding ecosystem and
must be expunged from the list.

Kris was such a crazy bitch. Who needed her pol-
luted PCB salmon anyway! I tried to get my work done,
but her e-mails kept rolling in.

Conman:
I've begun the arduous task of con-
vincing my Smith classmates (aka
the bridesmaids) that the petal
pink, strapless mini sheath from
the JLo collection is in fact age-
appropriate. I emailed Rhonda some
pix, and she is claiming that we
are infantilizing her (in addition
to being uniformist, conformist,
patriarchal, and size-ist!). She's
rescinded the hallowed position of
maid of honor. I'm terrified she'll
call Joan, LuAnn, and Marge and
create some sort of mass walkout.
Might want to look into backups! Do

you think Marnie could pinch-hit if
need be? What's her dress size?

PS—Have Marnie order two sets of
bride-&-groom figurines from Wal-
mart.com. I read in Real Simple
that you can saw them in half and
glue the two brides together!

PPS—I was thinking from now until
our big day, you should switch over
to lite beer. Just a thought.

When I got to work the next morning, Juniper came
running to my desk in tears. Her face was red and
puffy. "Did you hear? Did you hear?"

"Hear what?" I asked.

"Juan is dead!"

A shiver ran down my spine. This place was turning
into a *Law & Order* episode. First Charlotte Warlick was
in a coma, and now Juan was dead.

"What happened?" I asked.

"I don't know. I saw them taking him away. He was
slumped over Pampa's makeup counter." Pampa was
Gentry's replacement after Gentry had gone up the river.

Murfy and Jarret joined us. "What do you think he
was doing at the makeup counter?" Murfy wondered.

"Maybe he was leaving some mail for Pampa and he
had some sort of congenital heart condition and had a
massive coronary," I said, having a Nancy Drew moment.

"With his naked booty sticking up in the air?" asked
Jarret.

"What? His pants were down?" I asked, my interest
more than piqued.

"Yes, I saw it with my own eyes right before they put him in the body bag," Murfy said.

"He had the cutest rear imaginable," added Juniper.

"Beyond," Jarret said.

"Let's go take a look," I said as the four of us rushed over to the area. Cops were crawling all over the crime scene, and the place had been cordoned off with yellow tape. There was even a chalk outline where Juan's prone body had been lying.

"I heard a detective say it happened some time last night," whispered Juniper.

"Look at all that blood," I said, pointing to a coagulating pool on the makeup counter.

"They found him with a blush brush plunged right through his eye," Jarret revealed.

Poor Juan. What a way to go, I thought. The blood was pooled around a cluster of brushes in a tester unit, their pointy wooden tips sticking upward. "Maybe he had a stroke or something, fell over the tester unit, and the blush brush impaled him through the eye," I said. I looked over at Juan's mail cart. It was cast off to the side, alone and unattended. "But why were his pants down?" I wondered.

"Maybe he was receiving fellatio and something went wrong. Very wrong," said Murfy.

"Fellatio from Pampa?" I said.

"I hope not," said Juniper uneasily.

"Do you think it was Summer? Haven't you seen those two carousing around? Lord knows I have," Jarret said.

"That slut's finally going to get hers," hissed Juniper.

"Or maybe he was murdered," I offered offhandedly.

"Don't even go there," Juniper said.

"Whoa. That's heavy, Marnie," Murfy said, backing up a few paces.

"Don't look at me," said Jarret.

"Don't look at me," Juniper said, wiping away her tears.

Then they all stared at me. "Well, don't look at me either," I retorted.

Somehow word had leaked out about Summer and Juan's affair, and reporters were calling, wanting to know the dirt, insinuating that she had screwed him to death. The *New York Post* had Summer on the cover, coolly shrugging her shoulders in a "don't look at me" pose. The headline read I DIDN'T DO IT! I WAS DOLLED UP ON TYLENOL PM!

I wondered who had squealed to the press. It might have been anyone on the floor. Summer and Juan hadn't exactly been discreet.

Juan's death put Connie over the edge. This was worse than Charlotte Warlick's coma. Juan had died in the LeVigne offices under mysterious circumstances, and the press had made Summer their prime suspect. Connie was afraid that Summer's Gene Cream would sink under the weight of this mushrooming scandal. By now, Ronson had probably stolen the DNA formula and was getting ready to launch its own cream.

I sat at my desk in a daze. It was beginning to feel like the LeVigne offices were cursed. Were the offices built on ancient Indian burial grounds? I kept looking over my shoulder, afraid of what would happen next.

Sidney, Summer, and her high-powered attorney marched by my desk.

"Daddy, please. I know who I blow, thank you very much," Summer said as Connie hustled them into her office and shut the door.

That night I stayed over at Paul's and told him the story. I told him how Juan had always been so nice to me, and that although the coroner's report was not back yet, there were rumors that he had been murdered. Paul could see how shaken up I was about it, and we stayed up for hours talking through all kinds of scenarios and possibilities.

"Marnie, you realize you might have been there when it happened."

"What?"

"Didn't you tell me the cops said it happened last night? What time did you get over here?"

I jumped out of bed. "You're not thinking I did it?"

"What, are you nuts? Of course not, baby. It's just that they'll probably question everyone who was anywhere near the crime scene last night."

The next morning, Summer was brought down to the precinct for questioning, and it turned out that her alibi was pat. The detectives had reviewed her Park Avenue co-op's surveillance tapes and, sure enough, she was seen entering the lobby at five P.M., laden with shopping bags, and she hadn't left until the following morning. Unbelievably, it was the first night in years Summer had stayed at home. If Summer, the obvious suspect, was off the hook, then who had done it? Maybe Juan's girlfriend had found out about his affair with Summer, and she'd killed him. I was a little nervous, because if they questioned me, I had no alibi. And I signed out in the security log book, so there would be no point in lying and saying that I had left work earlier. I wanted to tell my dad, but I didn't want to worry him unnecessarily. With Trudy's death, he had a lot on his plate.

Connie escorted a detective down the hall. He was big and burly and very intimidating. They stopped at Juniper's desk, and the detective stared at her.

"Please don't arrest me," Juniper begged. "Juan and I only fooled around. Once. In the service elevator. Okay, and once again in the messenger center, but I didn't off him. I swear I didn't."

"Ma'am, thanks for the confession, but that's not why I'm here," he said.

"What?" Juniper said in an embarrassed voice that was ten octaves too high. "Well, forget what I just said, then. Scratch it from the record."

"Tell it to the court reporter," the cop said snidely. "Okay, everybody. Listen up. I'm taking you all to the station for questioning. Two at a time."

Of course Tinsley had lucked out. She was away in Austria on a communications-free mountaineering trip. The bitch was off the hook.

"We have a wedding to plan," Connie shouted as she and I were hauled off to the station house together.

After a grueling interrogation in a dirty tiled room, I was required to give a saliva sample. Apparently they'd found DNA on Juan's genital area, and it needed to be matched. Due to the physiological state of Juan's exposed penis at the time of rigor mortis and the way he had fallen, forensics determined that someone had probably been underneath the makeup counter, giving him oral sex.

Everyone but me had an alibi. Juniper and Murfy had been at the Park Avenue Borders, listening to Lauren Weisberger read from her new book. Jarret had been pumping iron at the gym. Saskia had been at the Learning Annex, taking a class called "How to Cash in on Costa Rican Real Estate." Connie had been at an autism charity ball. "And furthermore," Connie said, recounting her shakedown at the precinct, "I haven't done that kind of thing to a trouser snake since '71 when I was tripping on acid."

Sidney, Marion, and Rebecca had alibis too: They had all been in the building at nine P.M., but they were huddled together in Sidney's office in a family therapy session with a Jungian shrink.

I called my father in a panic, telling him the abridged version of the story. I told him that they took my DNA, but I left out the part about the blow job.

"You're not telling me something," he said sternly.

Did he know this because of his years as a trial attorney or because I was his daughter? I begrudgingly told him about Juan's dropped trou.

"You must tell me the truth, Marnie. Were you or were you not intimate with this man Juan?" he asked.

"That's a ridiculous question. Of course I wasn't. I would never cheat on Paul."

"Then listen, Marnie. Don't worry. There's nothing they can do to you. If you weren't at the scene of the crime, your DNA can't be on him. They'll find the guilty party. I'm going to e-mail you the name of a very good lawyer friend in the city. If you should need him, do not hesitate to call."

"Okay," I said apprehensively.

"I love you, Marn," my dad said. "Keep the faith. I know it's hard, but try and relax."

The talk with my dad helped, but even still, I really wanted to talk to Holly. Regrettably, she was away on a midnight parrot rescue at a Queens pet shop. Then Paul called to say that everything was going to be all right. I tossed and turned all night, hoping that when the DNA results came back, the true culprit would be revealed.

Defense Mechanism

As my butt hit my chair a few days later, Connie called me into her office. A detective was sitting in her guest chair. My heart raced, and my palms began to drip cold sweat.

"Marnie, I wish I could make this easier for you," said Connie. "So let me give it to you straight. They found you all over Juan."

"What? That's impossible! Connie, it must be a mistake. You've got to believe me. Yes, I worked late that night on your wedding list, but I never went near the makeup counter, and I never saw Juan."

The detective got up. "I'm sorry, Ms. Mann, but we've got to take you back down for more questioning," he said.

"This is ridiculous! I was at my desk and then I went to my boyfriend's house."

"There is incontrovertible evidence, Marnie. Your DNA was found all over Juan's body, and it was concentrated around"—Connie gagged a little—"his . . . his . . . johnson."

"That's impossible. I need to use the phone," I said. "I want to call my lawyer."

Connie and the detective stepped out to give me some privacy. I called Barry Tanner, my father's lawyer friend. Then the detective came back in and escorted me down the hall. This was the perp walk, the walk of shame, as all the CAPs jeered and stared at me.

"You didn't have to kill him," hissed Juniper.

"I didn't do anything," I yelled back at her. "It wasn't me."

Now that I was a suspect in a potential murder, the second interrogation was far more brutal than the first. Thank God Barry Tanner was with me. I stuck by my story, and they couldn't arrest me because they were still awaiting the autopsy report. There was still a chance that Juan had died accidentally.

The next morning, Tinsley returned from her Austrian vacation looking trimmer and more rested than she deserved to be. She told us with much bravado that she had been stuck in an avalanche but somehow survived.

Juniper and Murfy went into Tinsley's office to fill her in on all the tawdry news. All I could hear was, "Marnie . . . ssssp . . . ssssp . . . Marnie."

"You're still here?" Tinsley said when she stopped at my desk later on. "It's a shame about Juan, but when I look at the bigger picture, he never picked up my FedExes on time," she said. "Please hold all my calls this morning. I've got a gazillion e-mails to go through." And then she went back to her office.

An hour later, Tinsley let out a shriek and buzzed me on the phone. "I need to speak to Connie immediately. There's something she needs to . . ." she shouted as my phone cord somehow dislodged itself and the phone went dead.

Shit, I thought as I scrambled to reconnect the cord, but by then Tinsley had stormed out of the office. Why did she need to speak to Connie so desperately? Did she know something? Were they coming to haul my ass off, and she didn't want to be here when it happened? Maybe I should sneak away. Dye my hair. Get a one-way ticket to Mexico. Go Greyhound.

I snuck into Tinsley's office. Her computer was in sleep mode, but it would take just the tap of a key, any key, to see what was on her screen. I hit "b" for bitch. Sure enough, a startling e-mail popped up. It was from Rebecca to Summer, and it had been sent two days before Juan's death.

Hey Summy Sum,
Since you're older and wiser and everything, I have an important girl2girl question 4 ya. Don't laugh, ok??? Yikes. Breathe in. Breathe out. Here it is. Do guys ever pee on you? Listen. Here's the skinny. Juan peed on me when we were fooling around late one night in Daddy's private office bathroom, and it kinda freaked me out. And then he did it again! Besides it being messy and stinky, it just doesn't seem normal.

I tried to Google some info, but I didn't know how to phrase the question ("showers, golden" or "golden" and "showers"??), so that's why I'm axing you. Btw, thx 4 your sloppy seconds. For real. Juan's a wild man, mami!

Later, Rebecca

PS—Do you ever get road rage without the road?

Oh my freaking gawd. I was having a hard time wrapping my mind around this. Innocent little Rebecca had been doing the nasty with Juan. It just proved that you could never judge a book by its cover. I closed the e-mail and looked at the list of incoming ones. I noticed that the e-mail right before this was from Rebecca to Tinsley with the subject line "When the hell are we getting ceramic flat irons in the PR bathroom?" Rebecca must have mistakenly sent the one meant for Summer to Tinsley right after the one she really sent to Tinsley. I clicked on the Summer e-mail and printed it out. I needed evidence in case Tinsley tried to delete it to protect Rebecca and frame moi.

I shoved the e-mail into my pocket and went back to my desk. I had to put my thinking cap on. Think. Think. What did this all mean? If Rebecca was having an affair with Juan, and she was the one who gave him the blow job under the makeup counter, how had my DNA gotten on him? How was this possible?

Suddenly it all became crystal clear. It was that day when I was labeling Dr. Von Heedle's Gene Creams. I must have mixed up the labels and given Rebecca my jar by mistake. I'd felt feverish that morning, but when I called Tinsley from home, she'd made me come in anyway.

I raced down the hall to Rebecca's office. That little bitch was trying to make me take the fall, but she was sorely mistaken. Luckily she wasn't there, but her jar of Gene Cream (with my DNA in it!) was sitting on her desk. I swiped it and marched into Connie's office. She was back from her meeting. "Rebecca did it," I said, holding the jar and the e-mail in the air, my two pieces of incontrovertible evidence.

"What the hell are you saying, Marnie?" asked Connie. "Who are you to make such defamatory accusations? Your DNA was all over Juan, and when the autopsy comes back, you may very well be arrested. But first, did you get the estimates from the florist and the DJ? I need to give them to Kris."

"Not so fast, Connie. Innocent until proven guilty," I said, slamming the jar down on her desk. "It's Rebecca's DNA all over Juan. I figured out what happened. When I got the creams back from Vector 21, I must have mixed up my jar with Rebecca's. I was just in her office and I took this off her desk. It has my DNA in it. I'm sure of it. And the cream I've been using—it must have her DNA."

"How can you be so certain?"

"Go test it."

Connie shook her head. "How do I know you're telling the truth? You could have switched the jars, putting yours in her office and vice versa."

"There's more. Here, read this," I said, pushing the e-mail into her hand.

Connie turned white as she scanned it. "What the hell is going on here?" she yelled.

"Rebecca accidentally sent that e-mail to Tinsley, and apparently it was sitting in Tinsley's Outlook inbox while she was on her communications-free vacation. She opened it this morning."

"Then why didn't Tinsley come forward and tell me about this?"

"Because she hates me and she probably had a Ferragamo sample sale."

"Get Tinsley in here now."

"She's not back yet," I said.

Connie tried to get her on her cell, but Tinsley didn't answer. When Tinsley finally returned, Connie had me tell her the whole sordid story. The first thing Tinsley did was scold me for snooping on her computer. Then Connie called Sidney in and told him everything. He was beyond irate, dragging me down to Rebecca's office. When we got there, Rebecca was playing Tetris on her computer and licking the inside of a Splenda packet.

"What up, Daddy-o?" asked Rebecca.

"Marnie has something she'd like to tell you," said Sidney, trying to control his temper.

I clenched my fists, trying not to lunge across the desk and rip her hair out. That little bitch was not going to let me take the fall. Oh no no no.

I cleared my throat. "Rebecca, I think I've been using your Gene Cream and you've been using mine," I said calmly.

Rebecca's defenses immediately went up. "I don't think so, you ugly crack-whore bitch! Why would I want your raggedy-ass lowlife DNA all over my body?"

This was the classic cycle of abuse. Just as Sidney and Marion had told Rebecca that no one wanted her DNA, she was telling me the same.

"Calm down, daughter," said Sidney. "What Marnie is trying to say is that there was an apparent mix-up. Your cream was switched with hers. A labeling mistake."

"What kind of retards are you hiring here, Dad?" Rebecca exclaimed.

"Let's bottom-line this, Rebecca. If Marnie is correct, that would be why her DNA was found on Juan's, well, you know . . ." he said.

"That doesn't mean anything. How do you know she's not framing me?" asked Rebecca.

"Unfortunately there's more," said Sidney, sliding Rebecca's damning e-mail across her desk.

"I'm bulletproof," Rebecca said, waving it away.

"Goddamn it, child! Read it!" roared Sidney.

Rebecca took one look at the e-mail and gasped. She tore it into tiny little pieces, shoved it in her mouth, and attempted to swallow it.

Sidney rushed over to Rebecca. "Spit that out," he said, trying to make her cough it up. "That's going to make you sick."

"I need to get sick. I had curly fries for lunch."

"Stop it, Rebecca," Sidney said, trying to pry his daughter's mouth open.

Rebecca finally spat it out into the trash. "Did Summer give you the e-mail?" she asked Sidney.

"She never received it," said Sidney. "Apparently you sent it to Tinsley by mistake."

Rebecca got up and paced the room, sliding into one major meltdown. "Oh shit, oh shit, oh shit. No one pees on a LeVigne! And gets away with it. No one!" She collapsed on the floor and curled up into a shivering little ball. "I didn't mean to kill him. I didn't mean to push him that hard. It was an accident."

Sidney tried to shush her. "Don't talk until your lawyer is present," he said.

Just then the attorney that had been representing Summer and a detective appeared at the door.

"It's not me! I didn't do anything!" shouted Rebecca. "It's Marnie. She did it," she shrieked, trying to run out of her office. Sidney grabbed her arm.

"Please don't send me to Grandma's!" she screamed as Sidney dragged her down the hall. "I'll go wherever you say, but just not there."

So it was true. Hattie was alive! But how alive? Was she a spry ninety-year-old, or a recluse in a wheelchair with the curtains drawn? Now that we were launching Beautyfarm, I wanted so badly to meet her. I had so many questions racing through my mind about starting a skin care business.

When I got back to my desk, Juniper and Murfy seemed disturbingly disappointed by my innocence. I called my dad. I told him all about Rebecca and what really happened. "That's great news, Marnie. Those makeup heirs just keep getting in trouble, don't they?"

Then I called Paul to tell him the good news. I had been exonerated!

"That's so great, Marn," he purred. "I knew they'd figure it all out. I'm craving a glass of wine, a piece of Roquefort, and you."

"I hope not in that order," I replied.

He laughed. "I have a proposition for you. In two weeks from now, I'm going out to Wisconsin on a cheese buying trip. I'm planning on staying with my parents. Would you like to come?"

"I'd love to," I said excitedly. I wanted to ask him whether, in addition to this being a business trip, it was also a Meet the Parents journey. But I lost my nerve.

After work, I went to Barnes & Noble and bought a Cantonese phrase book.

BREAKING THE MOLD

Holly and I were in her kitchen, poring over a bunch of soap-making books. We were attempting to make shea butter soap, which helps heal dry and scaly skin.

"What do you think about using royal jelly?" I asked, munching on a chocolate Easter bunny. "It's supposed to have amazing healing properties."

"We can't use it. It's made with honey," Holly replied.

"Refresh my memory. What's wrong with honey?"

"The bees make it. You see, with bees, it's an unfair division of labor. It's forty thousand workers to one queen. Marn, I thought we were in agreement on using only fair labor practices."

"Sorry," I said.

As I worked, I channeled the young Hattie and recalled the scratchy black-and-white footage of her bubbling kitchen laboratory.

On the counter, I set out all the instruments and equipment I had purchased from a supply company in Queens: a seven-quart enamel kettle, wooden spoons, a thermometer, and plastic molds. In Holly's well-ventilated kitchen, she and I donned protective goggles, dust masks, heavy rubber aprons, and latex gloves. We spent the day melting, mixing, and melding, using grape seed oil, almond meal, and shea butter as a moisturizing base.

I stirred the mixture nice and slowly until I thought my hand was going to fall off. After about an hour, when the consistency became satiny and puddinglike, it had successfully reached saponification. Now we were ready to add scents and color. We used burnt brown sugar for a coloring agent and a few drops of rose geranium oil and lime basil for scent. We poured the soap batches into plastic ice cube trays to harden for twenty-four hours.

"Did you hear that they found a three-thousand-year-old moisturizer in King Tut's tomb made out of animal fat and perfumed resin?" I asked Holly. "Think about what they'll find in our coffins in the next three thousand: silicone boob bags, pacemakers, tooth veneers."

"And hair extensions, cheek implants, and hip replacements," Holly said, continuing the list. "Kinda freaky, huh?"

"We're plastic fantastic, girl," I said.

After we finished the soap, we took a quick coffee break, then made moisturizer using beeswax with olive oil, which we melted into a velvety paste, adding rose water and senna leaf. (After much hand-wringing, Holly agreed to use beeswax: even though it's an animal derivative, neither the bees nor the hive are harmed when it's removed.)

Holly and I peered into the living room. Dwayne was sound asleep in front of the tube. "Perfect," she whispered with sadistic glee.

We snuck in and smeared cream all over his face. By the time I left, it was one A.M. I was exhausted, and Holly's kitchen was as sticky as I'd ever seen it.

Things finally calmed down at work. Juan's death was ruled an accident, and Rebecca was shipped off to an undisclosed location. But something didn't make sense to me. At the time of Juan's death, Rebecca was purported to have been in a family therapy session in Sidney's office. I never understood how she could have been in two places at one time. It was later revealed that, as part of Sidney, Marion, and Rebecca's therapy sessions, the shrink often hypnotized them. The night Juan died, Rebecca snuck out and rendezvoused with him while Sidney and Marion were under and the shrink was catnapping. Another mystery solved!

Even though I had been cleared of all charges, Tinsley—and to a lesser extent Juniper and Murfy—still treated me like a criminal. It crystallized my decision to leave the job. I planned to stay a little while longer to bank more money for Beautyfarm, and then I'd bid them all adieu.

As Connie and Kris's wedding date drew closer, a

beautiful and mysterious woman named Ming suddenly began calling Connie. The more Ming called, the
less Connie took Kris's calls. "Business before pleasure," Connie hummed brightly as I took messages
from a huffy Kris.

When Ming, Connie's spring fling, came to the office, I
could see why Connie had fallen for her. She was a stunning Eurasian woman with a simple, understated style.
That first day, she wore a crisp white shirt, perfectly worn-
in butt-hugging Levi's, and a pair of gorgeous leather flats
that looked handmade and très expensive. Connie ushered Ming into her office and shut the door. Three hours
later, the door burst open and Connie whisked a tousled
Ming, shirttails out, down the hall to the elevator.

Things had been quiet on the e-mail front until Ming
appeared, and now they were heating up again. One
afternoon an e-mail came in from Ming to Connie:

```
You can book the lair for tonite.
```

Oh my God. Connie was about to get married. Was
she getting cold loafers? Kris must have had a vibe
about Connie's betrayal, because her e-mails became
even more insecure and pleading.

```
Conch shell:
Just wanted to let you know that
I'm back safe and sound from my
skin peel. Dr. Lurvey says I'll be
"restaurant ready" in about three
days. Hint, hint: I'm craving Nobu.
The girls aren't handling my hugely
swollen face very well. They
screamed when they saw me and are
```

```
presently hiding under Bernice's
bed. So bring home some carob bars
for them, will ya?
Luv, your soon-to-be-glowing wifey-
poo
```

I felt worse for the kids. Couldn't they at least get Fudgsicles? And then this doozy came in:

```
Con-dodo:
I forgot to tell you. When I was
walking the girls to school, Seiko
said, "Brita and I don't like you
anymore. We want to go back to
mainland China." Needless to say, I
have a double with Dr. Apfelbaum.
```

Shit. Which reminded me, I had to pay her shrink bill.

The next morning, Connie was as chipper as ever. She even complimented me on my hair. As she walked into her office, she dumped two receipts from the decidedly downscale Milford Plaza Hotel on my desk. One was from the Lullaby of Broadway lounge, with "dinner" scrawled on it. "Dinner" had consisted of two shots of Wild Turkey. And the other receipt was for room 201. . . . This must have been the "lair."

Sensing something was awry, Kris really let Connie have it:

```
Constance Craving:
I didn't appreciate you sneaking in
and sleeping in the guest room last
night. I know I look scary, but
```

you're supposed to be there for me
while my face heals. I really needed
my mojo humming! Can you come home
early on Thursday? I have scream
therapy, and it's Bernice's night
off. The girls really miss you.

Kris, face the music—she's just not that into you.
Meanwhile, e-mails between Ming and Connie were
flowing at a rapid clip.
Ming wrote:

Miss your little yoni already. Na-
maste.

Connie responded with:

Miss you too, my little tomato.

Ming answered:

Tomatoes are nightshade veggies
and I'm deathly allergic to them.
See you at the lair tonight. But
don't forget: fingernails!

"Goddamn her," Connie screamed. I minimized my
screen a millisecond before Connie barreled over to
my desk. She was holding the strap of her Coach sad-
dlebag with pincered fingers and sadistically dropped
the heavy deadweight into my lap. "I got French tips
put on for the 2008 Hillary fundraiser, and my nails are
still wet. Open up my wallet, take out a twenty, get me

some sugar-free Binaca spray, and buy yourself one. Do you ever smell meat on my breath?" she asked as she threw an imaginary football at my head and disappeared into her office.

In one e-mail to Ming, Connie impudently suggested that while Kris was away on a three-day Civil War reenactment, Connie would take a train trip with the girls and secretly book a berth next to theirs for Ming. Her life was turning into a perilous *North by Northwest*. I thought about forwarding the message on to poor clueless Kris. She deserved to be warned, especially after Connie said in an e-mail to Ming that she'd prefer the girls had an Asian mother.

But Kris found out soon enough. Later in the week, she discovered a love note from Ming in Connie's suit jacket, and she went berserk, calling Connie over a hundred times in a row, which subsequently shut down the entire LeVigne phone system. When it was up and running again, Kris called me and began to sob. She started in on a long, meandering rant about her "suspicions" and how Connie had had affairs before. She said she wanted to lock herself in her study and do something really self-destructive . . . like eat a Kozy Shack pudding four-pack. When I finally talked her down from this vomit-inducing cry for help, I realized that some training in hostage negotiation might have been useful in this loony bin. She told me that Connie had moved into the guest room and they were consulting a divorce attorney. Just great. After all my hard work, their "special day" had been cancelled.

Though the wedding bells had been silenced, there was no stopping a baby. The following week, a bloodcurdling wail sailed out of Diana's office. Jarret skipped by my desk, waving a pair of latex examining gloves in the air. "God bless the child who got his own," he crooned like Billie Holiday. "Marnie, we're about to deliver a baby!"

He handed me a bunch of trash bags, and I jogged behind him. As I passed Jarret's office, his phone rang. Like a good secretary, I went in and picked it up.

"Jarret Andrew's office," I said officiously.

"Tell him his shoes are shined and he can pick them up at the Cobbler," said a creepy male voice. The guy hung up before I could ask who was calling.

When I got to Diana's office, she was lying on the floor, writhing in pain, but not only because of her impending childbirth. "That cipher's going to destroy us! Schotzie's launching a teen acne line just like ours. He stole all our kids!" she screamed, checking her lipstick in the reflection of her desk's metal leg.

I hovered over Diana, and she grabbed my arm. "Marnie, get Legal on the phone. We've been cannibalized!" she yelled.

As the paramedics arrived, Diana reached for her Balenciaga weekender and pulled out a wad of cash.

"Diana, put your money away. You don't tip EMTs," I instructed.

"I would. They're pretty hot," Jarret said, cruising the guys.

"Shut up, you idiots," Diana whimpered, holding up a wad of bills. "This is Schotzie's pimple cream designed like a squeezable stack of cash. It's called 'Pimps n' Holes for Jills n' Johns'. It smells like Crest, because kids put toothpaste on their zits. We're sunk," she cried as she blacked out.

After Diana was put on a stretcher and carted away,

I walked back with Jarret to his office and reminded him to pick up his shoes at the Cobbler.

"Thanks, Marn. And by the way, I'm calling in sick tomorrow. Lifetime's running a *Golden Girls* marathon."

The next morning, there was a commotion outside of Jarret's office.

"What a perv!" Murfy screamed. She and Juniper were clutching a bunch of photographs.

"Marnie, you're not going to believe what your freaky friend did," said Juniper, shoving the pictures into my hand. My eyes widened as I looked at a series of pornographic stills. Jarret had photoshopped various CAPs' heads onto the bodies of some morbidly obese women. There was even one of Tinsley's head on the body of an SS guard. Jarret skewered Connie by creating a portrait of her using a thousand tiny penis images, and there was a picture of Kris in a pilgrim bonnet, performing a lewd act on a butter churner.

"What a sicko!" I feigned, playing along, secretly thinking that the pictures were utterly hilarious, but in a weird way, I felt kind of left out that he hadn't skewered me too.

MANN-CHURIAN CANDIDATE

I wanted so much for Paul's parents to like me. I tried to imagine how they would react to me, a Jewish-Italian girl whose only experience with things Chinese was eating at Ah Fong's on Ventura Boulevard every Sunday night growing up.

As I packed for the trip to Wisconsin, a dream from

the night before popped into my head. Paul had proposed to me in front of his parents. "Chinese people believe in fate," said his father, Eddie Shun, upon hearing
the joyous news. "Evidently it is my son's destiny to
marry someone international." My prospective new
name came to mind: Marnie Mann-Shun. How posh. I'd
be Marnie Mansion. Trudy would have liked that. I envisioned myself as an international woman of mystery
wearing a white patent leather Courrèges minidress and
zipping around Wisconsin in a vintage Aston Martin.

After an hour's delay at Kennedy, Paul and I were finally airborne. The flight got bumpy and I ordered a
vodka tonic, sucking it down in one thirsty gulp.

"You seem really nervous, Marnie. Is it the turbu-
lence?"

I told him I was nervous about meeting his parents,
which was certainly part of the story.

"Don't worry. My parents are going to love you. It's just
that the last time I brought a girl—" He cut himself off.

"Did Kendra meet your parents?"

"Yeah, and it was a total disaster. She tried to get all
Chinese on them."

*There goes that twenty-six-dollar Cantonese phrase
book,* I thought.

Actually, some of my anxiety had to do with the fact
that Jarret had been fired that morning. Everyone assumed it was because of the porno pictures, but I was
convinced that he had been spying for Ronson. Thinking back on it, I wondered whether his getting his
shoes shined at the Cobbler was some kind of code for
going across the street to Ronson's office. And Jarret always did wear Schotzie cologne. Would someone discover that I had given him the AKNY Blemish Brigade
finalist photos? That must have been how Ronson had

stolen the kids away. I was totally skeeved out. He had completely duped me, and now I might get booted before I had saved up my goal amount for Beautyfarm. I had aided and abetted a mole!

As we walked through the Madison airport, I pushed all the worrisome thoughts out of my mind, straightened my posture, and put on a big, happy face. I wanted very much to make a good impression on Paul's parents. Eddie Shun was not hard to spot. He was the only Chinese person in a sea of large-boned blonds. Paul looked just like his father, so I knew exactly what Paul would look like when he got older: handsome and distinguished. Annamarie Shun was a foot taller than Eddie, an attractive, sturdy woman with a gray bob and a face refreshingly free of makeup.

"Marnie, we've heard all about you," Eddie said. He gave me a warm hug. I went to hug Annamarie, and she backed away.

"Zionist problem," she mumbled, wincing and holding her head in her hands.

I was sickened. Paul's mother was an anti-Semite and she wasn't even trying to hide it. But wait a minute. She was Dutch. Hadn't Holland harbored Jews during World War Two? This was truly horrible. How was I going to spend the next three days with her? I was tempted to run back into the terminal and take the next flight home.

Annamarie leaned her head on Paul's shoulder as we walked to the parking lot. I was furious at her. And at him! How could Paul let her touch him after what she said to me?

"What's wrong?" Paul asked as we got into their rusty, trusty Subaru wagon.

"Your mother wouldn't hug me. She says she has a Zionist problem," I whispered.

Paul laughed. "A sinus problem, silly. The pollen gives her headaches."

Oh my God. I felt like such an idiot. When we got back to their 1960s ranch–style house, Annamarie excused herself and went to lie down before preparing dinner.

Dinner was a delicious garlicky feast. It was better than any Chinese food I'd ever eaten in a restaurant. No gloopy sauces. No cornstarch. Nothing breaded. I told them that my Bat Mitzvah had been catered by a kosher Chinese restaurant called Shang-Chai, and that in Hebrew *chai* means "living." I didn't tell them that Dwayne facetiously called Hunan Delight, our neighborhood Chinese joint, *Human* Delight because they served meat.

"Do you work in cheese too?" asked Annamarie.

"No, I work for a cosmetics company—which reminds me, I have something for both of you." I rushed into the bedroom and came back out with two gift bags, one for Annamarie and one for Eddie.

"Thank you, Marnie," they said in unison as they excitedly rooted through their bags. Eddie pulled out a bottle of Sidney from his.

"What about a cologne called 'Eddie'?" he snickered, liberally spraying the toxic stuff all over himself.

Eddie's quirkiness reminded me of my father, and Paul reminded me of Eddie. Did I have an Oedi-Paul complex?

After dinner, Paul and I did the dishes. "Marnie, come see," shouted Annamarie from her bedroom. When I went in, Annamarie was at her dresser, neatly lining up the creams and colors I had given her. "I don't usually wear makeup, but tomorrow will you do me?" she asked.

"Absolutely," I said.

Annamarie took my hand, and we sat down on the bed. "Do you think you two will get married?" she asked.

"Maybe someday, but first I think we should move in together. See how that goes."

"That makes sense. I'm happy Paul found such a wonderful woman."

"Thank you, Annamarie."

"Please call me Ma."

I smiled, so happy to have her blessing. After we said our good-nights, Paul and I retired to his bedroom. He went into the bathroom to wash up, and he came out looking like a samurai warrior in a white bathrobe and shower sandals. We both climbed into our respective race car beds, left over from Paul's childhood. I was PMSing and horny, so I tried to carjack my way into his, but the bed was too small to cuddle and there was no point in pushing them together, since they were their own self-contained units.

In the morning, I surreptitiously downed a couple of Lactaid tablets, and we motored to the first farm. Despite the beautiful May day, Paul was not in the best mood, but I tried to ignore this. Cedar Tree Farms was on 140 acres of lush rolling hills that were used as sheep-grazing pastures. Their specialty was a robust sheep's-milk cheese that was aged in cedar-planked caves.

While Pia and Bob, the owners of the farm, took a real shine to Paul, their sheepherding collie took an annoying shine to me. Probably because I had just gotten my period. We went into the tasting room and sampled some cheese. "Pure heaven," said Paul, trying a Bergere Bleue, a sheep's-milk blue cheese.

"Um. Yum," I stiffly added, coughing up some phlegm. Paul shot me a look and then gazed beatifically at pretty, big-boned Pia. "Cheese this addictive should only be served with a doctor's prescription," Paul teased.

"Your man's a real cheesemonger, ain't he?" Bob said with a wink.

I winced as I rode out a wave of stomach cramps.

Then Paul took a bite of a green, moldy cheese. "It's buttery, but slightly acidic. I taste fruity, earthy undertones with a nutty finish." He sounded like a LeVignette talking about a new perfume. He gave me a piece.

When I thought no one was looking, I flicked the mold off the wedge with my nail.

Pia gently took my hand. "Marnie, you must always remember: furry is your friend," she said.

Paul picked up a wedge of ivory cheese and raised it like a goblet. "Here's to the other white meat," he toasted, explaining how since Caesar's time, cheese has been an important source of protein.

Paul placed a large cheese order for Dean & DeLuca, and in return we each received a "Got Mold?" T-shirt and a sweaty complimentary cheese wheel. Paul had me lug it to the car.

"Not gonna find anything that good at Highland Hills," Bob called out as Paul gunned it down the gravel driveway. "We hear they pump their cows with hormones."

Very catty, I thought. Cheese people were almost as bad as fashionistas.

Highland Hills Cheese Company was run by yet another earthy husband-and-wife team (Darlene and Ron). They made award-winning artisanal cheese from the milk of a single herd of Guernsey cows. "This cheese is patterned after provincial Alpine farmstead cheeses, reminiscent of French Gruyère," said Ron as he gave us a tour of where it was stored.

"Each wheel gets a daily washing, and then it's aged for five months," Darlene proudly added.

It seemed to be their version of Siesta's Parachute fermentation process in the wooden vats. Then it was out to the pasture to admire the herd. The scenery was placid and beautiful, but these bucolic images quickly dissipated as I imagined this plebeian farm life as my own. Getting up with the roosters, constant UV exposure, the subsequent premature aging, chaffed hands from milking, in bed by eight, too tired for whoopee, up with the roosters . . . No, thank you!

"Look at those milkers," cooed Ron. "They're happier and more content than their confined friends at Cedar Tree Farms."

Meeeeow! As we drove to the third and final dairy farm, I began thinking about the possibility of adding a milk-based line to Beautyfarm. It could be a great angle for us.

"Hey, Paul, what do you think about Holly and me making soaps and body creams from dairy?" I excitedly asked without giving him a chance to answer. "After visiting the farms today, I think it could be really cool to make some fromage blanc shampoo. We could put it in mason jars. And goat milk soap wrapped in white butcher paper. Scented bath puddings made with yogurt and the yolk of an egg. And deliciously soothing lemon ricotta foot scrub."

I was getting so carried away, I had almost forgotten I was lactose intolerant. Paul didn't seem to be listening, but I kept at it excitedly. "And I thought with your cheese expertise," I continued, "maybe you could help us formulate some dairy-based products."

Suddenly we were at a dead stop in a traffic jam.

Shriners in go-carts were doing figure eights at the tail end of what looked like a parade. "Damn it," Paul said. "We'll never make it to Milkstone Farms in time."

"Maybe we can squeeze it in tomorrow before we leave," I said as we drove by a mammoth ferris wheel. "Since we're here, why don't we stop at the fair?" I offered brightly, thinking if we had some childish fun, maybe Paul's mood would shift. "Can you call Milkstone and reschedule?"

We parked and got out of the car. Paul found a quiet place to make his call, and I stretched my legs. A few minutes later, Paul came back. "We're not going to Milkstone," he said testily.

What a relief, I thought. "Then can we get some food? I'm starved," I said, laying hungry eyes on a concession stand. "I see fried cheese over there." If anything was going to perk him up, that would. As I stealthily reached into my bag for more Lactaid just in case Paul tried to give me a bite, the strap broke and the bag fell to the ground. The Lactaid bottle rolled out and stopped right between Paul's feet.

"Well, will you look at that," he said, crossing his arms tightly over his chest. "You seem to have dropped your vitamins."

I was so busted. I stood there, speechless. It was a beautiful warm afternoon, but suddenly I was freezing. Happy fairgoing couples walked past us in a colored blur, smiling and holding hands. "Paul, let me explain. I can't do dairy."

"I'm lactose-intolerant intolerant," he shot back.

"What? You don't believe me? There are fifty million Americans in the same boat."

"I don't know what to believe," Paul said, backing away. "You misled me."

"I never meant to. It's just something that got out of hand. That first night, on our first date, I should have told you, but I wanted everything to go just right. And then when you mentioned how Kendra didn't like cheese, you sounded so disappointed that I panicked. It was a little white lie that spiraled out of control."

"What else have you lied to me about?"

"Nothing. I swear."

"You're freaking me out. First the Botox. Now this cheese lie. Your name really suits you, Marnie. Just like Tippi Hedren in the movie. You're an imposter."

"Now that's low," I said.

"At least I don't lie," he said.

"Except for maybe about Sofia," I muttered.

"Who? What?"

"Sofia 'We Talked for Hours and Hours about Chevre' Coppola. Did you forget that sweet little note she sent you about hooking up in New York? I found it in your desk drawer when I was looking for a pen."

"Big deal. Sofia was launching her champagne line and she had a tasting at D & D. I didn't go because I was with you!"

"Paul, it seems every cheese maker you talk about is a woman. There's the Sonoma goat girl, Laura Chenel." I deepened my voice to imitate him. " 'Laura's chèvre is to die for. She's like a goat whisperer,' " I said. "And how about Soyoung Scanlan's Nocturne cheese. 'Soyoung's a shepherd protecting her microbial flocks, but she's also a classically trained pianist.' And let's not forget Sue and Peggy of Cowgirl Creamery. It's like you've fallen in love with them all."

"Marnie, I've fallen in love with their cheeses."

"I mean, even a Benedictine nun isn't off-limits," I said, imitating him again. " 'Marn, you can't believe how Sister Noella uses her microscope to solve cheese problems. She's amazing.' "

Paul looked really angry. He stared at the ground, kicked some dirt with his sneaker, and, after what seemed like an eternity, finally spoke. "So tell me something. What's this about you and me moving in?" he asked.

So this was what he was really mad about. "Did your mother say something to you?"

"No. I was passing by the bedroom and I heard you two scheming up some plan."

"Excuse me, but your mom's the one who brought it up, so don't be so paranoid. I feel like we're in some kind of limbo land. We tell each other we love one another, but there's no real talk about our future. I mean, truth be told, yes, I would like us to move in one day. Wouldn't you?"

"I don't know. This is taking me off guard. I like where we're at. At least for right now. Look, I'm not feeling financially secure yet. When I go out on my own as a cheese consultant, it's going to be risky. It means I have to quit my job, and I won't have a steady salary for a while. If I'm going to start a life with someone, I want to bank some money first. I want to have my ducks in a row."

Paul walked over to the concession stand and got in line. It was amazing. Even after his coldhearted honesty, he still had an appetite. How could he eat anything at a time like this? I couldn't imagine ever eating again. They would have to hook me up to a feeding tube. Paul bought me a lemonade, and when I saw the Sweetheart brand name on the cup's plastic lid, I threw the cup in the trash. Just seeing the word "sweetheart" made me want to sob. Was he even my sweetheart anymore? All I could feel was sadness and confusion.

A mime followed us to our car. He imitated my scowl and my depressed, shlumpy walk. A crowd of cheeseheads laughed as we walked by them. Ha, ha, ha. I never realized how insensitive Midwesterners could be. They could keep their flat state and their cloying blond cheerfulness.

"Listen," Paul said as we pulled into his parents' driveway. "When we get back to New York, I think I need some space."

"Are we breaking up?"

"No. I don't know. I just need some time to think things through."

Suddenly my merrily imagined soap molds shaped like leaves and pinecones morphed into Zoloft tablets and razor blades. Where had the love gone?

When we walked into the house, another feast was in the making. I wasn't hungry, but I forced myself to eat a little. "Annamarie and Eddie, your dishes are delicious. Have you thought about opening a restaurant? Maybe near the university?" I asked brightly, determined not to let Paul ruin this evening.

Eddie patted me on the back. "Now that's a fine idea." He looked at Paul. "This girl sure has a good head on her shoulders."

"*Xie xie, Ma. Wei dao zhen hao!*" I said to Eddie and Annamarie, impressing them with my phrase book Cantonese.

"You really enjoyed our meal?" asked Eddie.

"Yes," I said emphatically. "It was superb."

"She's a keeper, Paul," continued Eddie.

Paul glared at me. Tonight I would be grateful for the refuge of my own race car bed. Later, as Paul blissfully snored the night away, I lay awake, wishing I could drive my race car back to Brooklyn.

WAR PAINT

I was so glad to be back at work. I needed something to distract me from Paul and the Wisconsin disaster. I called Holly and told her all about the dairy idea, and she was really into it. She said she would just have some explaining to do to vegan Dwayne.

"Did you know that Marie Antoinette used buttermilk as her favorite wrinkle preventer?" I whispered as Tinsley walked by. "And goat's milk is easier to incorporate into soap because it's heavier and has more fat than cow's milk."

"Gosh, you sound like Paul now, with all your dairy stats," said Holly.

When she mentioned Paul's name, I broke down and began to cry, and gave her a brief rundown of what happened in Wisconsin.

"Yikes, bad times," Holly said sympathetically.

Through my veil of tears, I asked Holly how her weekend went.

"Dwayne surprised me and took me to this fancy day spa in Woodstock. We had a five-course feast made from these detoxifying matsutake mushrooms. When we got back, we were totally energized."

"Wow. Sounds really fun," I said, so happy that Dwayne was venturing out of the house more.

"I'm really sorry about Paul, Marn. Come over later," said Holly. "We'll work on Beautyfarm. It'll be therapeutic."

With my interest piqued after visiting the cheese farms, I did some internet research on milk-based soaps. They were creamier than regular soaps, with a richer lather. It turned out they were especially good for sensitive or irritated derma. They could help psoriasis and eczema by balancing the oils in your skin. Since milk was packed with proteins, fats, and vitamins, the skin readily absorbed it, giving it a lustrous, hydrated appearance. Apparently women had used dairy-based folk remedies since the beginning of time. I read how colonial ladies made masks out of milk, lemon juice, and brandy, and body scrubs from oatmeal, milk, and the off-limits honey.

That night, Paparazzi was hosting a party at the Metropolitan Museum of Art to launch their new "War Paint" color story (berry-stained lips and cheeks, smoldering muddy-brown eyes). It was a tie-in with the museum's new armor and weaponry exhibit, and Connie was attending. Connie had left for a meeting at four and said she'd be back in an hour. I was so engrossed in my Beautyfarm research that when I looked at the clock, it was seven and everyone had gone home. I poked my head into Connie's office. She was nowhere to be found. I called her cell. No answer. She must have been off having an afternoon-into-evening delight with Ming. Finally, at 7:25, she stumbled in whistling a happy tune.

"Any calls?" she muttered as she went into her office. The trail of her boozy *sillage* was potent and telling. She shouted to me from behind her door, "Marn, I see the girls have left. Could you do me a huge favor? I need you to do my makeup."

I was speechless. I couldn't believe she was entrusting me to do this.

She stuck her head out through the crack in the door. "Pretty please," she slurred. "I need my eyes to pop!"

I could tell she wasn't going to take no for an answer. "Okay," I said reluctantly.

"You can come with me to the event if you want," she said.

"Thanks, but I have plans with a friend," I replied. I grabbed Juniper's voluminous makeup case, and Connie pushed a plate of food off to the side of her desk to make room for it. "Can you believe this? Dr. Lurvey put me on this weird skin diet. I have to eat the skin of a boiled potato, the peel of an apple, and the rind of a slice of Camembert. All I want is a steak."

"That sounds really horrible," I said, working my feeble magic on Connie's face.

"But he didn't say I couldn't have a drinky-poo. Marnie, can I pour you one?" she asked. She opened her bottom desk drawer to reveal a veritable minibar of top-shelf alcohol.

"Don't want to mix business with pleasure," I said, sifting through the vast array of brushes.

Connie fixed herself a Scotch and soda. "To women," she toasted, raising her glass in the air. "Can't live with them, can't live without them."

Since I had no glass, I raised a blush brush and clicked it against her tumbler.

"You can get closer. I don't bite," continued Connie, her eyes shut, her face jutting toward me as I gingerly applied some foundation. "Gentry worked so fast. You're much slower. I like that."

I carefully applied eye shadow, mascara, eyeliner, and lipstick. Connie grew impatient, tapping her loafered foot. "Is it soup yet?"

"Not quite," I said, lightly powdering her face with a large buff brush.

She opened her eyes. I was impressed by my handi-work. Connie looked really good.

"You're a wonderful gal, Marnie," Connie slurred as she suddenly grabbed the puffy brush out of my hand and thrust it between my thighs, quickly sweeping it over my crotch. It was so fast, I wasn't sure it even happened. I suppose it could have been considered sexual harassment, but she was drunk and I was sort of flattered. After all, Ming was really hot.

"Gotta get dressed," said Connie, ushering me out and shutting the door. I packed up my desk, ready to make a mad dash over to Holly's.

Connie shouted from behind the door, "Marnie, get your arse in here. I need ya to tie me up." If this was some sort of S and M thing, Cross Temps was going to have to cough up more than $24.75 per hour! I took a deep breath and opened the door. My eyes widened when I saw her in a medieval wench's gown, her surprisingly ample décolletage lifted up and out for all to see. "I need you to tie the bodice," she said, turning her back to me. If "Hut, Hut" Connie was trying to reinvent herself as a fembot in this Alexander McQueen creation, it was far from working, but I wasn't going to tell her that. I tightened the corset, tied it, and started for the door. "Not so fast, Marnie. On your way home, I need you to drop this box off at Mount Sinai," she said, kicking a carton out from under her desk. "Kris knitted some preemie caps, and even though she's taking me to the cleaners, I promised to deliver them."

I leaned down and opened the box. "They're huge," I said, putting one on my head. "It fits me."

"I told Kris they're for fetal alcohol babies," Connie cackled.

Like hell I was going to drop off those horrible cro-
cheted helmets. The hospital was way uptown, in the
opposite direction from my trek back to Brooklyn. I'd
give them to Holly. They could be mock nests, and she
could donate them to a spotted owl sanctuary.

When I got to Holly's, she was lounging on the
couch with a joint in her hand. "I just spent the last
hour contemplating my split ends," she said. "I was
thinking we really need a product to tame them."

"I thought we were contemplating our dairy line
idea," I said as I yanked the joint from her and stubbed it
out. "Did you know that Cleopatra bathed in donkey's
milk?"

"Get your head out of your ass," she said, giggling.
"Now, where are we going to get donkey's milk?"

"C'mon, I'm serious," I said. "Let's brainstorm."

"Okay, I'm seeing it, Marn. We should make a
sheep's-milk soap called Let Them Bleat Cake," she said.

"Sounds good."

"And Goat Bloat, with goat milk, marjoram, and
lavender, to soothe cramps. And what about Baaabar-
ian, a sheep's-milk shaving cream with patchouli and
ginger. And . . ."

"Damn, girl. What's in that weed?" I asked, scribbling
her clever names into my notebook.

"Fingers and Does, a peppermint . . ."

I cut her off. "Is that a deer's-milk soap?"

"No, silly. A goat's-milk hand-and-foot exfoliator scrub."

I came up with some good ones too, and I wasn't
even stoned: Ewe Called, a sheep's-milk lotion with
rose water. And Wool Over My Eyes, a sheep's-milk
eye cream infused with soothing calendula extract,
sandalwood, and vitamin E.

"How about Rambunctious, an energizing exfoliating cream with rosemary and sage?" said Holly.

I countered with Buck Fifty, an inexpensive goat's-milk facial cleanser.

Holly had made a concession to Dwayne. We would not use tallow, an animal fat normally used in soap making. We would make only vegetable-based soaps with preservative-free oils. In appreciation, Dwayne was building us a beautiful walnut display case.

When I got to work the next morning, Connie's borrowed medieval gown was heaped on my desk with a note attached: *You missed a great party. Please take to dry cleaner. Must return to Alexander McQueen's showroom ASAP.* I lifted up the dress and gasped when I saw the glutinous stains that ran from the shoelaced bodice all the way around to the padded derriere. The gala's theme had been a medieval banquet. I imagined the sallow socialites and female fossils politely drinking the beeves broth, an easily sippable consommé, while Connie, away from prying eyes, gobbled the evening's greasy roast cockerel and slurped the indelible mold wine. The dress looked like a battle scene.

I wasted my lunch hour haggling with an Eighth Avenue dry cleaner who was less than confident that he could remove the stains. When I got back to my desk, I was shocked to find that all my belongings had been cleared away. I stood by my chair in stunned silence. Had Connie finally found out that I was reading her private e-mails, and fired me? Or was it the two-hour lunch I'd taken the other day to buy Beautyfarm supplies?

I sat down and kicked off my shoes. My phone rang. Tinsley's name lit up on the caller ID, and I froze. After many foreboding rings, I finally picked it up. "If you're wondering where your things are, they're upstairs."

"What do you mean, my things are upstairs?" I asked.

"We just hired a new PR director for Deeva, and since we've run out of office space on the GMR floor, you and she will be sitting upstairs with the rest of the Deeva team. I'll escort you up in a few minutes."

I was pissed off beyond belief. I felt like things were starting to wind down for me at LeVigne, and the thought of leaving Connie and starting fresh with a new boss seemed pointless and energy-zapping. On the upside, the eco-friendly Deeva brand was more in line with Beautyfarm. I was sure there'd be a lot to learn.

Tinsley took me upstairs and walked me through the Deeva area. Although Deeva was only two floors up from where the CAPs resided, it felt like a world away. The verdant hallways were decorated like a tropical jungle, with rubber tree plants, a rain forest photo mural, and a waterfall that trickled soothingly in a corner. I would later discover that while the CAPs spent their weekends power-shopping and power-exercising, the Deeva crew cleaned abandoned lots and fed AIDS babies. Deeva was more than a brand; it was a lifestyle centered on spiritual healing and socially conscious living. The brand espoused beauty from within. But beauty from within didn't come cheap. Spearmint-and-mango shampoo cost sixteen dollars a bottle, and a tiny vial of essential oil was twenty-two dollars. And beauty from within didn't necessarily come chem-free either. If you carefully read the label, there were toxic ingredients sandwiched in between the tourmaline and shiitake extract.

Tinsley ushered me into an office that faced north. The view was spectacular, but the room was very small, very brown, and shockingly DIY; the furniture was made out of honeycombed recycled cardboard and reclaimed wood.

"So I guess my cube is out there with the Deeva support staff?" I asked.

"There's no room out there. Until some space frees up, you'll be sitting in here with Brenda Dargon, the new hire, on the boxes," she said with a demonic smile.

My heart sank. I had never thought of a cubicle as private until that very moment. My personal phone calls would no longer be personal. No more all-access Internet pass to Connie's love life. No more open-air chin-hair plucks.

"Where is Brenda coming from?" I asked.

"Connie and Jacquie hired her away from Rogaine, of all places. It's a mystery to me why she's leaving her job in plugs," said Tinsley.

I looked forward to meeting Brenda. The fact that she wasn't coming from the beauty industry was refreshing, but I hoped she knew what she was getting herself into. From bald spots to age spots. Follicles to fingernails. Dandruff to dermal treatments.

I sat down at the corrugated desk and opened the top drawer. There were a few chewed pencils and an old black-and-white publicity photo of Hattie on a state visit to China, applying cream to Chairman Mao's face. I smiled because it made me think of Paul. I was trying to keep a positive attitude about his need for space, hoping that he would come to his senses and move in with me.

Hair 'Em, Scare 'Em

Monday, 9:15 A.M. I had been up until three A.M., working with Holly on a new batch of soaps, and I was late for my first day with the new hire, Brenda Dargon. As I hurried blearily down the hall, clutching a soy latte and a chocolate croissant, energizing aromatherapy scents misted me, and piped-in nature sounds and birdcalls chirped from tiny speakers camouflaged behind the rubber tree plants.

To the sound of clapping thunder, I readied myself for Brenda, shaking out my hair and putting on a big smile. But there was no one there, only a new *sillage* that lingered in the room, brassy and cloying.

I could hear Tinsley's evil voice down the hall. "Marnie, look who's here," she gushed as she burst into the office, her eyes glowing with perverse and sadistic satisfaction. "Brenda Dargon, I'd like you to meet your new assistant, Marnie Mann."

Before I could say a word, my hand was hoisted up and vigorously pumped by my new boss. "Very nice to meet you," said Brenda, her own voice overwrought with a reedy pent-up quiver.

Tinsley walked in a circle, inhaling the air like a drug-sniffing beagle. "That's not Schotzie you're wearing?" she asked Brenda.

"No, of course not. It's Smitty, by Coty," Brenda proudly replied. "My mother and I have been wearing it for years."

Tinsley blanched visibly. "Word to the wise. On weekends, you and your mother should feel free to spray yourselves with Poison, Passion, Pleasures, whatever tickles your fancy," said Tinsley, adjusting her striped grosgrain headband. "But at LeVigne, it must be only Vienna, Hattie's original scent.

"I'm sure you two have lots to talk about. Ta ta, then." She turned on her Ferragamo flats and left.

"So the shiksa's putting the shiv in me already," hissed Brenda as she unfastened the gold buttons on her George Steinbrenner blazer. I was perplexed by her outfit. It was very Liz Claiborne bridgewear. Her hair, more red than brown, was worn in a blown-under shoulder-length bob that framed her long horsey face like a pony's mane. She was all gums and Popsicle legs.

Brenda sat down at her desk and thumbed through a pile of memos I had placed there. She looked at me. I looked at her. We had known each other for all of ten minutes, and already the air was fraught with steely tension. I stared uneasily into her hawklike eyes, waiting to see who would blink first. Finally she spoke.

"I didn't know we'd be sharing an office. Funny what they don't tell you in the interviews. It has nothing to do with you, exactly, but I find this wholly unacceptable. I'm a director. Doesn't it bother you, sharing such close quarters?"

I wondered how she had made it through the rigorous and fashioncentric interview process with those sinister eyebrows that were neatly arched into two thick suspension bridges, but then again, this was Deeva, where beauty was supposed to came from within.

"I just roll with the punches," I said. "Oh, and by the way, your printer should be here sometime next week."

She curled her lip. "Will that be cardboard too? Is everything this slapdash around here?"

"There's a lot of red tape. Things have to be signed

off by a series of people. I'm far from an expert. I'm only a floater."

She stared at me incredulously. "Let me get this straight. They gave me a temp?"

"Floater," I corrected.

"Now, that speaks volumes," said Brenda. "It's abundantly clear they don't think I rate a real secretary."

I am a floater. I can float away, I chanted to myself. Her condescending remarks couldn't pierce me. I had decided that my leave date would be in six weeks from now, and just knowing that made everything at work so much more bearable.

When Brenda left, I called my mom to wish her a happy Mother's Day, then went to lunch. On the way out, Dobie Nesbitt, the Deeva art director, stopped me in the hallway. With his foppish Southern drawl, small paunch, and nerdy black glasses, he was a dead ringer for Truman Capote. He was barefoot and wearing a Lycra one-piece yoga outfit. "Do you smell butter?"

"Yes, and it's making me sick," I said.

"Those Legal Department bastards have started up again with that vile microwave popcorn. Two can play at this game," he said, pouring some peppermint essential oil into the hallway aromatherapy misters and cranking them up to full blast. "That'll teach those fat corporate fucks," he shouted.

For a brand that focused on Ayurvedic mind-body balance, Deeva sure had a lot of negative energy. When I got back from lunch, Brenda was at her desk, eating a very non-Deeva-ish lunch of Cup Noodles and Pringles. There were product comps, makeup samples, and testers spread out in front of her. Deeva was launching a new product called Gleam, which claimed to have real quartz crystals in it. They positioned it as a makeup that wasn't really makeup. It was a diffuser with light-reflecting properties and was supposed to give you an ethereal, lit-from-within luminescence. With healing properties too.

Brenda stared quizzically at a small lipstick tube that was shaped like a tiny vibrator. "Jacquie Wires wants me to write a press release about how Gleam gives the 'appearance' of tighter, more luminous skin." She read from a marketing report, " 'Silica quartz crystals soft-focus the skin. Intuitive face-firming gel imparts a restful effulgence. Gleam forms a matrix for seamless skin-reflecting coverage.' " She looked up at me. "Where is the raw empirical data? It is abundantly clear that this stuff is just a bunch of smoke and mirrors. At Rogaine it was very straightforward. Massage minoxidil into head. Wash hands. Grow hair."

I sat down at my desk and suppressed a yawn. I was picking up my dad at the airport that night, and I didn't know if I would make it through the day without falling asleep.

The phone rang, and Brenda jumped to answer it. "No, Jacquie Wires is not in charge anymore. I am Brenda Dargon, and I am in charge. Paris Hilton wants ten Gleams? Can't she afford to buy her own?"

Oh my God. Her PR skills were hideous! I didn't like how we pampered celebrities either, but you just did it. No questions asked. I picked up my extension. "Hi, Becky. It's Marnie here. We'll be glad to send some right over."

When I hung up, Brenda went berserk. "Why did you embarrass me like that?"

"I don't know how it was done at Rogaine, but I've worked for Systems, Paparazzi, and Siesta. The protocol is, you send out whatever the celebs want."

"We are not the other brands. We are Deeva."

"But Deeva's a hot brand with the stars. They all want it."

"I really don't like this idea of coddling Paris Hilton, especially when she can afford to buy the entire company. Why can't she purchase her lotions and potions at Bloomie's like the rest of us?" said Brenda, her flushed face backlighting her bleached-blond mustache, turning it hot pink. "And where in the heck do you get a cup of coffee around here? Or are we just supposed to drink wheatgrass for pep?"

It was obvious that Brenda was not a tree hugger. Maybe a cellphone-tree hugger.

THEY'VE PAVED PARADISE

Instead of the usual Larry/Trudy airport sing-alongs and bedazzling sweat suits, my father got off the plane alone, a silent, bedraggled widower. His eyes were swollen and puffy, and he was disheveled and out of sorts. He had a squished sandwich sticking out of his jacket pocket and had tied a dingy tube sock around his wheelie suitcase as an identifier—something Trudy would never have tolerated. She always tied sequined bandannas on their luggage handles.

"Dad, are you okay? You look really beat," I said as we got into a cab.

"This is all that's left of her," he said, clutching onto the small box that held Trudy's ashes. "It's very hard, Marn. I sure miss her."

"I know you do, Dad. I do too. She meant the world to you."

"Now give me some sugar," he said, reaching over to hug me. I noticed that he was wearing Trudy's diamond-encrusted "T" ring on his pinky.

My dad slept on the pullout sofa, and in the morning, we got up early and drove out to Bridgeport, Connecticut, to spread Trudy's ashes on the first house she ever sold. Unfortunately that house was no longer there. It was now a strip mall filled with the usual motley businesses: suntan center, one-hour photo, nail shop, Chinese restaurant. Since Trudy had always loved egg rolls and duck sauce, my father decided to sprinkle the ashes in front of Foo's Palace.

"Hurry up," I said, peering through the restaurant's vertical blinds. "They're going to come out and wonder what you're up to."

Once the deed was done, Dad's mood brightened. "I'm starved," he said. "Let's go in and have all the things Trudy would have eaten, had she not been on the Atkins diet at the time of her tragic death."

We happily lunched on egg foo young and moo goo gai pan, reminiscing about old times, but when the pineapple chunks and fortune cookies were placed on the table, my father got serious again.

"There's something I want to talk to you about, Marnie," he said, holding back the tears. He pulled out a tan slip of paper that was tucked inside his wallet and placed it on the table. It was a check. Made out to me, for $10,000.

I looked at it, then at him. I was speechless and confused. "Huh? I don't get it."

My father cleared his throat. "It's from me and Trudy. I know how serious you and Holly are about your business. So I—we—wanted you to have this. The day before Trudy died, she said that when you became successful, she was going to broker your first home. A sun-drenched jewel," he said.

"That was so sweet of her to say, but I can't accept this," I said, pushing the check across the table.

He pushed the check back toward me. "Yes, you can."

"I can't."

"You better take it before the next wife snatches it up."

If he was going to put it that way, then damn! Hand over those Benjamins. I took the check and tucked it carefully into my wallet. This would be Beautyfarm's much-needed start-up funds. I was going to prove to him that I could make something out of myself.

"Thanks so much, Dad," I said, getting up to hug him. "I don't know what else to say."

"Just say that you'll work hard and make your old man proud. And when am I going to meet your fella Paul? I'm starting to think he doesn't exist. I want to see what kind of man works in cheese."

I didn't think Dad needed any more to worry about, so I didn't tell him that Paul and I were estranged. Paul, like his stinky wash-rind cheeses, seemed happy to stand alone.

The next day, I took my dad to the World Trade Center site, and then we ate lunch in Little Italy. Afterward I took him to JFK, and as we walked into the terminal, I shared an idea I was hatching. "In honor of Trudy, I was thinking of dedicating a line of skin care products to her."

"Hey, that's swell. You could call it Tru Blue, 'cause that's what she was," he said wistfully. And with that, we hugged, and he disappeared through the metal detector and back to his new, uncharted life.

* * *

Holly was so blown away about the money, she started to cry and asked for my dad's number so she could thank him. The windfall had come just in time: a buyer from Bendel had gone to Holly's spa for a massage, bought a few of our products, and adored them. She wanted to meet with us. How amazing would it be to have our line at the esteemed Fifth Avenue store!

It was getting harder and harder to show up at work every day, but I derived secret pleasure from knowing that the CAPs and Brenda couldn't possibly imagine someone like me owning her own company, especially a competitor to theirs.

After about two weeks of working for Brenda, I noticed a major change in her. First, she did a Post-it sweep, throwing out every sticky pad that wasn't white, recycled, and one inch by one inch. Then she stopped eating her processed Frankenfood and started ordering fancy to-go lunches that I had to transfer from the plastic take-out containers onto a black ceramic platter she purchased at Takashimaya. One day when I was doing a sushi transfer in the pantry, I bumped into Jacquie Wires's assistant, Deirdre.

"So, tell me, what's it like working with your new boss? She's so uptight. That one really needs her chimney swept," Deirdre said with a complicitous wink. "I hear she doesn't wash her hands in the bathroom."

Even though Deirdre seemed pretty cool, I was sure she was an interminable gossip just like the rest of the CAPs. "Can't really go into it now," I said. "Gotta get this sushi to the great unwashed."

We both chuckled as Jacquie Wires came rushing by. "Sushi looks great, but must dash," she said in her staccatoed shorthand. "Going to lunch. An expensive lunch that I don't have to pay for. Bergdorf Goodman. Men's store. Their lobster-crab salad is to die for."

The next morning, Brenda was dressed in high-hippie attire. She was wearing an embroidered peasant dress, Pocahontas braids, and a leather beaded pouch slung across her chest. I picked up one of the Gleam products on my desk. "The real illusion is how Deeva magically extracts the money from your wallet," I said.

Brenda sat stone-faced. "We're supposed to be working *with* this brand, not against it," she snapped. One minute she was dissing Deeva, the next defending it. Go fig.

Since Brenda didn't trust me to do any real work, I had officially become her valet. I felt like Max the butler to her Norma Desmond—scheduling her doctor's appointments; writing threatening letters to the tenant in the apartment above her, who seemed to be dragging dead bodies across his floor; and, most important, being the go-between in an ongoing battle with It's Only Yogurt, a dating service. Apparently Brenda had paid one thousand dollars for a guaranteed nine dates, and thus far she had gone out on only two.

I had become friendly with Cheryl, the date coordinator, and I told her about my problems with Paul. She said that if and when I was ready to venture into the yogurt dating arena, she would hook me up. She also told me that Brenda had three strikes against her: her age and her eyebrows.

I told Cheryl that Brenda was unhappy and that she wanted her money back. "She won't take no for an answer," I complained.

"I can't do that, but you've been really nice. Marnie, I'm sending you over a gift."

The following day, Juan's replacement, Santiago, came whistling down the hall, carrying a lush bouquet of flowers. Was this the gift from Cheryl?

Brenda came rushing toward the arrangement with outstretched arms. "Oh, they're so beautiful! My yogurt date shouldn't have. No, he should have. Let me see the card," she demanded, ripping the envelope off the clear protective wrapping. "Marnie Mann? I didn't know you had a boyfriend."

You never asked, bitch. And thanks for ruining my surprise.

Santiago gave me a wink and handed me the flowers. I put them down, quickly sniffed the beautiful bouquet, grabbed the envelope and my cell, and ran to the ladies' room. I went into a stall and read Paul's card. He had written me the sweetest note.

<u>Kraft Single in Search of Swiss Miss
for a Feta-Compli</u>
You: Eyes the color of Danish blue
cheese. Skin the creamy texture of
mascarpone.
Me: Brie-zy l'Explorateur with big
pecorino.

Sorry for stinking up the joint
like a piece of Limburger. I'm no
Muenster.
Have a Havarti. ♥ I miss you so
much!
Love, Paul

My stomach was in knots. I spent the rest of the day sitting at my desk, trying to figure out how to respond to him. Though I was ecstatic to hear from him, I wanted a straight-up commitment. Nothing else would fly.

When I got home that night, Paul was sitting on my stoop. "What are you doing here?" I asked.

"I wanted to apologize in person. Did you get the flowers?" he asked as we silently walked upstairs to my apartment.

"Yes, I did get the flowers," I said. "Thank you. They're beautiful, but that doesn't make it all right."

"Didn't you get my note?"

"Yes, of course I got your note. And while it was sweet and quite creative, it still doesn't make things kosher. How did things go so far off course?"

"I don't know. We were so close. We were getting along so well."

"Wasn't that a good thing?"

"Maybe it scared me a little that something could be so good, so I shut down. I thought I might screw it up."

"And you did. Royally."

Paul looked like he was going to cry. "You've got to give me another chance. I was such an idiot."

"I really, really want to, but . . . Tell me that it will be good this time. That you're not going to freak out on me. Tell me what it is that's so good about us, what's so good about me."

Paul took my hands in his. "I love your sense of humor. I love your gorgeous smile. I love that I can tell you anything. We fit together like a puzzle." Paul grabbed me tight and whispered in my ear, "And I don't really care that you don't eat cheese."

I could feel his heart pounding in his chest like a strong warrior beat. My own heart melted, and I felt safe in his arms again.

SHE'S IM*PAST*ABLE

As part of Connie's ongoing product-placement crusade, she convinced a well-known playwright to write some Deeva products into the story line she was developing about the muslim women of Iraq. In exchange, Connie agreed to give an undisclosed sum of money to fund the production. As part of the deal, Connie insisted the play be named *Bombshell*, merging the seemingly disparate themes of war and beauty.

Bombshell was the story of a group of American businesswomen and social workers who travel to wartorn Iraq to help a town of female refugees open a beauty shop. In the midst of bombs dropping and severe food shortages, the women learn to master hairstyling and skin care techniques. By the end of the play, the primitive salon has been turned into a fancy full-service Deeva spa, complete with laser resurfacing, waxing, and colonic irrigations.

Since Brenda was incredibly frustrated with her regular work (everything she did was closely nitpicked by Jacquie), she dove into the play like she was Joseph Papp. Her self-appointed role as producer and dramaturge was beyond irksome. She went to the theater via car service every evening to check in on rehearsals and, like Condoleezza Rice, had me compile a daily briefing of political events in the Middle East. Then Brenda began to psychotically dictate bossy e-mails to

the director into a minirecorder, which I had to transcribe and send.

```
Evie,
1. The refugee camp set definitely
   needs more cots and mosquito
   netting. And the latrine—this
   isn't the Four Seasons! Have
   your design team dinge it up a
   little.
2. What's happening in the search
   for a less temperamental don-
   key? I know he's an angel on-
   stage, but we can't have another
   teeth-baring tantrum offstage.
   He back-kicked an understudy
   and now she's suing!
```

I flipped the Dictaphone off. I didn't know who was
more moronic, Brenda or Evie.

Today was the annual Deeva lunch, and Brenda
came to work wearing an orange T-shirt inscribed with
the numbers 563-483. It looked like the upper half of a
prison jumpsuit.

"What do those numbers mean?" I asked.

"They're the dates of Buddha's birth and death," she
said eating a gluten-free poppy seed bagel. "I'm awak-
ening the Buddha within."

"Oh. Interesting," I said, trying to hide my disdain for
her phoniness.

"I pray they don't seat me next to Jacquie, because I
just might stab her with a salad fork," Brenda said, fingering her Tibetan prayer beads.

"Sounds like you really need your chakras balanced," I muttered as I printed out Brenda's itinerary for a Deeva executive off-site weekend. They were going to an Indian reservation in upstate New York to partake in bonding exercises that included blindfolded trust circles.

Brenda snatched the sheet of paper out of my hand. "I just can't wait for the retreat. They will be anointing me with a native Indian name," she said. "I've already picked one out. Chippewa. What do you think? It means 'to pucker up.' How perfect is that?"

"Beyond perfect," I said, egging her on. I actually preferred Chief Snarly Face, but I kept that to myself.

The mail arrived, and Brenda grabbed for it. "Looks like those bastards finally sent me my refund check. I calculated it out. Minus the two dates I went on, I should be getting back $778. Thank you, Marnie, for all your hard work," she said excitedly as she opened the It's Only Yogurt envelope, which was actually addressed to me. Brenda gasped. Inside was a stack of yogurt coupons, apparently my gift from Cheryl. "This speaks volumes as to what a shoddy operation this is." She threw the coupons into her purse. "You are not done with them, my friend. I want my money back, not some free cups of yogurt. Marnie, I want you to stick on them like glue," she said like a hard-boiled Hollywood villainess.

"Stick on them like glue," I repeated robotically, surreptitiously doing a Beautyfarm flowchart. Brenda tightened the straps on her Birkenstocks and grabbed her purse from under her desk. "Time to go. Any poppies?" she asked as she bared her teeth like a braying horse. "I'll be back in a couple of hours."

I waited a few minutes to make sure the coast was clear, then checked my phone messages.

"Hi, it's Holly," said a squeaky, non-Holly-like voice. "I

have really bad period cramps. I can't make it tonight. Maybe you should call Paul and see if he wants to do something." It was my prankster Paul. After I called him back, I raided the product closet. As I filled up a FedEx box to send to my mom, I heard footsteps and turned around. Brenda was looming large in the doorway.

"What are you doing, Marnie?" Brenda demanded.

I quickly came up with a lie. "Uh. Chessy Pierson from *Cosmo* called. She's working on a color story for their December issue, and she wants everything we have that's red and green."

"Hold on there just one minute, missy. It's only the beginning of June. Her deadline can't be for another couple of months. And furthermore, packages like that should go out via regular mail."

"What happened to your lunch?"

"I looked through the window and they hadn't saved me a seat, so screw them. How about you and me go to lunch on LeVigne? I'll charge it on my corporate card."

"I'm not really hungry. I just ate," I lied. The thought of sitting across from her for lunch was unbearable.

"Oh, come on, Marnie. Bloomie's does such a nice lunch. Or better yet, let's order in and have a working lunch at our desks. They do a wonderful lobster ravioli. Real light. And a great spinach salad we can both nibble off of."

When the food arrived, I put it all on Brenda's desk and went back to mine.

"Marn, you're so far away. Scootch over here so we can really talk," said Brenda.

I reluctantly rolled my chair over to the edge of her desk, desperately searching for things to say. "Did you know that the average woman eats between four and ten pounds of lipstick in her lifetime?" I asked.

"Well, I don't know about that," she responded dismissively, "but what I do know is that I'm absolutely starved." Brenda divvied up the salad. She put the majority of it on her ceramic platter, and I got a smidgen on a paper plate. "Tell me what it's like temping," she said with a mean-spirited brightness.

I wanted to tell her about Beautyfarm and my former film career, but I had sworn myself to secrecy, and pretended I was the directionless dolt they all thought I was.

"Oh, it's great," I deadpanned.

Brenda brought her voice down to a whisper. "Don't tell anyone, but I'm working with a headhunter to find a new job. I wanted to give you a heads-up on this, but please don't quit before I do."

What a selfish creep. I had a good mind to quit that afternoon just to irk her. In the meantime, I played waiter and cleared the salad plates away.

Brenda opened the entrée tin and ran a finger over the ravioli to make sure that the chef had followed her butter-free instructions. "This is very peculiar," she said, staring intently at the food. "Last month, I ordered this very same dish, and I distinctly remember ten ravioli. Here there are only nine."

"I did notice the delivery guy chewing on something at the messenger center," I said, just to mess with her.

"You don't think he . . ." she said, madly spinning her Rolodex. "Marnie, call the restaurant now, and put it on speakerphone."

Gritting my teeth, I explained the situation to the manager.

"I'm terribly sorry," said the manager. "There should have been ten. I don't know what happened."

Brenda's face reddened with anger, and she screamed

into the phone, "Do you have any idea how much money I spend in your store? Just last week I bought two cashmere sweaters with the underpinnings. I want my other ravioli!"

"I will credit you one ravioli the next time you grace us with your presence, Ms. Dargon."

Brenda hung up and turned to me. "Since you said you weren't hungry, I'll take seven," she declared, moving the now-cold ravioli onto her plate. She scooped two onto my plate and spooned some sauce over them. I glared at her. "Okay. Okay. I'll give you another one," Brenda continued, reluctantly pushing a third my way. "Bon appetit."

Love Shack

After Paul and I ate dinner at Chestnut on Smith Street, we went for a stroll through the neighborhood. Paul had seemed nervous all night, and was asking really strange questions.

"If you were on death row, what would your last meal on earth be?" he asked.

"Gross stuff like five Big Macs in a row. Spaghetti and meatballs, maybe some really good onion rings," I said. "What about you?"

"A big round of Brillat-Savarin. It's a French triple-cream with over sixty percent fat."

"You wouldn't need old Sparky to do you in if you ate that," I joked.

"Marnie, I'm really excited about your Beautyfarm dairy idea," said Paul. "Whatever I can do to help, count me in."

"That would be great," I said, smiling an extrawide jumbo smile.

"I have a good feeling about it. I can really see people eating it up."

"I don't think it'll taste very good," I said.

"But I can vouch for the smell," he said, snogging my neck. "I have to tell you something, Marn. Manhattan's really been getting on my nerves."

"It is?" I said, completely stunned by his confession.

"Is your vacancy light still on?"

I had goose bumps all over my body. "Why? Do you need a room?"

Paul nodded. "Only if the inn is cat-friendly."

I was over the moon. Jeffrey, Paul, and I were about to become a blended family. I was going to learn what it felt like to be a stepmother.

I woke up in a cold sweat. Paul was moving in next week. Did this mean that the honeymoon period would be officially over? Would the bloom be permanently off the rose? Now that we would be living together, would we hiss at each other, pacing the floor like captive animals?

Yesterday at my place, we'd had a serious powwow about co-habiting. I told him what I liked and didn't like of his. My "didn't like" list was quite long, while his list for me was short and specific.

"It's like *Night Gallery* in here," Paul said, looking at my portrait collection. "Their eyes follow me around the room. Doesn't it bother you that you don't know who these people are?"

"No. I like it."

By the time we were done hashing everything out, Paul had agreed to throw out all the dusty candles and

cherubs and display his Yao Ming memorabilia in his
office at work. In turn, I agreed to take down all the
portraits in my (our) bedroom. He said they were giving him funky dreams.

The big news at work was that Tinsley handed in her res-
ignation, which really cheered me up. Despite the fact
that as her final parting gesture Tinsley denied everyone's raises, we all went to her going-away lunch at La
Grenouille. Diana Duvall came with Zulu Marie, her severely underweight trophy baby, who was wearing tiny
leather chaps, a rhinestoned mini–cowboy hat, and a
doll-sized motorcycle jacket, all from Prada Preemie.

Juniper took a sip of Perrier. "Question. If cottonseed
oil is made from cotton, and olive oil is made from
olives, what is baby oil made from?" she asked us.

"Babies!" I said, incredibly sick of her daftness.

Everyone at the table gasped, and someone grabbed
Zulu Marie as if to protect her from the likes of me.

"She's got your eyes," purred Murfy.

"And her father's Semitic profile," said Diana. "Let's
not forget, Hickory Jones used to be Hershel Jankowitz.
But nothing a good plastic surgeon can't fix."

Zulu Marie's cowboy hat slipped down into her face,
and Diana reached over to adjust it. The baby's arms
flailed, almost hitting Diana in the face. "Unless you
have an extra twenty grand, Zulu Marie, don't get anywhere near Mommy's cheek implants," Diana said.

I was surprised to see Diana playing mommy. While
Zulu Marie spent her first few weeks on earth in a
heated incubator, Diana spent that same time blissfully
baby-free—in the gym and at the office, until her Outlook beeped every day at six P.M. to remind her to go to
the hospital.

As ghastly as it was to be in Tinsley's presence, it turned out to be a great lunch. I got to take home six doggy bags—basically everyone's uneaten food. The minute Tinsley was gone forever, the vultures (Murfy, Juniper, and I) descended upon her office, but the wicked witch had left her larders bare. A lone *New York Times* crossword puzzle sat on her desk, with only two clues filled in—"OLEO" for margarine, and "EVA" for Hitler's Braun.

Paul called from the apartment. He had taken a couple days off to try and finish unpacking his boxes. Unfortunately, we were having a terrible mid-June heat wave.

"I wish I was there to help you," I said.

"This place is an oven, Marnie. We've got to get a better air conditioner," he said. "Let's go to Circuit City on the weekend and buy one."

"Sounds great," I said, faking enthusiasm for a dreaded trip to testosteroneville. "Since it's too hot to cook, how about I bring in dinner?" I said, thinking about the leftovers from Tinsley's good-bye lunch that were in the pantry fridge.

"Sounds great, baby. I'll set the table."

We were already sounding like the perfect housebroken couple.

I called my dad to tell him that Paul had officially moved in, and also that Holly and I scored a Beautyfarm account with Bigelow Chemists in the Village. I told him we'd found a great place in Far Rockaway to buy discount raw materials.

"What? You're going to throw it all away?" he asked.

"No, Dad. I found a wholesaler in Far Rockaway." He could be so exasperating at times.

"That's just great, kiddo. Keep up the good work.

When are you gonna send us some samples? You're gonna love my new gal, Rhoni. She rides a Harley and grows avocados."

I couldn't believe my dad was dating, but I was really glad for him.

"She sounds so earthy, Dad. Is she there right now?"

"Yeah. She's in the kitchen, mixing up a batch of frozen margies."

"Could I talk to her? Maybe say a quick hello?"

"Rhoni's not really a phone person. You'll meet her when you come out next time."

I smiled to myself. The Karmic tables had turned. I'd be chasing after her.

TALES FROM THE CRYPT

The day of the *Bombshell* press preview had finally arrived. Brenda and I were at each other's throats. We were totally haggard from days of readying for this event.

It was five P.M. Brenda was already in her theater garb: an orange sari and bare feet. I grabbed my outfit, which included the Manolo Blahnik pumps that Summer had begrudgingly given me in the stairwell, and I headed for the bathroom to change. On the way back to the office, I noticed a small, stooped figure in the distance: a tiny old woman zooming toward me on one of those electric scooters. She hit the breaks in front of our office and then made a sharp, screeching turn inside. I ran in after her. Brenda was obliviously applying a golden bindi to the center of her forehead.

Dobie Nesbitt came running in and stopped dead in

his tracks. "Oh my God. It's Hattie LeVigne! I've got to go get Sidney and Marion," he yelled, running back out.

I didn't know how Dobie could have recognized her. This wild-haired crone in a velour jogging suit and Velcro-fastened sneakers bore no resemblance to the polished, stately woman in the old publicity photos. No more than ninety-nine pounds wet, she looked like a spooky apparition in a ratty, full-length fur coat. Her ashen, liver-spotted face was covered in flour-barrel powder; her chalky lips were wan and ghostly white. She had what you might call the "dug-up" look.

Hattie looked around the room. "This place is in shambles," Hattie screamed. "What have you clowns done to my office? Where are my Tiffany lamps? My Chippendale desk? Who has stolen my priceless Fabergé eggs?"

A group of people gathered at the door. Impervious to Hattie's fury, barefooted Brenda got up from her desk, calmly padded over, and offered Hattie her mend-hied hand. "It's an honor and a privilege to meet you, Ms. LeVigne."

Hattie recoiled. "My husband may have croaked thirty years ago, but it's *Mrs.* LeVigne, you feminist fool, and I don't care if you're Indira Gandhi—you're loitering in my office."

More people crowded in the doorway. Hattie leaned in and closely examined Brenda's skin and sari. "Since when did they let untouchables work here? Poor thing's been hit by the ugly stick. My eyes want to see perfection. Now get out."

Then Hattie plucked a letter off my desk and gave me the once-over. "Your skin is shiny, but your letter is neatly typed," she said. "I like the way this swanky dame dresses. I wore a dress like that in the summer of '52. It's obvious you can't afford diamonds, but paste looks just the same. What's your name, miss?"

"Marnie. Marnie Mann," I said nervously.

Hattie got behind me and, with her bambooed fingers on my slouching shoulders, she straightened out my posture. "This broad is going places. Remember, Marnie, never wear makeup to bed. Always wash your face no matter how tired you are, and don't forget to cream your neck."

"I do. Every night," I said. I couldn't believe she had singled me out. I felt like I had been touched by greatness.

Breathless, Dobie came running back in, and Hattie gave him a working-over.

"And you, mister-sister," Hattie said to him. "How do you leave the house like that? You have a face like a foot. Droopy jowls and a corded, ropelike neck." Dobie slunk to the corner of the room, completely crestfallen.

Hattie looked around at the ever-growing crowd. "Why are you all in my office? This is my eminent domain, my citadel of glamour."

"No, you're a bit confused," said Brenda, completely undaunted. "The executive offices are downstairs. This floor belongs to Deeva."

"What? I'm the diva! I'm the pioneer of beauty," Hattie exclaimed. "And what is that terrible stench?" she said, pointing to the aromatherapy candles burning on my desk. She zoomed around the perimeter of the office, taking it all in—the rubber tree plants and a series of aura paintings that Brenda was working on. "Could someone please tell me why this place looks like a Pygmy jungle?"

Hattie abruptly tore out into the hallway. We followed her, and when she whipped the scooter around a tight corner, we clung, heels to the wall, as she practically mowed us down. "Don't mess with me, kids. I could pull a two-ton truck with this thing. As my dear friend Bette Davis used to say, growing old ain't for sissies," she hooted. Hattie grabbed her four-pronged cane and began poking at some boxes that were lined up in the hallway. "This is a disgrace. Doesn't anyone remember my memo, spring 1979, about leaving detritus on the floor?"

Jacquie Wires ran in and stood in uncharacteristic silence, staring at the woman who had started it all.

Hattie looked around and shook her mighty cane in the air. "Who are you people? You look like a bunch of boxcar hoboes." Then she gave Jacquie a swift kick to the shin. "Don't they have mirrors where you bought that outfit? That jacket needs a scarf. With a knot to put a pin on. And your face! It's colorless. The little makeup you wear was done with a sloppy hand. Beauty isn't vanity. It's a woman's duty. The only time you ever leave your house barefaced is for a family emergency."

Sidney and Marion finally arrived, and Sidney snuck up behind Hattie just before she pulverized a large ceramic Buddha with her heavy cane.

"Well, good afternoon, Mister Ed," said Hattie, looking directly into Sidney's mouth. "Son, I could play mah-jongg with those dentures."

"Mother, what in God's name are you doing here?" he asked.

"I've been taking Dr. Lurvey's feel-good pills, and he's been pumping me up with cortisone," she said as she revved up her ambulatory engine.

Marion placed a loving hand on her mother-in-law's forearm. "Hello, Mother," said Marion. "What do you think? This is our brand Deeva. It's really dyna-mite. It's all natural"—*Not!* I thought—"and the sales are through the roof." She grabbed a tube of Crevasse lotion and massaged it into Hattie's fingertips. "It's got sage and elm bark. Doesn't it smell delicious?" she said as she led Hattie's hand to her already twitching nose.

Hattie recoiled and pulled a pair of bifocals from the straw basket attached to her chair. "What's the shelf life on this crap?" she said, reading the ingredients on the tube.

"Isn't it wonderful? It has such a light scent," said Marion.

"If you don't smell it, I can't sell it," shouted Hattie. "And put on some crimson lipstick, Marion. It will make your teeth shine like pearls, not little corn niblets."

Dobie looked nervously at Sidney. "We've got to leave for the theater," he whispered.

Rebecca and Summer came rushing in. Summer was wearing a tight vintage Gucci jumpsuit, and her hair was matted into thick blond dreads.

"We just heard," said a winded Rebecca, who had recently returned to work from what was rumored to be a boot camp for troubled trust-funders.

"Give Grandma a kiss, my shaineh maidel," Hattie said, reaching out to touch Rebecca's lacquered helmet-head. Rebecca backed away.

"Honey, not to worry. My encephalitis cleared up a year ago."

While Hattie looked Summer up and down, Sum-mer looked at her former shoes and shot me a resent-ful glare.

"And who, pray tell, is this strumpet?" Hattie shouted.

"You're pretty now, but you have the kind of sallow skin that will look sixty when you're forty."

Summer looked devastated.

"And get your cooch out of your throat," continued Hattie, pointing to Summer's exaggerated camel-toe, her crotch flossed by the jumpsuit's seam.

"Don't mind her, Summer. It's the pills talking," whispered Marion.

"How did you ever convince me to let this company go public, Sidney?" said Hattie, dramatically clutching her heart. "I think I'm dying." Hattie pushed a button on her scooter, and the seat reclined into a little daybed. In this supine position, she appeared to be napping.

Sidney pulled Marion aside. "Honey, maybe her liver and lung transplants aren't taking," he whispered.

"Sidney, you get what you pay for," explained Marion. "I told you we should have waited for her name to come up on the official donor list, instead of getting Brazilian organs on the cheap."

Oh my God! I thought about the poor indigent souls who harvested their body parts for a mere pittance. Some young able-bodied person had lost a liver and a lung to give an old woman a couple more years of life. *But wait a minute, it's kidneys you have two of. . . .* I pushed the awful thought out of my mind.

Sidney leaned down to speak to Hattie. "Mother, I must let you know: we're leaving for a Broadway show. I'm going to bring the car around so you can go home and rest."

"Shut your piehole. I want to go to the show," she said in a suspiciously stronger voice.

"No, you can't," chided Marion.

Hattie was indignant. She grabbed Sidney's hand. "I've been cooped up for so long. My dear son, show your mother what she's been missing," she said, batting her eyelashes like Baby Jane Hudson.

"Sidney, should we get her a walker?" whispered Marion.

"What's wrong with the scooter?" Rebecca asked.

"Your mother's talking about an escort," Sidney explained to Rebecca.

"I want my favorite walker, Mason. Have him washed and sent to my tent," shouted Hattie.

Rebecca reached out to touch Hattie's chalky white face. "Let's get her down to Pampa. He could do a rad job on her makeup."

Hattie perked up a little and looked at Summer. "Let's make sure this Pampers fellow puts some nice cream blush on you, missy. Blondes tend to fade out at night. And bring me a big bottle of Vienna. You never know who might be sitting downwind at the theater."

As they took Hattie away, Marion whispered to Rebecca, "Get her out of that monkey fur and into something au courant. Also, make sure they clip her toenails. It's a press event. You don't want her clicking around like a German shepherd."

Once the LeVignes were gone, Dobie put the essential-oil misters on full blast, and he and Brenda got into the lotus position. While they were chanting, I called Sidney's secretary. She put me on hold while she made some inquiries about a walker.

"Dearie, it doesn't look the least bit promising," she said. "Mason passed away several years ago. When Nan Kempner died, Dudley retired, and Brooke's booked Gilford until midnight. I think Mrs. LeVigne's going stag. So sorry."

*   *   *

At the theater, the LeVigne family occupied the front row, center. Hattie sat in the aisle in her scooter. The press sat right behind them, and us lipstick lackeys sat behind the press. Brenda was extremely agitated because she had expected to be seated in the VIP section.

Hattie looked beautiful. Thanks to a little help from Pampa, her hair was swept up into a Blond Ambition–Madonna ponytail extension with a braided coil at the point of entry, and he must have Gleamed the shit out of her, because her face was misty and glowing.

During intermission, Brenda and I went down to the first row. Brenda tried to ingratiate herself with Hattie, but she was duly ignored. From the aisle, I watched as Sidney introduced Hattie to the rapper 2 Cent Plain. He was recording a duet with Summer for a cross-promotional tie-in for her new fragrance, Summer's Yves.

"Sidney's my homie," 2 Cent Plain said to Hattie as he bumped knuckles with her sixty-five-year-old son.

"Nigga, please," jived Sidney, his shoulders rolled forward in a menacing hip-hop stance.

Brenda leaned over and whispered to me, "I don't care if it's cool. I wish they would all stop using the N-word."

Hattie grabbed on to 2 Cent's arm. "In my day, sonny, they'd deliver a case of seltzer to the door, and the following week they'd pick up the empties. Now, that was service."

"No one touches 2 Cent," said one of his bodyguards, extricating the rapper from Hattie's bony grip.

The play was horrendously bad, but the press (who were employees of the magazines and newspapers that profited from LeVigne's substantial ad dollars) behaved politely, laughing at the few funny moments and sniffling at the sad ones. But what an embarrassment to see the Deeva products so shamelessly promoted. In the Iraqi beauty salon, a cornucopia of Deeva products sat on a counter, labels blatantly facing the audience like little blinking neon signs. "Buy me. Buy me," they seemed to scream.

But no one was really focusing on the play: Hattie's performance was far more riveting. She turned the show into a call-and-response, shouting things out like she was at a gospel revival. Sidney tried to shush her, but she just kept at it.

In the final scene, the Iraqi women gave one another facials, smearing Mask-er-ade, a lemon yellow Deeva mud pack, all over their grimy unwashed faces.

One teenage girl used an empty mask jar and a soiled rag to create a sad little doll, which she cradled as she sang:

> Dolly, I'm so dirty and I cry all night
> But my skin sure looks pretty.
> And my pores are nice and tight.

While the burka-clad girl spun her legless little waltz partner around, Hattie went nuts. "Save it for Riverdance, you licorice stick," she heckled.

There were several curtain calls, where the actors, still covered in the lemony gunk, came out and took bows, much deeper and more heartfelt than the play or their performances warranted.

When the lights came up, there was a commotion in the front row. I immediately noticed that the electric scooter was gone. Apparently so was Hattie.

Brenda and I rushed toward the stage. Sidney was frantically pacing the floor like a headwaiter, with Hattie's fur coat draped over his arm. "My mother. She's out of it!" he shouted. "Look alive, everybody. We've got to find her!"

The side door opened, and we all streamed out into the humid night. "Maybe she's outside," I said, looking around. It would have been hard to miss an old woman popping wheelies, but there was no one that fit that description in the milling, cab-hailing crowd.

"There she is! She's heading into Times Square," a theater usher yelled as he pointed toward Broadway.

"We'll scope it out from the Bentley, Dad," Summer said as she and Rebecca sped away into the night. The Bentley had been painted fuchsia and orange in keeping with the new Systems "Sangria Nights" color story.

"Don't all stay together," Sidney shouted. "Break up into groups of two, and if you feel safe enough, go alone. We have a bounty on my mother's head. If you bring her back safely, there'll be a handsome reward."

"And one more thing," Marion said as Sidney barked out his cell phone number over the din of a street preacher. "She's wearing Vienna. So use your eyes *and* your nose." Sidney and Marion must have had Botox boosters before the show: despite their vocal hysterics, their faces were as placid as the Dead Sea.

Brenda and I teamed up and searched together. Like bloodhounds, we poked our heads into every dingy doorway and brightly lit fast-food joint. At some point I lost Brenda, which was for the best because all she could talk about was the reward money. Yes, the money would have been nice, but I was truly concerned about Hattie. It figured that the day I finally got to meet my Beautyfarm role model, she disappeared into thin air. I made a plan of attack. First I would search the hotel

lobbies. After that, I'd hit the dark alleys behind the the-
aters. Maybe Hattie's electric scooter had gotten stuck
in a pothole. The white-light neon of Times Square
blinked day for night, illuminating the streets in a beautiful preternatural glow. From up on high, the gargan-
tuan Cup-a-Soup container languorously puffed out
blasts of ramen smoke.

I felt defeated. It was two A.M. What if this were Pom-
peii, and the volcano erupted right now? I would be
frozen in place for all of eternity in a dirty Pizza Hut,
searching for Hattie. It was time to go home.

At the Forty-second Street subway entrance, I
thought I smelled traces of Vienna. Or was it stale urine?
I spotted an elevator. Maybe Hattie and her scooter had
descended into the hole in the ground, because surely
no one would look for the doyenne down there. One
thing was certain: that tough old broad would definitely outlive the cockroaches. I took one last look
around. The sign for the 1, 2, 3, 7, N, Q, R, W, A, C, E, and
S trains hovered before me like a scrambled language,
an anagram that I could finally decipher.

We had eighteen thousand dollars in the bank. It
was finally time to give my notice at work.

The next morning, I marched into Connie's office to
tell her I was quitting. Connie had Human Resources
on speakerphone. From what I overheard, a temp, who
had been hired to stuff press kits, had had a miscar-
riage at her desk.

"Make sure she didn't get any goop on the goody
bags," Connie cackled as she hung up and turned to
me. "Well, hello there, Marnie."

I looked around her office. All the photos of Kris
were gone.

"Did you hear?" Connie continued. "Kris got the kids in the galimony suit, but I get to keep the Jag. Sweet."

"You know, Connie, the best things in life aren't things," I said.

"Hey, that would make a great bumper sticker for my car."

She so wasn't getting it.

"So, Marnie, what can I do for you today?"

"I'm quitting," I blurted out. "I'm giving you my two weeks' notice."

"Hold that thought. Before we get into that, I want to ask you something. I had the most absurd conversation with the president of NOW. She accused us of not doing enough for women. We're doing plenty for women. We're making them beautiful."

"And broke. And toxic," I said with pointed relish.

"Seems like you've gone to the other side. Anything I can do to persuade you to stay?"

"I'm kinda working on my own line," I said brazenly. "Holistic skin care. It's important to me."

"Good for you," Connie said as she shook my hand and thanked me for a job well-done. "But don't forget: we buy out our competition."

GERITOL CHIC

The day after Hattie's disappearing act, she had made the front page of the *New York Post*. In the photo, she was holding court with a bunch of hookers and homeless people at a Dunkin' Donuts on Eighth Avenue. The headline read, SHE'S BAAAAACK! According to the article, after Hattie left the theater, she spent a couple hours zooming around Times Square and ended up at Dunkin' Donuts, wetting her whistle with a bottomless cup of, as she liked to call it, "decrap." It was reported that she gave complimentary makeovers to a half-dozen prostitutes, and they returned the favor by stealing her electric scooter and her fake ponytail. Hattie had been stripped for parts like an old Toyota Corolla.

"Those soiled doves need it more than I," she said diplomatically when a reporter asked if she would press charges.

And the media continued to feast on the "lost Hattie" story like a pack of bulimic starlets gobbling up a secret stash of full-fat cupcakes. She was doing the talk-show circuit, and Barbara Walters booked the hookers on *The View* to talk about their night with the old-fashioned Cream Queen.

"Dang," said a beautiful tranny named Peanut. "Hattie got it goin' on. Not all high-falutin' like her boo-boo don't stink."

After the hooker interviews aired and Hattie appeared on *Larry King Live*, Hattie's street cred went through the roof. She had gone from a crotchety old lady to a senior superstar. Connie and Sidney wanted to take full advantage of Hattie's reemergence and newfound popularity by giving it some serious spin, so they brought back the image consultants, Gainsley and Khaki. A bunch of us sat in the conference room. In my final days, I was sent back to work for Connie. I took notes, I hoped, for the last time.

"We've got to tap into the market while Hattie still has her fifteen minutes," said Gainsley.

"At her age, it could be fifteen seconds," added Marion.

"The H to the A to the T to the T to the I to the E," rapped Summer as she zoomed in on a tricked-out Jazzy electric scooter. "Look, Daddy. I pimped my ride," she said as the gold wheel-rims spun wildly. She'd had a blue rinse put in her hair and sported coral-frosted lipstick. Her skintight denim-look polyester leisure suit left nothing to the imagination, and she was sporting putty-colored Velcro orthopedic shoes. She was also wearing big dark wraparound glaucoma sunglasses.

"Summer, take off those horse blinders. I don't even wear those things," Marion said. "And get out of that chair and sit at the table like a lady."

"Cute pants," said Khaki, sucking up to Summer.

"Don't they make my bedonkadonk look big?" Summer said, pushing her padded booty in Khaki's face.

"Let's get down to business, folks," said Gainsley as he laid out Hattie's marketing plan on a dry erase board. "The public is in love with the curmudgeonly Hattie, and to our great surprise, the kids are eating her up. Maybe they think of her as a grandma figure. We're not really sure. All we know is that the elusive concept of reverse-cool is in play here, and while she's hot, we want to run with it."

Khaki got up and spoke. "There's a whole host of cross-promotional opportunities for Hattie—her own line of sneakers, apparel, energy drinks, ring tones, and video games."

"If we hone in on getting the youth market to embrace senior chic, we can make a killing."

"We need a name for the launch. Any ideas, folks?" asked Connie, looking around the room. "Marnie, you seem to be good with these things."

"What about Gen Rx?" I said off the top of my head.

Sidney and Marion looked delighted.

"No, no. Sounds way too clinical," said Khaki, visibly upset that she hadn't come up with the moniker.

"Gen Rx. I like that. Very catchy, Marnie," said Sidney.

"You hang out with that hip and funky crowd," Marion said to Summer. "What do you think of Gen Rx?"

"Fo' shizzle, but be quiet, beeatch. I'm banging out some lyrics," said Summer, handing a sheet of paper to Khaki.

Khaki quickly scanned over the page. "That's wonderful, Summer. Is this for your duet with 2 Cent Plain?"

Summer nodded.

"I have an idea," I said to Summer. "What if you do a trio—you, 2 Cent, and Hattie?"

"I guess I could get my groove on with her," said Summer.

"I was thinking that you could do a rap song called 'Black Don't Crack,'" said Khaki. "Because black skin is so supple and wrinkle free."

"I be thinkin' more like redoing that Ol' Dirty Bastard song called 'Proteck Ya Neck II The Zoo,'" said Summer.

"You could do a tie-in with a neck cream," I said.

"Great idea, Marnie. It's really too bad you're leaving us," said Marion wistfully. "You've been a wonderful asset to our company."

I wasn't one bit sorry about leaving, but I wished I had asked to be paid for my rockin' marketing concepts.

Summer began to sing. *"Bite my style, I'll bite your—"*

"Go Summer. Go Summer," chanted Khaki, seeing the dollars pouring in.

"Yo, chillax, dawgs. I've got an intravenous vitamin drip with Dr. Lurvey in five," said Summer.

"Honey, I thought you were back on solids," said Marion.

"Not if I'm doing a video with slenderella Grandma. I've got to lose some serious poundage. Or else I'll be breaking some ribs to get into a size-two dress."

After Summer left, Gainsley continued his plan of attack. "We'll get Summer to take Hattie to all the rad hot spots."

"Is my mother really up for stumbling out of the Meatpacking District at four A.M.?" asked Sidney.

"Of course she is, honey," said Marion. "Don't forget, she's the one with the new organs."

In preparation for Hattie's foray into all things hip hop and happening, Khaki and Gainsley created a slang "cheat sheet" for her. Connie had asked me to spend some time with Hattie, reviewing the vocabulary list. I jumped at the chance to have a one-on-one with my American idol.

I made sure I dressed in a way I thought Hattie would appreciate. I wore a forties-style vintage floral-print dress, and cherry red ankle strap wedgies. Very Andrews Sisters.

When I got to Hattie's office, her door was ajar. She was sitting at her desk, eating a soft-boiled egg and melba toast. She looked frail in a floral turban and thick, tinted Carol Channing glasses. It was hard to believe that in just a few weeks she would be unveiled as the newest supa-dupa fly girl.

Hattie motioned for me to sit down. I surveyed the room as she drank a cup of black coffee. So this was the shrine to the grand old ballbuster. It was frozen in time. It had a fusty, old-fashioned feel to it, and everything was tinged in a yellow film. I remembered hearing that although Hattie was never photographed with a cigarette in hand, she had been a very heavy smoker. The walls were papered in hand-painted pink petunias. The windows were swagged in floral chintz. There were lipstick tubes and perfume vials set out on a Chippendale desk, ready to be sniffed and tested. A vase of American Beauty roses (Hattie's favorite) sat on a glass occasional table. A Wedgwood tea service sat on a silver tray. The room smelled of pressed powder and, of course, Vienna. And there behind her desk sat a heavy silver safe that housed the closely guarded "juice" formulations.

In my hands, I was holding the Gen Rx rapspeak file and a prototype of a gaudy gold Adidas high-top (orthotics included) that Hattie would be "hawking." The idea that they were trotting out this superannuated woman like some show pony was starting to feel very wrong.

"Hello, Marnie, you sassy, classy dame," said Hattie, taking her last bite of lunch.

I was flattered she remembered my name.

Hattie pulled out a tube of her original cream and moisturized her hands. "You know, Marion and Sidney took this away from me when I was sick. They made me use Vaseline."

"How could they?" I cried, not believing this sadistic form of elder abuse.

"They thought I was six feet under. Well, guess what: I'm not," she said mischievously. "This ain't no farewell tour. I'm like Cher. I'll be back. Care for some Sanka, child?"

"No, thanks," I said. I was too nervous to drink. My hand would probably shake and I would drop the china cup. I cleared my throat. "Connie asked that I go over some things with you. And also," I said, holding up the ridiculous sneaker, "if you could be so kind as to sign off on this shoe?"

"Remove that hideous boat from my sight line. I've told them a thousand times: I am not a fan of casual dress," she said. Between sentences, Hattie's little parrot tongue darted out of her mouth to moisten her dry lips.

"But Connie . . ."

Hattie cut me off. "I don't care what that bulldagger wants. I don't take orders from anyone!"

Hattie's outburst made some coffee slosh onto her blouse. "Dagnabbit!" she said.

I handed her a linen napkin to dab the stain. "While I'm here, I need to go over some words with you. Phrases and things that you should be familiar with when you make your public appearances."

I looked at Hattie for a reaction, but there was none. She was staring off into the middle distance, so I proceeded with caution.

"Hattie, how do you refer to men?"

Hattie pondered the question for a moment. "Gents, if they have clean fingernails. Fish sticks, if they're bums."

I laughed. "Believe it or not, Hattie, these days, men are sometimes called pimps, homies, OGs. If there's a bunch of them, they become a posse or a G-unit."

Hattie looked puzzled by this, but she didn't say anything, so I trudged along.

"Let's work with the word 'dame,' which you like to use so much. Today, when you refer to a woman, you should call her either a bitch or a ho."

"What kind of sauce are you on, child?" groaned Hattie.

That brought us to the next subject: liquor.

"Hattie, sauce isn't called sauce anymore. It is now known as gin and juice, Alizé, Colt 45."

"Get me a pistol, because I'm going to shoot myself," Hattie shouted.

"Speaking of weaponry, there's this East Coast–West Coast rivalry. There was a singer Tupac. He was gunned down. And Biggie Smalls . . ."

"Did you say big band, child? Now that's something I understand. Duke Ellington. Louie Armstrong. Those balmy, serendipitous nights at the Stork Club."

I once read that Mae West had a radio transmitter built into her wigs to feed her one-liners. This could work for Hattie.

"Hattie, what's your favorite color? Hummer is pimping your ride," I said.

"Chicken yellow, Marion," she snapped, suddenly confusing me with her daughter-in-law.

She must have been tired. There were more ludicrous things to review, but instead I shut the folder. Hattie spun around in her seat and faced Central Park. "Marion, you and Sidney thought I was going to drop dead years ago. But I'm a barracuda. I'm the Cream Queen of Fifth Avenue. I started out with nothing, and I built an empire," she said, sweeping her hand majestically across the skyline. Hattie leaned in toward me, put her bony elbows on the desk, and put her head in her hands. She looked me straight in the eye and spoke. "Has my dear Sidney told you the formula, Marion? I swore him to secrecy years ago, and I know he listens to everything his mother says. It's just me, Sidney, and the chemists who know it, but maybe I should tell you too. In case anything happens to my dear son."

I sat on the edge of my seat, speechless. Of course I wanted to know the formula. It was like finding out what makes Coke Coke, but if I opened my mouth to speak, I would be pretending that I was Marion. I didn't want to snow her. As I pondered this dilemma, she continued.

"If memory serves me, my original cream was made

from elder flower and chicken fat. I always used dried rose petals. Never rose oil. Let's see. There was the freckle remover and a very popular mustache wax. Don't remember what was in those, but to make a good face mask, whip up some oil, eggs, and scraps of leftover fruit."

That sounded like a great concoction. I picked up my notepad. Maybe it was something I could use in a Beautyfarm formulation.

"And let's not forget the most important ingredients: snips and snails and puppy-dog tails," Hattie cackled dementedly.

My heart stopped. Had she totally lost it?

"Just kidding," continued Hattie as she looked me right in the eye. "Oh, hello, Marnie. How nice of you to come visit me."

"Hi," I said.

Had she forgotten that I had been there all along?

"I see you have oily skin, Miss Mann. Try brewing up some walnuts and aloe leaves for a bracing skin tonic."

"Is there anything else you can share?" I asked, hungry for more data. "What are some of the other ingredients in your products?"

"My dear, young Marnie, don't call them products. It sounds too commercial. Call them preparations. And the secret formula isn't only in the preparations; it's how you treat each customer. If a woman feels beautiful, she looks beautiful. That's the secret to my success! At House of Brownettes, where I sold my very first creams, I would approach a woman under a hair dryer, look her squarely in the eye, and speak directly to her soul. Always remember, your best customer is a captive customer."

I scribbled it all down. "Can you go back to the oily-skin potion? What's the ratio of walnuts to leaves?"

Hattie ignored me. "I didn't get here by wishing for it. I got here by working for it. Whatever you choose to do, do it well and with passion. Follow your dreams. You've got to have confidence in each and every item you make. And don't ever stereotype a customer. I'll never forget the Mexican woman who came into that San Antonio department store years ago. She was carrying a child in a papoose on her back. She was barefoot and dusty and looked like she had walked a thousand miles just to get there. Didn't speak a word of English, but her dollar was as good as anyone else's, and she put it right down and bought herself a lipstick."

There was such an innocence about the way Hattie spoke of the business. It was as if she had transported herself back to the early days, when you were able to appreciate each sale, each smiling, satisfied customer. Where corporate conceits like globalization and hostile takeovers were light-years away.

I didn't want to stop listening, but Connie would be wondering where I was. As I reluctantly gathered my things, Hattie stood up and began to ramble from what sounded like one of her stockholder speeches, or maybe her self-penned eulogy. "And if there is a world beyond this planet, it will certainly be filled with tiny cherubic creatures who will surely need the littlest sweep of Paparazzi Red Carpet rouge, the tiniest smear of Systems Whipped-Cream All Over Lotion Potion, and the most infinitesimal spritz of Vienna parfum to make them look and smell exceptionally beatific. Have no fear, little ones! For you will find me there, ready to do the daubing!"

On my last day of work, Juniper and Murfy sent me out to buy low-fat cupcakes and champagne splits for my final LeVigne "life event." When I got back, a bunch of CAPs crowded into the pantry to eat and drink, including Tanaquil, my replacement. Tanaquil looked and acted just like Murfy. They knew better than to hire another me.

"Marnie, I've been nipping at the bit to ask you," Juniper said, a little tipsy from the bubbly. "You stuff your face, and you're not *that* fat. Do you poop more than once a day?"

"Three, at the very least," I said as I watched Juniper's eyes widen and then glaze over.

Murfy stared at my clear forehead. "Wow. Those chocolate-chippy age spots finally cleared up. Which LeVigne product got rid of them?"

"It's actually a cream called Crop Circles. From a new product line called Beautyfarm."

"Haven't heard of it."

"You will."

"Did you leave a contact number in case we might need you again?" asked Tawny. "'Cuz you're the best. Where are you going now?"

"I'll be working from home for a while," I said.

"Word to the wise: Don't wear elastic waistbands, 'cause you'll just keep eating," intoned Juniper.

"Thanks for the tip," I replied as I wished them all a buh-bye. Hugs were administered, and I was bashed by many rock-hard boobies and jabbed by their razor-sharp pelvic bones.

Before I left, I gave Summer's Manolo pumps to Saskia. I adored them, but they gave me blisters, and I wanted to repay Saskia for giving me her extra pair of shoes on the day of the fire.

I was ecstatic about leaving LeVigne. I waltzed out the door and leisurely strolled down Fifth Avenue. It

was broiling hot, but the cool winds of freedom caressed my blemish- and eczema-free skin. On the way
to the train, I could feel my haunches getting sore from
the nasty bruises I had received from the girls' pointy
arrowhead hip bones. I'd have some explaining to do
when I got home to my stinky cheese guy.

About a month later, on a muggy August afternoon, the
beauty buyer from Bendel finally called to set up an
appointment. We were meeting with her at the end of
the week. Paul, Holly, Dwayne, and I were leaving for a
celebratory picnic in Prospect Park when it began to
pour, so we resorted to Plan B. Instead of going out, we
unfurled the blanket on our living room floor and happily gorged on our yummy food. I looked out the window as the world was washed clean. It could rain
forever, for all I cared. Beautyfarm was taking off, and
there was no stopping us now. Holly and I had so much
to do. Important decisions needed to be made. Packaging colors. Logo design. Popcorn or pretzels for office snacks. Poland Spring or Fiji water.

In the background, MTV was on. Suddenly something caught my eye. I pointed to the TV, and all four of
us were riveted by what was happening on the tube.

"Get ready, 'cause we're bringing you the phattest,
hippest export straight outta Palm Beach, F-L-A,"
shouted VJ Vanessa Minnillo over the din of a gaggle of
screaming studio audience teens. "Put your hands together for the one, the only Hattie LeVigne and her
spankin' new breakout single, 'Don't Call Me Grandma.'
Give it up for the mad rappin' Gen Rx Hattie."

I clapped a hand over my mouth as this supa senior
fly girl stepped out of a graffittied subway car. Hattie
wore a baggy pink velour Fubu sweatsuit, and she was

dripping in bling (probably out of the vault from her own personal collection). Jeri curls sprung out from her sideways newsboy cap. She had crazy long nails, and when she smiled, I could see a glistening gold grill. Hattie's formerly pale skin had been sprayed nut brown.

Hattie was bringing down the house, with Summer and 2 Cent Plain flanking on either side. Summer, who had been sprayed Al Jolson black, was rocking a Sporty Spice porno star look, with her boobs spilling out of a tiny tube top, and 2 Cent was in his usual gangsta attire. I didn't know if I should laugh or cry.

"You go," shouted Dwayne as he leaned in to Holly and sweetly nuzzled her neck.

Summer jived sexily across the stage.

"Looking good," said Paul. I elbowed him. "I meant Hattie," he corrected.

Summer looked over her shoulder. "This place is hot with police."

"What should we do?" shouted 2 Cent.

"Let's cap their asses," jived Hattie in an unusually husky voice. (Later we found out that Missy Elliott had done the voice-overs and all of Hattie's rapping.)

We were all cracking up.

Summer raised a gun in the air. "Bam, bam, coppa man. You're nuthin' but some funky flim-flam," she sang.

"C'mon, Grandma, let's blow this copsicle stand," 2 Cent rapped as he grabbed Hattie's arm to make a run for it.

Hattie yanked away from him. "Don't call me Grandma, 'cuz I ain't your mama jamma," she sang. And with that the kids went crazy, jumping to their feet and rocking out. Hattie used a rhinestone-studded cane to hobble across the stage. Summer threw Hattie a can of spray paint, and in big childish letters Hattie scrawled "Taggaz" on the subway car. Oh my God! They were promoting the newest LeVigne product, Taggaz, a suntan in a can. Watching this blatant adver-tainment, I realized we had just gone to hell in a wait-listed Louis Vuitton handbasket.

When the song was over, we all fell over laughing. They were somehow able to pull off something that could have been in really bad taste. Hattie had been given another chance at life, at communicating with her public, and she was eating it up. Hattie was such an inspiration to me. Do what you love, work your ovaries off, and you'll succeed.

We turned off the tube and continued to eat our indoor picnic. Believe it or not, I took a bite of a delicious chèvre called Purple Haze, a tangy goat cheese dusted with lavender buds and wild fennel pollen. In the past few weeks, I had gingerly tried certain cheeses, and I kind of liked them. Holly and I had been whipping up a batch of goat cheese soaps, and I had gotten hungry and smeared some on a cracker. Since goat cheese is much easier to digest than cow's-milk cheese, it hadn't given me the usual problems. Today I also sampled another kind of goat cheese, called Gariotin, which Paul described as ripe, saggy, and wrinkled.

Paul shook his head as he watched me eat it. "Marn, all those years you didn't eat cheese, you'll never get them back," he said wistfully.

Je ne regrette rien, I thought, smiling at Paul. "I'd prefer to think of all the yummy years ahead of me—us," I said, happily taking another nibble of Gariotin—possibly the only thing on the planet that was considered better saggy and wrinkled.

LYNSAY SANDS

The BRAT

All the knights have heard tales of Lady Murie, King Edward III's goddaughter. It is said she is stunningly beautiful. It is also said that the king dotes on the girl and spoils her rotten.

But there is more to Murie than meets the eye, and Sir Balan soon learns that he'll be lucky indeed to deserve such a bride. Yet he is not the only one to discern the truth, and the other hopeful hubby is not quite as honorable. Soon will come a reckoning, a time to show who is chivalrous, who is a cad...and who has won the love of a heart unspoiled.

ISBN 10: 0-8439-5501-5
ISBN 13: 978-0-8439-5501-9 $6.99 US/$8.99 CAN

To order a book or to request a catalog call:
1-800-481-9191

This book is also available at your local bookstore, or you can check out our Web site **www.dorchesterpub.com** where you can look up your favorite authors, read excerpts, or glance at our discussion forum to see what people have to say about your favorite books.